FEARLESS KING

MAYA HUGHES

PROLOGUE

I could still taste her. The soft, full press of her lips against mine and her raspberry smell lingered on my skin. Olivia peered over her shoulder at me and ran her fingers along her bottom lip, those same lips that were swollen and glistening from my kiss.

The trees in the courtyard bowed and swayed in a canopy that separated us from the people wandering around the hotel. Only we weren't alone anymore.

"You okay?" Colm walked over and stood in front of her, doing his brotherly duty. He ran his hands up and down her arms. "You've got goose bumps." Goose bumps I'd given her, ones that didn't come from the light June breeze but from my demanding kiss and lingering touch on her body, though we might as well have been an ocean apart now with him standing between us. He was my best friend, but if he knew what I'd been doing, the thick, metallic taste of blood would be filling my mouth.

Her gaze darted around his shoulder to me and dropped to my lips.

The kiss I'd wanted to give her since the previous summer...

The kiss that had unlocked a part of my soul and cemented it to hers...

The kiss was something I never should have taken from her because I'd spend the rest of my life wanting one more, and one more would never be enough.

I'd seen the nude thigh-highs hidden underneath the pale pink dress that skimmed across her knees. She'd answered the hotel suite door in her robe. The fabric had parted and I'd gotten the briefest glimpse, but it had been enough. It only made it harder to tamp down the desire boiling inside of me.

"I did, and Ford offered me his jacket, but I'm going to head back inside." She lifted her chin, motioning to the glass doors leading back into the chaos inside.

Shaking my head, I tried to focus on their words. Their conversation had been secondary to my daydreams of Liv.

Her small smile calmed Colm, but the glint in her bright blue eyes when they darted to mine matched the tug I felt toward her, the one I'd been fighting since she'd graduated high school just over a year ago.

She took off toward the ballroom, leaving us out in the courtyard. The bass from the music in the reception traveled in the light summer air. The wedding was for one of our own, one of the Kings.

Declan had been the first to fall, and he'd fallen hard, but there hadn't been much of a choice when Makenna was his bride. They'd been giving each other hell since high school. Mak never let him get away with anything and always called him on his shit. It had been inevitable that their sparks turned into a full-blown inferno, and I'd never seen them happier.

"Is she okay?" Colm turned to me, his eyes filled with concern.

A pit formed in my stomach. I licked my dry lips and cleared my throat. "Seeing Mak and Declan on the dance floor with their parents got to her. I followed her out here to make sure she was okay." A thin layer of sweat that had nothing to do with the summer temperature broke out on my forehead.

Colm's eyes narrowed for a second before some of the tension in his shoulders relaxed and he squeezed my shoulder. "I should have realized. I'm glad you were here. She's got two brothers around looking out for her." He stared after Liv through the glass doors.

Nothing could have been further from the truth. I couldn't see her as a sister no matter how many times Colm tried to cram her into that box. It was like he subconsciously knew what was happening and kept unsuccessfully trying to head it off.

"You go ahead. I'll catch up in a bit." I took a step back.

"When are you going to get over the whole crowds thing. You're a professional hockey player. You play in stadiums filled with thousands of screaming people."

I shrugged. "I'd rather be buried under ten opposing players than stuck out on a dance floor trying to do the chicken dance. I'll meet you in there."

He stopped and his eyes narrowed. Before, he'd never second-guessed anything I'd done. Everything had been taken at face value, but now there was a hesitation, a pause other people might not even notice. It was a side effect of accidentally sleeping with someone's fiancée.

His forehead smoothed out, and he nodded before heading back inside.

As I paced in the courtyard, surrounded by ballrooms

with different events going on, I stared through the glass at everyone on all sides of me smiling and laughing. The melody from the live band filled the warm summer air around me. I could still feel Liv's lips on mine. The way she'd stared into my eyes made me drunk and eager to taste her again. Even after the promise I'd just made to myself, even knowing the fallout that would come when Colm found out, I needed to see her.

I walked through the hotel and took out my phone.

Me: Meet me by the garden at the entrance of the hotel
Liv: When?

An immediate response, like she'd been waiting for this message.

Me: In ten minutes
Liv: I'll be there.

I slipped my phone back into my pocket. Grabbing a bottle of champagne and a couple of glasses from behind the abandoned pre-reception bar, I kept out of sight. I ducked and dodged wedding attendees and hotel guests to get back to the lobby.

Rushing down the front steps two at a time, I held my contraband close to my chest. I hit the bottom and spotted the entrance to the garden. Someone in a car in the long line along the front of the building rolled down their window. Getting recognized was my own personal nightmare. On the streets, outside the stadium, I wanted to duck my head and run for the hills the second anyone squinted in my direction, trying to place my face. I did a double take at the flash of red hair streaming out of the open window.

The blood leached out of my face like a vampire had attached itself to my neck. It wasn't an actual vampire, but it was a close second. Angelica stepped out of the car and wobbled on her towering, pencil-thin heels. *Fuck.* I should have smelled her crazy from a mile away.

I whipped around, looking for an escape. If she saw me, it was all over. Her heels clicked on the pavement, and her voice bounced off every available surface.

"Ford!" Her call cut through the thick evening air like a bullet.

Spinning around, I faced her like she was the executioner and my time had come. "Angelica, what are you doing here?" I wrapped my hand around her arm and tugged her away from the entrance to the hotel, closer to the garden.

Liv would be there any second, and I needed to get rid of Angelica. She stared at me, batting her mile-long fake eyelashes.

"What are you doing here?" I asked again. *Please let her be here for dinner or some other event and not for me.*

"Aren't you happy to see me?" She held out her arms and pulled me in for a hug. I kept my hands at my sides. "I wanted to surprise you."

Hope died a fiery death. I shrugged off her hold as people getting out of the cars looked over at us. "How did you even know where I was?" I nudged her away from the line of cars, farther into the garden. I considered whether to make a scene there in front of everyone and embarrass myself, or try to get her meltdown to happen away from prying eyes, even if it was stupid to be alone with her. Stupidity won time and time again when it was up against making a public spectacle of myself.

She held up her phone, shaking the glowing screen in my face. "I follow all the Kings on social media. Someone posted about the wedding, and I saw you in the pictures." She looked so pleased with herself, like she'd followed some bread crumbs I'd left her and now was waiting for her prize.

"If I'd wanted you here, I would have invited you."

"Ready for round two." She slid her arms around my neck like I hadn't just made it clear she wasn't invited. Her perfume clogged my nose and made my eyes water. "I can't stop thinking about our incredible night together."

As I stepped back, the gravel of the garden path crunched under my shoes. "That was months ago." Maybe I'd had too many drinks that night and somehow I'd missed the crazy in Angelica's eyes. Usually I could spot it and avoided those women at all costs. They made puck bunnies look like nuns, but no, I'd walked right into the jaws of this lioness.

"I know you're busy. I'm very understanding." She stalked closer with her eyes focused on my neck like a predator ready to take down its prey. "We can work things out."

"There are no things to work out. It's not about being busy. It's about what we had being a one-night thing." I never made bullshit promises to get anyone into bed. It wasn't my style, and it only brought on more complications. "And there is no *we*."

"Ford, I know you don't mean that." She lunged forward with a speed I wouldn't have thought possible with her teetering. Angelica's lips were on mine in a blink. She tasted like cheap vodka and desperation. I turned my head, but her lips were magnetized to mine. My legs hit a stone bench, cutting off my retreat.

"Ford?" Liv's choked whisper was a dagger shoved deep into my heart with both hands on the hilt.

I dropped the champagne glasses and bottle and shook Angelica free. The glass exploded against the gravel on the path, shards hitting my pants, and Liv's gaze shot to the remnants of my shattered surprise. The sheen in her eyes reflected in the moonlight. My heart dropped.

"Liv—" I stepped toward her, but Angelica blocked my path, winding her arms around my waist. She swayed and tightened her hold.

"What's going on?" The words caught in Liv's throat as though she had to push them out.

"Nothing's going on. I'll meet you back inside." I wrapped my hands around Angelica's arms, trying to be gentle, breathing deeply to keep from flinging her to the ground.

"Ford, who's your friend?" Angelica spun toward Liv. Now it was my turn to grab her around the waist. Knowing her, she'd attack Liv or do something equally insane.

Liv, go. I pleaded with my eyes. I didn't want Angelica to know anything about Liv, not even her name. *Just go.* I tried to force the words into Liv's head.

Angelica was a hell of a lot stronger than she looked. She tried to step forward, her heels slipping on the gravel, but I wasn't letting go.

"Yes, run along, sweetheart. We've got business to finish."

"Shut up, Angelica." I held on as her muscles tensed like she was poising for an attack.

"Just go, Olive." My voice came out as a harsh yell as Angelica twisted in my hold and tried to plant another kiss on me. I needed to keep her contained and not let anyone hear about this. That was the last thing I needed to do—tarnish Declan and Mak's wedding.

Liv stumbled back.

Angelica ran her hand along my cheek. I flinched, not only at Angelica's touch but at the look in Liv's eyes. I watched her turn and walk—no, sprint away from me. Grant showed up at the end of the path. His gaze darted over her shoulder toward me and the goddamn octopus of a woman wriggling in my arms.

He tucked Liv under his arm and escorted her out of the garden. His face was a mask of disappointment and anger that bridged the distance between us to kick me straight in the teeth like only a brother could. *Thanks, little bro.*

I managed to flag down someone from security to get the Angelica situation under control. I also didn't need Colm to have yet another reason to get pissed at me for my past in the bedroom blowing up in my face. It was a lesson I'd learned the hard way. It was much easier to talk to a woman in the bedroom where our bodies said everything that needed to be said than in the light of day, but that trail of bedroom partners had ended abruptly after what happened with Colm.

Rushing out of the security office while they contained Angelica, I ducked back into the reception. Heath called out my name and waved me over, his blond-haired head bobbing out on the dance floor.

I scanned the room for Liv, but none of the blondes had the glow she did. None with Liv's updo with strands skimming along her smooth, soft skin. I'd had those silky, golden curls between my fingers less than an hour earlier. The sinking in my stomach multiplied with each passing minute she thought something was going on with me and Angelica.

"Have you seen Liv?" I grabbed Emmett's shoulder as he passed. Stopping, he glanced around and shrugged, slipping his arm over his fiancée Avery's shoulder, probably trying to find a quiet place to make out.

My pulse throbbed in my veins. I dragged my hands along my hair and interlocked them behind my head, drowning, standing in a sea full of people. Rushing back out of the reception room, I caught a flash of pink out of the corner of my eye.

Alcoves dotted the hallway, each with a padded bench. I skidded to a stop when I heard Grant's voice.

"I'm sorry he hurt you, Liver."

Liv let out a watery laugh. Grant was the only one who got away with calling her that. They'd grown up together, less than two months apart, much less than the nearly five years and truck ton of baggage between her and me.

"I told you back in eighth grade if you called me that one more time, I'd never play tag with you again."

"I know, but it made you smile."

I peered around the corner.

Grant tucked a strand of her hair behind her ear and looked at her like she was the air he breathed. My jaw slammed shut, biting the inside of my cheek so hard I tasted blood.

"Thank you, Grant. I needed that." She dropped her head onto his shoulder. He closed his eyes and ran his hand along the back of her head.

Jerking away, I pressed my back against the wall and ran my fingers along my beard.

I wanted to rip his hands out of her hair.

I wanted to explain everything to her and tell her it was all a mistake.

I wanted to not be the guy who'd betrayed his best friend and his own brother for a woman he'd had no business being near in the first place.

Olivia was everything I wanted and everything I should've never dared to hope I'd have. Their murmured conversation barely reached my ears. The bitter punch of regret rose in my throat as her sweet taste was seared into my soul.

Walking into my hotel room, I tried to catch my breath. My chest was squeezed tight like I'd been kicked in the ribs with a pair of freshly sharpened skates. I cracked open the mini bar and downed five mini bottles of whiskey. They'd probably want an arm and a leg when I checked out, but this was a liquor emergency. Sitting on the edge of the bed, I stared at the open bottle clutched in my hand. I'd made myself a promise back in the garden that I wouldn't kiss her again. This time it would stick. It had to.

And I kept that promise for another 544 days.

1

FORD

I wrenched the shower handles to the side, turning off the cascade of water. Picking up a towel, I began to dry off, sweating even more as my heart rate slowed. Cooling off after games was always a pain in the ass. Grabbing my shirt and shorts off the hook in the stall, I stared at my hands. I squeezed them tighter around my clothes as the adrenaline rush shot through me. The crash was inevitable. I pulled my clothes on. Every second I stayed in the shower shielded me from the circus that was post-win locker room chaos: the industrial lighting, the reporters, and the cameras.

After a game I needed quiet. The energy from the ice sent me looking for refuge. I hated how that was the only thing to calm me down after my time trapped in front of a goal with just the ice and the pounding determination not to let the team down.

Without the cover of the showers, the sweat and Icy Hot smell hit me the second I entered the main locker room. Orange, black, and white jerseys were strewn all over the wooden benches, and the team staff members were rushing around to clean up. Some of my teammates trudged in and out of rehab—AKA torture—sessions that included ice baths and brutal stretches that had you biting your fist to keep from screaming.

I dropped my towel into the bin piled high with others—like we could wash away the intensity of the game with a quick shower and a towel off. The bright lights from the news cameras made the hairs on the back of my neck stand up, like being under a microscope even though I was halfway across the room.

There were too many people. This was when the switch flipped and I was outside myself, observing and keeping my distance. It was easier that way. On the ice, surrounded by thousands of screaming fans with all eyes on me for every shot on goal, I could deal, but the one-on-one stuff might as well have been squeezing lemons with a papercut-covered hand.

On the other side of the room Heath rushed up and smiled wide, jumping with his hands on Emmett's shoulders and nearly knocking him over in front of the camera crew. Heath's surfer-dude look always caught the reporters' attention no matter where we went. Emmett shook him off and finished talking to the reporter with the mic shoved in his scruffy-bearded face. I ran my hands over my stubble. The one time I let Declan talk me into going to a barber for a shave and the guy practically took the whole thing off. I felt exposed.

I slipped past some of my teammates, a few clapping me on the back with cheers of "Good job." I attempted a smile and kept my head down, making it to my locker. The flood lighting shut off, and the room dimmed as the cameras were turned off and the local news crew left after the team interviews. The answer from me was always no, so they'd stopped asking.

"Our last weekend off in a while—what are you up to?" Heath sat on the bench beside me, staring at me like he was afraid I'd try to disappear into a puff of smoke in front of his eyes. If it were possible, I'd have learned that trick a long time ago.

I shrugged. What did I do with any of my free time? Read, cook, visit my family, and avoid most other social interactions. There was also my personal favorite activity: staying out of trouble.

"I'll see you guys tomorrow." Emmett waved and disappeared so fast I wouldn't have been surprised if a plume of dust appeared behind him.

"Avery's got the day off, so I'm surprised he showed up for the game at all." Heath chuckled and brushed his blond hair back off his face, then tied it up.

Emmett had gotten traded back to Philly a year earlier and had finally gotten to move in with Avery. They'd gone from wanting to kill each other to head over heels in love in the course of a couple of months two summers back. Talk about whiplash of epic proportions.

"She's persuasive." I slipped on my shoes. She'd probably told him if he did blow off the game, he wasn't getting any.

"Meaning she threatened him." Heath grinned and snagged his shirt out of his bag beside him. "Kara and I are having everyone over tomorrow for dinner."

"And he's cooking." Declan slid in next to him and tugged on his shoes. Water dripped from his curly brown hair, dotting a pattern on his T-shirt. "Nice hair." He smacked the blond knot on the top of Heath's head.

"Shut up." Heath pushed him. "If you want chicken

parm and garlic bread, you'd better leave my man bun alone."

Declan held up his hands in mock surrender and turned to me. "Ford, you're coming, right?"

Excuses about putting together my new furniture, painting my apartment, or exploring my neighborhood weren't going to cut it anymore. I'd been moved in since the beginning of the season. Letting out a deep breath, I met his gaze. "I'll be there."

"Hell yes." Declan jumped up from the bench.

"And you believe him? Remember the Halloween party?" Heath lifted his eyebrow, staring right at me. I ducked my head and zipped up my bag. "The one he bailed on because he had to take the cat to the vet?"

"Emergencies happen." I shrugged.

"You don't even have a cat."

It had been my neighbor's cat. So sue me.

"I need your word you'll be there." Declan held out his hand. "We miss you, man. The only time we see you is at practices and games."

Damn, I was letting the guys down. I grabbed his hand and changed up the hold, tugging him in for a hug. "I'll be there. I promise."

"Oh, and Mak invited Liv, so you two can bond over your joint happiness at finally being Colm-free. He's on the plane, right?"

Those words hit me like a deer bolting in front of my car in the middle of the night.

"At the airport." The words came out automatically, but my mind had just been shot into the past. My mouth went dry, and my fingers tightened around the strap of my duffel. "He flies out in a couple hours."

My stomach knotted. If Liv was going to be there, I

needed to stay far away. The kiss at Declan and Mak's wedding a year and a half ago still kept me up some nights. She'd steered clear after that night, since she'd backed away like I'd plunged a dagger into her heart. That night she had decided to go on a date with my brother—not that I blamed her. I probably should have thanked her. Their date had hammered home the fact that she and I were never going to be anything more than what we were: Colm's best friend, on a good day, and his sister.

"Actually, I—"

"Too late to back out now. You said yes. You promised you'd be there." Heath joined Declan with the double stare down.

I let out a deep breath and shook my head. The depths of how screwed I was hadn't even been discovered by the scientists exploring the Mariana Trench. We gathered our stuff and headed out to the cars, signing a few autographs for some fans who had stuck around. The puck bunnies were out in full force. If I hadn't already sworn them off a year and a half earlier, that old fallback routine to wind down after a game had just been blown out of the water. I'd be seeing Liv the next day.

"We'll see you at Heath's, Ford," Declan yelled as we went opposite ways in the parking lot. The sun skated along the horizon, doing absolutely nothing to warm anything.

I waved and climbed into my black S-Class Mercedes. I'd retired my Honda Accord when I'd made the move to Philly. They'd had to special order a model without leather seats. I preferred the fabric, nothing sticking to your arms or legs when it was hot out. If the dealership hadn't cut us a sweet deal, I'd have probably stuck to something less flashy, but I had to admit, it was a smooth ride.

Blowing into my hands, I stared up at the stadium in

front of me. How was it colder in there than outside? Sometimes it seemed like a dream I'd wake up from. I was living the pro hockey dream. In my head I was still the same screwed-up twelve-year-old with bruised knuckles, holding on to my guilt about my parents splitting up so tightly I wore it like a shield. The engine purred, and I cranked up the heat.

The hamster wheel of my mind was in overdrive. Hours of my gears working out on the ice, keeping my eyes on everything, left me too unable to settle. My phone buzzed in my cupholder. I grabbed it and tapped the screen.

Colm: Good game.

Me: Two made it past me

Colm: You can't win by yourself. It's not like it was all your fault.

Me: You sure? Sometimes that doesn't matter...

He jumped right over that shit like the minefield it was. Even two years later he still wore that pain on his sleeve—at least to me. No one else saw it, but I did.

Colm: Headed out to get some strange?

Me: I gave that shit up

Our friendship had become a poisoned pill, but I swallowed it because that was what I always did. I wanted to get back to how things used to be, before I'd screwed up his future.

Colm: You act like I don't know who you are.

It didn't deserve a response. He'd banged up his knee. He was probably still loopy on pain meds.

Pulling out of the lot, I drove aimlessly. Philly was where I'd wanted to be, closer to my mom and little brother, and the rest of the Kings, too.

After parking in the garage under my building, I jogged across the street to my version of Cheers, Fish's Bar & Grill. I pushed through the doors, and Jack, the bartender, looked up, nodding his head. I took off toward my stool at the far end of the bar. Fish's was a place where, even if they knew your name, they sure as hell didn't shout it out loud.

"Ford." Jack slung a towel over his shoulder and leaned on the bar.

"Jack." I nodded at him. "I'll have the Forester 1920 and the usual." I drummed my fingers along the nicked and dinged wood.

He nodded. The old-school bar wasn't flashy and it sure as hell didn't serve any artisanal waters or tapas, but it kept me from drinking alone in my apartment. Although Jack had taken the place over from his dad, he seemed content to leave it just as it was, which was fine by me.

My Netflix queue called to me from my apartment. I'd have to people for a solid few hours the next day, so I needed to save my energy reserves. I ran my fingers along my chin. *How will I make it through tomorrow with Liv?*

The throwback decor of green glass lamps hanging over each table, wood paneling, and worn leather booths and stools kept the trendier crowds at bay. It also made it the perfect place for me. I might have been a shut-in, but I wasn't going to turn into an alcoholic. I'd seen some guys go down that path before. Practices were only a couple of hours a day when we weren't traveling for games, and that left a hell of a lot of time to mess yourself up.

My phone rang on the bar. Colm.

"Way to not respond to my text."

"Didn't think it needed a response. Aren't you getting on a plane soon?"

"I am, but we need to talk."

Like when a woman said those words to me, the hairs on the back of my neck stood up.

"What?"

"Olive."

If I'd been wearing a button-down, I'd have tugged at my collar. I cleared my throat. "What about her?" I picked up my glass, trying to gulp down some of my drink past the tightness in my throat.

"She's being weird lately." The concern in his voice bled through the coolness of his words.

"Weird how?"

"Not responding to my texts and calls. She's ducked out of our family dinners at least three times. Since I've moved to Philly, she's fallen off the face of the Earth."

"What do you think it is?" Was she seeing someone? In trouble of some kind?

"No idea, but her grades are slipping."

"Slipping to what?"

"She got three A minuses last semester."

I choked on my bourbon. "You think an A minus is tanking? Do you remember my grades in college?"

"You had a lot of other recreational activities going on." There was an edge to his voice that I'd gotten used to over the past couple years, and I fucking hated it. "You also weren't trying to become a doctor. Listen, do me a favor..." He paused so long I checked to make sure the call hadn't dropped.

"What do you want me to do?" I leaned my elbow against the bar. He hadn't come to me for a favor in a long time.

"I wouldn't be asking, but she'll listen to you."

My fist tightened around the glass at the way he asked, like it was a last resort. Tension gnawed at my chest.

He let out a deep sigh. "Talk to Olive. See if you can figure out what's going on with her. She's distracted. I asked

Mak to find out, but she told me to ask Liv. Olive's just so damn tight-lipped lately, and I need to know she's okay, especially when I'm not there."

"I'm sure she's fine. You're acting like she's still a little kid." He'd always treated her like she was the same scared twelve-year-old clutching his hand and standing beside the gravesite of their parents as her tears mixed with the rain.

"She's my baby sister. I love her more than anything. I need to know she's not screwing up her future. She's all I've got, man."

A lump formed in my throat. Colm didn't trust me, not anymore. If he'd known the thoughts about Liv that were running through my head, he'd have punched my lights out —not that I didn't deserve it and more.

"She's stronger than you think." My appetite was gone. I motioned for Jack that I'd take my food to go.

"But I don't want her to have to be. Just please do this for me. I've got to call her before my flight. I'll talk to you later." He ended the call before I could get in another word. The next day I'd see her, and Colm wanted me to drag information out of her. I was the last person she'd want to see, let alone open up to.

Jack held out the bag for me at the bar, and I grabbed it, buttoned my coat, and headed outside.

"Still looking for that Macallan," he called out, wiping down the bar. I waved and the door slammed behind me.

The elevator in my building dinged, and I got out at my floor. I had no idea who most of my neighbors were, cat lady aside. There were only three apartments on this floor anyway. It was nice and quiet, just how I liked it.

The loft with exposed brick walls had been home for half a year, but it still felt like I was house-sitting. Even with only one bedroom, the twenty-foot ceilings and top-of-the-line finishes were a world away from how things had been for me growing up. I closed the door to my apartment.

Some bottles rattled in my fridge, and Grant shot up straight, closing the stainless-steel door with a slice of cold pizza shoved in his mouth and holding two beers.

"What are you doing here?" *How the hell did he get in?*

"I thought you'd be celebrating after your game. What are *you* doing here?"

"It's only my apartment. I took your key after you brought that girl back here last semester. How'd you get in?"

He bit off another chunk of pizza. "You didn't take Mom's key." He grinned, cracking open his beer on the edge of my granite countertop.

I slid my food onto the counter.

"Fresh food." He reached for the bag, and I punched his shoulder. He winced, and I smiled at the hollow thud.

He glared at me and rubbed the spot. "What was that for?"

"It's bad enough that you break into my apartment and steal my leftovers—now you're trying to steal my meal too?"

"It's not like you can't get more. I'm sure they'd rush over here right away to get another order for the amazing home-town goalie."

"That could have been you." I opened my food and took a plate out of the cabinet.

"With your leftover pads and hand-me-down sticks? No thanks." He snatched a fry off my plate.

"How's school?"

"It's school." Leaning back against the counter, he gulped down his beer.

"Slow down, man. It's not water."

"Gee thanks, Dad."

I hated when he called me that, mainly because I hated

stomach drop and the tips of my ears burn. His words still rang in my head, right along with the image of his arms around another woman.

Once I'd figured out it was a *date* date Grant was after, I'd actually hoped I'd feel something more than friendship for him, hoped maybe I'd been hung up on the wrong brother all this time, but our kiss had produced no toe-curling spark. It had been...nice. I'd gone the easy route and used my premed studying as a cover for why I couldn't go on any more dates. I supposed that was better than "I'm secretly in love with your brother who wants nothing to do with me, so I think being with you might make the holidays a bit awkward." *Kill me now.*

Every crosswalk threw me right into the devil's alley of a swirling vortex of air that seemed to come straight from Antarctica. Tugging my hat down farther onto my head, I crossed the street to my apartment. My legs cried uncle as I made it to the fourth-floor landing. A walk-up wasn't my first choice, but it meant I could split the rent with my room-mate, Marisa, who absolutely refused to let me pay more than half even though it might have eased some of the financial pressure of the situation with her and her dad. She hated that he could hold paying for college over her head.

It wasn't like I needed the money.

It had been that way since we met freshman year when we'd split some appetizers at a restaurant. She refused to ever let me pay more than my share, and even though it frustrated the hell out of me sometimes, she was a real friend, one of the few I'd ever had. That was the hazard of having a famous brother and a trust fund—people inevitably tried to take advantage.

The music from the surrounding apartments thumped as I hit the landing for our floor. Colm's overreaction at the "squalor" I lived in told me I had been right to choose to live off campus this year. Jamming my key into the lock, I jiggled it twice and lifted up on the knob at the same time before the *click*, then I turned it.

Pushing the door open, I yelped when a sock hit me in the middle of my forehead.

"Shit. Sorry, Liv. I was doing a little laundry." Marisa jumped up from the couch. LJ, her "best friend, definitely not boyfriend" as she'd said about a hundred times, lounged on the dark gray cushions.

I closed the door and spotted the laundry basket. "Sock shoot-out?"

"It's the only way to get her to do anything as boring as laundry." LJ hopped up and headed into the kitchen. The gray Henley stretching tight across his chest matched his eyes. Marisa's gaze followed him the entire way. *Just friends, sure...*

I dropped my bag beside the door. Our hodgepodge of furniture filled the living room; posters and art prints graced the walls. We'd really pulled the place together over the past few months. "I'm watching the game in twenty."

They both groaned. "Do you have to watch every. Single. Game?" Marisa pushed LJ out of the way to grab a drink from the fridge.

"Says the girl who watches every one of his games." I jerked my thumb at him, standing in front of the open fridge drinking directly out of a carton of my orange juice.

Her cheeks turned bright red, and she chugged her beer, avoiding eye contact with him.

"This is why I posted the schedule." I pointed to the wall calendar with every home game clearly marked in red and all of LJ's games in barely readable pencil.

"Aww, Risa, you watch all my games?" He chased after

Marisa, who dodged his grip and jumped over the coffee table to get away from him.

"Thanks a lot, Liv. Now he'll never let me live it down."

I grabbed a handful of Twizzlers from the cookie jar on the breakfast bar. "Just trying to make sure everyone's being open and honest. Pop some popcorn." My drenched clothes clung to me. I headed to my room to peel them off.

The white string lights around my room lit it up with a soft glow. Rows of string lined my walls with clothespins holding up pictures from the previous summer. Almost every available surface was covered in a memory, and these were just from the last year. The collection of shoeboxes filled with pictures under my bed had grown, a box for every few years.

I'd stolen every picture I could from our old house before Colm cleared the place out. I'd always loved photographs. There was something about holding the physical photos in my hands. While reading my mom's words on the back, I'd trace my fingers over her terrible doctor's handwriting, usually scribbled when I'd cornered her after getting the pictures printed.

Opening my nightstand drawer, I spotted a picture in the small gap between my bed and the nightstand. With pincer-like finger power, I grabbed the edge, slipped it out, and flipped it over.

It was from Mak and Declan's wedding two summers ago. I'd been a bridesmaid on the arm of Ford. He and Colm were usually joined at the hip, but things had been off at the wedding. They'd been off for a while with those two, but it wasn't like I'd been around either of them much to find out what had happened. But that night wasn't about questions circling Ford and my brother.

I'd looped my arm through Ford's as the doors to the

ceremony opened. His smile had been big and wide as he'd stared into my eyes. For a split second I'd been able to pretend we hadn't been assigned to be together for the ceremony and reception, had pretended he'd picked me—and then our incredible kiss had ruined everything.

For so many major moments in my life, he'd been there for me, and now he was gone. Standing in that same spot, I'd blinked back my tears as he'd made it clear in no uncertain terms that there was nothing more than friendship between us, and now I didn't even have that. I dropped the picture on the bed and wrapped my arms around my waist.

The horrified look on his face when Colm had almost spotted us should have been my first clue. Ford had been trying to cheer me up, and I'd thrown myself at him. His text had probably been sent to let me down gently, to make sure I hadn't gotten the wrong idea. *Stupid!* I smacked my palm against my forehead. Why was the brain always so good at replaying embarrassing moments in high-definition detail? Maybe I'd study it in medical school.

Hockey season was the only justifiable, consistent time I got to see Ford. I was starting to feel like a psycho, puckbunny stalker. I knew his stats for the season, which was shaping up to be his best ever. Watching Philly play wasn't really a choice when Declan, Heath, and Emmett also played for the team. At least that's what I kept telling myself when my gaze drifted to the masked man standing in the center of the goal during every game. Shaking my head, I picked up my towel rushed into the bathroom and jumped into the shower.

Wiping away the steam on the mirror, I stared at my reflection. Why did I do this? Why was I torturing myself by watching every one of his games? I could pretend it was just to watch Colm and I hadn't been doing it since Ford joined the Philly team, but my eyes sought him out in the net, piled with pads, every second he was on screen.

I ran my fingers over my lips. Two summers already? I still thought about that kiss, the way his hands had felt on my waist and how my heart had nearly leaped out of my chest when I'd stood on my toes to taste him. The moment had stretched on for an eternity. I'd compared every kiss I'd had since then to the intensity of it. None had measured up, but the sadness and pain of what had come after always tainted those memories.

My skin broke out into goose bumps. He'd made it abundantly clear how he felt being around me, and the fact that he'd disappeared from my life spoke volumes. With my towel wrapped around myself, I stepped into the hallway and tiptoed into my room. I closed the door and whipped it off, and grabbed my folded pajamas off my bed. The pregame announcements blared from the living room. Jerks were starting it without me. I glanced up and eyed my dresser. Tucked inside was another one of my torture devices. I would not wear his jersey. I wasn't going to do it.

Opening my middle dresser drawer, I hesitated before shoving my hands in and taking out the jersey. A sigh burst out of my lips, and I shook my head. I was even lying to myself now. The jersey had been a gift from him back when we were still friends. Had we even been friends? Or was I just the little sister he humored and had given a toe-curling kiss to before sending me on my way?

I put my hair up into a ponytail. Staring at myself in the mirror, I ran my hands over the roomy jersey.

Yes, I was pissed at him.

Yes, I needed to forget about him.

Yes, I was going to follow my own advice...right after this

game. This night was the last time I was going to think about Ford, about the kiss, and about what had come after.

Move on, Liv. Suck it up and stop obsessing.

Picking up the frame on top of my dresser, I ran my finger along the edge of the picture of my parents before heading out into the living room. "You'd be able to tell me what to do, Mom." Well, if I'd made an appointment through her office to get a few minutes of time with her.

Everything was set up in front of the TV. I quickly whipped up a batch of drinks and returned to the couch. LJ and Marisa had cleared a spot for me. Drinks, popcorn, dip, and chips along with some killer sports action coming my way—who needed anything else?

The crowd in the stadium drowned out the announcers. Every possession and turnover had them on their feet, and I was on mine often, too. I sloshed my drink onto LJ more than a few times.

"Is any of this making it into your mouth?" He wrung out his sleeve.

"Sorry." I cringed and went right back to the game.

Philly was up three to one when a breakaway ended with one shot making it through Ford's defenses. I gritted my teeth at the blare of the goal buzzer.

"Bad call, ref." I shot out of my seat and chucked a handful of popcorn at the TV. Ignoring the looks from LJ and Marisa, I grabbed my glass and drained the last of it. The sweet raspberry flavor warred with the bite of the rum. If Colm could have seen me, he'd have had a fit. My lips lifted in a smirk. One of these days he'd stop seeing me as a little kid.

The seconds ticked by on the game clock. Philly was up by one, but a small mistake was the difference between a solid win and dragging it out into overtime.

Two wings blazed down the ice on the screen. I held my breath at the double team Ford was up against. He blocked the first shot and lunged to stop the second. "Where the hell is the rest of the team?"

Declan, Heath, and Emmett had to be coming out of their skin on the bench. Ignoring the yelps from LJ and Marisa, I dug my fingers into their arms as the puck shot straight for the gap between Ford's skates. He shifted, closing the hole, and the buzzer sounded, signaling the end of the game.

"Christ, Liv. If I'd wanted a dead arm, I'd have sat next to Marisa." LJ rubbed his bicep.

"All those muscles and you're hurting from little old me." I put on my best innocent face, tucking my hands under my chin and batting my eyelashes.

"I stopped buying that act when you challenged me to do those crazy ballet moves." He pushed against my shoulder.

"Aww, the big football player can't do a few pliés?"

"Shut up." He chucked a pillow at my head. I ducked and it hit the half-full plastic pitcher on the table, spilling the last of the sangria all over Marisa, who'd crouched down to grab some popcorn.

"LJ!" she screamed. He grabbed some napkins and started dabbing at the spreading wet spots on her boobs and crotch. Nope, totally not awkward at all. She batted his hands away, and his cheeks turned fire-engine red. "I'm going to kill you. Just for that, I should tell your mom it was you who spray-painted the garage when we were eleven."

He jumped up, and she rushed after him. I collapsed back onto the couch. That small knot forming in my stomach with reminders of what I'd missed out on rose to the surface. They'd been best friends since third grade. Back in third grade, the biggest tragedy in my life had been not getting an invite to the most popular girl in my class's party. Little had I known, just a few years later I'd know what real loss was. My life had been ripped apart in the seventh grade. Sometimes it felt like a part of my life had frozen at that point, and I didn't know if I'd ever feel whole again.

3

FORD

Ducking behind the half wall, I crawled across the floor using only my arms. The noises got closer, and I held my breath, keeping myself as still as possible. A herd of footsteps headed straight for my spot. Rolling over onto my back, I prepared for the attack.

Five heads popped around the corner with huge smiles on their faces.

"You got me," I yelled, holding my hands up in surrender.

They laughed and jumped onto my stomach, barely missing my junk. *Oof.* More kids rounded the corner and added to the pile on. Reminder: toddlers do not have any sense of danger zones.

Tiny, sticky hands went straight for my nose and mouth. Flipping onto my stomach, I covered my head. I opened my eyes and glanced up at the adult legs standing in front of me.

"Hey, Mom." I smiled and went up on all fours. The kids held on, grabbing my shirt and climbing aboard their own personal horse.

"You always show up right before nap time." Her smile was bright and wide, just as pristine as all my childhood memories, wisps of her salt-and-pepper hair flying out of her braid.

She'd dealt with so much since my dad had bailed, but she'd never let it stop her. I didn't know a stronger person.

"I'll help you get them to sleep." I stood and wrapped my arms around my back to catch the kids as they let go of my shirt.

"You'd better or Marianne is going to kick your butt." She laughed.

I ducked my head and waved at Marianne where she was sitting in the corner finishing up snacks with the other half of the kids.

"Don't worry, Mari. I can take them to the soft playroom if they're too hyper after our game of hide-and-seek."

"They wouldn't be too hyper if someone hadn't barreled in here like the Macy's Thanksgiving Day Parade." Her lips thinned.

"Next time I'll keep my parading to a minimum."

She shot me a glare that singed my eyebrows. Turning back to the kids, she was all smiles.

Walking toward the door, I stepped extra high with the additional cargo wrapped around my legs. "Are you guys coming to soft play?" The two kids on each leg peered up at me and nodded. "Hold on, then." Their tiny fingers tightened around my jean-covered calves.

Shuffle-stomping out of the room, I walked across the hall to the soft playroom. The walls were covered in framed paintings the kids had done and pictures of the classes over the years. There were a bunch of Polaroids arranged in the shape of a star with all the kids striking their best dance moves, along with the local childcare award plaques. Joy radiated from the walls. This place was so different than it had been back when we'd first moved in, but we'd made it a home.

Mom had refused to give the place up once I bought her new house. She probably spent more time here than at home. Relaxing wasn't in her nature. Instead of taking the yearlong cruise I'd booked for her, she'd added two more classes and after-school care to the preschool using her bedroom and Grant's, and she'd converted my room into a mini planetarium with projected star charts and meteor showers on the ceiling and walls. She'd also introduced a sliding scale tuition program to help give people who wouldn't normally be able to pay a chance for a spot, not that the waiting list wasn't a year long already.

Falling into the foam blocks, I battled it out with the four non-sleepers.

Running on my knees through a foam pit was harder than it looked. If the team strength and cardio coaches could have seen me then, they'd have been shaking their heads. Hell, if Heath could have seen me, he'd have banished me to the treadmill for the next year. I fell back into the soft blocks, and the kids took turns trying to bury me in a foamy grave.

Their muffled voices muted all around as they slowly covered me. Maybe I could hide out here? Pretend I'd fallen asleep until the dinner was over? I took a deep breath, the foam cubes shifting on top of me. *Things should be okay. She's probably forgotten all about the kiss. Of course she has.* Not even the voice in my head could convince me of that.

For the next twenty minutes the kids helped me with my therapy session AKA distraction from thinking about Liv, complete with slobbery hands, foam to the skull, and a few near-miss nut shots. I stared at the upside-down child hovering above my head. He looked at me with pity before a sneak attack finger to the nose, followed by a yawn. Sitting up and rising from the foam pit, I gathered up the other yawning kids.

"Okay, little people, looks like some of you are tired." They all shook their heads with mops of curls, dark and light, bouncing around. "I think it's time for a nap. Let's get you some water, and then I'll read you a story."

We joined hands, walking into the now empty classroom, everyone else already in the nap room. I grabbed a book and settled onto a beanbag. Narrowly missing knees and elbows flailing as they tried to get comfortable, I opened the book and read some of *The Very Hungry Caterpillar*.

"You know you've always got a backup career whenever you're finished with hockey." Mom stood in the doorway with her arms folded across her chest.

I lifted my head from the wall and glanced down at the four kids piled onto the beanbag with me.

"They're all asleep. You've got the magic touch." She picked up some of the toy carnage.

"More like a lot of energy to burn, but I'm beat. How can kids tire me out more than hockey?"

"They drain the power of the sun like Superman. Most of the time it's a nearly bottomless pit of energy until they crash or have a meltdown—or both." She helped pick them up off me; then Marianne came in and helped us get them into the nap room. The dim lighting, gentle classical versions of pop songs, and soft cots made me want to curl up in there, too.

Creeping out of the room, I closed the door behind me with barely a click.

"I'm so glad you're back in town." Mom squeezed her

arms around my neck. "Now I've got my two best guys together again." Mom and I put away some of the toy explosion in the Butterfly Room. "Grant's been coming by more often too, and not just for laundry. I think he's trying to orchestrate a run-in with Olivia."

I froze, bent over as I picked the dress-up costumes off the floor. "Olivia? As in Olivia Frost? You see Liv?"

"Sure. She comes by a couple times a month to do a little dance class for the kids. They always get a kick out of it. Grant's always asking before he comes over to see if she's going to be here."

The muscles in my neck tightened, and I glanced around the room like I'd be able to sense where she'd been. "How long has she been coming by?"

"This past year. I've helped her out with some motherly advice types of things. It must be so hard growing up and not having a mom to talk to. I know Colm does his best, but it's not the same." She let out a sigh and clutched the toys to her chest.

That night at the wedding, Liv had been upset during Mak's father-daughter dance. Of course it had been hard on her. How had I not thought about that? About what it might be like for her on her own in the city? And I hadn't tried to help with anything at all.

"I haven't seen her much lately." More like I'd avoided her at all costs.

"That's a shame. It's nice having her around. I get to do girlie things without having to hear my men moan about being dragged along."

Liv had been hanging out with my mom and I'd had no idea.

"She usually called to check if you were around. She

must have wanted to see you." She grinned, but I knew the opposite was true.

Seemed like I hadn't needed to avoid Liv at all—she'd been avoiding me too. She probably regretted the kiss, wished it hadn't happened, and didn't want to make things awkward. Sure, she'd had a crush on me back in middle school, but that was a little kid thing. When I'd kissed her at the wedding after her freshman year of college, she'd probably realized reality didn't measure up to the fantasy.

My stomach knotted at the thought of the meet up at Heath's place later today. If I bailed, I had no doubt they'd track me down. Maybe Liv would back out if she knew I was going to be there. That made the knot tighter.

"Your dad's birthday is coming up."

"Is he still alive?"

"He sent a birthday card a few weeks ago." She sighed, taking it out of her pocket.

"There's nothing I need to say to him." I hadn't spoken to him since he'd left, since he'd packed up after I told Mom about his affair. Mom had still been in the hospital when she'd broken her leg cleaning out the gutters like he was supposed to. He'd packed up his bags and cleared out the family account. The image of Mom sitting at the kitchen table, staring at the stack of bills with tears streaming down her face would always stay with me. Where had he been then? Fucking gone. The guilt ate at me for keeping that secret from my mom for two weeks before I told him I was telling her, spilled everything, and then he bolted on us.

After everything he'd done, she tried to get us to talk to him and shared updates here and there. He didn't deserve any of our time, especially not hers. I took the card so she wouldn't worry about it and shoved it into my back pocket.

"I don't like you hanging on to that anger in your heart,

sweetie." She ran her hand over my chest. I closed my hand over top of hers and squeezed it.

I embraced the anger; it helped melt away some of the guilt. What if I hadn't said anything? Would he have stayed? Saved Mom from all that stress and pain? It was guilt I'd carried with me for a long time with little bits added on with each secret I kept. It clung to me like a magnet, finding me no matter how much I tried to avoid it. My parents' divorce, that kiss with Liv, Colm's ex-fiancée—the strikes against me kept piling up.

Mom straightened up the bookshelf and walked over to me. She looped her arm through mine. "When are you going to introduce us to your girlfriend?"

"Not this again, Mom. I'd have to have a girlfriend first." I groaned and slowed my steps, but she held on tight to my arm. Damn, she was strong. Must have come with the territory of lifting all those little kids all day. "There's no girl to introduce you to. If there were, you'd be the first to know."

"And why not? You're very handsome, a professional athlete—a catch, if I do say so myself." She stepped in front of me with her hands on her hips like she was ready to rip any woman who didn't want to be with me a new one.

"It's hard with traveling so much and avoiding the fake people out there. It's better to keep things casual." I squeezed the back of my neck and stared down at the floor.

She grabbed me by my chin, lifting my head. "That means you're playing the field, huh?"

I met her eyes. It was the same disapproving look I used to get when I came into the house with busted and bruised knuckles as a kid.

My gaze darted away from hers. "I'm weighing my options."

"Don't weigh them for too long. I don't like you bumping

around all by yourself. You can't count on the Kings to force you out of being a hermit. Where's Colm been? He's back in town, and I've barely seen him. Oh, these are for you." She handed over a box of cookies. The colorful sprinkles peeked out from under the plastic on the top of the box.

"He's in LA now because of his knee. Why are you acting like I'm an eternal bachelor at twenty-five? I promise you'll be the first to know when I find that special someone."

"I'd better be."

"I'm heading out. I'll see you when I'm back from my next stretch of away games. Do you need me to do anything before I leave?"

"I need a hug." She plastered a kiss on my cheek, and I squeezed her tight. She squirmed in my hold and laughed. "And can you take out the trash? It's always a nightmare after lunch." She pinched my cheeks before disappearing into her office by the front door. Always ducking out on the dirty work.

"On it." Balancing the box of cookies in one hand, I grabbed my coat, shrugged it on, and picked up the trash bags. A woman pushed through the front door of the school and skidded to a halt when she spotted me in the entryway. Her gaze darted from the black bags in my hand to my face.

"You're the hottest trash man I've ever seen." She snapped her mouth shut, and her cheeks turned even pinker.

"Thanks," I mumbled, holding the bags in front of me.

"Don't I know you from somewhere?" Her eyebrows dropped, and I averted my eyes. "I don't usually do this..." She licked her lips, and I grimaced. "But here." She scribbled something down using the pen from the sign in/sign out sheet, then shoved a folded-up piece of paper into my pocket as I skirted by her. There were a number of rules I'd set for myself about women who were absolutely off-limits, and anyone whose kid went to my mom's school fell solidly into that territory. Shouldering the door open, I escaped into the sharp, freezing February air.

Making sure she wasn't looking, I dumped the bags and her number into the dumpster right along with the card from my dad. He didn't deserve any better than that. I got into my car and snagged one of the cookies from the top, showering myself in pink and purple sugar crystals. Brushing at my shirt, I devoured the cookie, which was the perfect blend of sugar and vanilla.

My phone pinged.

Declan: If you don't show, we're driving over to your apartment and bringing the party to you.

Heath: Hell, if you don't show, we might all decide to have a slumber party at your place!

Emmett: Just make sure you show up so these two don't get any crazy ideas...

All I needed to do was get Liv to tell me what was going on with her. It wasn't like her to shut Colm out, and worry nagged at the back of my mind. Was she in trouble? She knew she could come to me if anything big happened, right? How the hell would she when I'd stayed so far away? Squeezing the back of my neck, I started my car and headed toward Heath's place. *Be cool, it's fine. I'm sure she thinks about it like a distant memory.*

I grimaced and shook my head. What had I been thinking? This was Olive. Olive Oil forever. *Ask a few questions, give Colm the update, and back the hell off. Easy as that.*

LIV

My black boots clicked on the cobblestone sidewalk, and I tugged on my braid, which was draped over my shoulder, my fingers tingling inside my gloves. Closing my books earlier and shutting down my brain to come had been the highlight of my week. These dinners were hard to pull off during the season because the guys were always traveling, and seeing everyone in one room was like being transported to a simpler time, back when I'd sneaked into Colm's room at home while they were all in there playing video games and discussing "guy things," eavesdropping like any good sister would.

They'd talked about their games and hot girls at school. Declan had always squawked about something Mak had said that got under his skin. The biggest things anyone had to worry about were sports, grades, and how much beer they could get from Emmett's booze hookup.

Then there was the juicy stuff. The crap Declan, Heath, and Colm would give Ford because of the expectations the girls at Rittenhouse Prep had after being with him always came up in conversation. He kept it to himself, never being big on locker room talk, but it seemed the girls had no trouble shouting about their time with him from the rooftops. The jealousy burned brightly even though my curiosity hadn't kept me from wanting to hear more.

This group was the closest I had to childhood friends. Sure, they were really Colm's friends, but I wasn't opposed to barging in on get-togethers if they came with awesome food and memories I wanted to snapshot in my mind. Plus, Ford usually steered clear, so it was a win-win-win.

The morning had been rough. Marisa had had a blowup with her mom on the phone over something, her raised voice filtering through the closed door to her bedroom. Even with how screwed up that relationship was, not to mention the one with her dad, there was still the chance of change, the glimmer of hope that they could repair things. The possibility wasn't even an option for me, and I hated the pangs of envy scratching at my gut.

Those feelings had bubbled up more and more lately, and that wasn't fair. I was sure I'd have been having those same issues with my mom—if she'd been around and not working 100 hours a week. It was why my trips to Ford's mom's had become more frequent over the last year.

Sinking into her hugs, I could pretend for an instant she was my mom. I dreaded graduating from college. Everyone would be there with their proud parents for pictures and parties. High school graduation had been an unexpected blow, a milestone people took for granted while bitching about dressing up and posing for photographs. I'd have given anything for Mom to come up and wipe a smudge off my cheek with a spit-covered finger.

The father-daughter dance at Mak's wedding had started the highlight reel of everything I'd miss out on with Mom and Dad gone. Stopping in the middle of the sidewalk,

I stared up at the sky and blinked back the moisture there. *Stupid wind, making my eyes water. Get it together, Liv. This is ancient history. Nothing you can do about it. Just keep swimming.*

Heath and Kara's brick town house was tucked in alongside all the other red brick historical homes not too far away from our old high school—well, what would have been my old high school if I hadn't shuffled along to Boston with Colm just before my freshman year.

Being thrown in the deep end with boarding school girls at the peak of puberty had been the gift that kept on giving. My photo album from the first few months included a hell of a lot of pictures of the landscaping around the school and the library. Learning to make friends, mixing drinks, and having a college-aged brother who picked me up for weekly dinners had saved me from abject isolation and shunning.

I stood at the bottom of the steps to the house and smoothed my gloved hands down the front of my camel-colored cashmere coat. Laughter filtered out from inside, and I smiled. I'd never been happier to get folded into a group of friends as the little tagalong sister than I was with the Kings. Lifting my hand to knock on the door, I froze, and the hairs on the back of my neck stood up.

"Hey, Liv."

My back went ramrod straight. I spun on my heel. "Ford." The word was almost swallowed up by the sharp winter air.

His hands were shoved into his pockets as he took two hesitant steps closer to me like I was a wild animal who might bolt at any second.

He had on a double-breasted black pea coat and jeans that hugged his thighs, powerful muscles honed over years on the ice and daily workouts. Our breath hung between us in small puffs of frozen air. Why did he have to look so good in winter clothing?

"Why are you here?"

"You look good."

We spoke at the same time. He looked back at me with wide eyes like when you say that one thing you've been telling yourself not to say or focus on. Like one day in class, my stomach was rumbling and the teacher called on me and I just yelled out "Bread!"—exactly like that. Ford was probably hoping I wouldn't take it the wrong way and attempt to jump his bones right there on the sidewalk.

"Thanks."

"Why are you here?" I repeated, hoping maybe he'd decided to go for a walk and happened to be in the neighborhood and wasn't, in fact, going inside where I'd have to be around him for the next few hours.

His eyebrows dropped and pulled together like he wasn't even sure himself. Someone passed by on the sidewalk, casting a sidelong glance at the two of us doing living statue impersonations.

His gaze landed on mine. That sparking, skin-on-fire feeling rushed through my body, and I couldn't move. The fullness of his lips contrasted with the scruff on his cheeks, reminding me how they'd felt on my mouth. Seeing every light brown fleck in his gray eyes was like reacquainting myself with a painting I'd once stared at every day. My heart pounded in my chest. Everything I'd promised myself went out the window the second I was within three feet of him.

My stomach turned itself into an intricate balloon animal with each passing second. I'd seen him on the TV screen the day before, but this was the living, breathing man standing in front of me. All those same giddy feelings I'd felt back when I'd discovered what a crush was rushed forward, but they were now tinged with reality. I clamped down on those schoolgirl sensations; I wasn't one anymore. I wasn't mindlessly following him around searching for a sliver of his attention. I'd had it, full on. My lips had felt the ghost of his touch for days, and my heart had borne the bruises from his rejection for months.

The front door flew open, and Kara stood in the doorway. Her black curls were pinned up by a pencil jammed into her bun. "I thought I saw you walk up. Hi, Ford. Come in! Everyone's here already." She stepped out of the doorway and waved us inside. Ford tugged his hat off. His shaggy hair. With the short beard, he looked a bit more like the Ford I'd had a crush on back when I was in middle school, and somehow that hurt a little bit more. Back then I'd had the hope of possibility. He shoved the hat into his coat pocket.

I unbuttoned my coat and shrugged it off. Kara grabbed them both and put them in the coat closet. Kara and Heath had been together since his senior year of college when she was a master's student and, scandalously, his TA.

"Look who I found hiding out on the doorstep!" She tugged Ford forward by the arm, and a big cheer went up from the rest of the guys in the dining room. They barreled forward and swarmed him with limbs flying like they hadn't seen each other the day before.

"I thought we'd have to burn down your place to get you out of there." Declan clapped him on the back. The muscles in Ford's neck tensed so tightly it looked like it hurt, and then he relaxed and smiled back.

"And I also found someone else out there." Kara pulled me forward. I stepped up out of the shadows, and the pile of hockey players transferred from Ford to me.

"Olive!"

"Liv!"

I rolled my eyes at the collective yell. My childhood nickname hadn't died the death it deserved. I'd been tall for my age at eleven and then had just...stopped growing. Olive Oil had been my name back then when everyone thought I'd inherited my parents' height. Colm was over six feet tall, as were the rest of the guys. I, however, had capped out at five-four, which wasn't that short, but around them I felt like a teacup poodle.

Delicious smells wafted out of the kitchen, sweet and savory dueling for top billing on what I was going to devour first. Ford made himself scarce over by the bar cart, checking out Heath's bourbon collection. Of course he did.

"You guys are going to crush her." Mak batted them off me and pulled me in for a hug. "How's the biochem prep going?" Mak had been a godsend with my premed requirements trying to eat my life, consuming any free time, and destroying my brain. Her note-card method kept everything organized. She was going to make an amazing doctor.

"It's going. I took the practice exams, and I'm hitting the high eighties on them, so I'm no longer ready to pull my hair out, but not doing as well as I need to be."

"You'll get there, and you know I'm just a phone call away if you need anything."

"Remember that when the organic chemistry final is coming up and I'm knocking on your door."

Avery leaned out of the kitchen with a glass pitcher filled with mint leaves. "Liv, get in here and make us some raspberry mojitos." Her standard uniform of jeans and ripped sweatshirt showed she hadn't changed one bit over the years. There may or may not have been little bits of icing stuck in her chestnut hair, a hazard of owning a bakery.

Ford's head snapped up from his intense study of the

five liquor bottles in front of him over at the bar tucked in the corner.

"Duty calls." I saluted the guys and departed for my kitchen escape route.

"Jesus Christ, you're right. It's like she stepped out of a catalog," was my greeting the second I crossed the threshold into the kitchen.

I whipped around at the new girl's voice. "Thank you?" Black boots, dark blue jeans, and my sweater with the bow accent on the shoulder didn't seem catalog-worthy to me.

"Max, this is Liv. Liv, this is Max. She works at my bakery and creates things like this." Avery pushed her turquoise-haired friend out of the way, and I gasped. Behind her on the counter was a small two-tiered cake. The icing matched Max's hair, and she'd also created an intricate pattern in gold that looked like a cross between paisley and henna designs you'd see covering someone's hands.

"That's gorgeous." I walked toward the cake and clasped my hands in front of me to beat down the temptation to touch it. It wasn't a cake—it was a piece of art. "You did all this?"

Max's peacock-blue head bobbed. "Trying something new. Avery's trying to pimp me out to the high-society party set for weddings and stuff." She shrugged, resting her hands on her paint-splattered jeans. "It probably pays better than she does." A sneaky smirk curled her lips.

"Hey!" A shout of mock outrage came from Avery.

Emmett, with his regrown scruffy facial hair, popped his head into the kitchen and made his way to Avery immediately.

"Everything okay in here?" Nuzzling her cheek and wrapping his arms around her waist, he rocked the two of them back and forth to music no one else could hear. The dark days of brooding Emmett were over, and now he was like an eager puppy whenever she was near him.

"We're fine. Max is just being an ass, as usual." She covered his hands with hers. The massive ring on her finger caught all the available light in the room, bathing us in a rainbow kaleidoscope of colors.

"Leave us to our work, Cinderella. Your ring is burning a hole straight through my retinas." Max spun back around and picked up the tiniest piping bag I'd ever seen, going back to her detailed work on the cake.

"I'll be right back, Liv. Everything you need should be there." Emmett rushed Avery out of the room. They were probably going to find a nice secluded nook to make out in.

I sighed. Maybe I needed a date. It had been almost five months since I'd left the house with anyone other than Marisa.

"What's your deal, Disney princess?" Max swung back around, propping her feet up on the bottom rung of the stool.

"My deal?" I scrunched my eyebrows.

"How'd you end up with this ragtag group? You're kind of young, aren't you?" She lifted an eyebrow.

"I'm the younger sister tagging along. The guys all played hockey with my brother, Colm, who got traded down here a few months ago."

"Weird being around so many pro athletes, huh?" She peered out the open kitchen doorway.

"I'm used to it. I've been around these guys since they first got on the ice. Sometimes I forget they're famous now. What about you? What's your deal, tough girl?"

Her head jerked back, and her eyes widened. A big smile spread across her face. "I knew I liked you." She set down her gold icing and leaned against the counter. "My deal:

orphan, baker, candlestick maker, resident big mouth, and tough girl, as you mentioned." She flexed her arm and kissed her bicep. Staring at me, she lifted her chin toward me. My turn.

"My deal: orphan, little sister, dancer, resident fashionista." I swooped my arms out in front of me to show off the outfit she'd already commented on.

"No college?" She lifted an eyebrow.

"Right, that too. I'm premed in college." Why hadn't I said college student?

"And a brainiac to boot. Go you. I hear you're also a master mixologist. Avery, Kara, and Mak have been going on and on about your cocktails since I got here. I'm excited to try them, but no skimping on the booze." She winked at me and spun back around to face her sugar-laden masterpiece.

Her work was mesmerizing. The precision of her movements and the patterns she created entranced me. She was in a world where nothing else existed other than buttercream and a painstaking attention to detail.

I grabbed a pan out of the cabinet, threw in some water and sugar, and then cranked up the heat. Turning to get the pitcher of mint leaves, I spotted a tall, scruffy-cheeked figure in the doorway. I took a deep breath and beat back the flutters in my stomach. Did this have to happen every damn time I saw him? It'd only been eight minutes.

"Hi, Ford." That sounded nonchalant, right?

He froze, like if he didn't move I wouldn't see him. "They need some more glasses out there."

The air around us crackled. Was it all in my head? Maybe it was. He'd shouted at me to get lost after the wedding with that puck bunny all over him, the smear of her lipstick on his cheek. I'd gone over it so many times. Why had he kissed me? Had he just been trying to cheer me up? Had he done the one thing he knew could stop me from thinking about everything I'd lost? If so, he'd done one hell of a job. My body had hummed in anticipation of more, and then that future had been ripped away.

I felt the heat from his fingers, which were less than an inch away from mine on the cool counter.

"Holy sexual tension, Batman, you two are going to melt the icing on my cake." Max's laughter broke the thin line that stretched between me and Ford, releasing us from its grip. "How long has this thing been going on?"

I stared at her with wide eyes, shaking my head. My chest tightened.

"No!" he shouted.

"Not even a little bit. We've known each other forever. He's...we're...there's no sexual tension here, not at all, and we're certainly not dating." Had someone broken out a flamethrower? Because my cheeks were on fire. I might have overdone the denial the *tiniest* bit. This was my worst nightmare come to life. Did he think I was in there talking about him to Max? Did he think I was still hung up on him? I mean, I kind of was, but he didn't need to know that. Did he think I was there hoping to run into him? Or that I'd been pining away for him? I pumped up that outrage. It would keep me from doing something stupid like trying to talk to him.

"Whatever you say," Max sing songed.

"I'll get the glasses." I wrenched the cabinet open. The handle flew out of my hand, and the glass rattled. I winced at my clumsiness and nearly cleared out the entire shelf of glasses, gently putting them on the counter. Avoiding eye contact, I stirred the pot, which was now at a rolling boil, and then turned off the burner.

He gathered up all ten glasses at once and left the kitchen, showing off with his massive hands.

I lifted the pot and swung around, skidding to a halt and nearly sloshing piping-hot simple syrup all over us both when he reappeared behind me.

"How did you become the designated cocktail maker?" He leaned against the edge of the counter like we were old friends catching up. Well, we were old friends, but this was the first time he'd initiated a conversation with me in a long time.

"I picked it up a little bit here and there." I wasn't going to tell him it had been at boarding school. All I needed was an earful from Colm when that made its way back to him. I'd promised him two summers ago that my mixology skills would be on ice until I was officially twenty-one. Grabbing a handful of the mint leaves, I stuck them in the simple syrup. "Good game yesterday." I kept my eyes trained on the pitcher in front of me.

"You watched?"

"I watch every game you guys play. It's a compulsion Colm's drilled into me over the years." It wasn't to watch him, though—totally definitely not to watch him.

Ford opened his mouth before snapping it shut. He was a regular chatty Cathy, just like old times.

I went back to work on the drinks.

"How's school?" His hands were shoved in his pockets, and he rocked back on his heels.

"Why do you want to know?" I lifted an eyebrow and sighed. "It's going well. Mak's been helping me study."

"That's great. No issues? Nothing upsetting you?"

My gaze narrowed. "Everything's fine, Ford." I grabbed the muddler off the counter.

"No guy trouble or anyone giving you problems?" His gaze locked on to mine.

"Nothing to report, inquisitor." The raspberries met the business end of the short wooden dowel.

"I just wanted to be sure you know if you need anything, you can always ask."

"Ask who? You? Yeah, right." This was the most he'd said to me in over a year.

"Of course from me."

I scoffed. Now he was pissing me off. "You made it clear that I shouldn't count on you for anything." The swirling red mess at the bottom of the pitcher looked like a crime scene. There weren't a lot of people I was close to, and he'd been one of them until suddenly he wasn't.

"Liv, I never meant—"

My chest tightened, and it was hard to catch my breath. "Can you go now?" I didn't look up from my work. I was tempted to check his forehead and see if he was running a fever and delirious. Had he gotten his bell rung during the game the night before and I'd missed it?

He let out a deep sigh and left the room.

I stared after him, trying to figure out what the hell had just happened. One minute he was running away from me like I had a chronic case of halitosis, and the next he was playing twenty questions.

"You know he's into you." Max's voice broke through the intense fruit-mashing session I had going on.

"Maybe he was once for a split second, but it's too complicated now." I glanced over at her. Swallowing past the lump in my throat, I squeezed my eyes shut. Even if he was, there wasn't anything I could do about it. The things Grant had confided in me... We'd gone to the Rittenhouse Prep playground after grabbing a bite to eat. Sitting on the swings, he'd talked about how relieved he was that I'd said yes to the date, about how much he'd always had a crush on me and the worry he'd had about never measuring up against his all-star brother.

I'd dropped my gaze to the wooden mulch covering the ground and hadn't said anything. He'd figured Ford had already beaten him to the punch in asking me out. Ford had always been the first at everything: state championships, getting dates, going pro. Grant had talked about how he'd always felt like Ford had become the man of the house and he'd been relegated to kid status. I identified with that hardcore.

I had choked back the tightness in my chest and let him know he definitely didn't have to worry about Ford, said I wasn't interested anymore. Replaying it over and over in my head, I shook my head at how I'd tried to convince myself through Grant that I was over Ford. Stupidity had had a field day that summer.

Then there was the rocky relationship between Ford and Colm. I didn't have all the details, but things had been off for a long time—too long. Even if Ford had been an option once, he wasn't anymore. It was time to button up that old dream and lock it away.

Even if that weren't enough, he was a hockey player, and I knew that life: puck bunnies throwing themselves at him, always on the road, over eighty games a season. That wasn't a settled life, all the staticky phone calls, the missed and delayed flights and general mayhem. Even if he wanted me —which he didn't—what kind of life would that be when I craved stability above all else?

"If you say so, but you didn't see the way he checked out your ass when he was lurking in the doorway."

"Right, to make sure I hadn't accidentally sat in something or gotten dirt on my pants by playing on the monkey bars after school." I grabbed more raspberries that had escaped my berry massacre and crushed them in the pitcher. Anything to do with Ford was a one-way trip to heartache. *Been there, done that, got the jersey.*

FORD

Real freaking smooth. I resisted slamming my head against the wall.

How was I supposed to be in the same room with her and not watch her? Not think about her laugh? Her lips? Want to feel her pressed against me? Her hair hung in a thick golden braid over her shoulder. She'd only gotten more beautiful, and she hated me. Hell, even I hated me sometimes.

The streak of white hair straight up the back of her head was tucked away in her blonde strands. Colm had the same one through his hair at the front. It was one of the only things that made people believe they were siblings.

When she was standing there in front of me, she wasn't Colm's little sister or the girl Grant had had a crush on since third grade. She was Liv, the woman who'd haunted my dreams for so long I'd stopped wanting to wake up because when I opened my eyes, I knew I could never have her. I was the frog and she was the boiling water, slowly turning up the heat, and soon I'd be cooked, which was why I'd pushed her away so hard.

A choir of timers went off with phones buzzing across the table. "Dinner's ready!" Heath jumped up from his seat and dashed into the kitchen. He was a hell of a cook. Even after eating my mom's cookies, the smells filling the air had my stomach rumbling.

The guys were so much like family, and I didn't want to let them down and drive the wedge even further between me and Colm. Easier to stay away and not take the risk. Secrets and lies had a way of coming back at the worst possible moment.

Like Colm's not-quite fiancée, for one. No one else knew. It was bad enough hooking up with the team owner's daughter. Sleeping with someone like that was bad news. If I'd known who she was, I wouldn't have gone near her. Turned out there was more than one reason it was a night I regretted.

Eventually Colm had introduced me to the woman he'd been sneaking around seeing. He had thought it would look bad, sleeping with someone from the opposing team, so he'd kept it quiet, so quiet he hadn't even told me he was seeing someone. *Felicity.* A drunken hookup when I was new to the city had turned into one of the worst moments of my life when he opened the door to the restaurant with his girlfriend—her—on his arm.

When her eyes landed on me, they'd gotten so wide and scared. I was the guy she'd fucked in the coat closet of the club after the season opener celebration. Happiness radiated off Colm, and I didn't say a word. I sat across the table from him, chewing food that tasted like sawdust and keeping my mouth shut. I couldn't break his heart like that, not for a one-time thing.

She begged me not to tell him, promised me it would never happen again. I should have said something, should

have told him right then and there, but the ultimatum I'd
given my dad when I was a kid had come roaring back. He'd
broken my mom's heart. I'd heard her crying behind closed
doors after the divorce. I'd wanted to spare Colm that, but
turned out I'd only made it worse.

"Are you casing the place? Sit down—you're making us
nervous." Emmett dragged the chair beside him out from
the table and motioned for me to sit. Pushing off the wall, I
dragged my fingers through my hair. I dropped into the seat.
Declan slid a glass of bourbon across the table to me.

"It looks like you could use that." He dropped into a
chair on the other side of the table and looked over our
shoulders into the kitchen. "What's going on with you and
Liv?" His eyes bored into mine.

I lifted the crystal tumbler to my lips to buy myself some
more time. The sweet and smoky burn shot down my throat.

"Nothing."

"Bullshit, dude. This is us you're talking to, and Colm
isn't here." Emmett peered over his shoulder into the
kitchen where bodies crisscrossed in front of the doorway.

"There's nothing to tell. I'm keeping my distance. All is
right with the world."

"If nothing's going on, why would you need to keep your
distance?" Declan's *gotcha* smirk made me want to throw
something at him.

"You can tell us." Emmett dropped his voice. "We saw
you two at the wedding. Avery and I saw you kiss her." His
whispered words sent a shock through my body. Bourbon
sloshed onto my hand, and the smoky aftertaste of my drink
turned sour in my mouth.

I gripped the edge of the table. "It was a mistake." My
jaw tightened, and I slammed my lips together. Could
everyone else hear my heart pounding? Or was that the

blood thrumming in my ears and drowning out everything else after the words *I saw you kiss her*?

My moment of weakness... Being so close to her with tears swimming in her eyes, I hadn't been able to walk away. I should have found Colm and told him Liv was upset instead of rushing out of the wedding reception after her. The tears had done me in, and I'd been the one to put them in her eyes again later that damn night.

She was my weakness. It was so easy to give in, but that dam bursting would flood the plains, drown my oldest friendship, and leave nothing behind.

"Dude, chill the hell out. You look like you're going to blow a blood vessel. We're not going to rat you out or anything—or does Colm already know? Is that why things have been so...weird?" Emmett stared at me like I could clue him in to what was going on, but I couldn't.

I took a deep breath and ran my hand over my face. "No, he doesn't know. That's not why things are...weird." I rubbed my hands along the sides of my glass, the cool condensation doing nothing to beat back the heat rising along the back of my neck. "The kiss"—I licked my dry-as-ash lips—"was a one-time thing. She was upset."

"Makes perfect sense—you decided to calm her down with your tongue?" Declan laughed from the other side of the table.

I shot him a glare that would melt steel, and he did his best clam impersonation. His Adam's apple bobbed up and down as the ceiling became the most interesting part of the room.

"Listen, no judgment. She's been crushing on you since forever."

I squeezed the back of my neck. "That's part of the problem. It's like a habit for her, ingrained back when she was a preteen. I'm not about to be the guy going after a teenager."

"But she's not a teenager anymore. She'll be twenty-one in a couple of months. If she's into you and you're into her, what's the problem?" Declan leaned back in his seat like it was that easy.

"What about Colm?" He'd treated her like Bubble Boy since their parents died. She'd been a kid then, but he thought he could protect her after one of the worst things that could happen to a kid had already ripped away any sense that the world was a safe place.

Emmett took a swig from his glass. "He realizes she needs to grow up sometime, right?"

"I'm not going to be the one to break that to him. You remember the beach house." My stomach turned.

Coming back from our guys fishing trip three summers ago, we'd walked into the house and right into Liv coming down the stairs with some guy. It had been bad enough sharing a room with her and Colm, but watching her run around in bikinis and sleep shorts had been straight-up torture.

Walking into the house as she slipped the strap of her tank back up with that fucker coming down the stairs behind her, I had wanted to break something. I had no right to dictate anything about who she wanted to date, kiss, or do anything else with, but it had killed me nonetheless.

"Emmett probably doesn't remember because he was grudge-fucking Avery in the back bedroom."

Emmett jumped across the table, rocketing a fork straight at Declan's head. Declan dodged the flying utensil, which clattered against the wall.

"Hey, no denting the walls. This is a new place." Heath walked out of the kitchen with a huge dish in his ovenmitted hands. A steady flow of food followed behind him, and Liv carried a pitcher.

"Is everyone having mojitos?" She rattled the container.

"That's a silly question—of course we are!" Avery yelped as Emmett tugged her down onto his lap, nearly toppling over the tray of glasses. "Em, hands off. I'm carrying glassware." She laughed and kissed the side of his face.

The table turned into a scene of chaos and mayhem as everyone lunged for the food, trying to secure the biggest piece of chicken parmesan. The ladies ducked out of the way, protecting their drinks from the encroaching horde.

Liv poured more of the red and pink mixture into everyone's cups, ducking and dodging flying limbs. She stood at my end of the table. "Did you want one?"

Lifting my glass, I held it out to her. She wrapped her hand around my cup, our fingers brushing against each other. I jerked my hand back though I wanted to slip it under hers and feel her palm pressed against my skin. It was death by a thousand looks and touches.

Her gaze bounced around the room, trying to find another seat, any seat other than the open one to my right. There weren't any. Pinching her lips together, she took it, every muscle in her body tensed like I might pounce on her at any second.

Easy conversation flowed around me as the gentle brush of her leg against mine every couple of minutes sent a pulsing throb through my body.

The food in the serving dishes was piled high even after the chicken parm bandits had their fill. Heath cooked for a small army, which was saying something when he was cooking for pro athletes. They'd have leftovers for weeks.

"Heath, if you weren't such a good hockey player, I'd say

you have a future as a chef." Avery patted her stomach, and Emmett nuzzled her neck. They were just as vomit-inducing as they'd been back in high school.

"Can I have another one, Liv?" Mak shook her glass in the air and smacked her lips. Declan plucked it out of her hand.

"You've already had two."

"I can handle it." She smacked her lips together again, and Declan shook his head.

"Liv, how about some virgin ones? Otherwise I'll be on hair-holding duty tonight." He wrapped his fingers around her reddish curls and held them back from her face. She stuck her tongue out and batted his hands away. Grabbing her glass away from him, Mak held it out to Liv, who poured her half a glass.

"Ready for dessert?" The new addition, Max, hopped up from the table and disappeared back into the kitchen. A second later she came back balancing the two-tiered cake with gold and blue designs on it, everyone oohing and aahing at the intricate details. The gold icing reminded me of Liv's hair, shimmering and breathtaking.

Max shrugged and tucked her turquoise hair behind her ear. It matched the icing. "This is a practice cake. I needed to make sure I could get the flowers right."

"I don't want to cut it." The look on Kara's face was straight-up distress. "How can you cut this? It's so beautiful." Her fingers ghosted along the edge of the edible flowers piled on top.

Without warning, a huge knife sliced through all the delicate petals. Max wielded it like the cake had slapped her mother. "It tastes better than it looks."

"But...we didn't even get to take a picture." Kara glanced

up at Max like she'd taken a club to a baby seal in her dining room.

"You get used to it." Avery laughed, holding out her plate for a slice. "Max makes the most beautiful desserts and loves to watch the world burn when she destroys them."

"What can I say? I'm a rebel." Max rolled her eyes and continued cutting and doling out the pieces to everyone at the table. "Cakes are meant to be eaten. They're pretty things to look at and then they go away." With everyone served, she sat down and dug into her slice.

Liv inhaled her piece.

"Someone grab the plate before she accidentally eats it," Heath called out before shoving another forkful of cake into his mouth.

Liv ran her finger across the plate to catch every last bit of chocolate.

"Wow." The word was out before I could stop it.

She glanced up at me like a deer in headlights. Her cheeks turned beet red, and her eyes narrowed.

"It's really good." Chocolate coated her teeth and covered the side of her cheek.

"You've got some cake on your face." I pointed to the spot.

She picked up a napkin and wiped at it, spreading it even more.

"Gone?" She stuck out her chin, turning to Kara to give her a better look. Before Kara could say anything, I jumped in.

"No, right here." I pointed to the same spot on my face.

Her gaze darted back to mine, and she hesitated, like speaking another word to me pained her. She rubbed the napkin and smeared even more along her skin.

"Is there chocolate on the napkin? You're making it worse." I laughed and held out a fresh napkin.

Her lips pressed together in a firm line. Like my hand was a bear trap, she took it from my hands. The temptation to wipe away the chocolate with my fingers had me squeezing my fist against my leg under the table. With the way she looked at me, she'd have stabbed me with the fork if I'd done it—not that I'd blame her.

After a few more wipes, she was chocolate-free and I was locked in a cage match with what I knew I should do and what I'd wanted to do since the first time I kissed her. There were two things I knew: I'd have to win back her trust to get her to open up to me, and that was the last thing I should do. Opening up to her was a one-way ticket to something I'd regret, and I didn't know if I could stop myself again if I went hurtling down that path.

"You've got to try out for the company. How can you not? The only things you ever talk about are dancing and hockey, and I think the ship has probably sailed on your pro hockey career." Marisa ran the brush across her nail before dipping it back into the bottle of silver polish.

"I don't want to go pro with dancing. I like teaching. If I was in the company, I couldn't teach anywhere near as many classes and I'd have to tour. Sometimes they're gone for months at a time." I shook the glittery bottle. Being in one place and building a home had way more appeal to me than roaming the country, dancing in front of strangers every night. Working with my students and seeing them grow was what made what I did worth it.

"At least try. Even if you don't want to join, you should give it a shot. Then if there's ever a doubt in your mind, you'll know, 'Nah, I totally could have danced my ass off across the country.'" She hopped up and shimmied while walking on her heels with her wet toes in the air.

"I'll think about it. How's calc tutoring going?"

She let out a cross between a scream and a groan. "They're driving me to drink." The clink of ice against glass sounded from the kitchen. "They think me being their tutor means I'm supposed to do the work for them. It makes me want to strangle someone."

"The people you're tutoring aren't putting in the effort?"

"An effort in getting into my pants, yes. LJ and his roommates can be a pain sometimes, but some of those other football players on his team are straight-up assholes. I'm putting a ban on them for my tutoring schedule next semester. Someone else can deal with their bullshit."

"Tell LJ—he'll straighten them out."

She laughed and plunked down a glass of sangria in front of me. "He's got enough to deal with on the team. I'm not adding anything else to his plate." She stared down into her glass, swirling the ice around in the pink mix.

Careful of my nails, I picked it up and took a sip—so sweet and delicious. "What's going on with the team?"

Her gaze snapped to mine like she'd forgotten I was there. "It's nothing." She waved her hand in the air. "There's one guy, Kevin—I swear I'll stab him with a mechanical pencil the next time I see him."

"You're tutoring him?"

She took a sip and nodded. "He keeps asking me out. At first it was flattering, but now it's just creepy. His breath always smells like cat food. Anyway, enough about me. How'd the dinner go?" She deftly changed the subject.

"Ford showed up, surprised the hell out of me. We had to sit next to each other! It was insanely awkward."

"That sucks. Do you think things will ever not be weird?"

"No." I dragged my hands over my face. "I went on a couple dates with his little brother. One kiss was as far as it went, but there's nowhere good that can go." A small part of me had wanted my kiss with Grant to be a toe-curling, steal-my-breath-away kind of thing, the same kind I'd had with Ford. Maybe deep down I'd thought that would fix things. Ford could have gone his own way and I'd finally have found someone I was really into, who didn't run the other way the second I stepped into the room, but that hadn't happened. It had been a nice kiss, pleasant, like a kiss on the playground under the slide, not something that lit my soul on fire—not like when Ford's lips had been on mine.

"Damn, you hit the awkward ball out of the park on that one."

"You have no idea."

Then there was the weirdness between Ford and Colm. It was an all-around recipe for disaster, but if the pattern held, I wouldn't see Ford for another year and a half. I could handle that as long as the thoughts about him stopped playing in surround sound in my mind.

"The game's on in a few. LJ was bitching about sharing a hotel room on the road, but the coach said it's for team-building purposes. I told him to suck it up. He'll just have to spank it in the shower like a normal guy."

"Why do you bust his balls so much?" I scrunched my eyebrows and looked at her.

She shrugged. "Habit. It also helps keep the lines of our friendship crystal clear. You watching the game with me?"

"No, I've got to study."

"You've been studying all day."

"Not all day." I wiggled my newly painted fingers at her. "Organic chemistry is a serial killer standing behind a shower curtain, and my grade is about to get sliced and diced if I don't get this material down."

She crinkled up her nose. "It's the worst. Let me know if

you need any help, and by help I mean someone to help set those books on fire."

"I will." I closed the door to my bedroom and sat back at the desk I'd been chained to for days. Colm would kill me if I didn't ace the semester. I should have just switched majors and been done with it, changed it to something I'd actually use like business, archery, or underwater basket weaving. I could sell my baskets at an artisanal farmers' market or run away with the circus.

Cracking open the books, I took a deep breath and dived back in. *Rip that Band-Aid off.*

"Olivia!"

The cheerful sound hit me dead center in my chest every single time, the way I imagined it would feel to come home from college if my mom were still around. I closed the taxi door and smiled so wide my cheeks hurt.

"Hi, Sylvia."

She wrapped me up in her arms. I leaned into her, probably more than I should have, and squeezed her back.

"How are you?" She brushed back the hair from my face and cupped my cheek. "Come inside; it's so cold. The kids are so excited."

She pulled me inside and closed the door behind us. Shrugging off my coat, I wiggled my toes trying to warm up. The smells of Elmer's glue, goldfish crackers, and construction paper always brought back so many childhood memories. I adjusted my tights. I wasn't normally a tutu type of girl, but the kids loved it. Their laughter and joy bounced off the walls and poured out of every nook and cranny of the house.

"They're energetic as usual and ready to show you what they remember from last time."

"Perfect." I stepped through the doorway. The kids screamed and jumped up and down before rushing me. I crouched down and was nearly bowled over by the kiddie stampede. *Is this what being a rock star feels like?* "I can't wait to see what you all remember, and I hope you're ready for some fun today."

Cheers and even more jumping. How did kids always have so much energy?

With everyone bouncing off the walls half an hour later, I ended our lesson. I'd put them up against anyone in my regular classes when it came to stamina. These children could run for hours and not get tired. Giving them a curtsy with my sheer ballet skirt, I let their teacher take over.

I grabbed my sweats from my bag and walked into Sylvia's office, a small room off the kitchen. When they'd lived there, it had been the TV room. Grant and I had hung out in there while waiting for Colm and Ford to finish up practice or get back from a game. Those childhood memories of freshly baked cookies, microwave popcorn, and cartoons were so bright and innocent. Then things had gotten complicated. I tapped my knuckles against her open door.

"I've got some hot chocolate with mini marshmallows, and I can make you a sandwich if you're hungry." She popped up from her desk.

My stomach rumbled.

"Sounds like you are." Her laughter was always so full of life and happiness.

I followed her back into the kitchen. "You don't have to make me anything. I can grab something on the way back to campus."

"Nonsense, of course I'll make you something." She spun around with the jar of mayo clutched against her chest. "Unless you need to go. I can whip up something quickly and you can take it with you."

The only thing waiting for me back at home was a pile of coursework that made my brain hurt. Marisa was at the library and then off to her torture dinner with her dad. Going back to an empty apartment versus staying there with Sylvia?

"There's nowhere else I'd rather be."

"Perfect. Have a seat." She smacked her hand on the black cushioned stool and went to the fridge.

I hopped up behind the island.

Sylvia moved around the kitchen like she could do it blindfolded, her black and silver hair hanging down her back like a curtain.

"Sorry it's not more, but I had everything handy." She slid a plate with the biggest BLT I'd ever seen across the counter to me, and there was even a heaping helping of potato chips on the side.

My mouth watered as the bacony smell wafted up from the toasted bread. "Never apologize for a BLT."

She laughed and sat beside me on her own stool. "I've got some cookies too, once you're finished. I made way too many for the parents' night. You can take a box home if you want. They're chocolate chip."

"Has anyone in the history of the world ever turned down a box of your chocolate chip cookies? Never. Maybe I'll share them with my roommate. *Maybe*." I'd also push my classes extra hard to burn off those calories.

"Good, because every one of those is another five pounds added to my hips." Laughing, she took a bite of her sandwich. "How's school?"

I regaled her with my ineptitude in biology, organic chemistry, and biochem. This was how I imagined it would be with my mom: sitting in the kitchen, making lunch together, talking about what was going on with me at college. She'd have done it, right? Taken time out as I got older? Maybe over time it would have dawned on her how little time we had before I left for good. Maybe...and maybe we wouldn't have even been discussing my science classes because I wouldn't be premed at all. Perhaps I'd have seen even less of her as I got older. She'd never made making time for me a priority...

Then the guilt came. What was more important for her to do, performing actual brain surgery or showing up to my dance recital? Saving lives, or sitting with me in the kitchen midday on a Tuesday and eating a sandwich?

"What's up, Liv? You look a thousand miles away." Sylvia leaned in with concern swimming in her eyes.

"Sorry, I...I was just thinking about my mom, worrying I'm letting her down...letting them down."

Sylvia's eyes softened, and she scooted closer. The chair scraped against the tile floor. Covering my hand with hers, she stared into my eyes. "There's nothing you could do that would. I wouldn't care if Ford was a street sweeper or doing what he does now. He's happy, loves his job, and makes good money. Your parents would care about your happiness itself, not the exact path you took to find it."

"You don't understand how important medicine was to them—is to me." It was one of the last connections I had to them.

"I'd imagine anyone who does all that work to become a doctor would have to care about it deeply."

"They were so proud when I said I wanted to be a doctor."

"What parent wouldn't be? But that's not an easy journey. I've been around my fair share of doctors, and it's an unforgiving lifestyle sometimes."

"It is." I crushed a chip remnant under my finger. "And I'm not always sure it's a life I want." My gaze snapped to hers, and my eyes widened. I hadn't meant to say that. Of course it was the life I wanted.

"It's not something you should take on lightly. There's nothing that says you have to make that decision today. You're young, and there's time."

Not when you're a doctor. There was never enough time. No life for years on end, living inside the hospital, sleeping in on-call beds during twenty-four-hour shifts, eating standing up at the counter because you know if you sit, you'll pass out. *Is that what I want?* "This was always the kind of stuff I thought I'd get to talk to her about. I thought I'd have her to help me figure all this out."

"I know I'm a poor substitute, but you're always welcome here, Olivia. Always. I'm here to talk to you whenever you need me."

My throat tightened, and I covered her hands with mine. "You're not a poor substitute at all. You're an amazing mom. Ford and Grant are lucky to have you." She made time for them. Hell, she made time for me and I wasn't even her kid. I was never rushed out of the room. She never disappeared mid-conversation, and she didn't check her phone every few minutes like something more important was always a text or a page away.

The time I spent with her was special to me. If I screwed things up with Grant or Ford, I might lose her too, and I'd already lost enough people. I couldn't handle losing more.

She chuckled and picked up my plate. "You try telling them that. All I get are moans about my gripes that they don't come visit more often." Her phone lit up on the counter. "Speak of the devil." She tapped the screen and picked it up, a big smile spreading across her face. "Were your ears burning? We were just talking about you." A short pause. "Olivia. She's here."

An ice bucket might as well have been poured over my head. Just what I needed, Ford thinking I was talking about him to his mom. I got down from the stool and picked up my sweats off the counter. Motioning to the bathroom, I darted out of the room. Quickly taking off my leotard of death, I looked at myself in the mirror. How long had those dark circles been there? The long study days were taking their toll. I got into my clothes and rolled up my ballet gear under my arm.

"She's back now—did you want to talk to her?" She paused. "Okay, no problem. I'll see you soon. Love you." Ending the call, she grabbed our plates and put them into the dishwasher alongside a collection of bright plastic plates, cups, and utensils.

"That was Ford."

Why would he have wanted to talk to me? I ran my hand over the pang at the center of my chest. *Get a grip, Liv.*

"He didn't know you've been stopping by." She eyed me from the stove.

"It's not a big deal. He's always traveling so much, and it just never came up." I shrugged.

"What about Grant? The three of you always seem to be doing a dance of checking on who's here and who isn't."

I stared down at the floor. Did she know I'd kissed both her sons? My stomach backflipped.

She wiped her hands on the towel and gave me a hug. "It's okay, sweetie. It will all get figured out."

Sylvia sent me on my way with two boxes of soft baked

chocolate chip cookies after I inhaled five with a glass of milk. I was a ten-year-old all over again. Colm and I had tried our hand at baking for my school bake sale once right after our parents died. Eighty percent of the cookies had ended up a charred mess at the bottom of the trash can and he'd given up, eventually going out to the bakery for a few dozen.

The messes weren't as easy to clean up now. Real life loomed ahead, and the choices I had to make only got harder. Ford had popped up twice in one week after almost eighteen months of distance. Maybe his guilt had finally caught up with him. *Good.* It was a test, and I was not going to fail.

It was a new resolution, a few months late, but whatever. I wasn't spending another minute thinking about him. I had enough problems to deal with. I didn't need to add a scruffy-faced, six-one goalie into the mix.

7
___

FORD

I peeled my eyelids open at the annoying chirp that wouldn't stop. Lifting my phone, I stabbed at the glowing screen.

"What?"

"I've called you five times already." Colm's annoyance matched my own.

"I'd have thought me not answering the first four would have given you a hint." Squinting my eyes, I checked the time: nearly three a.m. "Why the hell are you calling so late?"

"Oh shit, I forgot about the time difference."

I grumbled under my breath.

"Have you gotten a chance to talk to Liv?"

"No. I mean yes." I wiped the sleep from my eyes, pushing away the dreams filled with a blue-eyed woman whose head fit perfectly under my chin.

"Is it yes or no?"

"I talked to her a couple days ago at Heath's. She said school was going well and she's fine."

"Seriously? You think she's going to spill just like that? I need to know what's going on with her, need to know she's okay. Being this far away is going to drive me crazy. You owe me." The concern in his voice bled through the line. I pushed aside the bitter pill of his anger, focusing on why he needed me to do this.

"I'll meet up with her again after these away games, and I'll turn up the interrogation."

He let out a deep breath. The past year, his worry about her had shot through the roof. I knew all about being protective of a younger sibling, especially when you turned into a default parental figure, but the pressure he was putting on her was insane. Maybe by talking to her, I'd be able to figure out why he was going off the deep end.

"Thanks. I'm glad I can still count on you."

I squeezed the bridge of my nose. Before, he'd never have thought twice about it.

"You know you can." Guilt knotted in my stomach. He might not think so if he knew what I'd just been dreaming about. He'd probably break my nose.

We ended the call, and I picked up my phone again.

Me: Hey Liv, want to get ice cream on Thursday?

What was she, five? *Delete!*

Me: Liv, we should go to a movie this week

That would be the perfect way to pick her brain: sitting in a dark theater for two hours while laser focused on where our arms touched on the armrest. *Delete!*

Me: I'm back in town Thursday. Can we meet up?

The second I hit send, my gaze shot to the time and I smacked myself on the forehead. Who sends a text like that at three a.m.? This moron, that's who. Slamming my head down on the pillow, I tugged it from behind my head and shoved it over my face. If I was lucky, I'd smother myself by morning. The minutes ticked by as I pretended I wasn't waiting for her reply.

Eventually the morning sun streaked through the curtains. Nothing.

Talk about fucking things up in five seconds flat.

~

"Ford, get your head in the game." Our coach's voice boomed across the ice.

Emmett skated over to me, stopping short, sending a sharp spray of ice showering over me. "Wake up, man. What's up with you today?"

"Got a lot on my mind." Like the fact that even though I'd sent the text at three in the morning, Liv still hadn't replied. We'd been on the road for three days, and it was another two before I'd be back home. Back when we used to text, I'd always gotten an immediate reply.

That was a good thing, right? She wasn't still hung up on me. Distancing myself had worked, maybe too well, but at least this meant we'd be able to hang out and talk without anything other than platonic feelings—if she talked to me at all. So why was I counting down the minutes until I could get to the locker room to see if she'd replied?

"Earth to Ford!" Heath knocked on my helmet.

My head snapped up, and I lifted my face mask. "Would everyone just leave me alone?"

"Dude, you're spacing big-time. You coming down with something?"

I batted his hand away as he feigned concern, trying to feel my forehead. "Everyone back off. I've got some stuff to handle, that's all."

"Maybe if you came out of your shell, we could help you, little hermit crab." Emmett leaned against the goal.

Glaring at him, I shoved my mask back down. "Nothing I can't handle. Would you two get back out there to practice and stop stalling over here with me?" I pushed my thoughts about Liv, the text, and my phone deep down until practice was over.

Throwing on my T-shirt in the shower stall, I trudged out into the locker room and sat to put on my shoes.

"I could barely see straight, she was such a fucking vacuum on my dick." The words of our resident team asshole, Axel, carried across the bustling room like nails on a chalkboard.

Gritting my teeth, I shoved my feet into my sneakers.

"I was actually going to call her again, but she sent me a text the next day. Talk about needy." Axhole's voice grated on my nerves.

My jaw popped. It was one thing to sleep around, and I'd been there. It was another to scream about your conquests from the rooftops like a braying jackass.

"Maybe I'll bang—"

"Maybe you should shut the hell up!" The words were out of my mouth before I could stop them, and everyone in the locker room froze. It might as well have been filled with mannequins. "Why do you think everyone wants to hear this shit, man? No one wants to hear about you being an asshole twenty-four-seven."

"What the hell is it to you?" Axel shot up from the bench and glared at me.

"Just shut up about it." I stood and grabbed my duffel off the floor. "We already know you're a douche—no need to announce it to the entire locker room every chance you get."

"Just because puck bunnies only sleep with you because

they feel sorry for you doesn't mean you've got to shit on everyone else's good time." He got right up in my face.

Adrenaline from our practice pumped through my veins. I was seconds from knocking him on his ass. "Shouting to everyone within earshot about the kind of garbage you are and how you treat women shows everyone exactly the kind of *boy* you are."

He shoved both hands into the center of my chest. The back of my knee hit the bench, and I stumbled. Whipping back around with my fists ready to knock that smug smile off his face, my arm was jerked back a split second before my fist connected.

Glaring behind me, I tensed my muscles in Heath's grip. His whole arm wrapped around mine. Emmett and Declan descended, and their hands tightened around my arms and shoulders, getting between us.

"You're lucky we're here," Emmett ground out at Axel. "If we weren't, you'd be down a couple of teeth before the next game even started."

"You need your friends to fight your battles for you, Ford?" Axel taunted behind the wall of guys.

Heath held on to me, and Declan pushed me back. "Don't do it. You hit him and you're not playing the next game. We need you." Declan then turned to Axel. "You'd be lucky if you loosened one of his teeth, but you wouldn't be walking out of here on your own two legs if we hadn't stepped in. Back up, Axel." His words cooled my temper. Letting the guys down was the last thing I wanted to do, even if it meant I couldn't beat the shit out of Axhole.

Shaking off their holds, I slammed my lips shut tight and breathed deeply to get myself under control. I slung my bag over my head and stormed out of the locker room. On the team bus, my blood slowed to a dull pounding from the raging drumbeat it had escalated to back inside. Close quarters were a bitch when we were on the road. At least Axel was smart enough to sit at the front of the bus, and the drive to the hotel was quiet. I pulled on my headphones and kept them on until I got to my room.

My phone buzzed in my duffel the second the door closed behind me. I fished it out and stared at the screen.

Liv: Wrong person?

I ran my hand over my face. Three days later and that was what I got. Damn, things were worse than I'd thought. If only she knew how many drafts I'd gone through to send that to her, and she didn't even think I'd meant to send it at all.

Me: It was meant for you

Liv: Oh...

Me: We're back on Thursday. We could do something?

Liv: Are the guys having another dinner?

Me: No, I meant just me and you

Liv: Why?

Me: Why not?

Liv: I don't think that should need an explanation. You made it all abundantly clear.

My fingers hovered over the screen, the words that were already so hard to come stalling worse than ever.

Liv: You've been a ghost for the last year and a half and avoided me at all costs. I got the message.

I tapped on her name. She picked up on the fifth ring, like she'd contemplated not picking up at all. My heart slammed against my ribs.

"Hello?"

I smiled at the hesitant sound in her voice. "Hello? Yes, it's me. Why are you acting like we weren't just having a text conversation?"

"Because you haven't called me in years."

My mouth went dry, and I ran my fingers along my hairline. She had me there. "I'm calling you now." And I shouldn't have been. Grant would be crushed if he knew and Colm would never forgive me if it went beyond a friendly check-in, but I couldn't stop wanting her—even if it was just to talk. I couldn't stop thinking about her.

"Did you hit your head at practice?"

I drummed the hotel pen against the bed. "What? No. Why would you say that?"

Because she's pissed you're calling her.

"Do you suddenly think it's two years ago and I should jump up and down like a happy puppy because you called?"

"Liv—" I squeezed the base of my neck.

"Don't *Liv* me, Ford. You're the one who made these rules. We've been playing by them just fine. Why are you changing them now?" I envisioned the angry crease in her forehead between her eyebrows.

"I never made any rules."

"Then why have you avoided me?" She spoke to me like I was Hannibal Lecter inviting her over for dinner.

"Can't we have a cordial conversation?"

"Fine." The word jumped out through gritted teeth. "How was practice? Ready for your game?" Her pleasant tone was like whiplash.

"The usual. Why haven't you come to any games this season? I'm surprised Colm hasn't reserved a sky box for you."

"He has, though I keep telling him not to. I can't make it, but you know how he can be. Once he gets something stuck in his head, he's a pit bull who refuses to let go."

Didn't I know it. It had been years since Felicity and he still acted like it had happened just the day before.

"He loves wasting money. My nights are usually booked."

That perked up my ears. "Doing what?" *If you say boyfriend, I'll only die a little.*

"Stuff. School stuff and classes."

Relief washed over me. "You have classes late at night?" Was she okay walking to and from campus? I knew she lived off campus now because Colm had sent me the address.

"Study sessions and other things." Her cageyness had my spidey senses tingling.

"What kinds of things?"

"What's up with you calling me and asking a thousand questions?"

I cleared my throat. "I figured with Colm away, you might need someone to talk to."

"I do *not* need another person breathing down my neck every second of the day, okay? Colm's only been back in town since September and I was just fine without him. It didn't bother you before that I might need someone to talk to. I don't need you taking pity on me like a high school kid who's been left alone while my parents are out of town." Her words poured out of her like a volcanic eruption.

"It's not like that."

"How is it? You don't get to kiss another woman five seconds after I've kissed you, then tell me to get lost. You can't just text out of the blue, then call me and start grilling me."

"I'm not grilling you, and I didn't tell you to get lost that night."

"You might as well have." Her voice drifted off.

"It's not like you didn't get in a little payback." The way Grant had rolled into the hotel room gloating about his date with Liv, I'd wanted to knock him out—my own brother, who I'd protected since he was born.

She sucked in a sharp breath. "Grant wasn't payback. We just went on a couple of dates." Her voice rose an octave.

A couple dates too many. "Maybe, but he doesn't think of it that way."

"He said that." Her words were low and whispered.

"He asked me to find out how you're doing. It wasn't a one-and-done thing with him, Liv." I swallowed past the lump in my throat.

"I... It was never anything serious."

"But he's still my brother." My jaw clenched. It was a line that wasn't crossed, just like not dating your best friend's sister.

"And Colm's still *my* brother. Why make this harder, Ford? We've been getting along fine since then."

"As in not at all."

"I like to think of it as a cold war."

"Can we hit pause or reset or something? Colm's injured and in LA. He's gone for a while. I wanted to make sure you're okay."

"I'm great, and I don't need a nanny."

"That's not what—"

"I could use a friend, though. If you decide you're up for that task, you know my number."

The call ended before I could say another word. Banging the phone against my head, I flopped onto the bed. I could be her friend. I could totally friend the hell out of her. I would get to the bottom of what was going on with her, tell Colm, and then quietly extricate myself from the situation before I crossed a line I shouldn't—again. I would make sure she wasn't in trouble, and I would make sure no one else got hurt—except maybe me.

8

LIV

"This is not healthy." Marisa stood in the doorway to my room.

"It's not like I have a choice." I dropped my pen onto my notebook and stretched my back. The bones cracked all the way down my spine.

"Of course you have a choice. Fun is also a vital part of college. Remember fun? You've been studying nonstop for eight hours straight. I'm tempted to check for a bottle filled with pee under your desk."

"Gross! I'm not that bad."

"Liv, it's almost nine p.m." She jerked her arm out toward my window.

My head snapped up, and I glanced outside. The glow of the streetlights below and the pitch-black sky were the only things I could see. Two awkward texts to Ford before his flight had been my only break all day before I shut off my phone to avoid distractions.

The stilted weirdness was still there, but at least he'd stopped with the interrogation.

"Give me another half an hour." I spun back around in

my chair.

"No." She closed my laptop. "My friend Seph told me data proves studying past a certain threshold is actually worse for information retention. Every extra minute you sit in this chair, you're making it harder for yourself."

"You don't understand what will happen if I don't ace this test." I needed to prove I could do it and make my parents and Colm proud.

She sat on my bed. "Burnout is a real thing, and it's going to be your future if you don't slow the hell down."

"Slowing down isn't an option."

"You can think about that tomorrow—with a well-rested brain. Come on, Liv. It'll only be for a couple of hours. LJ's here. They're having a party at the Brothel. We go for a couple of hours, then you can run off and sneak in some more hours of studying. You can't sit by the phone waiting for another text from Ford."

"I'm not!" I knew I shouldn't have told her about that. Waking up to his middle-of-the-night text had screamed booty call to me. My stomach had dropped when I'd rolled over and read the message, not that I didn't know the deal. Single hockey players weren't exactly known for their restraint in the bedroom. But apparently it hadn't been a booty call for someone else.

"Prove it to me, then."

"Ten more minutes."

"You've been saying that for days. Take a break. Dancing and studying are all you do. Come hang out with me. I miss you."

I mentally kicked myself. I wouldn't get these years back. This was what it was like when you had friends. Making time for them was just as important as studying or work. I'd fallen into the old pattern my parents had modeled for me, and I still had a lot to learn.

"Okay, I'll go. Let me get dressed."

She threw her arms around my shoulders and squeezed me tight. "Yes! Oh, and the toaster kind of exploded, so we need to buy a new one."

"What the hell did you do?" My words stopped her hasty retreat.

"I didn't do anything! I turned it on, and the freaking wall outlet started sparking. I grabbed an oven mitt and unplugged it, then left a message with the super."

Maybe Colm was right about this place.

"Hurry up and get dressed or I'll make you go in that." Bounding out of the room like a deer hopped up on caffeine, she closed the door behind her.

Getting outside would be good for me. How the hell did you connect with anyone when working ninety-hour weeks and cramming in vacations on top of surgeries, conferences, and everything else? More than half the pictures in the boxes under my bed had been taken during our annual family trips. Three weeks, six countries—it was the most uninterrupted time we got with our parents, and then they'd disappear for another eleven months.

Yes, I'm a total asshole for being sad my parents were out saving lives instead of coming to my middle school graduation, my school plays, or anything that didn't have to do with me wanting to be a doctor, but those aren't the things a kid should have to worry about. Their parents should be there.

I threw on the first dress I found and attempted to do something with my hair. A party was the last place I wanted to be, but I'd dragged Marisa to so many dance company parties over the summer, and I owed her. Now she got to do the dragging, and I got to do the moping.

I turned on my phone: three texts from Colm, one from Grant, and one from Ford. I opened his.

Ford: Landed. Headed home now.

The temptation to reply was strong, but I didn't. I refused to fall back into that pattern of lapping up any bit of attention he threw my way.

I responded to Colm first.

Me: Just finished studying for the night. Turning in and turning off my phone so I can catch some shut-eye. Talk later?

Colm: Okay. Proud of you. Love you.

Then to Grant.

Me: Hey, Grant, midterms are eating my life right now. I'm heading to bed in a bit.

Grant: I could bring you some study fuel.

Me: If I have any more caffeine, I'll probably launch myself to the moon. Thanks for thinking of me though.

Grant: Always.

My stomach knotted. I had to talk to him. Regardless of what happened with Ford, Grant deserved to know there would never be anything between us.

Opening my bedroom door, I checked myself again in the mirror on my dresser. I walked down the hall. "Can we leave by one? I'd like to wake up before noon. And for the love of God, no shots."

I turned the corner at the end of the hallway to the two of them slamming back shots of light brown liquor. Marisa shuddered and set her glass down on the counter, then slid one closer to me. "Just one?"

LJ picked his beer up off the counter. Marisa served up another shot, licked her hand, and sprinkled on some salt. Lime wedges seesawed on the counter.

"I'm not holding your hair tonight." I jabbed a finger in her direction and picked up the glass. "Being bent over behind you is not how I want to end my evening. He can take care of you—right, LJ? You wouldn't mind being bent over behind her, would you?"

He choked on his beer, spraying us in a fine mist. He hunched over, holding on to his knees while coughing and sucking in air.

Marisa grabbed some paper towels and held them out to him, patting him on the back. "Careful, L. I thought you football players knew how to drink."

"We do." His words were choppy and wheezy. "I do. It just went down the wrong pipe." Wiping the tears from his eyes, LJ thumped on his chest.

She grabbed her coat off the hook by the door. I snapped a pic of the three of us with my instant camera, then stashed the pic in the photo collage beside the door. The two of them continued to bicker as I put on my coat and we walked downstairs.

The strong icy blast of air hit me the second the door opened, nearly blowing me back into the stairwell. Shoving my glove-covered hands into my pockets, I danced in place as our taxi pulled up.

LJ opened the door, and Marisa and I slid inside first. Then the cab pulled away from the curb and joined the rest of the Thursday night traffic.

The phantom buzzes from my phone had me checking in my bag a couple times on the drive over. *Stop checking. Do not text him.* We pulled up in front of the house, AKA the Brothel. The name was an unfortunate holdover from when the place had been a frat house, but on this night it seemed to live up to the reputation.

The front of the house was barely visible from the street. People swarmed the porch and steps leading up to the house. Near-freezing temperatures didn't mean much when people were lit up.

Thumping music from the rows of houses along the street vibrated the walls as college students streamed in and out. Laughter, whistles, and shouting filled the air.

"Ladies." LJ climbed out and held the door open.

People on the steps made way as LJ climbed up, a perk of being a member of the most successful football team in the past ten years. Sweat, cheap beer, and way too much body spray hit us the second we crossed the threshold. We wove our way through the crush of a hundred partygoers, and LJ's party wake did not extend to us. The heat of their bodies turned the house into a sauna. LJ high-fived guys along the way, and appreciative glances came from all directions. Heads turned as Marisa and I walked through the living room, and I thought maybe the party was a good idea after all, at least for an ego boost.

He whipped around when we got to the kitchen. "Do you guys want some drinks?"

"No, we came here for enthralling conversation." Marisa pushed at his shoulder and smirked. "Hell yeah, we want some drinks."

"Be right back," he shouted over the volume of the party, which was increasing by the minute.

"It's a million degrees in here." Sweat rolled down my back. That was the bitch of winter parties: dress for the sauna and hope you didn't catch hypothermia when you went outside, or dress for the weather and die of dehydration inside. I fanned myself while we looked for a good place to stand and people watch. LJ came back with the drinks and disappeared again.

The first sip tasted like pure booze. If it had been rubbing alcohol, it wouldn't have surprised me.

"Jesus, are they making this themselves in the bathtub?" I coughed into my hand.

"Probably." She winced and took another sip. "Do I still have my eyebrows?"

I laughed and choked down another gulp. We danced along to the music, singing the lyrics at the top of our lungs, and our voices could actually be heard over the pounding music.

Marisa leaned over and shouted into my ear. "I told you this was a good idea."

We danced together and drifted around the party, my body buzzing with the warm, fuzzy feeling the booze delivered. With each drink, the heat on my neck and cheeks increased, but I hadn't been out in so long. I thought I better make the most of it before Colm came back and sent me off to some isolation chamber with only a toilet, sink, and my textbooks.

LJ's roommates stopped by for hugs before being torn away by the crowd. Damn, they were hot—for football players. My tastes tended to fall more toward the hockey variety. Marisa introduced me to Seph, short for Persephone, who was dating one of LJ's teammates and disappeared upstairs with him within seconds. Somebody was getting some.

A new drink was never far off with LJ taking care of us. Tugging the front of my dress away from my super sweaty body, I motioned to the bathroom. Marisa looped her arm through mine, and we wove our way to the stairs.

Standing at the bottom of the steps, I grabbed the railing. The woozy picture in front of me knocked me over into Marisa.

"Are you okay?" She steadied me.

"I'm fine, just feeling a little dizzy." The steps multiplied with each lift of my foot. *Who the hell designed these stairs?*

She steadied me as we made it to the top. "We've been going drink for drink so far, and I'm fine. When's the last time you ate?"

I ran through my schedule for the day. "Breakfast?"

"As in this morning?" Nodding, I braced my hand on the banister as she spoke. "Shit! You're totally tanked, aren't you?"

Leaning against the wall in the bathroom line, I laughed at the look of concern on her face. "I'm not tanked, you're tanked." I ran my fingers over her lips, a giggling fit seconds from overtaking me.

Her hand shot out as the floor seemed to be rushing up to meet me. *Hello, floor.* Marisa leaned her shoulder into me and pushed me back against the wall. *Nice to almost meet you, Mr. Floor.* Marisa and I inched forward in the bathroom line.

"Damn it, I thought I had a granola bar or something in here." She rummaged around in the purse slung over her shoulder.

The bathroom door opened, and the person in front of me darted inside. My phone lit up in my hand. I danced from foot to foot. There was the slightest chance I'd had too many drinks. *Was it four or five?* I stared down at the screen, and my breath caught in my throat.

Ford: How are you?

I fumbled the phone, nearly dropping it on the floor. Turning away from Marisa, I tapped out my reply.

Me: Feeling awesome! How are you?

Ford: Awesome huh?

Me: Totally. I feel amazing. So good. Out with my roommate.

Ford: Oh, I'll let you go then

Me: Wait! How are you? Out partying? Picking up some bunnies?

I laughed at my own joke.

Ford: Back in my apartment. Crazy traffic. Want to get something to eat tomorrow?

Someone came out of the bathroom, and I ducked inside, closing the door in Marisa's concerned face. Tapping on his name on my screen, I held it up to my face. I tried to steady my body as the floor dipped. *They need to get this floor fixed—it isn't level.* I held on to the sink.

"Hey, Ford!" The words came out way louder than I meant them to.

"Hey, Liv. Sounds like you're having fun."

"I'm having a wonderful, responsible time out with friends." I smacked my lips together.

"And getting drunk off your ass."

"Not even a little bit." I closed the lid on the toilet and sat, but the damn thing moved when I wasn't looking and I ended up on the bathroom floor. I didn't even want to think about the last time it had been cleaned.

He chuckled, and that deep laughter did something to me. The warm, tingling feeling spreading throughout my body traveled a little lower.

I pushed myself up off the floor. "You should come to the party!" Getting all sweaty pressed up against Ford sounded like the perfect way to end the night. I'd already made enough bad decisions—why not add another and stop his little let's-be-friends act dead in its tracks? I couldn't deal with being friends with Ford. It was better if we stayed away, but he was the flame and I was the moth, flapping my wings as hard as I could. We were caught in each other's orbit and unable to escape our gravitational pull.

"To a college party?" The smile in his voice made me smile wider. "I'm not going to be that guy." He laughed.

Someone knocked on the door. "I'll be out in a second. What guy?"

"The old guy at a college party."

"You're not old."

"Anyone in college would think so."

"I don't think so." There was a louder knock on the door.

"I'll be right there." I tripped over the bathroom mat and nearly face-planted on the floor. My phone slipped out of my hand and clattered onto the black-and-white tiles.

"Are you okay?" His voice blared out of the speaker.

I picked it up. "I'm fine. Just tripped."

"Send me your location."

"It's fine, Ford. I'll go dance and drown my worries in some more booze. You don't have to come. Forget I asked. I'm sure you've got other things to do."

"No, I don't. Send me the address."

After accidentally snapping a couple of pictures of myself, I tapped the button to share my current location.

"I've got it. Do not go anywhere and don't drink anything other than water until I get there."

"Yes, sir." I saluted the air. Quickly using the toilet, then washing my hands, I tugged the door open and wrapped my arms around Marisa. "He's coming."

She crinkled her eyebrows. "Who's coming?"

"Ford." My mouth had never been dryer. It was like I'd been eating dryer lint all night.

"You called him?"

"He texted me first. I need to get some water."

She wrapped her hands around my arms and stared into my eyes. "I'm going to the bathroom. Do *not* move from this spot until I get back."

I danced to the music from downstairs, which was vibrating the floor, while she disappeared inside. Maybe Ford would have a couple of drinks and loosen up a bit. Maybe I'd get a repeat of the kiss from Declan and Mak's wedding and then Ford would reject me again. That would be fun. *Maybe my stomach should stop churning like this.*

Marisa popped out of the bathroom door. The light from inside it nearly blinded me, and I did my best vampire impersonation.

"We should get out of here. I'm getting you some water, and I'll take you home."

"No way—Ford is coming." I sat on the steps, splintered wood poking the backs of my thighs.

"Even more reason to bail. If he sees you trashed like this, your brother will be on the first plane back here."

"Ford won't narc on me. He said he's my friend now." I folded my arms over my chest.

"I'm going to go get you some water. Stay right here. Don't try to walk down these steps on your own."

People stumbled and fell around my spot on the staircase; then Marisa reappeared with a bottle of water. She held it out to me, and I gulped it down, dripping water all over my chest.

"Let's get you downstairs." She grabbed my arm and helped me stand; then we made our way down the winding steps. *Were they winding before?* The house had gotten more packed, if that were even possible. I missed the last step and stumbled as the door opened. Framed by the doorway was the man of the hour.

"Ford! You—" The blackness rushed up so quickly I hoped it didn't hurt when I kissed the floor.

9

FORD

The cab pulled up to the curb, and it was definitely a college party. The only way it could have been more of one is if everyone were wearing togas, but they didn't go with late February weather so much. A few heads turned as I walked up to the house. Some kids ran off, probably thinking I was a cop or something.

A wall of cheap beer smell and heat slammed into me as I stepped inside, followed by a familiar voice. "Ford! You—"

That was the only warning I got before Liv's body hurtled toward me and the floor. I grabbed her, shoving my hands under her arms and cradling her against my chest. Lifting her up, I checked her face. Her cheeks were flushed, and she was sweaty. Her eyes fluttered open.

"Hi, Ford." Her friend, who'd tried to grab her before she fell, made it down the last step and greeted me.

"Hi, Ford," Liv parroted, running her hand along my chest.

"How much has she had to drink?" I looked over her shoulder to her friend.

"Four?"

Liv held her liquor way better than that. "Only four? Did someone put something in her drink?" I'd kick the ass of every guy in there if I needed to.

"No, she just hasn't eaten anything since this morning. She'd been studying at her desk all day. I didn't realize she hadn't eaten anything or I'd have made something for her before we left." She bit her bottom lip, her eyebrows furrowed with worry. "I'm Marisa." She held out her hand, so I shifted Liv and shook it.

A few heads turned in our direction. I couldn't tell if it was because of super-drunk Liv or me, but I didn't want to stick around to find out.

"I'm totally fine; put me down." Liv shoved against my chest.

My lips pressed together in a grim line, and I set her down. Her first step turned into a wobble, which then became a stumble, and back into my arms she went.

"Let me take her home." Marisa craned her neck around the party.

"There's no way you'll be able to get her home like this." Liv was deadweight, a completely floppy noodle. "I can take her to my place. Colm will freak if he knows I saw her like this and didn't take care of her."

Marisa nibbled on her thumb, probably weighing the guilt factor of trying to muscle Liv home on her own or letting me take her.

"Give me your number, and I'll text you when we're home safely. I don't want you to worry. My phone's in my back pocket." I told her the pass code.

She slipped it out and unlocked it. As she put her number in, some of her tension ebbed away.

"Can you order a taxi while you've got that?" I gave her my address and let her order the cab.

"It'll be here in two minutes."

The words *hockey*, *goalie*, and a few more terms came from the crowd. Phones came out, and I wished I had a hat on or something.

"I'll take her out there." Cradling her against my chest, I lifted her off her feet.

"I'll come too—don't want the cab driver thinking you're picking up passed-out women at college parties."

"Good point."

The cab arrived, and I hurried Liv inside.

Marisa knocked on the window. "Don't forget to message me."

"I won't," I shouted through the glass.

She stepped back from the car and waved to us as we pulled away.

Liv's head rested against the back of the seat with her eyes closed. I itched to reach for my phone to call Colm. He'd want to know, but I'd made the promise to Liv.

"How are you feeling?" I put my hand on the back of her sweaty, heated neck. She was going to be hurting in the morning.

"I feel awesome." Her head lolled to the side, and her eyes widened, recognition lighting up her face. "Ford, you came!"

So we're dealing with a Dory Drunk tonight. The corner of my mouth lifted. "I told you I would."

"You've been avoiding me for so long, I figured it was all lies, figured you'd never want to speak to me again."

Guilt hammered at my gut. "The way that night went down is something I've always regretted, Liv."

She lifted her head from the back of the seat. "I'm drunk off my ass, and even I know a bad lie when I hear one."

Streetlights flooded the car in a steady rhythm, each

pass showing off her profile, the delicate curve of her nose, the length of her neck, the way she filled out that dress.

Shaking my head, I stared out the window. Ogling Liv while she was drunk felt so damn wrong, not that ogling her while she was sober felt any better. The nagging voice in the back of my head telling me to stay the hell away was getting drowned out a little more each day.

A soft, warm hand slid across my thigh and I jumped. Turning back to Liv, I shot back against the door as she leaned in closer. Her hand inched higher up my leg, and the rush of blood straight to my dick was a disaster waiting to happen.

"I'm glad you came tonight."

"I'm glad I did too. There's no way Marisa would have gotten you home." I put my hand over hers and stopped her steady upward progress.

"That's not why." Her breasts pressed against my arm.

"Liv, you're drunk. You don't know what you're doing right now."

"I know exactly what I'm doing." She licked her lips and inched even closer.

My head was wedged between the back of the seat and the window. Taking advantage of a drunk Liv wasn't going to happen.

"I'm kissing you," she said with a small smile.

"Let's talk about this in the morning." If I'd gotten any farther away, I'd have been running along beside the car.

"Enough talk."

"Liv—" My words were cut off by her lips landing on mine. The sweet taste of rum and Coke danced on her tongue, and she smelled so good, even through the college-party funk that clung to both of us. I threaded my fingers through her hair. Our lips mashed together. Her hungry tug on my lips sent a shot down my spine, and I wanted to rip the dress off her body.

Her sleepy moan snapped me back to my senses. She was drunk off her ass. She didn't know what the hell she was doing, and I was not taking advantage of that.

I jerked my head away, slamming it hard against the glass.

"See, I told you—terrible liar. You don't want me." Even through the drunkenness, the sadness-laced words sliced at me. "It's okay, though. I won't make you say it again." Her head dropped onto my shoulder. She toyed with the buttons on my shirt before her hand stilled against my chest.

Craning my neck, I looked down at her and brushed the hair off her face. A steady snore came from her mouth.

"You don't know how much it kills me. There's no one else I want in the world, but I can't have you," she mumbled, and I wrapped my arm around her shoulder. Her body pressed even tighter against mine as she burrowed into my side.

The taxi pulled up in front of my apartment, and I lifted her out, cradling her in my arms. With any luck she wouldn't remember any of this, but I sure as hell would.

Shifting her weight, I opened my apartment door and kicked it closed. I flicked on a couple lights, and she picked up her head from my shoulder.

"Taking me back to your place—this should be fun." Her drunk, unfocused gaze tried to lock onto mine like she'd forgotten what was said in the car. "I don't feel so good."

She clutched her hands to her stomach, and that was all the warning I got before receiving a baptism of sorts. Doing my best to get us cleaned up, I kept my eyes averted as I peeled the dress off her body.

Her grumbles reassured me as I tucked her into bed

after making her drink a couple glasses of water. I replied to her roommate's text and let her know Liv was sleeping it off safely at my place.

Grabbing some pillows and blankets, I made up the couch and settled in for a long night filled with tossing, pillow punching, and memories of our last non-puke-tainted kiss. I stared up at the ceiling before dropping into the most fitful sleep I'd had in a long time.

10

LIV

Nails on a chalkboard mixed with a jackhammer topped with a cottonmouth cherry on top. The only thing rivaling that was the sour, stomach-turning taste on my tongue. *Did I gargle a handful of pennies?*

I squeezed my head, pressing the heels of my hands into my temples. This was how I usually felt after cramming all night for a big test—or hell, most nights. Well, the pounding headache part was more usual, but not the stomach that was trying to climb out of my mouth. Slowly cracking my eyelids, I snapped them shut at the bright, surface-of-the-sun light from outside.

My eyes shot back open, and I whipped my arm up to cover my face. This was not my bed. Shoving the sheets back, I stared at my body, swimming in an oversize T-shirt. *Oh shit!*

I still had on my underwear and bra. *Please tell me I didn't blackout hook up with someone.* I rolled over twice on the bed, and my feet landed on the wood floor. The trash can and glass of water beside the bed told me everything I needed to know about how my night had ended.

A pop and sizzle from the other side of the wall that didn't reach the industrial-height ceiling got me off my ass. I tried to run my fingers through my hair and nearly yanked myself off my feet when my fingers got stuck in the tangles.

On my tiptoes I walked down the two steps leading from the bedroom. Rounding the corner, I shielded my eyes from even more sun. Was this apartment somehow closer to the sun than normal human dwellings? Had I been abducted by an alien approximating a regular apartment but getting the lighting wrong?

In front of me, standing at the stove, was the broad back I'd committed to memory. His ruffled hair and thick, corded muscles under his light blue T-shirt did crazy stuff to my stomach that had nothing to do with how much I'd had to drink last night. *I'm delirious. That's it. It's a fever dream and my head is still in the toilet at the Brothel. Please let that be the case, and not that I got blackout drunk and puked in front of Ford.* My silent prayer was cut off when I came face-to-face with the chef.

"Morning." Ford turned around with a pan in his hand, sliding a golden-brown pancake onto the big stack already teetering on a plate.

"Morning." My voice sounded like I'd been gargling broken glass.

"How are you feeling?" Pity swam in his eyes.

"Like death? Would that be too overdramatic? I feel like I've been dug up after two weeks underground."

"There's an extra toothbrush for you in the bathroom." He pointed to the hallway behind me.

The words were barely out of his mouth before I shot down the darkened corridor, closing the door behind me.

Don't freak out. This is totally fine. Ford saw you in your underwear, heard you puke, and put you to bed. No biggie.

I spotted the dirty clothes hamper in the corner. I walked toward it like a person in a horror movie opening the closet door with a gently swaying hanger on the handle. The smells emanating from the hamper as well as the tangled fabric, namely my dress and a men's button-down shirt, were my own silent horror reel. Not only had he heard me puke, I'd blown chunks all over him.

I gingerly rested my forehead on the cold granite counter. How many floors up were we? Could I crawl out a window to escape and preserve some of my dignity? I stared into my bleary-eyed reflection. Of course not.

Brushing my teeth, I ran my fingers through my hair to get rid of the rest of the rat's nest as much as possible and then turned to face the music. Actual music pumped through the Bluetooth speakers, and the smells from the kitchen made my stomach clench.

"Here, have this first, and then we'll slowly move you up the food chain." He pushed a churning glass of pink liquid toward me.

I smacked my hand over my mouth. "I don't think that's a good idea."

"It's the perfect hangover cure." His cheeks fought against the smile he held back.

Eyeing it suspiciously, I lifted it to my nose.

"Don't smell. Just drink. Bottom's up."

Pinching my nose, I choked down the glass of pure evil and waited for the detonation, maybe a geyser erupting from my mouth or, if I were seriously lucky, it would be from the other end and the humiliation would be complete. The drink settled into my stomach like lead and I braced for the inevitable rewind, but instead of creating the seventh level of hell in my intestines, the churning stopped.

Ford set a plate of bacon in front of me, and the salty

sweetness called to me like cherubs on clouds playing harps. I picked up a piece, not sure if the truce in my stomach would hold. My first crispy bite set off every taste bud. Each bite got quicker as I was assured I wasn't going to have a repeat of the night before. I devoured the plate like a zombie at a brain buffet, each strip restoring some of my bodily functions.

"How are you feeling now?"

Full, I leaned against the counter and licked my fingers. "Better." The word was muffled by all the bacon shoved in my mouth.

"If that's sitting okay in your stomach, try a couple of these." He lifted two fluffy pancakes from the big stack and put them on my plate. *Carbs, glorious carbs.* He slid a bottle of syrup toward me, but I picked up the warm pancake and broke it apart with my fingers.

"It'll help soak up some of that hangover." He sat on the stool on the other side of the counter and dug into the other full plate of pancakes and bacon.

With the imminent eruption from my body canceled, the guilt and humiliation of the night before slammed into me.

I'd puked on him.

Had I said anything? Done anything I should run for cover from? He wasn't acting weird. Maybe we *could* do this friendship thing. He *had* rescued me from myself the previous night, after all.

"About last night..." I picked at the pancake on my plate.

"Don't worry about it. You're in college."

"I know, but puking on you—" I cringed. "I'll pay for the dry cleaning or a new shirt or whatever else you need."

He glanced up from his plate. "Seriously, don't worry

about it. I've helped Grant out loads of times before." His face fell the second Grant's name passed his lips.

Yeah, Grant. I winced. I needed to have that conversation with him and let him know, one more time, we were better as friends. It reminded me a hell of a lot of the one Ford had probably wanted to have with me after the kiss...and now my stomach churning was back.

"Are you going to tell Colm? Have you already told him?" My shoulders shot up to my ears as I braced for the earful I'd get from my brother. Ford had probably already told him. I could just envision the angry messages rolling in on my phone.

"I'm not your babysitter. I'm your friend, remember? He doesn't need to know unless you want to tell him."

The tension in my shoulders relaxed a little. My friend. I played with that phrase in my head for a bit, and it almost fit...almost. It was a puzzle piece with the right picture, but the grooves were off.

"So what happened last night?"

He stared into my eyes, and I prayed to the drunk gods it hadn't been as bad as I thought.

"I brought you here, you puked, and that was it." He shoved a forkful of pancakes into his mouth.

"That's it?" I leaned in and kept my eyes trained on him.

"That's it." His words were muffled by pancakes and syrup.

A sigh of relief whooshed out of my lungs. "Thank God. I was worried I'd tried to kiss you or something."

He froze with his fork midway to his mouth, and a sharp cough broke free from his throat. He grabbed his glass of orange juice to wash it down, and that small ray of hope that what he'd said was the end of the story was washed away as he downed the glass, not quite meeting my gaze. I sent up a silent prayer. *Please let me be wrong.*

11

LIV

The pungent smell of fear, textbooks, and no. 2 pencils mixed with the scribbled scratching of lead on the exam booklets. Running my pencil down the last few equations on my paper, I glanced up at the clock. *Crap!*

There wasn't time to triple check my work. The oxygen in the room thinned, and it was hard to catch my breath. My chicken-scratch answers covered in eraser fuzz and the remnants of previous answers I'd corrected would have to do.

I hopped up from my seat and dropped off my exam in the pile on the desk at the front of the room before darting back down the aisle. I packed up my things, grabbed my coat, and bolted from the room. Outside, the sharpness of the winter freeze didn't seem to care that March was fast approaching. I turned on my phone, and a message from Ford popped up.

Things had been different since my drunken night out. There hadn't been any angry messages from Colm about how irresponsible I was or how I was screwing up my future.

Ford had kept his word, and our texts were less stilted. Every call from him wasn't a butt dial until proven otherwise, but in some ways that made it harder. Every little joke made me smile. Each notification sent my pulse racing. The sweet, strong side of him I'd crushed on so hard was right back in my face.

Shaking my head, I jogged the last few blocks to the studio. Inside those walls, the tension seeped out of my muscles, and the tight clench of my jaw that I didn't notice until I walked through the door relaxed. Dance kept me sane. Exams, med school, Colm, Grant, Ford—life was throwing everything it had at me.

The freezing brass handle of the studio door made my teeth chatter, the alcove between doors warming me the slightest bit before I made it inside. My squeaking boots made their own soundtrack on my way up to my classroom. The remix version would be coming out the following week. I checked the time again: only fifteen minutes before class. I'd have barely enough time to change, stretch, and run through the choreography to make sure I didn't screw it up. If I was lucky, I'd have a few minutes to inhale a protein bar in my face. After ducking into the changing room, I put on my dance clothes and shoved my street outfit into my bag.

I scurried back out into the studio. Voices echoed up the stairwell, and people climbed the steps, spilling onto the floor.

I leaned out the door as they got closer to the room. "Give me five minutes."

Rolling my head and stretching out my bad case of exam-taker's neck, I shook out my arms and shoulders. With my eyes on my reflection, I went through the entire routine, my ease of movement returning with each step, bringing the dance that had only lived in my head to life. In the mirror I tracked my arms and legs, correcting myself as I went. There wasn't the same pressure that weighed me down inside the classroom or on the pages of my textbook.

Slamming out the last move, I laughed at myself in the mirror. My heart raced, my skin tingled, and every worry I'd had before I stepped into that room had melted away.

The class began, and for sixty minutes, nothing outside those walls existed.

This was where I was alive.

Where nothing bad could touch me.

Where I'd always found the pieces of me that were lost out in the real world.

Still sweaty from the studio, I jogged up the steps to my apartment.

Opening the door, I stopped short. A tangle of limbs and bright colors greeted me by the couch.

"Hey, Liv," they chorused together. Marisa blew her hair out of her face, her cheeks flushed red and her body contorted half over and half under LJ.

"She tried to take the last Snickers." His words tumbled out as a breathless, choppy mess.

"Sharing is caring." She wheezed and shoved at his shoulders. Shimmying out from under him, she redid her ponytail, laughing and popping a piece of the candy into her mouth. LJ grumbled and pouted, but the undercurrent of their caring for each other shined so bright it almost hurt. They had this connection that didn't come around too often. I couldn't hold back my smile that they had each other, but it also constantly reminded me of my third-wheel status.

"Maybe I do, maybe I don't, but you know what's mine?"

He lunged under the coffee table and shoved the last lonely fun-sized Snickers into his mouth, grinning the whole time.

"You'll pay for that later." Marisa picked up a pillow and chucked it at his head before turning to me. "How was class?"

"They are blowing me away. I keep throwing these moves at them, and every class everyone is getting better and better. I've got some new routines I'm planning in my head. It's going to be insane. They'll hate me at first, but once everything's flowing, I'll get them on board."

She laughed and gathered up her books on the coffee table. "I meant biochem. Didn't you have a test today?"

"Don't remind me." I flopped down onto the couch. "It was a bloodbath. If I get an A minus this semester, it will be a miracle, which means I'm screwed." The knot in my stomach and tension in my shoulders that had relaxed over the sixty minutes of dance were firmly back in place. If I made it out of college without an ulcer, I'd be shocked.

"That's what happens when you're at the studio nearly every night."

"You're the one who told me I can't stay chained to my desk every day."

She held up her hands in mock surrender. "There's a difference between taking a break and hiding from what's coming."

I shrugged as LJ took a bite of a Twizzler.

"Where did you get that?" Marisa's gaze darted to the candy in his hand.

"I have my secrets." He waggled his eyebrows at her.

"You're like a piñata. Maybe I should shake you to find out what other secrets you're hiding."

"Maybe you should." He stared down at her. She froze with her fingers poised at his sides, mid-tickle.

Clearing her throat, she stepped back and turned to me. "When's your brother back? Maybe you should talk to him about putting off med school for a bit, travel or something."

I flopped back against the cushions. "It's not that easy. I wish it were. You don't understand how important med school is to him, to our family."

"But he's not the one who's actually going to med school. How important it is to him doesn't really matter."

"It's been the plan since forever. It would be a big adjustment from 'yay, I'm going to be a doctor' to 'screw that, I'm going to be a dance teacher.' It doesn't exactly roll off the tongue."

"The longer you wait, the harder it will be—for both of you. Ease him into it. At least tell him your doubts about it. You can't exactly spring it on him at graduation. 'Hey, remember that whole med school thing? Yeah, not doing it. Going to teach dance. Bye!'"

"I know." I leaned my head against the back of the couch and closed my eyes. Wasn't I supposed to know what the hell I was doing as I got older? Instead the questions got harder, and someone had stolen my study guide. My phone buzzed in my pocket.

Ford: There is no way in hell you can beat me in Scrabble.

Our earlier argument picked up right where we'd left it. He hadn't run away, but I was once again friend-zoned.

I tried my best to squash the giddy anticipation that came with each notification.

Me: We'll have to wait and see because I'm the reigning champ in this apartment.

Marisa had banned all board games after I'd beaten her in everything from Candyland to Risk.

Ford: I eat those tiles for breakfast. I'll spank the hell out of you.

The phone nearly fell out of my hand, and I snorted. I could just imagine the way his eyes would bug out when he realized what he'd typed.

Ford: I mean I'll cream you!

Ford: Shit, not what I meant. Not that you think I meant anything

The text bubble popped up and disappeared at least three times.

Ford: I'll kick your butt in a fair and square game of Scrabble

Me: I'd like to see you try!

Three days later he got his chance.

"Seems someone was a little overconfident." Ford grinned at me across the board.

"You got a lucky hand," I grumbled before shoving another handful of popcorn into my mouth.

He looked larger than life sitting across from me at our small dining room table.

"These chairs could be used for torture." He stretched his back.

"It's how I get my competitive edge. How long until practice?"

"Another couple of hours. The practice rink's all screwed up, so at least I don't have to go all the way out to Jersey."

My phone rang from my bedroom where I'd plugged it in to charge. I hopped up, stopped short, and squinted at him. He whistled a tuneless melody, staring up at the ceiling, twiddling his thumbs. I raced back and grabbed my tiles, taking them with me. Lunging for my phone, I tapped the screen.

"Hey, what's up?"

"Thank God you're there." The dance studio receptionist's relief seeped through the phone.

"I am indeed here." Ford walked by my room, and the bathroom door closed.

"Emergency situation—can you pretty please teach the three o'clock class?"

That was soon, and Ford hadn't been at my place long. I stared out into the hallway. We didn't get much time together. I wanted to tell her no, maybe pretend she'd gotten a convincing version of my new voice mail, but the students would be disappointed. Canceling a class with some people traveling from all over the city sucked, especially when I could do it, even if at that moment I'd rather have been curled up on my bed with Ford. I checked the time: half an hour to get ready and get there.

"Sure, I can do it."

"You're a lifesaver, Liv!"

She hung up before I got to say another word, probably hoping I wouldn't back out.

"What are those?" He leaned against the doorway and pointed to the boxes under my bed.

Hanging down over the side, I looked at where he pointed. "Pictures. I've been hoarding them since forever. These"—I tapped the two in the back—"are the ones of my parents before they had us. My mom wrote whole stories on the backs. They're my favorites, but I'm afraid to take them out too often. Before Mom and Dad started med school, they were totally different people. There were hikes, dinners out on the town, celebrations with friends we never met. When Colm sold our parents' house, I had to go rescue them."

"Why didn't he want them?"

I shrugged. Colm and I'd dealt with losing our parents in different ways. Sometimes it was like he wanted to erase them from his memory, like when he'd sold the house, and other times he clung to their legacy like it was the only thing keeping his head above water.

"Have you backed them up?"

"It's a lot of pictures to scan." There was never enough time. I'd calculated it would take me nearly three days to get them all done, and putting the boxes in someone else's care freaked me out. What if they lost them?

"Someone can do that for you." He leaned against the doorjamb.

"And it costs an arm and a leg. Trust me, I've checked. Colm does not have fun and frivolity budgeted into what he sends me every semester." I paused briefly. "That was the chem lab calling. One of their lab assistants bailed and they need me to fill in." He didn't need to know about my dancing. I tucked my hair behind my ear. There'd be more questions, maybe something like, *Can I watch?*

"No problem, I can go."

"There's no point in you going home just to come back to this side of town for practice. Hang out here for a while and lock the door behind you when you go. I'll tell Marisa not to be alarmed if an overly large man is lounging in our living room."

"Thanks for keeping me safe." He winked.

"And I'll even let you have some of the chocolate chunk brownies hiding in the back of the fridge. I don't part with those easily, so you should feel honored."

He bowed. "I absolutely do." Peering up at me, he smirked. "Now where are those brownies?" He rubbed his hands together.

"I'll be out in a couple minutes, so don't go rummaging

through the fridge like a bear. Also, I'm taking my tiles with me. We'll finish this butt kicking next time."

He scoffed and disappeared from the doorway. I ran my hands through my hair and stared after him. This was a tightrope we were walking, but the longer I was with him, the more I convinced myself it wasn't one-sided. It wasn't all in my head. The sidelong glances, the lingering touches that sent tingles up my spine—it was real, but what could we do about it? It wasn't the time. Rushing around the room, I gathered up everything I'd need.

I threw my bag over my shoulder and ran into the living room. Slinging the fridge door open, I pushed the V8 and celery aside and pulled out the small bag of edamame.

Ford's eyebrows furrowed; then he smiled when I pulled two wrapped brownies out of the bag.

"Perfect disguise."

"Desperate times call for desperate measures." I plunked the chocolate square into his hand. "I'll talk to you later. Have a good practice." I leaned in. He smelled like honeycomb, which he'd used on his leather bag back in high school. Did he still use it? It had been so long since I'd been close enough to know. Like I was outside myself, the scene in front of me unfolded: rushing off to work and giving my boyfriend a kiss to remember me by until I came back home to him.

Ford's eyes got wide, and it dawned on me how close my lips were to his.

"Sorry." I bolted across the room. "See you later." My fingers fumbling with the knob, I opened the door and nearly closed it on myself before I made a break for it down the steps.

Wasn't being away from him supposed to be the hardest part? This was worse. This was so much worse, being this close but not acting on every little urge to touch him floating through my head. Not jumping into his lap and feeling his hands on my body, lying on the couch together watching TV, tasting his soft yet firm lips on mine as he pulled every bit of pleasure out of me...

With a new determination, I bounded down the last flight of steps. This new Ford had gotten inside my head. Late-night texts, playing board games, watching TV—we'd slipped into a comfortable routine when he was home, and it didn't make sense to me. I didn't know how far we could push things, but I didn't want to lose him again.

Liv: Sure, dinner would be nice. See you in a couple hours. I'm not at my apartment. I'll send over the location where we can meet.

Me: Ok

The team's killer schedule over the past two weeks hadn't left time for anything other than airports, hotels, the team bus, practices, and games. Road stretches like these left everyone drained, bleary-eyed, and ready for a little time off. Four days off, then a home game meant no planes for a week, and that was as settled as things got during the pro hockey season.

Liv had crept up in the forefront of my mind more over the past few weeks. Long stretches away from home sucked a bit more, and texts were all I'd had to sustain me. Her energized chatter late at night and the weary words she squeezed in while studying weren't enough.

The Kings had gotten back together at a dinner with Colm while we were out in LA for a game. It was cut short when he'd excused himself from the table and hadn't come back. I'd pushed back from the table and gone to look for him.

He'd been standing out on the pier overlooking the water.

"You okay?" I'd stood beside him, leaning onto the railing.

"Why wouldn't I be? You guys are on fire this season, skating better than ever, and I'm not there with you." His face had looked like he'd been sucking on a bag of Sour Patch Kids.

"My game's been off without you there on the front lines." It hadn't been, but the easy rhythm we'd once had was long gone. "You'll be back. The month's almost up."

He'd turned his face away. "My rehab isn't finished."

"The coaches said a month."

"Looks like the damage is deeper than they thought. It's going to be a few more weeks."

"Shit, I'm sorry." I'd dropped my hand onto his shoulder.

He'd turned, shaking my hand free. I'd clenched my hands at my sides. "What are you sorry about? It's not like you did anything. You're never to blame." He'd glared at me, and the churning fire in my gut had burned brighter.

"You're throwing this at me too? Haven't I paid my penance already for something you admit I'm not to blame for?"

"You might not have been to blame, but that doesn't mean I can't still be pissed about it, can't be angry about your lies." The bitter words were a sore spot between us. He'd blown out a big breath, shaking his head, and dragged his hands through his hair. "How's Liv?"

A lump had formed in my throat like a jawbreaker shoved down deep, making it hard to swallow. "She's sorting through some stuff."

His head had snapped up.

"But she's working through it. There's nothing to worry about."

He'd nodded, staring out at the water. The cool, salty air washed over us, no sounds but the gentle roll of the waves and the caws of the seagulls circling, looking for food. Once, the silence between us had felt comfortable, but now it felt stifling.

"What are you two doing out there? Get back in here." Declan's hands had cupped his mouth as he'd shouted out to us.

"I need to go." Colm had waved him off and disappeared into the night, leaving without another word.

"What the hell crawled up his ass?" Declan had held the door open for me.

I'd shrugged and gone back inside. We got back on the road the next day, and he hadn't answered any of my messages since.

At first the travel had been one of my favorite parts of playing because it meant no expectations from anyone you met when they knew you'd only be in town for a night or two. I had my family, the Kings had been an extension of that since high school, and that had been all I needed. Even knowing they were out in the world and had my back was enough, but now the travel meant more time away from family and friends. There were only so many hotel parking lots, stadium locker rooms, and airport lounges I could stare at before they all ran together.

A message came in from Liv with her current location. It was a dance studio, according to the map. I looked the place up and saw a picture of her on the home page. Clicking on the schedule, I spotted her name. *She teaches dance classes?*

The screen went blank, and the call screen popped up.

I cursed under my breath. "Hey, Grant."

"I got a text back from Liv."

"Not even a hello." The rough texture of my jeans scraped against my palms as I rubbed them down my legs.

He ignored me and kept talking. "She said she wanted to talk to me."

"I mentioned you wanted to talk to her." I clenched my jaw.

He let out a deep breath. "Perfect. Midterms are almost over. I'll see if she wants to get dinner."

"Good luck. I've got to go." I jammed my finger against the screen and shoved my hands into my pockets as I shouldered my way into the parking garage. I grabbed my key and headed toward her location.

She had said a couple hours, so why was I going immediately? *Since when has she taught dance to anyone other than little kids? Does Colm know? What kind of dance?*

The entire drive over, it was the same loop that had been playing in my head since that dinner at Heath's. Her lips on mine, so soft and smooth... The switch inside of me that only flipped on when the lights went out was on a hair trigger around her. My blood pounded in my veins and my fingers itched to touch her, and that was why I should have turned around and told Liv I'd see her the next day.

Instead, I parked and jogged up the steps of the dance school, pushing through the glass doors. Dragging my hat off my head, I checked out the lobby. Pictures hung on the walls. Pictures of Liv with a huge smile on her face surrounded by other people. I hadn't seen her smile like that in a long time.

A woman at the reception desk popped her head up. "Can I help you?"

"I'm looking for Olivia Frost."

"Class starts in ten minutes."

"No, I'm not here—"

"Second floor, second door on the right."

I wasn't sure what about me screamed dancer, but I went along with it, nodding then climbing the stairs two at a time. People milled around in the hallway as music filtered out of the door and filled the hallway with a muted ballad. Peering in the small window, I spotted her.

In front of the mirrored wall, she had on tights and a sheer skirt that floated around her like magic as she danced. She ran from one side of the room to the other, coming up to her full height and lifting her other leg up and over her head almost in a midair split. Time stood still as she moved in time to the beat.

Her partner followed her through the moves. She jumped into the air and straight into the guy's arms with her legs wrapped around his waist. His hands crisscrossed her back.

My jaw clenched at the way he looked at her. It wasn't a look of professional appreciation. Their bodies pressed together, and they swayed to the music, each movement more frantic but fluid as the music built. The final explosion of sound ended with her wrapped around the guy, his hands cradling her ass. I slammed my lips together, tension creeping up my neck as their bodies moved together, touching, entwined, completely focused on the other.

They stopped, and Liv's face broke out in a cloud-clearing smile. She jumped up and down, high-fiving the guy who'd had his hands all over her.

More people walked up the stairs behind me and went through the second door. I turned back to the cutout window in the door, and Liv's face popped up, her down-turned lips cooling some of the tension running through my body.

She tugged the door open with a duffel bag over her shoulder. "I said an hour, right?"

I nodded.

She pulled out her phone and checked the message. "You're here early."

"Your name was on the class schedule on the website."

She chewed on her thumb. "My class is an hour. You might want to go get a coffee or something until I'm finished." The sweat clung to her skin like a warm glow. She rushed away toward the changing rooms.

"Can I stay and watch?"

She turned around, walking backward. "It's not interesting. You'll be bored." Adjusting the strap of her bag, she nibbled on her bottom lip.

I could never be bored watching you. "I won't."

She hesitated like she was going to tell me I couldn't watch, and her fingers tightened their grip. "I need to go change. I'll be right back. The second door." She pointed toward the room everyone else was filing into and rushed off.

People poured into the space, dropped their bags, and stretched. This was not my scene at all. A few heads turned, eyeing me up. No, I didn't belong there. Yes, I was trying to figure out why I'd come, too.

Liv burst into the room with an energy radiating off her I hadn't seen before. She'd traded the more traditional dance leotard for pants that hugged her ass like a second skin and a bright green top that rode up a little when she put her arms in the air, exposing a band of her taut stomach.

"Thanks for coming tonight! We're going to have an awesome class. I've got some new choreography that's killer.

I hope you're ready to sweat." Her lips curved into a mischievous smile.

Everyone in the room's attention was riveted to her while she clicked the music on with her phone and the beat poured out of the speakers.

She ran everyone through the routine. The warmup was probably the only thing my body could have handled. The entire class's attention followed her every move as she broke down the dance she'd shown them into smaller pieces.

I'd seen her dance when she was younger, kid ballet recitals that had dragged on forever, but this was different. The way her body moved, she was so in tune with every muscle, every line creating a picture that stole my breath away.

I grabbed a chair and sat, not wanting to miss a second of her dancing. She broke the class into groups and bounced around the room to each one, helping them work through the spots where they couldn't quite get it.

I'd never seen her like this before, so in control, running the room like it was second nature. These people were so eager to learn from her. Her smile and happiness racing from group to group, reworking the same moves over and over again were absolute.

She jogged over to me once everyone got the help they needed. "You sure you don't want to jump in?"

"That would be a terrifying experience for everyone here." Dancing had to be avoided at all costs.

"I'm sure you've got some moves." Her gaze ran up and down my body, and the playfulness of her look didn't stop my muscles from snapping to attention.

"And those moves are best left out on the ice. How long have you been doing this?"

"Dancing?"

"Teaching."

She nibbled on her thumb. "Almost a year. I started last summer, and I took on more classes in the fall. I was here so much, and it can get expensive. It felt weird using the money Colm gave me to pay for dance classes, so I asked if they might have an instructor spot open."

"Just like that."

"Just like that." She snapped her fingers. "Someone bailed last minute, and I got in. It was meant to be. Free classes and workshops whenever someone big comes into town, plus I get to come up with new ideas all the time and see these guys bring it to life." She turned around with her arms folded over her chest, looking every bit the proud parent. "I love it." She grinned back at me like I'd just promised her a trip to Disneyworld. There wasn't a tenth of that joy when she talked about medical school.

"I can tell. Does Colm know how important this is to you?"

She shoved that water bottle up to her lips so quickly she looked like a hamster in its cage, chugging away.

"That's a no." Wiping her mouth with the back of her hand, she dropped the bottle to her side. "It's complicated. Med school has always been the plan." She ran her hand over her face. "That's always been the goal. It was what they'd have wanted, what I want for them. It's an important part of the legacy they saw for me and Colm." Sadness flickered in her eyes.

"They'd be proud no matter what you did."

"Would they? Would they have even cared if it didn't have to do with medicine?" Her gaze filled with the honest question of whether or not they'd have been on the sidelines cheering her on no matter what path she chose, and given what I remembered of them, it was a fair question.

How many of Colm's games had they missed? How many times were Liv and Grant holed up at my house being lugged to our games because her parents were stuck at the hospital?

The volume in the room increased as people finished up their practice.

"You sure you don't want to jump in?" She nodded back toward the class behind her.

"Not if my life depended on it." I sat back in my seat, and Liv returned to the front. They all moved as one as she turned the music on again. The driving rhythm pounded louder and faster, arms and legs moving in unison. Hair flew through the air, and everyone followed in Liv's footsteps, taking her moves and making them their own.

The smaller groups performed the choreography for the rest of the class. Liv took out her phone and recorded them all. Whoops and cheers rang out as they hit their marks, throwing their own improvisational moves into the routine.

There was one last burst of kinetic energy as everyone did the routine together. Panting and resting her hands on her knees, Liv called it. "Until next time, everyone!" she declared over the laughter and applause. Her class slowly left the room, their giddy excitement over what they'd just done together radiating off them.

I helped her pick up things people had left behind and dropped them into the lost and found box. In the span of an hour, she'd transformed into a different person, every bend and dip so much more precise than I'd noticed before. Her movements were controlled and fluid at the same time.

"Why don't you show me something?"

Her head snapped up and a smile curved her lips. "Changed your mind?"

I lifted my chin.

"I can show you a little of what I just taught."

"Show me what you were doing before...in the other room."

"The lift? That's pretty advanced. I don't want to end up cracking my tailbone." She ran her palm over her butt.

"You think I can't hold you?"

She eyed my skeptically. "I'm not saying you aren't strong enough, but handling someone else's weight can be tricky."

I tugged her close to me, my chest flush against hers. "I promise I won't drop you."

Her eyes widened, and she nodded, licking her lips. "O-Okay. I trust you."

My hold tightened around her waist. "I know. Now show me, teach."

13

LIV

He was early. We were supposed to meet after class, maybe get some food, try to make sense of whatever was going on. I'd maybe ask him how I should handle the Grant situation. The last thing I wanted to do was cause issues between them; there was enough sibling dysfunction in our little group already.

This should have been easy. I was on my turf in the studio, but there was nowhere to hide with the mirrored glass showing every part of yourself to anyone in the room. My stomach had been in knots since he'd arrived.

His gaze had landed on me, and I'd felt him. Even through the door, peering through the small window, my body had known he was there. The crackling energy of the room had shifted. I'd been a split second from claiming I'd been struck with a sudden bout of food poisoning and canceling the whole class, but deep down, maybe I'd hoped he'd come.

I could have sent him a location a few blocks away, but I'd sent this location. Maybe that voice in the back of my head had known he'd show up and see me, not like any Liv he'd seen before, but as someone different. Someone he didn't know and think of as his friend's little sister.

He didn't watch me like a friend. He watched me like he'd looked at me the night we'd kissed, the crackling heat of desire pouring out of every pore in pools so deep it threatened to drown me. That was the Ford I'd known and really seen for the first time after the wedding, and I wanted him to see me again.

During the class, I'd danced for him, wanting him to see me in a way that couldn't be denied. This was the place I knew more about myself than I'd ever thought possible. It wasn't another dancer's hands on me; they were Ford's, and now it wasn't just in my head.

And now we were alone in my territory.

"Put your hands here." I covered his hands with mine and pressed them against my waist. He readjusted his hold, his fingers sinking in deeper. The top I had on rode up higher, and his fingertips brushed against my skin.

There was a slight jerk of his arm like he wanted to pull away, but he didn't. The wisps of hair that fell free from my ponytail brushed against my neck in time with his breathing as the rise and fall of his chest played against my back, charging the room and the energy between us.

"Like this?" His words licked the curve of my neck.

I nodded, not trusting my voice. I'd never doubted his strength. The tireless practice sessions and hours in the weight room took care of that, but having his hands on me again would only bring us back to what we were both fighting so hard. I was a step away from dragging him into the nearest broom closet to maul him. Restraint would be a feat of strength on my part.

"Let's start it slow."

"Slow is good."

"It's as much about the emotion as it is about the movement."

His fingers tightened against my body.

Taking a deep breath, I shoved those butterflies down and locked them away. I walked him through the moves at a tenth of the pace, making sure he got every movement before we went on to the next.

His arms wrapped around me, and we moved together for a while before I gave him space to watch him move by himself. His solo work wasn't bad, but I couldn't hold back my laugh at his serious face in the mirror. He never half-assed anything.

"We can stop here." I walked to him from my spot halfway across the room.

"How was that?" His gaze landed on mine. That sparking fire rushed through my body, and I couldn't move. My heart pounded in my chest. I ran my hands over my leggings.

"That was great. You're a natural."

"So are you." He ran his fingers along his jaw. "Let's try the lift thing."

I laughed. "That's not a good idea."

"Why not?"

"You might get hurt. It's trickier than it looks."

"Come on, Liv. Give me a chance."

I would have given you all the chances in the world.

"And what happens if I fall on you and you break a bone or something?"

"If you fell on me, I'd barely break a sweat. Let me try at least once. I swear if I drop you, you can kick me in the balls. Please." He licked his lips, and the word reached deep inside of me, adding a little more kindling to the flame I'd been trying to extinguish for years.

I closed the gap between us. "You need to put your

hands here." I stood facing him, our chests almost touching. The heat from his fingers seeped into my skin. *Why did I have to wear this top today? Should have stayed in the classic leotard from before.* A little breathless from dancing, he was the sexiest I'd ever seen him.

"When I bend my knees, that's when you lift. I'll push off the floor to help." I rested my hands on his shoulders.

I couldn't hold back my smile at the look on his face: peak concentration like every time he stepped onto the ice.

"It's not that serious. This is supposed to be fun." I ran my hand along his jaw. The softness of his newly grown-in beard caressed my hand, and his eyes peeled away the last layers of protection I'd placed around myself.

"This is more fun than I've had in a long time." His hold on me tightened. Our bodies pressed closer together.

My feet slipped in between his, our bodies the perfect puzzle pieces even with our height difference. The hammering of my heart drowned out the music track playing on a loop.

"Me too." My lips were a whisper away from his. The heat of his breath fanned across my face.

One of his hands lifted from my waist and ran along the side of my face. He cupped my cheek, and we were transported from the studio to the garden under the summer moonlight. My dress flowed around me, and his lips were the only thing that mattered.

"Liv." My name was an unanswered prayer that I wanted to sate.

The gap between us disappeared as his hand slid to the back of my neck, drawing me in closer. Our lips collided like two planets that had been circling one another for eons. He tasted like spicy citrus, like my ginger-lime margaritas.

My lips parted, and he deepened the kiss. His body

covered mine, and he bent me backward, invading every part of my mouth. My hold tightened around his neck. This was more than before. It was overpowering, all-consuming, with the possibility to be all-crushing.

I jerked back out of his hold, panting with my eyes trained on the floor.

My entire body shook with the pent-up energy that refused to dissipate.

He stepped toward me, and I took a step back. We were dancing a new dance now.

"Sorry." He reached toward me, and I sidestepped his touch.

"There's nothing to be sorry about. Sometimes people get carried away when they dance. It happens." My attempt at playing it off was failing badly. I rushed over to my bag. "I'm going to get changed. Can I get a rain check on our dinner? I have a big exam coming up, and I need to study." I stared at the wall, trying to get myself together.

He touched my shoulder. "Liv—"

"Don't worry." I shook my head and turned, forcing a porcelain smile on my face. "You don't have to wait for me." I darted out of the room, letting the door close behind me.

Inside the changing room, I rested my head against the wall. What the hell was all that talk about not falling for him again? *I'm not going to let him get under my skin. I'm not going to make the same mistakes. No, this time it's go big or go home.*

Quickly changing out of my gear and into my nice skin-fully-covered winter wear, I peeked out of the changing room. Ford leaned against the wall with one leg propped up. He dropped his foot when he spotted me.

I opened my mouth, trying to find the words.

"Good thing you wanted a rain check because I can't go to dinner anyway."

"Oh." Why did that hurt? I'd already canceled on him, already told him to go. "Looks like that rain check was perfect timing."

His lips smashed together in a thin grim line. "Right, perfect. I'll walk you out."

I zipped up my jacket and walked toward him, nibbling my bottom lip. I prayed my hat covered the red tips of my ears.

He moved to the top of the steps, standing stoically with his hands in his pockets. His broad shoulders and thick muscles showed though his winter coat. How could I not want him when he stared into my eyes like that, like there wasn't anyone else who saw into him like I did?

The lights from the stairway cast him in shadow. There was always a barrier between us, always things we wanted to say and do, but a force field shot up anytime the words bubbled up. The only time I couldn't hold it back was when he touched me. The wants and needs inside me warred with the shoulds.

We stepped outside in silence. The seasons were in a constant battle. One day spring was right around the corner, the next the freezing wind sliced right through my coat. My breath hung in the air in puffs between us.

"I fly out again tomorrow."

Shoving my hands in my pockets, I rocked on my heels. "I have all the games marked on my calendar."

"You'll watch?" He dipped his head and looked into my eyes.

"I always do. Have a safe trip." I spun on my heels and walked away, one foot in front of the other. *Just keep going and don't look back.* A little separation would be good, would help me get my head on straight. This was like an immunization to Ford. I was slowly building up my immunity, but I had a feeling I was about to catch a full-blown case of the Fords, and the recovery would leave permanent damage to my head and my heart.

14

LIV

"I give up, Mak. Seriously, this is insane." I threw down my pencil and slammed my book closed. Hysteria bubbled toward the surface. Disaster loomed on the horizon, and a light-headed wave rolled over me. I wrapped my hand tighter around the edge of my desk. *You've got to do this, Liv. You've got this.* Maybe I should cancel my dance classes this week. I could squeeze in a few more hours of studying before the next exam...

"You had it ten minutes ago. What happened?" She pushed her textbook aside and leaned over to look at mine.

"My brain doesn't want to hold on to the information. It's a sieve. One second it's there and the next it's gone." I flipped the book closed and leaned back in the chair, rubbing my eyes, the prickles of desperation scratching the backs of them. Crying in front of Mak wouldn't be cool.

"Why don't we take a break? We can go for a walk and get some dinner."

"I can't leave until I get this." Determination burning in my gut, I lifted the cover of my book. My usual tie-myself-to-the-chair-until-I-get-it method wasn't working, hadn't been working for days, not since Ford had left...not since our dance.

She pushed it closed, trapping my hand under the cover. "Taking a breather will help give your brain some time to absorb the material. Let's go." She squeezed my hand.

My shoulders slumped in defeat, and I squeezed the bridge of my nose. "You're right. I haven't had anything since seven."

"This morning? Liv! That was nearly ten hours ago."

"Really?" I double-checked the time. After waking up, I'd gone straight to the library until I met her. "I didn't even notice." My stomach disagreed, rumbling.

The Darth Vader ringtone blared from my phone. Pressing my lips together, I took a deep breath and tapped the screen.

"Hello, warden."

"Very funny. What are you up to?"

"Snorting lines of coke off a stripper's rock-hard abs."

"What are you really doing?" If Colm clenched his jaw any harder, he'd crack a tooth.

"What are *you* doing?"

"I just got back from a doctor's appointment. How did your bio exam go? And where are you?"

Leaving the table, I went into the living room to properly pace.

"I shouldn't have told you about the test." I groaned.

"All your course syllabi are online. I'd have looked them up anyway."

"Don't you ever get tired of monitoring every single thing I do?"

"Stop being so dramatic. You're my sister. It's us against the world. I'm here to look out for you." Lately that mantra felt more like a choke hold than the comfort it had once been. "What are you doing?"

He wasn't going to let up, and hanging up on him would only make it worse. "I'm at Mak and Declan's. Mak is helping me with my organic chemistry. I've got on a blue tank top, black cardigan, dark blue jeans, and I'm wearing black boots. We are going to get some food, and I'll maybe even have a glass of wine."

"Olive..." The warning tone in his voice set me off.

"There are fifty-two days between me and my twenty-first birthday—get over it."

"Would you rather I didn't care? That once Mom and Dad were gone, I dropped you off at boarding school and you never saw me again?"

"Now who's being dramatic? There's something in between abandonment and imprisonment, a happy medium where you get to live your life and I get to live mine and we don't have to be filled in on the smallest details of our days at all times. Like when you were dating Felicity. Remember that? You were ready to propose. We had our weekly dinners to catch up, talked a few times a week. You were so happy. You showed me the ring, and then poof she was gone and you started up your one-man surveillance operation on me."

"Drop it."

"No, you don't get to know every single thing going on with me and then not reciprocate at all. Every time I've tried to talk to you about her, you just clam up. If you want to keep grilling me, maybe I want to do the same to you."

"It's nothing for you to worry about."

"It is. It's obviously hurt you, but you won't talk to me about it. How am I supposed to open up when you've shut me out completely?"

I could hear his calming breaths on the other end, the ones he took when I kept needling him. Usually it was my cue to back off, but I didn't want to.

"You don't just go from 'I'm marrying her' to 'who?' in seconds flat."

"She wasn't who I thought she was, okay? We were building something and then she pulled the rug out from under me, so I broke up with her."

"Just like that? No compromise?"

"No, not when it comes to cheating."

My stomach knotted. "She cheated on you? With who? Why didn't you tell me this before?"

"It's not important." His jaw popped.

"Stop hiding things from me. Stop babying me."

"I'm on the other side of the country, and I worry about you."

"You don't need to. I'm studying hard. I'm worried about *you*."

"I know it's hard." He let out a deep, weary breath. "But you've got the smarts. Remember how happy Mom and Dad were when you got accepted into that middle school premed course? They took off work for a whole half-day to take you to the orientation session."

It had probably been one of the longest uninterrupted periods of time I was with both of them outside of our annual vacation.

"They'd be so proud you're following in their footsteps. You know how much they wanted you to become a doctor. Hell, there's money set aside in the trust expressly for that. They took care of everything you'd need, and part of my responsibility is looking after you."

"I know."

"It's a lot of pressure, but you can do it. You won't let them down."

I sank down onto the living room couch. My fingers dug into the soft cushions as my throat tightened. "Colm, I need to go. I've got a lot of material to cover and not a lot of time."

"Study hard. We can do this, Olive. It's us against the world. I'll talk to you later. I love you."

"Love you too." I ended the call and leaned back, covering my face with my hands. A noise to my left drew my attention, and my head snapped up. Mak stood in the doorway.

"I couldn't help but overhear." She sat on the coffee table in front of me with our coats draped across her lap. "Beating yourself up isn't going to make it better. After our break, I'm sure it will feel a lot easier."

I stared at the ceiling. "Maybe."

She handed me my coat, and we left the house in silence. Walking down the street, I shoved my hands into my pockets, the frigid wind chapping my hands.

"Liv, I've never asked this before, but maybe I should have." She turned to me while guiding the way to the restaurant. "Do you even want to be a doctor?"

"It's the only path there's ever been for me."

"That's not what I asked. Do you want to be a doctor? Want to finish out college, then do four more years of med school and then residency for another three to seven years? Does medicine light your soul on fire? Can you think of nothing else you'd rather do?"

Tears welled in my eyes. "It's the only thing I've ever allowed myself to think I could do."

She wrapped her arm around mine and pulled us to a stop. "You have a choice, Liv. I had the same doubts. I took some time for myself and realized it was what I wanted. You need to do that, too. You can't become a doctor for anyone else but you. Not for your parents, not for Colm, only yourself."

"Our parent's legacy is the most important thing to him. The life they envisioned for us is frozen in time eight years ago. Colm can't even think of any other options."

"But you're an adult, like you said. He can't force you to go to medical school."

"No, but I don't want to let them down either. It's my earliest dream." And I don't think he'd ever speak to me again if I didn't.

"Dreams change all the time. That's why I took a year off before going to med school. I needed to make sure it was what *I* wanted, not something I was doing out of obligation. He's your big brother, and he'd do anything for you."

I shook my head. "You don't understand how much this means to him, how much it meant to them."

"Maybe not, but this is *your* life. Talk to him—like, really talk. Not the bickering you do, but an actual adult conversation where he'll see you as the adult you are."

I blinked back my tears. "I don't even know if he can. I'm frozen in time as the little girl squeezing his hand at our parents' funeral."

"When he gets back, you need to find a way to make him understand what you want from your life or you'll never be happy."

I shrugged. We made it to the restaurant and ordered our food. Was Ford having dinner? Inviting someone into his bed? Watching Netflix in his hotel room alone?

"Is it weird being with Declan when he's gone so much?"

Mak slurped up the noodles hanging from her mouth. "It's taken some getting used to. I never realized how many games professional hockey players have every season."

"How are you two managing it?" My ramen swirled around my bowl as I poked at it with my chopsticks. I hated being away from Ford and we weren't even dating, let alone married.

"We've gotten creative." She cleared her throat and took a sip of her drink.

I glanced up at her with a smirk. Resting my hands under my chin, I scooted my chair closer. "Creative how?"

"You know." Her gaze darted away.

I set down my chopsticks and leaned over the table. "I think you're going to have to lay it out for me."

She chucked a spring onion at me. "Let's just say it's a good thing we don't have to pay our phone bill by the minute."

I laughed and ate more of the salty, broth-infused noodles. "You're running your own phone sex line, huh?"

"Practically. Being apart isn't that bad. Med school is insane most of the time, so it's good he's traveling. Then I don't feel as bad when I need to study for ten hours straight, and when he's home, I can keep the studying to a minimum so we get to spend time together."

"It sounds like you two have it worked out."

"It does, but we both live in mortal fear that he'll be traded, or I'll match at a residency program outside of Philly and then we're apart for eight months out of the year." She pushed around the chicken in her soup.

"If there's anyone who could do it, it's you two." They were that kind of couple that radiated lovey-dovey feelings from across a room.

"Declan would run himself ragged trying to fly to me whenever I had a full twelve hours off."

"He'd charter his own plane if he needed to."

She laughed and picked up the dessert menu. "Don't give him any ideas."

Back at the house, we sat together and went back to the other problem sets. Like she said, the material was clearer, and I finished the last set of questions in an hour.

"Next time take a break before the coronary, please."

"I will." I zipped up my backpack right as my phone pinged. "The taxi is here. I wouldn't have gotten it done without you."

"You'd have figured it out." She squeezed me in a big hug. Maybe I had a big sister after all. Mak let me go and stared into my eyes. "Should we meet next week?"

"Next week." We walked to the front door.

Pulling it open, she put her hand on my shoulder as I stepped out. "Take some deep breaths and remember to give yourself a break."

I sucked in a deep breath and blew it out, the air catching each puff and whisking it away into the inky night sky.

"See, you're already learning. Night, Liv."

"Night." I hopped into the taxi and waved to her. She stood in the doorway until I disappeared from view.

Slipping my phone out of my pocket, I spotted the game notification on my newly downloaded app. Swiping across the screen, I checked out the most recently posted word.

D-E-F-T-L-Y, picking up a triple letter score on the F, intersected with my S-T-Y-L-E-D. So, he wanted to play hardball. Going through the different options along the drive, I settled on S-O-B-E-R-L-Y.

Ford: Is that how you're doing things tonight? No parties or cocktail-making sessions?

Me: I don't drink every night.

Ford: I know, but I figured it's the weekend...

Me: Not after getting my exam back. Colm won't let up about it. Please don't add to the pile.

During my taxi ride over, we played a few more words. As I climbed the steps to my apartment, my phone buzzed in my hand.

"I wouldn't do that. I know you're working your ass off in school and devoting so much time to dance, too."

I opened my apartment door and dropped my bag beside the door. "Maybe I shouldn't be. I'll probably cut down on the classes I teach next month. Obviously three times a week is too much." Someone else could take over for a while. I could show them the routines and make sure everyone kept on track with their progress.

"You can't do that." His words came out rushed and forceful.

"Why not?"

"I saw you in that class in front of everyone. You loved it. There...you were different up there. I've never seen you happier."

"But med school—"

"Med school will still be there, but if you don't do something that makes you come alive, what's the point?"

The silence hung between us. It seemed like everyone was doling out that advice lately.

"Are you there?"

"Yeah, I'm here."

"Just think about it. I hate the idea of you giving up something you love to chase after a future you don't even want. I've got to go—our flight is boarding." His voice caught like he wanted to say more.

"Bye, Ford."

"Night, Liv."

I sat on the edge of my bed with his words running

through my head. The idea of giving up teaching made me want to scream, but all that time was time I could devote to studying. It was time I should have been devoting to studying, time lost and brain power devoted to new moves and choreography and energy expended until I was sweaty and barely able to breathe...time I'd never been happier. Which dream did I get to live? The one that had always been there and made my family proud, or the one that made my heart sing?

15

FORD

Sweaty and winded, I skated off the ice.

"Those saves were insane today." Emmett slapped me on the shoulder. We climbed out of the box and walked through the throng of fans who'd come to watch us play.

I nodded. A couple of kids shook a jersey with my number on it in front of the tunnel. It still blew my mind that people paid money to wear my jersey, that little kids could be excited to see me out on the ice.

Dropping my gear, I took their pen and scrawled my name across the number. Their faces lit up and they jumped up and down. I gave them high fives, then ducked inside the tunnel to the locker room.

Everyone got changed and onto the bus to the hotel. It had been a long stretch on the road. The bus was quiet on the way there, back-to-back games and travel having wiped everyone out. We'd be home soon, but not soon enough.

I had my headphones on but wasn't playing any music. I didn't need to add to the chaos in my brain. Declan, Emmett, and Heath bolted to their rooms before the bus had come to a complete stop in front of the hotel, probably for some quiet time with their better halves. I hung a hard right and headed into the hotel bar. Maybe a drink would quiet my mind. The dance with Liv ran through my head on a constant loop. I couldn't escape, not that I wanted to. She had stared into my eyes, resting her cheek against my hand, and I wanted to freeze that moment, preserve it forever and never leave it. The wedding kiss had been burned into my mind, but the one in her dance studio was seared into my soul.

Scanning the shelves, I looked for a bourbon I could sink my teeth into. After ordering a drink and some food, I took a spot at the far end of the bar as far away from the door as I could get. Up in the corner, a silent replay of the game and commentary from talking heads on a sports show glowed on the TV.

I checked the time, thinking maybe I should give Liv a call. It wasn't too late.

"What are you doing down here all alone?"

I grimaced as the long, thin fingers ran along my back up to my shoulder and down my arm.

"Don't worry, honey. I don't bite." The tall, slender brunette sat down, choosing the stool next to mine out of the thirty other empty seats in the entire place, and she didn't take her hand off my arm. Desire filled her eyes—and recognition. I bit back a curse. *Puck bunny.* It was the downside of team hotels—women like her knew exactly where we'd be.

Normally this wasn't an issue and cut down on a lot of the talking needed to get someone into bed, but that hadn't been my MO for a while. That eager look usually meant a night of mindless, sweaty sex, but hers was coupled with a greedy glint, like she was a hungry Rottweiler and I was a meaty pork chop.

I dropped my arm off the bar and slipped out of her hold. The bartender slid a glass across to me along with a plate piled with a bleu cheeseburger and fries. My stomach rumbled the second the smell hit my nose. Damn, I was hungrier than I'd thought. I turned and picked it up with both hands, broadcasting all the signals of *leave me alone*. The heft of the burger had my full attention as I took a bite. It wasn't as good as Fish's, but it hit the spot.

"It was a great game tonight," she purred beside me.

"One got past me," I grumbled, shoving a couple fries into my mouth.

"But you stopped eight other shots." She preened, leaning in. Her chest rubbed against my elbow.

The muscles in my back bunched. A year ago I might've considered her attention. I would have gotten out some of my pent-up energy in a sweaty, lust-fueled session that would have left her with an inability to walk and a satisfied smile she'd wear for a week, but all I wanted to do at the moment was eat my food and hope Liv could squeeze in a little time to talk to me before I passed out.

"If you're still feeling down about that goal, I'm sure I could find a way to help you get over it." She ran her hand along my knee. Chicks this gung-ho were always bad news. I'd learned that lesson back in college. Getting up from the stool, I threw my bourbon back, an oaky taste followed by a sharp burn. It was a shame—something like that deserved to be savored.

"I'll take this to go." I caught the eye of the bartender, threw some bills down, and stalked off to the bathroom. I'd barely gotten my dick out at the urinal when the door to the men's room banged open. The muscles in my neck tensed at the telltale click of heels against the black-and-white tile floor. *Shit!*

"Naughty boy." Once again her hands were on arm. What part of no eye contact and leaving within a minute of her sitting down had made her think I wanted to bang her in a bar bathroom? I clenched my jaw and willed the world's longest piss to end. The only thing worse than being stuck in there with her would have been walking home with piss-soaked clothes.

Shaking my shoulders, I tried to dislodge her arm. She walked around the front of me and I did my best to shield myself using the barrier between the urinals as she stood on her tiptoes, staring at me like I was an animal in the goddamn zoo.

"The stories are true. I should've made sure you were at the top of my list, sweetheart. There's only four of you left."

I stared into her eyes, and her gaze jumped up to meet mine. "What part of you telling me you've slept with most of my teammates makes you think I'd want to go anywhere near you? And I can sure as hell assure you that you're not getting anywhere near Declan, Heath, or Emmett, so it looks like your collection's going to remain incomplete."

I zipped up and stormed out of there before she tried to tackle me to the floor. That chick was insane.

Back in my room, I stared at my phone, hoping Liv would message or call. Standing up, I dropped it onto the bed and paced. *Don't suffocate her. You can go the night without talking to her.* I interlaced my fingers behind my head and stared at my phone like it was a bomb ready to go off. We'd kissed—again. She'd invaded my mind, and I was kind of okay with being pushed to the edge of crazy by her. It was driving me absolutely out of my skull with how much I wanted to see her again.

Had she watched the game like she'd said she would? I picked up my phone and tapped it against my palm. *Just do it.* I sent the message before the rational part of my brain kicked in, and her response was immediate.

Liv: You kicked ass tonight!

My wide grin hurt my cheeks. I tapped out a message and knew I'd probably pass out on my skates the next day, but I also knew it would be worth it.

Me: What did you think of the first play in the second period?

$\sim$

Flying in and out of the city so often, I felt like my apartment had a revolving door.

Another week gone and another long trip on the road. Why did I even have an apartment? It would've been less hassle to sleep in my car, and the trips seemed to stretch on a lot longer when I knew what was waiting for me at home.

I hadn't expected Liv's invite. It was a first, coming from her to me instead of the other way around. Remnants of hot chocolate and marshmallows sat at the bottom of our green and red mugs on her rug. It was a toasty, warm feeling that made me want to eat some cookies. This was what it felt like sitting in my mom's kitchen right before Christmas.

Liv's boxes of pictures were stacked on top of her bed.

"This was not what I expected when you invited me over."

"Did you think it would have to do with booze? Maybe carving a block of ice into an ice luge for shots?" She chuckled, flipping through more pictures.

"No, I figured you'd try to paint my nails or something."

She tugged open her bedside drawer and grabbed the

bottle of polish rolling around in there. I spotted the box of condoms shoved in the back, and my fingers tightened around the stack of pictures in my hand. *Paging Mr. Hypocrite.*

"That can be arranged. I think electric blue might be your color. There was a woman in my class with hair this color. She said my choreography made her think of a bright, crazy blue dance party." She slapped the bottle against her palm.

Shaking my head, I looked at the neon polish in her hand and backed up, slipping off the edge of the bed. She shot forward, grabbing my hand. Bracing my hand against the wall, I stopped my fall.

My fingers wrapped around hers, and the jump of her pulse beat against my callused fingers. Her eyes widened, and her full, pink lips parted. They were shiny from where she'd been nibbling them while she flipped through the pictures.

The taste of her, even masked by the alcohol, flooded my mind, the heat of her palm warming my skin through my jeans. Swallowing past the lump in my throat, I let go of her hand.

She gently shook her head like she was coming out of a trance, the same one that called to me whenever I was near her. It was for self-preservation, to maintain my sanity and because I knew what taking that step with Liv would mean.

My friendship with Colm was hanging on by a thread. It might never recover from what had happened with Felicity, but if I went after Liv, he'd probably try to kill me—or he'd tell Liv all the details of how I'd gotten between him and his fiancée and then how would she look at me? First Angelica and then Felicity? She'd hate me. What I needed to do was keep my hands and my lips to myself. It had been working so far...well, most of the time.

Pushing off the wall from my awkward spot in the gap beside her bed, I stood up and grabbed her desk chair.

"As if I don't get enough crap from the guys. Showing up with neon-blue nails would get me an earful."

Her gaze darted from my spot on the bed to my new seat as she lifted her lips in a half smile that didn't reach her eyes.

"Tell them it helps with wind resistance on the ice. With how you've been playing, they'd all be wearing it within a week." She picked up another box and flipped off the lid. It bounced with a muted thud. "Do you remember this one?" She tossed the picture into the stack I'd been flipping through, and I picked it up, the edges worn and tattered. Staring back at me was a younger version of myself. I looked so awkward and overly large, like my body had outgrown my ability to control it.

"I look like an insane person. Why would you take a picture of me like this? And why the hell is my hair all shoved up on one side?" I turned the picture around so she could look at it again.

"It was after the state championships junior year. You put the lucky sock in your helmet, remember?"

I threw my head back and laughed. It had started out as a joke someone played on me, shoving my helmet to me at the last minute with a used sock in it, but we'd won that game, had killed the other team five to nothing. They'd been our biggest rivals and had kept Rittenhouse Prep out of the state championships almost every year before we'd started high school.

The next game I'd played without the sock and everything had been off. At the end of the period, Declan had run into the locker room and come back with a sock. By then we'd have gone for anything, and the second our skates had hit the ice, we were a different team. "Damn, how could I forget that?"

My arm was around Colm and his was around Liv, who was standing in front of us.

"He was so upset Mom and Dad weren't there." She slid more pictures from the front of her stack to the back. Colm had been glancing up at the stands the whole time. They'd promised him they'd make it to that one.

"They missed a lot, didn't they?" That last season, our senior year, they hadn't been to one game, and their big accident had happened on the way to the state championship. They'd tried to rush back to surprise Colm.

"They did miss a lot." Her voice sounded far away. "Even if they did show up, we'd never know if it would last more than a few minutes. They were constantly one page away from disappearing in the middle of whatever might be going on."

"It couldn't have been easy."

She shrugged. "They were doing important work. What's a stupid hockey game or science fair when someone's life hangs in the balance?" Her laugh caught in her throat, and moisture gathered in her eyes.

I rolled the chair closer to the edge of her bed.

"It mattered because it mattered to you. Yes, they were doing great work, but you two also deserved some of their attention."

She wiped her face with her sleeve. "Doesn't matter much now, does it? They're gone. I'm sure I'll have a better idea of what they were going through once I'm a doctor."

Her words were flat, rote memorization with nothing else behind it, something said so many times it barely made sense anymore. She pushed herself too hard. Colm pushed her even harder.

"Do you want to be a doctor?'

Her head snapped up. "Why does everyone keep asking me that?"

"Colm talks about it constantly, but you almost never do unless you're talking about your parents or Colm. The only thing you bring up on your own is dance."

She scooped up the pictures and shoved them into the box. "And how would you know? We've had, what, ten conversations in the past two years and all of a sudden you think you know what I want?" Jumping off the bed, she plucked the picture from my hand. "I don't sit at that desk"—she jabbed her finger toward the desk behind me —"because I'm trying to decide. I don't bury myself in books until I can barely see straight so that I ace my exams to *not* become a doctor. Do you think I can't cut it?"

I held up my hands, palms facing her in surrender. "It was a question, that's all. Just an observation."

"An observation based on what? Going to one dance class? I'm going to med school. It's what they would have wanted. It's what Colm wants, and it's what *I* want." She jabbed her finger into the center of her chest.

"I just want you to be happy." It was all I'd ever wanted for her, even if it wasn't with me. Even if it ripped my heart out and skated over it a thousand times, she deserved to find someone who could give her the moon and the stars.

"Are you the happiness police? How do you know what makes me happy? You made it very clear that something I thought made me happy wasn't for me."

"I wasn't talking about that—"

"Maybe you weren't, but we need to get this out." She slammed the lid down on the box, crunching the stiff, cardboard sides. "We've been dancing around this since you decided you wanted to be my *friend*." Her fingers lifted in air quotes around the last word. "How happy do you think it made me when you kissed that woman? When you told me to go so you could be alone with her? How many tears do you think were spilled over that?"

She jumped up from the bed and stormed out into the living room.

My heart pounded in my chest and I chased after her.

"I never wanted to hurt you. Angelica just showed up. She was drunk and causing a scene. I had to get her out of there." My uselessness with words was failing me once again. Did I want to shove the fact that I'd slept with someone like Angelica in her face? Did I want her to think of me as that guy? Hell no. At the time it had seemed like the best way to handle things, but it had been a wrong move that haunted me like a Ghost of Christmas Past.

"And what about what you said?"

"What about what you did?" The flicker of anger and hurt I'd shut out came crackling back.

She took a step back. "What did I do?"

"You went out with Grant." I gritted my teeth.

"I—it was two dates."

"Two dates too many. I had hotel security put Angelica in a taxi fifteen minutes after I saw you, and then I came back to Grant floating around the hotel telling everyone about his date with you."

"What was I supposed to do?"

"I don't know, *not* date my brother?"

She squeezed her fists together and screamed at the ceiling. "I didn't date him. He asked me. I was distracted. I wasn't thinking straight, staring at you with another woman in your arms, not saying a single word while she talked about what she wanted to do to you. I thought it was a group thing, and then he shows up at my doorstep with flowers. That's when I knew there was more to it for him."

My breath came out short and choppy, matching hers. If she hadn't gone out with Grant, I could have talked to Colm. Maybe he'd have tried to punch my lights out, maybe not, but after what had happened with Felicity when I'd moved to Philly, there was no way in hell he'd let me near Liv.

"And it's still more to him." My shoulders slumped.

"I know." The pained look in her eyes matched mine, her features distressed. She stepped closer, staring up into my eyes. "What do we do now?"

"I don't know." I dragged my fingers through my hair and shook my head.

The front door jangled behind us and the cold air from the hallway whooshed in as it opened.

"So, lap dances are medicinal—is that what you're telling me?" Marisa laughed and dropped her bag beside the door.

Liv's gaze darted to Marisa's, who stopped when she spotted us.

"Maybe we should go." Marisa pushed against the guy behind her.

"No, it's fine. I'm leaving." I grabbed my jacket off the couch. "I'll talk to you later, Liv."

"Night," she called after me as the door closed.

I stopped at Fish's and grabbed a drink before going back to my place. Things couldn't go on like they were. I'd have to talk to Grant, would have to break things down and get him to understand how much she meant to me. The longer things went on, the harder it was to imagine my life without her.

16

LIV

After Ford left, I shoved the pictures back in their boxes and joined Marisa and LJ on the couch for an '80s movie marathon. There was no way I could have concentrated on my exams. A few days later I picked up some of the developed photos I hadn't put in their boxes yet. Sliding them out of the card stock envelope, I lifted the pictures out.

Turning each over, I wrote out the dates, the location, and what was going on in the picture. The summer at the beach house, love had been in the air as Heath and Kara, and Declan and Mak drowned us all in their PDA. There were also copious amounts of booze and the threat of homicide when Emmett and Avery first arrived. That had all been smoothed out over the course of the summer. If only my love life had followed the same path.

I grabbed the next few pictures.

My navy cap and gown and gold tassel dangled in front of my face. Colm stood beside me, beaming with happiness. I was peering up at Ford out of the corner of my eye. Shaking my head, I turned it over and wrote on the back.

My graduation, pictured: Colm, Ford, and me.

I plucked the next photo from the pile: the ladies lounging on beach towels, soaking up the sun the summer before Mak and Declan's wedding.

Summer after graduation on the beach, pictured: Kara, Avery, Mak, and me.

I flipped another over, and the smile on my face dropped.

Summer after high school graduation, pictured: me and Mason. I tapped the picture against my hand. The summer after Heath and Declan graduated from college, they'd rented a beautiful house down on the shore, right on the sand.

Having a summer fling with Mason, sneaking out under the watchful eye of Colm had been my little act of rebellion, but that had backfired when the guys all came back from a fishing trip early, interrupting our make-out session. The look on Ford's face when I'd stumbled down the steps had been a gut punch. He'd hid it well, but the expression was hard to miss. It was the same one I'd hid whenever women approached him time after time looking for an autograph and more that summer.

Maybe if I hadn't been so afraid back then, I could have just dragged him under the boardwalk and kissed the crap out of him, proven this wasn't some schoolyard crush back before everything had gotten even more complicated. I looked at the picture again and ripped it in half. Dumping it into the trash, I went through the rest of the pack. The bottle of wine beside my bed slowly disappeared, stolen by elves throughout the night.

Our conversations had been stilted since he'd walked out. It was awkward, but I didn't want to lose the tiny bit of *us* that we'd recovered.

Me: Do you fly in tonight or tomorrow morning?
Ford: Tomorrow morning. In my room now

The warm buzz of booze flowed through me. I imagined him in the bed in his hotel in gray sweatpants with a T-shirt stretched across his chest, pretty much the dirtiest and most delicious vision I could imagine.

Me: Alone?

I hit myself in the head with a pillow. *Why did I ask?* I didn't want to know. Actually I did, but one answer could kill me.

Ford: Of course

Me: You say that like it's not a possibility that you wouldn't be alone.

The phone buzzed in my hand.

"Why do you think I'd have someone here with me?"

"Come on, Ford. I've been around the guys long enough to know how you operate."

"What's that supposed mean? Have you been drinking?" There was a hint of teasing to his tone.

"Maybe a little bit. And it means people talk about things even when they think you aren't listening."

"You're totally lit up. Things like what?"

"Like your after-game rituals."

He chuckled. "I hardly think showering, grabbing some food, maybe a good bourbon, and collapsing in my hotel room or at home is newsworthy."

"Not that." I swallowed past the lump in my throat and squeezed my thighs together. There had been many nights I'd thought about all the stories I'd heard about Ford and his thorough attention to detail when it came to the opposite sex. It wasn't like I wanted to think of him out there picking up other women, but there had been more than a few drunken nights where the guys had teased him about his late-night activities.

"What do I do?" His voice was low on the other line.

"You bring them back to your room and fuck them until they can barely walk and they've got a huge smile on their face."

"Whoa, where the hell did you hear that?"

"Heath."

He muttered a curse under his breath.

"So it's true."

"Liv…" There was a warning tone to his voice.

"Just tell me if it's true." I licked my lips and rolled over onto my back.

"You're drunk and I hardly think it's—"

"I want to know. When you make love to them—"

"I don't make love. I fuck them."

Goose bumps spread all over my body, and my breath caught. "So the rumors *are* true."

"I've been told I go above and beyond in certain areas, yes."

"I'm going to need more details than that." Scooting higher in the bed, I rested my head on my pillow and squeezed my thighs together.

"You're not going to get them."

"Maybe I'll just guess what it's like, then." My chest rose and fell as my breathing sped up. All the dreams I'd had, the way my imagination had run wild thinking about a night alone with Ford, without the barriers that were always there between us…

There was dead silence on the other end.

I pulled the phone away from my ear. The call timer was still going. "Hello?"

"I'm here." His words came out strained.

"A play-by-play is in order, don't you think?" There were no objections. "You have a few drinks, get nice and toasted."

"Never more than two."

"Good. No one likes a sloppy drunk with a case of whiskey dick." There was a sharp exhale of breath that sounded a little like a laugh, and my drunk brain powered into overdrive. This wasn't a nameless woman he was bringing up to his hotel room; it was me. "You bring her up to your room and close the door behind you. She's standing in front of you and starts peeling off her clothes."

"I do it. I always do it."

"Okay, you slip your hands under the hem of her shirt and pull it up and over her head. The white lace cups of her bra are on full display. You run your lips along the curve of her neck, breathing her in and nipping at her skin. How am I doing so far?" My body was on high alert, a heated tingling traveling from head to toe. My nipples pebbled as his deep, rough breath filled the other end of the line.

"You're doing great."

"Then maybe you lead her to the bed. Take off your jeans."

He made a disapproving sound. "I push her up against the door and run my fingers along the insides of her thighs before slipping my fingers under her skirt."

"She feels the cool breeze from the AC across her skin and your warm hand pressed against her pussy."

There was silence again.

"You slide your hand up under the elastic of her thong and trace the outline of her lips. How wet is she?"

"She's hot and wet, but it's only the beginning. When I'm done, she won't remember her own name."

I slid my hand down my body and followed my own instructions.

"You squeeze her clit in time to a beat that lives in your head and slide two fingers inside of her."

"Three."

A moan I'd been holding back escaped from my lips as I pushed three fingers into myself.

"Then what?"

"Then I listen to her moans and find the rhythm of her body. That makes her cream even more on my fingers. Switching hands, I lick her heat off my skin. The taste is better than anything I've tasted before."

The unmistakable sound of his hand on his cock sent rolling tides of desire racing through my body.

"I pinch and rub her clit until her legs are shaking. Pinning her thighs open with one hand, I keep going, curling my fingers inside her until I find the spot so many men aren't patient enough to discover. Her pussy clamps around my fingers, and I keep pumping into her, giving her that high and stretching it out as long as I can." His words were choppy and strained.

"And then what?"

"I thought you were telling me."

"And then you take off your jeans."

"No, but since it's late, I'll give you the abbreviated version. She's getting at least one more orgasm on my tongue before I get my dick out, not because it's not the hardest it's ever been, not because I'm not seriously killing myself to hold back, but so I don't scare the crap out of her."

"Not possible." I licked my dry lips. "It's not possible. She's ready for all you have to give and more." I ran my fingers over my clit and my legs jumped.

"I want to give her everything." He groaned, a deep guttural sound that had me teetering on the edge.

I curled my fingers inside myself and nearly jumped off

the bed. The orgasm blindsided me, slamming into me so hard I dropped the phone and screamed. My back arched, and I rode the waves of my climax as spasms shot through my body.

It seemed like twenty minutes later when I finally came back to myself. Shoving the blankets around, I found my phone's glowing screen.

"Ford?"

$\sim$

FORD

"I want to give her everything." My hips shot up off the bed. I pumped my hand up and down at her shuddering breaths on the other end of the line. It wasn't my hand wrapped around me; it was Liv, and her keening cry shot me across the finish line.

Her moans and my whispered name across her lips... I bit my lip at the wet sound of her arousal. My mouth watered, wanting to taste her until she cried out again and keep tasting and touching until she couldn't stand it anymore.

My jaw snapped shut, and every nerve ending cried out in time to her moans. Panting like I'd skated sprints for the past hour, I slowed the stroke of my hand. My pulse pounded so loudly in my ears, I could only hope I wasn't saying all the dirty things running through my head.

I slammed my head back against the pillows. If she was this good over the phone, how good would she be in person? When I could skim my fingers along her skin and taste her goose-bump-pebbled flesh? Wrap my fingers in her hair and inhale every ounce of her? The fight was leaving me. I didn't want to fight what was between us anymore.

Grant didn't matter. Colm would have to suck it up. I wanted—no, I needed Liv. I needed to feel her wrapped around me, to bury my face in the crook of her neck and bury myself in her. I needed to wrap my fingers around her wrists and pin them above her head as I thrust into her velvety pussy. She was an addiction, and I hadn't even had a real taste yet.

"Ford?" Her shaky voice snapped me out of my drifting.

"I'm here." I licked my lips.

"That was…"

"Yeah, it was. I'm back on Monday morning. I need to see you."

"I have a lab session at eight in the morning. I'm free after that—we can grab lunch."

"Liv…" My throat worked up and down.

"I know. Just don't say anything else. I'll see you on Monday, and I'll be watching your games. Get some rest. Night, Ford." She rushed out the words like she knew exactly what was going through my mind: that the doubts would creep in once the orgasmic high wore off. She ended the call.

"Night, Liv."

Three excruciating days later, the town car from the airport might as well have been going backward. Her moans had gotten under my skin so deep I didn't think I'd ever be able to erase them. They were the soundtrack to every time I wrapped my hand around my cock. Her erratic breaths and sweet moans were an inescapable part of me now. I'd never be able to erase the memory, and I didn't want to.

My hands opened and closed in an involuntary rhythm. The tension rolled off me in waves, and I let out a deep breath. Maybe it was best I didn't see her yet. I needed to calm the hell down.

"Dude, you need to get laid."

My gaze snapped to Declan, sitting beside me in the back of the car. Usually, this was a chance to decompress without the rest of the team around, but now it made me want to scream.

"You don't need to worry about my bedroom habits."

"If you come out of the net like that again, Coach is going to ream you."

"I saw an opening and I took it." I shrugged. Yes, coming out of the net the way I had could have been a fatal error, but I'd seen my chance to end the game and I'd taken it.

"Don't give him too much shit. He's the highest-scoring goalie in the league after that little bit of mischief." Heath turned around from the front seat. "And I've never been prouder." He wiped a fake tear away from his eye. It was exactly the type of shit he loved.

"It's just a little out of character." Declan stared at me with suspicion swimming in his eyes.

"Maybe I'm trying to go for it a little more, trying to stop hiding in the net."

"You definitely can't hide now—they've been replaying those goals on *SportsCenter* nonstop. Welcome to the lime-light, buddy." Emmett nudged me with his elbow.

I stared out the window at the slowly thawing city whipping by. Liv's words had echoed in my head throughout the games. *I'll be watching.* That had been my focus, not trying to make the highlight reels. Liv's special tone chirped from my phone. Tilting it away from the guys, I checked my screen.

Liv: Great game! I've never seen you play like that before. The clips have been running on TV nonstop.

Looked like I'd managed to do both.

Liv: Do you want to get something to eat?

That was probably safest. Somewhere crowded, brightly lit, where I wouldn't think of laying her out on the nearest surface and burying my face between her thighs. We needed a place where the only trouble I'd get myself into was the mental ass kicking going on in my head. The weariness from travel wore off and tamped down the itch in my hands to run my fingers through her hair and get her back into my bed again. This time, she'd have a different type of hangover.

FORD

L *iv: Do you want to get something to eat?*

A simple invitation carried so much more weight now. Normally, I'd crash at my place until practice in a few days, but her message sent a surge of energy rushing through me.

We hadn't talked much after *the* call, only a few texts and chatting through the online Scrabble game we played. Her last play had been F-I-N-G-E-R-S. It seemed we'd both had that night constantly running through our minds. Words like *moan*, *suck*, *touch*, and *kissing* kept popping up when there were far harder and higher-scoring words available.

She came down the stairs of her apartment building, her radiant smile lighting up everything around her. Pulling on her gloves, she ducked under my arm as I held the door open for her. The leftover snow from the weekend had turned into sickly brown piles and dotted the street and sidewalk. Her cheeks were flushed, and I wanted to tuck her against my chest to warm her up.

"How'd your test go?"

"As well as can be expected when you're bleary-eyed

after ninety hours of studying. That's why I needed to get out of the house." Her hands were shoved deep in her pockets. "Can we walk?"

"Sure." I sent the car away and turned back to her. "Where are we going to eat?"

She turned to me and smiled, the kind of smile where you shared a secret with someone else. This time it just so happened that secret was that I knew what she sounded like when she came and I couldn't wait to hear it again. The smile was infectious, and I couldn't hold mine back.

"You're going to love it." She looped her arm through mine, and I filled her in on the latest behind-the-scenes news from the road as we walked.

Late-night tacos might as well have been heroin based on how packed the place was. The small taco shop had ten tables crammed into a space that could barely hold five. Someone stood up just as we walked in the door, so I snagged us a table.

The fluorescent lights above us washed the whole place out, except for Liv. She was like a glowing beacon in the crowded sea of people in need of a spicy meat fix. I smiled at her little dance from the counter to our table with our food. She'd nearly knocked her chair over when they called her number. Her entire body got in on the giddiness of tacos, and she wasn't even drunk like half the people who stumbled in and ordered.

Pushing back the paper lining in the plastic basket holding the tacos, she looked like she'd found the Holy Grail. "I swear, I eat at least ten of these a week." Lovingly picking one up, she caressed the side of the shell and stared at it like it was the Second Coming.

"Are you sure all you do is eat them? 'Cause right now it looks like I should leave you two alone for some private time." The breeze battled with the overheated interior of the restaurant whenever someone opened the door. Liv kept her coat on, and I unbuttoned mine.

A few heads had turned when we'd walked in, and someone stopped by the table and asked for an autograph. Being a sports figure, I was used to it, and Liv didn't seem to mind. Growing up with Colm as her brother, she'd been in the center of all this for a long time.

I hated when they stared, though, the people a couple tables over not even being discreet when snapping a few pictures. This was another reason I hated going out. Behind the mask on the ice, I could pretend they weren't looking at me. The driving energy of the game kept thoughts about how many sets of eyeballs were on me every second out on the ice. But up close and personal, once the mask came off, I couldn't deny it. I was a bug on a slide under the city's collective microscope.

"You'll stop talking crap when you taste these, and then you'll be sorry." She let out her best evil laugh.

I leaned back in my chair, content to watch her enjoy her meal.

"I ordered these for you. They're the best tacos you've ever had."

"Not possible. I've traveled all over the country, and I've had some pretty damn good tacos." My dinner from earlier had barely digested, but her love of them was infectious.

"I'm telling you." She held it out to me.

I eyed the taco. "Looks pretty basic." I pushed back the tortilla and checked out the contents: shredded meat, pico, some lettuce. No cheese? I'd suffer through it. My attempts at keeping my skepticism didn't seem to be working.

"Give it a chance," Liv sing-songed beside me.

Outside the large plate-glass windows, people stared. I

felt like a zoo animal on display. Flashes bounced off the surface, and I hoped it ruined their shots. At least Liv's back was to the windows; she didn't need to get roped into the circus of the hockey world any more than she already was.

"Ford Kenneth Atherton..." She shoved it toward my face. "Eat it. Now!"

I leaned forward, elbows on the table. She'd used my full name. My cheeks weren't cooperating with the scowl I was trying to pull off. Damn cheek muscles selling me out. Squeezing my lips, I gave a serious look my best shot.

I took it from her hands and had my first bite. I froze as the flavors invaded my mouth and pillaged my taste buds. My eyes widened.

"See, I told you." With her free hand, she picked up another from the basket and bit into it. "Great, right?"

The smirk on her face told the whole story.

Grabbing a napkin, I mumbled under my breath, "Not bad."

She cupped her hand over her ear. "Sorry, what was that? I didn't hear you."

Dropping my napkin, I leaned across the table, cupping my hands around my mouth. "I said, not bad."

A dab of spicy salsa hung out on her chin. Reaching over, I wiped away the spot on her face with my thumb, cupping her cheek with my hand. Her eyes got wide, and I snatched my hand back. There were too many people there. Heads were turning outside, more camera phones being pulled out. Our season had been hotter than usual, which meant more attention on us. And my goal had been making the rounds so even more people seemed to be recognizing me. No good deed goes unpunished, right?

Her lips curved up, and she crumpled her napkin, then

dropped it into her empty food basket. "Why can't someone come up with a taco shell that doesn't disintegrate on the trip home? I'd take a hundred and stash them in the freezer."

"Maybe that's why. You'd never make it out of your apartment, and they'd have to use a crane to lift you out."

She threw her head back and laughed. "You're not wrong." Slipping her gloves on, she scooted her chair away from the table. One second she was there, and the next she was completely engulfed by the giant black coat on the back of a guy throwing himself on her.

I jumped up out of my seat and grabbed the back of his jacket. *What the hell?*

"Liv! Is that my dance extraordinaire torturer?" His slurred words spilled out.

I jerked him back off Liv, holding him by the collar, and he stared back at me, glassy-eyed.

"Ford, it's okay. I know him. He takes my classes." She peeled my death grip off the back of his coat. "Hey, Tyler, looks like you've had some fun tonight." Getting up from her seat, she helped him stand straight.

"A little. Not too crazy." He swayed, and she kept her hands on him.

It shouldn't have bothered me. There was no reason for it to bother me, but damned if I didn't want her hands off him.

"You're on a date?" He wrapped his arms around her. "Lucky man! Dude, you should see how flexible she is! Or maybe you know already."

My head jerked back. Was this guy talking about her flexibility inside or outside of the classroom? And just how flexible *was* she? The barrage of images flooded my brain.

"She's the best dance teacher out there. I couldn't do this

before." He tried to lift his leg above his head and toppled over, nearly taking Liv with him.

I grabbed his arm and steadied him, putting myself between them. He was one of her students. Some of the tension in my neck eased up.

"Are you on a date?" His words were a slurred mess.

Her gaze darted to mine and back to his. "No, not a date. Just out with a friend." A zap straight to the central nervous system—and ego. I pressed my lips together to keep from saying anything I'd regret.

Colm would have killed me if he knew the things running through my head right then: staking my claim, taking her back home with me, seeing exactly how flexible she was.

She gave him the patronizing dealing-politely-with-a-drunk-person smile. "Who are you here with? Are your friends looking for you?" Standing on her tiptoes, she peered around.

"They're over there somewhere. I saw you and had to come say hi." He swung his arm around, and I ducked under his wildly flailing limb.

"Let's get you back to them." She nodded toward him, and I helped her get her incredibly drunk and flexibility-knowledgeable friend's order from the counter; then we escorted him back to his group of friends.

Liv shivered beside me when we stepped outside. Camera phone flashes went off, lighting up the front of the restaurant. I shoved my hands into my pockets to resist wrapping my arm around her and tugging her in close to my side. More people crowded around.

"Are you Ford Atherton?"

"Are you the goalie?"

"Great game!"

"You guys are kicking ass this season."

"Is that your girlfriend?" someone shouted.

I shook my head. "No, not my girlfriend." Glancing over my shoulder at Liv, my stomach knotted at the unreadable expression on her face. Had I just fucked up? She wasn't my girlfriend, and she'd just told Tyler we weren't on a date. We didn't even know what the hell we were, and the last thing we needed while we tried to figure it out was our pictures plastered all over social media.

The few people standing beside us became a crowd at whiplash speed. Selfies turned into signing anything the drunk people had handy. As is usually the case, these people had had too much to drink and got overly fixated on something, and that something was me.

People who'd probably never watched hockey in their lives jockeyed for position to get a picture with me in case I was somebody who could raise their social media profile. Nothing drew drunk people in like more drunk people. They were like a bunch of ants swarming all over a piece of candy, and I was the unwrapped lollipop sitting on the sidewalk.

Liv stepped back and let the inebriated mob take hold of me. Flashes dotted my vision long after the pictures had been taken. I hadn't been this blinded since my last trip to the eye doctor.

Taking one more picture, I waved to the ring of people surrounding me and offered up free tacos. Darting inside, I dropped a wad of bills on the counter, told them the deal, and barely made it out past the rushing tide of people swarming for free platters of tacos.

Liv watched it all, staying mostly clear of the mayhem.

I popped outside through the mob and joined her on the sidewalk.

"Sorry, I didn't think about what would happen if people recognized you." She nibbled on her lower lip.

"Don't worry about it. That's not how things usually go for me."

"You've had one of the best seasons in recent memory. Plus they've played your goals a lot while you were gone, and not just on the sports segments but on the regular news too."

I dragged my fingers through my hair. "Perfect." Not exactly fading into the background.

"We should probably go. You don't want more people to figure out you're here. You *are* a celebrity, after all." She held out her phone. Social media posts came pouring in and tagged the account the team had required me to make. I only had two posts, a picture of a hockey puck and my jersey, but the tag notifications pinged Liv's phone continuously.

"Let's go." I put my hand on her shoulder and ducked my head until we turned the corner.

"That back there doesn't happen to you often?" She thumbed her finger toward the crowd.

I shook my head. "Not even a little bit. The bar by my place is super quiet. No one ever goes in there. I tend to be a homebody beyond that."

"Maybe that's why Colm is always adamant about having family dinners at his place. I never thought about it before." Her eyebrows furrowed, and she kept her hands in her pockets.

The mention of his name should have thrown a cold bucket of water over my head, but it didn't. We stepped up to the entrance of her apartment. *Come back to my place* danced on the tip of my tongue. I opened my mouth, and my phone buzzed in my pocket at the same time hers went off. She reached for hers, and I took mine out.

"It's Grant," we said at the same time. I responded to his text, and she answered his call.

"Yes, that was me tagged in a few posts. Nothing, we ran into each other. Just grabbing some food. It wasn't a date. Someone in the crowd shouted that out."

Grant: *You're out with Liv.*

It wasn't a question. Of course he'd be following me on social media. With the jackals circling with their phones, it was a miracle I could take a piss without the world knowing.

Me: *Ran into her*

Grant: *Did she say anything about the date I invited her on?*

He'd asked her out again? I squeezed my eyes closed. Why couldn't this just have been a high school crush that blew over? My gaze cut to Liv. It was the same kind I'd sworn hers would be for me, and look where we were now. How did I stop him from getting hurt?

She ended the call and tapped her phone against her palm. Turning to me, her lips disappeared into her mouth as she looked like she was attempting to swallow them.

"He asked me out again." Her neck strained, and her eyes filled with that same lost worry that crept into mine when I thought about him around her. Dragging her hands through her hair, sending golden wisps up into the air, she looked to me like I'd have the answers. "I...I don't know what to do."

"I know." I ran the backs of my fingers along my chin.

"This is all my fault. I didn't think, after all this time, he still saw me like that."

I closed the gap between us and ran my fingers along her cheek. "How could he not? You're impossible to forget, impossible to stop thinking about."

Her fingers tightened around the front of my coat. "I feel the same way about you."

Our eyes locked, and that low undercurrent I'd been fighting sliced through all the buzzing distractions around us as it all faded away.

Her breath fanned across my face, warming it from the winter chill. I slid my hand along the back of her neck. Her soft strands ran through my fingers. She licked her lips, inviting me to take a sample. Wet, full, beautiful. Her eyelashes fluttered, and she stared deep into my eyes.

Dipping my head, I captured her lips. She parted them, and I savored the taste of her. Pressing her against the wall behind her, I bracketed her between my arms, the cold, rough brick a contrast against her warm, sweet softness.

She nipped my lip, and the sharp bite sent my body into overdrive. My cock strained against the leg of my jeans. How long had it been since I'd tasted her? Too long. Leaving her lips for more than a second was too much. Even a breath of air was too long.

We broke apart, panting, staring into each other's eyes. I wanted more with no winter coats, drunk passersby, or anyone or anything else in our way. The universe was conspiring to keep this from happening, and the roadblocks were driving me insane.

Resting my forehead against hers, I smiled against her lips.

"I missed you when you were away." She stared into my eyes like I'd hung the moon and the stars.

Her hands slipped under my coat, and she wrapped her arms around me. Her fingers trailed up and down my back in a short gentle path. Swallowing against the lump in my throat, I closed my eyes.

"Liv—" The twin chorus of our phones went off again.

We groaned. She held on to me, squeezing me tighter. For a second I thought she'd let it keep ringing and try to preserve this moment. Then she loosened her hold and dropped her arms, taking her phone out.

"Marisa's a little on edge. Dinner with her dad didn't go well. I'd better get back up there." She peered up at the building beside us.

I cursed under my breath. Snapping our phones in half or flushing them down the toilet the next time we saw each other seemed like a better idea by the minute.

She laughed and gave me another peck on the cheek. "Looks like our time's up again." A sad smile lifted the corner of her lips. "One of these days we'll get the timing right." She opened the door to her building and stepped inside.

The ringing in my pocket started up again. I watched her go, then grabbed my phone, frustration bubbling to the surface. "What?"

18

LIV

L aughs and screams came from the street below. People walked and ran on the sidewalks, enjoying a warm snap that would quickly be swallowed up by the cold weather the city hadn't seemed to be able to shake. The last pockets of snow clung to the pavement, holding on for dirty, nearly melted life.

Ford was away again, traveling the country and now on a plane back home, which meant I didn't get one of his nightly calls to kick me out of my textbooks before I passed out. On this night, though, I had another call to drag me away from the stack of practice exams with a stranglehold around my neck—a call with Grant. I fumbled my phone when the screen lit up. My knee bounced up and down as I tapped the green button on my screen. I'd been dreading this conversation, and I couldn't dodge it any longer.

"Hey, Grant."

I pinched the bridge of my nose and paced the length of my room. There wasn't much space for pacing, but it would have to do. This was not how I wanted to end my seven-hour study session.

"Hey, Liv." He was in a crowded place, voices mingling and mashing in the background into the soundtrack of college life. "I know you're busy, but I wanted to know if you wanted to go see a movie this weekend."

"I can't this weekend." *I can't ever. Just say the words.* It would make him hate me, and then Ford and I would really never happen—at least not until the dust settled. Once Grant found someone else, he'd forget about even asking me out on a date.

"How about next week?" Even through the phone, I could tell he had on his devil-may-care killer smile. It was an instant panty dropper to a lot of people, but it wasn't for me.

"It's not a great time. Midterms will be coming up soon. Then I've got to study for the MCAT again." I stared at the framed beach picture beside my bed. Grant had come down one weekend. The four of us stood smiling for the camera with the wind whipping my hair, our arms around each other's shoulders and big, broad smiles that only came from carefree times like those.

"All I'm talking about is going out for dinner."

"I know, but things are so busy. I'm sure you're dealing with that too."

"You weren't too busy to get something to eat with Ford." The sadness seeped through each word.

I stared up at the ceiling. This was me coming between them. This was me making it worse. Someone knocked on the front door. I peered out my bedroom door and saw Marisa walk out of her bedroom to answer it.

"That was just getting food with a friend."

Closing my door halfway, I sat on the edge of my bed.

My door creaked open, and Ford stood there blocking out most of the light from the hallway. The full-body awareness of his presence snapped into place. I couldn't hold back my smile. His forehead creased, and he stepped into the room, closing the door behind him.

I covered the end of the phone with my hand. "What are you doing here?"

"They moved my flight up earlier. Who are you talking to?" He motioned to the phone.

My eyes widened, and a lump formed in my throat.

"I'm not your friend?" Hurt radiated from his voice. "I could really use someone to talk to. We've known each other forever. I shared stuff with you, Liv, things I haven't shared with anyone else." Grant's voice brought me right back to this current issue.

My shoulders sank. "You did, and of course you're my friend, one of my oldest, and I wouldn't want to lose that." I took a deep breath. Ford's success and reputation had always cast a shadow over Grant. Coming in second no matter what could mess with someone's head. "I don't want to lose that." I ran my hand along the back of my neck, squeezing at the tension bunched there. "We can grab some coffee next week after my Tuesday class? There's a place on the far end of your campus. We can meet halfway?"

"Excellent. Just text me when and where and I'll be there."

I ended the call and dropped the phone onto my bed.

"Did you just set up a date with my brother?"

Lifting my head, I peered up at Ford. He'd shoved his hands in his pockets.

"Not a date. I need to tell him in person there's never going to be anything romantic between us, explain to him that he and I are better as friends. I should have just said that to him before even agreeing to that first date."

The bed sank beside me as Ford sat. His legs dwarfed mine.

"You were distracted...upset and hurting." His lips pinched together.

"It's no excuse for dragging someone else into this, and your brother..." I dropped my head into my hands.

Ford's strong hands kneaded my shoulders. The tightness there slowly relented under his methodical and persistent touch. I bit my lip to keep from moaning.

"We'll figure it out. I'll talk to Grant." He turned me sideways on the bed and shifted so I was nestled between his thighs. "Maybe I can help him understand." He dropped a kiss on the back of my neck, and my eyes fluttered closed. Another kiss along the curve of my neck and I sank back into him. My body pressed against his, sending sparks of electricity through me. It should have been the easiest thing I'd ever done.

"What about Colm?"

His body went rigid behind me. *Shit!* I shouldn't have said that. It was bad enough dealing with Grant; why did I have to bring up Colm? The electric charge of the room shifted, and he dropped his hands from my shoulders.

Shifting backward, he planted both feet back on the floor. Now it was his turn for a silent freak-out.

"That's going to be harder to handle." He glanced over at me with sadness in his eyes.

"What happened between you two? One minute you're inseparable and the next there's this weirdness." I ran my hand along his forearm. His muscles bunched under my touch.

He shook his head and stared down at the floor. "Sometimes things get complicated real fast and you don't know how to fix them."

"Complicated how?"

"It's something I need to work out with him first. It's been building for a while."

"Ford, tell me. Whatever it is, maybe I can help." I looked into his eyes and saw they were clouded with doubt. Running my hand down his arm, I slid my other hand under his larger one and threaded my fingers through his.

He put his other hand over top of mine and smiled back. "I swear, it'll be fine." Leaning his forehead against mine, he stared into my eyes, fanning the glowing embers of my soul.

My phone pinged, but I wasn't going to let someone else intrude on our moment again.

"Aren't you going to get it?" He leaned back, breaking contact.

"I don't want to." The interruptions from my phone had never been good news. They were always one more thing added onto the teetering pile towering over my head.

He picked up my phone off the bed and handed it to me. I stared at the notification on the screen. My heart jumped, and my mouth went dry. I let go of his hands and hopped up. With my hands shaking, I tapped. My exam grade had come in: 99. My heart hammered in my chest and my fingers tingled. *Are the lights going out or is that me?*

Ford rushed back over to me. His hands gripped my shoulders. "Liv, what's wrong?"

He sounded so far away. I was at the bottom of a well and the water was pouring down over me, filling my nose and throat. I couldn't catch my breath, and the screen swam in front of my eyes.

"Liv." He shook me, and my gaze shot to his.

I tried to breathe through the tightness in my chest. Licking my lips, I lifted the phone and turned it to him. He grabbed it and brought it closer to his face, staring at the screen.

His gaze bounced from the phone to me and back to the phone, keeping one hand on my shoulder. "You got an A. That's a great score." He turned on his megawatt smile, which always seemed to pull me out of whatever funk I was in, but it wasn't doing the trick now.

I licked my dry lips. "It is." So why did I feel like I was in need of a medical intervention? I kept waiting for that first inkling that I couldn't do this, that I wasn't cut out for med school. Wouldn't it be so much easier if I just sucked? If the concepts didn't stick and I couldn't do it?

Shaking my head, I took the phone from his hand. "I have an A in the class, a perfect match with the average GPA of a UPenn med student—a 3.8. With organic chemistry and bio, I'll have an A." I leaned back against the door to my closet, resting my head against the cold wood. "Colm's going to be so happy. I can retake the MCAT to give me an even better shot at acceptance."

I'd have to cut back on dance. My brain was mush after a seven-hour practice exam. No way I'd be able to come up with choreography, let alone drag myself out of my apartment after that.

I tapped my shopping app on my phone. "I can get some study guides and start working on that this weekend. I was waiting until after the semester ended, but I need to start now." My voice was desperation tinged with hysteria. A barrage of MCAT test prep options filled my phone; then it was plucked from my hands. "Give it back!" I reached for the glowing screen.

"Why does it sound like you're walking to your own execution?"

"I'm not. I'm fine." This was my life now. My good grade had cemented my future.

Ford traveling all the time would make things easier. I didn't have to make any hard choices. I'd be buried under coursework for the next seven years of my life. The whole room winked in and out. *Who is screwing with the lights?*

"You need to calm down, Liv." Ford grabbed my arms and held me up. "You're breathing crazy fast."

"Colm will be thrilled." I'd have to tell him in a call and hear the excitement in his voice. I stared at the picture of us on top of my dresser, me standing there in my little lab coat, Colm in his hockey gear, our parents beside him. It was one of the few games they'd gone to his freshman year.

"What about you?" Ford ducked his head to catch my eye.

I licked my lips again. "What about me?" Who was I without this plan?

"This is not how someone normally reacts to great news like this. You've been busting your ass for this, working so hard, and you look like someone just told you Santa's not real."

"Santa's not real?"

His lips thinned into a smooth line. "Knowing full well how this went the last time I asked this, I'm going to ask again: do you want to go to medical school?" His muscles tightened, bracing for my reaction.

"You don't think I can do it?"

"That isn't what I said. Stop looking for a reason to side-step the question, and of course I do. You can do anything you set your mind to and you're probably one of the most determined people I've ever met, but letting something suck out your soul, giving so much of yourself over to something you don't even enjoy—that sounds like a one-way ticket to hating your life."

"What else can I do? This has always been the plan." My back slumped against the door.

"Whose plan? Your plan? Because you don't look like someone who's living by a plan they made for themselves."

"My parents—"

Ford broke off and let go of my arms. "Exactly. Your parents didn't exactly have their priorities straight when it came to what was best for you or Colm."

I leaned over, resting my hands on my knees, feeling like I'd run a 5K.

"Look at how getting a grade most people would kill for makes you feel. How will this path ever make you happy? I've seen you when you dance, and you glow. Every word out of your mouth about it is like you've injected happiness straight into your veins."

"But I can't make a living off dancing."

"That's Colm talking. Your parents left you two more than enough to fend for yourselves, no matter what you decide to do."

"Like not become a doctor." It was the first time I'd said those words out loud. My chest tightened, and the room spun around me. Ford grabbed hold of me and helped me over to the bed.

"Lie down. Lie down and breathe, deep long breaths."

I held on to him like a lifeline in a raging storm. "What about Colm?" The fabric of Ford's shirt bunched under my grip.

"Don't worry about that now. Just close your eyes."

An overwhelming tiredness overcame me, like I hadn't slept in years. Using his arm as a pillow, I threaded my fingers through his and let the thump of his heart against my back break the clawing hysteria clouding my mind.

He ran his hands up and down my arms before wrapping his around my stomach and tugging me close. The sensation of free falling disappeared with Ford as my anchor, and I drifted off to sleep, basking in his warmth and his scent. If I hadn't been on the verge of a nervous breakdown, I might have tried something with him. We were finally in a bed together, after all. Maybe in the morning, I'd be more with it, would pounce on him and tie him down, but until then the safety of his arms was all I needed. Wrapped in them, I didn't feel like the world could ever be as scary as I imagined, as hard and cruel as I already knew it to be.

19

FORD

"This is bordering on obsession. It's been two years since you had two dates." I sliced into my steak. My mouth watered at the perfectly cooked meat as I tried to inhale it. Leaving Liv that morning before she woke had been one of the hardest things I'd ever done. I'd left her a note and hustled over to practice, though I had thought about taking the fine from the team for missing practice and staying in bed with her all day.

The Fish's crowd was heavier than usual, not that I usually came in on the weekend. It felt more like one of the trendier bars closer to Center City than my tucked-away hidden gem.

"It's not like I haven't dated anyone else since then, but I've always liked Liv." Grant took a bite of his burger, getting ketchup all over his chin in the process.

I dropped my knife to the plate. "And things ended."

"You think I don't know that?" He put his burger down and wiped his face.

"Doesn't sound like it to me."

"I like her. She said we couldn't date because premed

was intense and she wanted to devote herself to school. From what you said, she's killing it in school, so that's not even a problem. I'm not dating anyone. She's not dating anyone. It sounds to me like the stars have aligned."

"Maybe you need to be devoting more time to school." I pointed a steak fry at him.

Grant rolled his eyes. "My classes are going well, and you got me that internship for this summer, *Dad*, so everything's all set."

"You aren't exactly graduating with honors."

"College isn't just about grades. It's also about fun. You'd know that if you ever had any."

I took another bite of my steak. "Just remember our deal: you slip below a 2.0 and you have to foot half the bill."

"I have a 3.0, but thanks for the reminder." He glared at me from across the table. "I don't need you to remind me that I'm not a genius. Trust me, I know."

"No one said you have to be a genius."

"Could've fooled me. It's not like I got the athletic genes in the family." He jabbed his fork into his fries. "You wouldn't understand. The world doesn't lay everything out on a silver platter for mortals like me."

"Where is this coming from? How has the world served up anything on a silver platter for me?"

"Mom always busted her ass for you. She traveled to your hockey games, paid for all new equipment for you every single season, and once you went pro, it was all airline tickets, fancy hotels, and sky box seats for her. Of course she still wanted to support you. Fuck what Grant might be doing. Does he have a diving meet? Maybe some other event Mom might want to attend? Whatever. Doesn't matter." He kept his gaze trained on his plate.

I froze with my hand halfway to my face. He'd never

come on the trips I'd invited them both on, always saying he was busy. I had taken that as him not wanting to hang out with his mom and older brother. "Why are you only saying this now? How would I know if you didn't tell me?"

"Maybe you should've known your brother might have things going on in his life that didn't revolve around you."

"I'm sorry. I wanted Mom to get to enjoy things after all she sacrificed for us."

"For you—what she sacrificed for *you*. I didn't have to be shuttled to the rink at five a.m. with eighty pounds of equipment every day. I didn't make her go without anything for Christmas so she could buy new pads and gear when you outgrew your old stuff."

Guilt gnawed at the edges of my mind. "And I was doing my best to make sure those sacrifices paid off."

"Maybe I'm just sick of everything always being about Ford. You're all over the freaking news with your 'astounding goals,' then pictures show up online with you and Liv."

"How many times do I have to say this? It was just dinner. There's nothing going on between us." I sure as hell wanted to change that soon, though.

"But you'd like there to be. I've seen the way you look at her."

I hung my head. "That's the real reason she's always on your mind, isn't it?" Glaring up at him, I dropped my fork. "That's why you're texting her and calling her."

"Maybe just once I'd like there to be something I can have that you can't, unlike every other girl I've dated. More than a few made it real clear to me why they started talking to me in the first place."

As annoyed as I was with him, *that* was truly shitty. "I'm sorry you had to deal with that. I didn't know." Why was I always getting the blame for things I didn't know about? Although I did know I wanted Liv. I wanted my name on her lips when she came. I wanted to feel her in my arms, and I wrestled with that knowledge while staring into Grant's eyes as I swore up and down I didn't.

He shrugged one shoulder. "But now you do, so no more late-night taco dinners and other run-ins."

"What I do and who I do it with is none of your business."

"And I could say the same. Do you know why I asked her out that first time?"

I leaned back in my seat and crossed my arms over my chest. My jaw popped, and I stared at him.

"Because I saw how hurt she was when you were making out with that Angelica chick at Declan's wedding. I figured, damn, maybe now she'll see that you're always going to be toying with her, never serious, just loving that attention. You love to play the shy card, love everyone always asking you to come along, trying to draw you out of your shell. It's the world's longest con—why else would you play a position where the spotlight's always on you?"

"I'm sitting in a net behind a mask covered in equipment. I'm not there for attention." I got up from the booth and threw down some bills on the table. "Who I am isn't an act."

He stared back at me with a look I'd never seen before.

I left the bar and burst out the door into the crisp night air. It felt like I'd gotten a puck straight to the chest. To find out the little brother I'd thought looked up to me actually resented me was a tough pill to swallow.

Steam seemed to rise off my body. I only had the Henley on, not having grabbed my coat before I left my apartment, but I didn't want to go back there right then. My hands opened and closed as I walked, the blood pounding in my veins so hard my body pulsed to the racing rhythm of my heart.

Mom had sacrificed a shit ton for me. That was why I did everything I could to thank her, but it had hurt him. I'd never thought about how the spotlight being on me might mess with his head. None of the other guys had brothers. I was the only one, and how shitty of a brother did this make me?

I made it three blocks before the first double take from someone walking by turned into an ask for a picture. There was no blending in. I internally winced as I put my arms around the shoulders of the fans but kept my face neutral. Anonymity wasn't in the cards for me anymore. After signing a few autographs and posing for a picture, I went back to my apartment.

Kicking the door closed behind me, I could breathe again. I fell onto the couch. A text came in. If it was from Grant, there was nothing to keep me from launching my phone out the window. When I unlocked it, the tension melted away.

Liv: Do you think I'm too old to run away with the circus?
Me: You'd make a hell of a lion tamer

I tapped on her name. She picked up on the first ring. "I was thinking more of the person who cleans up after the animals."

"That bad, huh? How's studying going?"

She groaned. "I've taken every practice exam I could get my hands on, and I've been scoring in the 97 percent range. There's one more section I need to review before I go to dance tonight."

"I'm glad you didn't drop those dance classes." They

seemed to be the only thing keeping her going on those hard study days.

"Me too. You were right. Sometimes it feels like school and dance are the only times I leave my apartment."

"And for late-night tacos."

"And for late-night tacos with world-famous hockey players who are constantly surrounded by their adoring fans."

"World-famous is a stretch. Temporarily, locally famous would be more like it."

"Not with the way you've been playing." She paused. "I missed you this morning." I could hear her nibbling her lip.

"I missed you all day. When can I see you?" Playing it cool had never been my strong suit.

"This weekend?"

"I fly out on Friday morning."

"Shit, I forgot. Thursday night?"

"What about right now?"

Voices grew louder in the background. "Liv, come on, let's go."

"I can't." Regret laced her voice. "I told Marisa I'd help her with study prep for her midterm. We've got spectacular timing, as usual."

"Tell me about it." I dropped my head onto the back of the couch. "I'm on the road for five days this time."

"I'll clear the entire day you're back." The silence hung between us. "I'll miss you."

"I'll miss you too."

"Liv, we've got to get to the lab."

"Coming," she called out to her roommate. "I'll talk to you later. Night, Ford."

❧

The nightly phone calls from Liv had stretched well into the morning while I was on the road. I might have been a pro athlete, but she pushed herself to the limit between school and dancing.

Most nights had ended with the gentle rhythm of her breathing on the other end of the line, breathing I listened to for an embarrassingly long time. It became the steady soundtrack of my sleep, her little noises invading my dreams as I envisioned my arms around her, tangled up in the sheets on my bed.

On nights I played, the energy made it hard to concentrate on anything other than her once I got off the ice. She cleared her schedule to watch and wasn't on the verge of passing out the second the call connected. Those were the nights her moans and cries were the sweetest sounds of the evening. It wasn't the game-winning buzzer or the roar of the crowd; it was my name on her lips.

The wet sound of her fingers pumping into herself for me and the painful, driving need to bury myself in her were equal parts frustrating and satisfying. Each time I swore I'd hold off until I could see her in person, not torture myself like that, but after every game I bolted into my hotel room for the call.

Sweaty all over again, I'd lie there with my dick in my hand, cum on my stomach and her dirty, sweet words ringing in my ear.

"When you're back tomorrow night, I need to feel you inside me."

"Short of an extinction-level event, there's nothing on this Earth that will stop me." I grabbed a towel and cleaned myself up. Every reservation I'd had, every hesitation was eroded with each call.

She yawned. "I don't know why I'm so tired. I've just been sitting all day."

"You're pushing yourself too hard." Night after night, the weary tone in her voice got worse. Between our calls and her schedule, she couldn't have been getting more than four hours of sleep at night. A chivalrous guy would have put an end to the calls earlier and let her get some sleep. Apparently, chivalry was dead and buried.

"It's only for a few more months and then it's summer." She yawned again.

"What about after the summer? It's only going to get harder."

It took me a while to realize she wasn't mulling my words over.

"Liv?" The steady rhythm I knew so well came through the line. "Night, Liv." Setting the phone on my pillow, I propped my hands behind my head and stared up at the hotel room ceiling. The following night was too far away. There was no game or practice, and I needed to see her right then, which was how I'd ended up crammed into a town car with most of the Kings.

Headphones were the perfect isolation signal, the perfect way to ward off unwanted conversation. No one talked to you with headphones on—as long as the people around you actually thought you were listening to something.

I cursed mentioning to Declan, Heath, and Emmett that I was thinking of coming back early. It seemed I wasn't the only one eager to get back home after such a long stretch on the road, and they'd barged in on my solo return trip.

"He's probably living in his car, taking showers at the practice rink or the stadium." Heath leaned over, his blond hair dangling down between the seats. He stared at me and grinned.

"Maybe he's living in a box behind the stadium. Driving off after games and practices is all a big ruse to throw us off the scent." Emmett turned in his seat, giving me a look of pity.

"Maybe this is why he's such a man whore. All he's looking for is a warm place to sleep at night." Declan leaned over Emmett's seat and stared at me with puppy-dog sadness in his eyes.

Looked like the jig was up. I tore the headphones off my ears.

"Fine, everyone come over to my apartment. We can have a few drinks, I'll make dinner, and you can finally see my place, my actual apartment with four walls, a roof, and furniture." That shut them up for the rest of the trip.

Bleary-eyed, I finally made it home.

20

LIV

Sylvia's monthly dance extravaganza became a permanent fixture in my calendar, the first Thursday of every month. It also helped distract me from the fact that I'd be seeing Ford the next day.

My phone rang the second I stepped inside Sylvia's. "Hey, are you on your way to the airport?"

"Not exactly."

My stomach dropped. *Please not a delay.*

"Are you going to my mom's today?"

"I'm here already." I peered through the window in the door, laughing as the kids jumped up and down on the other side. "They're a ravenous pack. If I didn't get here in the mornings, I'd probably pass out. There's no way I can sustain this kind of energy in the afternoon."

He chuckled. "I guess I'll see you there."

"You're back?" My voice shot up three octaves. Hummingbird heartbeats took over.

"I skipped the team flight. I'm sure I'll get my ass chewed out for that, but I had to get back earlier."

"You did?" I cringed at the squeakiness in my voice.

"I did. I'll see you soon."

He ended the call, and I leaned against the wall with my phone clutched against my chest. He'd be there soon, and I'd finally be able to see him in the flesh, would finally be able to touch him, not just imagine him touching me.

"You ready, Liv?" Sylvia's voice snapped me out of my daydream about all the dirty things I wanted to do to her son.

"Yes, ready." I walked into the room of kids jumping up and down and screaming my name, thinking this must be what it felt like to skate out onto the ice before a big game.

Sweaty with cheeks hurting from laughing so much, I stepped out of the room an hour later. Ford had passed by while I was still inside, and it had taken everything in me to stay focused on the kids in front of me and not go rushing from the class.

Glancing up and down the hallway, I looked for him.

He stepped out of the kitchen and spotted me. I tamped down my urge to run to him.

"Hey." My voice was all breathy, but it had nothing to do with the running around I'd just done.

"Seems like I'm not the only one those kids push to exhaustion."

"Nope." The laughter and clamor from the rooms around me faded away. After almost a week of near nightly conversation with his words drawing out every ounce of pleasure from my body, all I wanted to do was touch him, have him touch me and finally fulfill the promises he'd made as he cried out his own release. I wanted to live out the dreams I'd had from back before we'd even had our first kiss.

He crossed the hallway and lifted his hand to the side of my face.

"Would you kids like some lunch, Liv?" Sylvia called out from the kitchen.

He dropped his hand, and the corners of his eyes crinkled, the mischief shining bright and naughty. His shoulders shook, and he dropped his head, taking a step back.

I shook mine and pressed the tips of my fingers to my mouth to hold back the laughter. Every damn time. I swore we'd have to find a bunker somewhere and stay there until I couldn't walk anymore. Was there a blue balls equivalent for women? Because I was sporting a pair, big time. It was either laugh at the game the universe was playing or cry in frustration.

"There you are." Sylvia came out of the kitchen wiping her hands on a towel. "Anyone hungry?"

"BLTs?" My voice sounded way more hopeful than I'd intended. She probably thought I was hanging around just to score some food.

"Close. Double bacon club sandwiches." The doors to all the rooms flew open, and the classes of kids filed out the door at the end of the hallway to the playground in the back.

"You're speaking my language, Sylvia." Letting my body brush against Ford's as I passed, I followed her into the kitchen.

We sat at the counter, our stools far enough apart, but every so often I'd reach out with my leg and run it along his calf. He dropped his hand from the counter and reached under the ledge to squeeze my thigh. His fingers danced along the tights I wore, and my body heated under his touch. Payback was a bitch.

Five minutes, he mouthed when Sylvia's back was turned.

"Ford, can you check out the planetarium room? I didn't want to get the ladder, but a few of the stars have fallen down and it's not feeling very celestial."

He snatched his hand back when she turned around. "Sure, I'll go do that now." He spun in his seat, sliding off the chair. With a noticeable bulge in his jeans, he sidestepped out of the room.

"Thanks, honey." She popped the dishes into the dishwasher.

"I'm going to change." I slung my bag onto my shoulder and went out the door, keeping my steps slow and even. The second I was out of the line of sight of the doorway, Ford grabbed my arm and spun me around, running his hand over the small of my back.

"Teasing me like that's going to get you into a world of trouble." He grabbed my hand and tugged me along the hallway.

"Promises, promises," I whispered after him.

The thrumming, hungry energy radiated off him. He reached out, turning the doorknob, and we tumbled into a pitch-black room. Glow-in-the-dark stars covered the ceiling and part of the walls.

He slipped his fingers along the base of my neck. "You're driving me crazy, Liv."

My eyes adjusted to the almost nonexistent light. The heat from his grip on me sent thundering pulses of pleasure rushing through my body.

"I could say the same thing about you." I ran my hands along his broad, solid chest. His hard muscles bunched under my touch.

"I wasn't the one playing footsie under the counter." His head dipped, and his breath fanned across the curve of my jaw, just under my ear.

Goose bumps broke out all over my body. "We're always getting interrupted. I thought we'd better take advantage of this while we can." Wrapping my fingers in his shirt, I bridged the gap between us.

The simmer shot off into a cascading fire that raced through my body. His lips crashed down on mine, and he tightened his grip on the hair at the base of my neck.

I yelped, and he used my slightly parted lips to take full control of my mouth. His tongue mimicked the dance his words had already done to bring that keen ache between my legs to the forefront of my mind.

There was nothing else but the flames he'd fanned in my body, and there was no one else who could put them out. There was only Ford.

He pushed me up against the wall. My body pinned under his, I hitched my leg up onto his hip and squeezed him closer, digging my heel into his denim-covered ass.

"We need to get to my place." He sucked on the soft spot on my neck. "Now." Giving my ass one firm squeeze, he let go and stepped back. I dropped my leg from his waist and nodded.

Working quickly, we picked up the stars from the floor and Ford stuck them to the wall, nearly pounding them into the drywall by hand. I slipped into the bathroom and changed my clothes, joining him and Sylvia back in the kitchen.

We wolfed down our food like it was our last meal on Earth.

Sylvia watched me with her mouth hanging open. "Do you have food at home? I can make you a plate to take with you."

"It was just so good." I tried to smile with my cheeks stuffed like a chipmunk.

She looked unconvinced.

"I've got to go, Mom. I'm beat from the trip. I couldn't even drive over here." He pecked her on the cheek.

"Okay, honey."

"And Liv, we can split a taxi—how's that sound?" His words were normal and even, but his eyes made promises my body hoped he'd keep.

21

FORD

"I should have called for one when we were still warm inside." I speed walked down the front path. Liv laughed behind me, trying to keep up. Glancing down at my phone, I willed the taxi icon flashing on my screen to move a hell of a lot faster.

She took a step closer to the curb, and the shiny glint along the concrete caught my eye.

Did you know there isn't a consensus from scientists about what makes ice slippery? Some say it's about the pressure from someone stepping onto it instantaneously melting it, others say it's a thin film of water that gathers on top. With all the time I spend on the ice, you'd think I'd know a bit more about it myself, but the only thing I know is that it hurts like hell when you wipe out on it.

Liv's arms flailed in a windmill, her phone clutched in her hand as her feet flew out from under her in those damn sexy purple shoes.

Lunging for her, I threw my arms out to steady her, but all I managed to do was find my own nice little patch of ice. For a hockey player, I'd like to think I'd be more graceful in a fall, but all bets are off when you're trying not to crush someone.

Folding myself over her as much as possible, I shifted my weight to take the brunt of the impact. My back slammed against the cold ground, and Liv landed squarely on my chest. Pain ricocheted up my back, and I knew it would leave a bruise. There was a bounce and a skid, then silence. Even the chirping birds had shut up to watch us bite it.

I kept my arms around her, her face buried in my chest. There was a faint tremble that ran through her body, and my fear ratcheted up.

"Are you hurt? Did I crush you?"

She looked up at me with tears in her eyes and a huge smile on her face. Her shoulders shook, and she gasped for air. "Dude, I thought you'd be more graceful than that." Her laughter continued as she wiped the tears off her face.

"I deserve a little credit. Who's the one who saved you from a face-plant?"

"You did, although you didn't save me from flashing the entire neighborhood my thong." She ran her hands along the back of her dress and pushed up off my chest.

A flash of her bare skin with my fingers sinking into her ass shot through my head. I groaned at the weight of her body shifting over mine. Was she made of eighty percent elbows and knees?

"Oh shut up, you big baby. You have two-hundred-pound hockey players slamming into you nonstop." She planted her foot, which slipped again, and everything moved in slow motion as her knee came back down.

There's a moment when you know the pain is coming, and it's almost worse than the actual pain—almost.

The pointiest knee in all of mankind made direct,

unflinching contact with my balls. The nauseating stomach-drop feeling slammed into me.

"Oh shit." She scrambled off me.

I lay there on the cold pavement, praying for death while curled up into a ball.

"Ford, oh God, I'm so sorry." She stood over me with her clenched fists pressed against her mouth, trying and failing not to let me see her laugh. Reaching out, she grabbed my arm.

I leaned against her as she helped me off the ground. Gritting my teeth, I sucked air into my lungs.

Bent over at the waist, I waved her off. "Totally fine." The words came out like a wheezy whistle.

"The taxi is here. Let's get you inside. I'm so sorry."

"Sure thing. Once the feeling returns to my legs, I'll walk it off." Barely able to fully stand, I braced my hands on my hips.

"I feel terrible." She stood in front of me, backlit by the midday sun, looking like an angelic bringer of pain. "I guess I'm stronger than I look."

I held the door open, and she slid across the seat with a worried look on her face, darting nervous glances at me.

I closed the door, and the taxi merged into the light afternoon traffic. "Really, I'm fine. It won't be the last time I get nailed in the nuts."

She stared at me, nibbling her lip.

"Seriously." I reached over to give her a reassuring pat on the leg. My mistake was made crystal clear the second my hand made contact with her skin. The sizzle of electricity that had been broken by the knee to my balls rekindled and pulsed between us.

She held my gaze. Her tongue darted out, and she bit her bottom lip. The expanse of skin I'd pushed out of my mind until that exact moment heated under my touch. Every cell of my body screamed, *Don't stop touching her.* All the air was sucked out of the cab, and the only sounds were my thundering heartbeat and her quickening breaths.

My thumb traced a path along her leg, and I tightened my grip on her thigh when the cab hit a pothole. The slow path of my thumb became the gentle caress of my whole hand.

I couldn't break the connection. Inside this cab, we were apart from the rest of the world. It was our bubble where everything we'd tried to hold back came rushing forward. The path of my touch widened, and so did her thighs. Her dress inched higher as she let her knees fall apart, and with a mind of its own, my hand traveled higher up her leg.

The light pink fabric of her underwear peeked out from under the skirt of her dress. My jeans got uncomfortably tight as my dick throbbed in time to my pulse. It was a bad idea to start something we couldn't finish right then.

The best worst fucking idea ever. Another interruption was bound to crop up, so I'd take what I could get. My hand moved higher, the rubbing long past comfort and straight into a tease, but I didn't know who for, me or her. Her shuddering breaths were a soundtrack I already knew so well, but in person they were even sweeter.

She covered my hand with hers, pushing me even closer to the apex of her thighs, to the fabric-covered prize that kept me up late into the night. My fingers danced along the edge of the lace as I lurched forward, nearly slamming into the plexiglass divider.

I'd never wanted to strangle someone more. Ford's fingers whispered across the fabric stretched over my wet core, and the driver screeched to a stop. It was the sharpest brakes in a taxi ever. He could have at least circled the block. *Seriously, help a girl out here, buddy.*

We rushed into the lobby of his building. Ford's grip tightened around my hand, and we beelined it straight for the elevator.

"There you are." Loud, familiar voices shook us right out of our foreplay-drunk haze.

We disentangled our hands like they'd caught fire, and turned the corner.

"Hey, Liv!" Mak hugged me. Not that I didn't love her, but why the hell were they there?

"I know we're early." Declan grinned.

If I could've, I'd have grabbed him by the back of his coat and launched him through the front door. I wanted to get down on my knees and scream up at the sky, *What did I ever do to you, universe? Why the cock block to the extreme?*

Ford's nostrils flared, and he clenched his hands at his sides.

At least I wasn't the only one hurting. *Let the torture begin.*

"I can see that. Luckily, so are we. Liv was at my mom's and wanted to come too."

Everyone's gaze swung to me. My cheeks did their best tomato impression.

"So, what's for dinner?" Emmett sat on the arm of the leather loungers in the lobby with Avery on his lap.

Ford's eyes got wide, and he clenched his teeth, sucking in a long breath. "Burgers and bourbon?"

"Hell yeah!"

"Sounds good to me."

"I knew you forgot."

It seemed the group was in agreement that this was an excellent plan.

"I just need to run across the street and pick them up. I'll be right back. Here's the key to my place. Ninth floor. Liv knows the way." He tossed the keys, and they landed in my hands as he bolted out the glass doors. I slowly spun on my heels with a sheepish smile. Once again, everyone's eyes were on me.

"He rescued me after a party and brought me back here because I was maybe a little drunk." I held up my thumb and pointer finger the slightest bit apart.

We all piled into the elevator and headed up to Ford's apartment.

"Don't worry, Liv, we've all been there—some of us more recently than others." Declan grinned at Mak, who shoved his shoulder.

This wasn't exactly how I'd imagined my next time at Ford's place would go. I had figured it would be more of a hazy blur, a tangle of limbs, and certainly without the entire Kings squad along for the ride.

I unlocked the door and held it open while everyone filed in.

The girls gathered around the bar setup while the guys unpacked some of the food they'd brought over and poked around the apartment.

"The expedition has found themselves in a rare position." Heath narrated with an imaginary microphone as he tiptoed around the apartment. "They are seeing the natural habitat of the elusive Kings goalie. Very few explorers have caught a glimpse of his territory, let alone been invited inside his den." He tugged open a closet door and jumped into a fighting stance like he imagined a wild tiger might jump out at him. "Why the hell does he have so many board games when he never has anyone over?" He pulled out a stack of five classic games. "Or has he been cheating on us?" Heath's eyes got wide, and he sniffed the games like he'd be able to smell other friends encroaching on the Kings' turf. "Has he been inviting other people over to play without us? Going out to drinks with them?" He dropped the games onto the table. "How dare he?"

The front door burst open, and Ford slammed it shut with sweat pouring down his face. "The burgers will be here in half an hour."

Raiding the bar area in his kitchen, I made a few drinks for everyone. The burgers arrived with a solid knock to the door. A sweaty guy with an unamused look on his face handed over the giant bag of food, and Ford slipped him a massive wad of bills.

I helped Ford unpack everything and get it onto plates. In the kitchen we worked together, every brush and bump bringing me right back to the taxi, right back to where his hands had been and where I wanted them again.

I had to keep reminding myself not to let my gaze linger for too long, not to reach out and touch him like I wanted to.

With full stomachs, everyone sipped their drinks, including the cranberry-orange mimosas I whipped up for dessert. Who said mimosas are only for brunch?

"You two are ringers. This isn't fair." Declan threw down his Scrabble tiles and walked away from the table in disgust.

"It's okay; you've got more than me. I only have thirty points." Mak laughed and set down her last tiles: I and S. She shrugged. "I tried, and I'm damn proud of my thirty points."

"You're killing me, Books. You're supposed to clean the floor with them." Declan wrapped his arms around her waist and hugged her to him.

"If we're talking purse-string sutures to close a wound, I'm your gal, but Scrabble...I'll leave that to the professionals." Mak dropped off her dishes in the kitchen.

The last two turns were me and Ford. I had 438. He had 442.

His gaze jumped from the game board to the tiles in front of him. He ran his hand across his forehead before squeezing his temples. The intense concentration looked sexy on him. He wasn't just a worthy competitor in online Scrabble.

I rearranged my tiles on my holder and sat up straight as the Scrabble gods smiled on me. Tapping two tiles on the table, I glanced around the room. Full stomachs, good drinks, and great friends—this was what I'd always wanted. I slipped two of my tiles back onto my holder and put down the rest: I-R-K-E-D, leaving the Q-U still on my tray.

"The fierce competitors are locked in a battle for dominance." Heath slipped back into commentator mode.

Emmett and Avery had long since excused themselves from the game. He was a second from re-consummating their engagement as she used him as her personal recliner. That ring of hers nearly blinded me from across the room. I still couldn't believe he'd bought it back in high school. Colm had never been that reckless with the money our parents left behind, but I guess people do crazy things when they're in love.

Ford lifted an eyebrow in my direction and put his word down on the board: B-U-S-T-E-D.

Heath picked up the notepad and scribbled down the scores. "We have a winner." He walked to the side of the table between us and leaned in for the dramatic pause. Covering both our hands with his, he lifted Ford's in the air. "The reigning champ continues to dominate."

Ford's gaze shot to mine, and my heart sped up.

With the first yawn from Avery, Emmett called it.

"We'll get out of your hair." Emmett stood up, bringing Avery with him. She pushed against his chest until he let her go. "Thanks for having us over."

The couples all grabbed their coats.

"We'll have to do it again sometime," Ford said, picking up the dishes around the apartment.

"Don't worry, man. Now that we know where you live, we'll be annoying the crap out of you." Declan clapped him on the back.

"Especially with burgers that good around the corner." Kara put her hand up to the side of her mouth, shielding it from Heath. "I think they're even better than his." She jerked her finger in Heath's direction.

"I heard that." Heath pushed his way toward us. "Next time, burger cook-off."

Ford grinned. "I look forward to that."

"Liv, do you need a ride?" Mak buttoned her coat. Everyone else stood at the door.

"No, it's okay. I'm going to a friend's place on my way home. It's right around the corner, so I can help Ford clean up and then get out of here." I hoped that sounded convincing.

Hugs from everyone and they made their exit. The silence in the apartment was louder than when everyone had been there.

"Are you ready for a rematch?" Ford's deep timbre tickled the shell of my ear, and a shudder shot through me. His chest pressed against my back, and the heat of his body set mine alight. "No holding back this time. I saw what tiles you had left. I'm not taking a pity win." He tucked the hair behind my ear and dropped a quick kiss on the curve of my neck.

I couldn't hold back my smile. Oh, this was going to be fun.

23

FORD

"You know you're technically breaking the law, don't you?" She shook the tumbler at me, the ice clinking against the side of the glass. I was seconds away from climbing over the table and ripping the thong off her body.

From the second we'd stepped out of the taxi, this had been bound to happen. There wasn't a thing in the world that was going to stop me. That didn't mean I didn't know it came with its complications, but right then I didn't care about those. All I cared about was hearing my name on Liv's lips as she screamed out her pleasure on my fingers, on my tongue, on my dick.

"Like you don't have a full bar in your apartment."

"True. So why did you bring this bottle out after everyone else left?"

"This is a twenty-five-year-old bottle of bourbon." It was a thing of beauty, only meant to be taken out for special occasions.

"Same age as you. And older than me." She lifted an

eyebrow like a challenge, to see if I was going to back down again.

"It deserves to be savored."

Tipping her glass back, she sipped it like I'd shown her. She let the flavors settle on her tongue, her expression changing the longer she held it in her mouth. "It's got a smooth burn. There are a lot of layers to it. I can see why you like it."

"Stop stalling—it's your turn." I lifted my chin toward the game board.

With the widest grin ever, she laid down the tiles. B-E-Z-I-Q-U-E.

"What the hell is a bezique?"

"No idea, but I know it's a killer scrabble word *and* gets a triple word score."

"No way. Give me that dictionary." I reached for the thick book on her side of the table.

She jumped up, clutching it to her chest. "You don't trust me?" she taunted.

"Not when it comes to Scrabble. Hand it over." I stood from my seat, and she hopped back. "Give it." I motioned for her to hand it over.

"I don't think so." She spun around and ran off. "It's a word. Take your defeat gracefully."

My apartment was a loft, so there weren't a lot of places for her to run to. She rushed into the corner of the open-plan living room where the brick met the drywall, refined meeting rough. With the dictionary wrapped in her arms, she leaned into the corner like she'd be able to keep it from me.

Coming up behind her, I wrapped my arms around her and grabbed for the book clutched in her hands. My body pressed against her, and our laughter filled the room.

"Just give it to me and take an honorable defeat." I reached around her, the back of my hand scraping against the brick.

"Not happening. It's a word!" She shoved her butt out and tried to open the dictionary.

Two things happened when she did that. My hand dropped off her arm and smacked into her leg—her bare leg —and the part of her body pressed up against me came into laser focus. Her ass, in that skirt, was right against me.

My fingers skimmed just below the hem of her skirt. I squeezed her thigh, and her head rocked back against my chest. The fire I'd tamped down while everyone was here came roaring back like we'd hit the snooze button and were finally ready to wake up.

I stepped closer, sandwiching her between me and the wall. I lifted her skirt, my fingers inching higher up her thighs. I ran my lips along the exposed nape of her neck. Goose bumps covered her skin, and her breath caught when my fingers brushed across the fabric covering her pussy.

The heat radiating from her body was off the charts. My cock thickened, and I bit back a groan as she ground herself against me.

Pushing my hand higher, I covered the only thing standing between me and the piece of her I'd tried to resist. Her legs parted. The *thunk* of the Scrabble dictionary falling to the floor did nothing to deter me.

My fingers danced along the lips of her pussy, slowly wetting my fingers through the fabric of her panties. Her hips rocked against me in a gentle rhythm, and I wanted to be nothing but closer.

I ran my lips along her skin, and her moans drove my need to be inside her even higher. I was going all in. I needed to have all of her—tonight.

24

LIV

I was suspended, pinned between the solid brick wall and the immovable force of Ford behind me. The weight of his desire was crashing down on me, threatening to bring me to my knees, but I didn't because he was there. He was holding me up while still giving me more than I could take.

The moment his fingers skimmed the top of the elastic, I prepared for him to stop, to hesitate. I balled my fists up against the brick to stop myself from putting his hand where I wanted it to be, but for the first time he didn't stop. The throbbing need threatened to consume me. A keen, blissful relief overtook me as his fingers dipped inside me. As he parted my slick folds, the sound of my arousal was nearly drowned out by my shallow breaths.

He groaned, and two of his fingers sank in deeper, stretching and teasing me. The heavy weight of his cock pressed against my ass. I wanted even more of him. This was a dance we'd been doing for far too long, and the only way for it to end was with him stretching me like only he could.

"You're so wet." His words were raw and primal, like a

switch inside him had been flipped. It was a side of Ford I'd never seen before. I'd heard a hint of it on the phone, but that had only been a taste. I craved more.

I licked my lips. "I'm always like this around you."

He groaned as his teeth sank into my shoulder, not hard enough to do more than make a dent, but enough. A shudder raced through me. My pussy clenched around his invading fingers. Plundering the control I had over my trembling body, he added another finger. Words were a distant memory. I'd once had the ability to speak, but now there were only moans and clawing at the brick in front of me. I came hard and fast. Spots danced in my vision as all the air left my lungs.

The coarse texture of the brick made me hyperaware of every point of contact, every rough spot, and every smooth one on him. The brutal climax didn't stop and neither did his fingers, driving me even higher than I'd thought possible. My thighs tightened around his hand, but he kept going. I was torn between begging for mercy and asking for more—so much more.

"Fuck, that's a beautiful sound."

It wasn't until he said it that I realized there was another sound over my panting and the wet heat between my legs coating his fingers. The babbling nonsense poured from my mouth as his hand slowed and my forehead dropped against the wall, the rough brick scraping against my skin.

Not giving me time to recover, Ford spun me around. His gaze roamed my body sending an uncontrollable shiver shooting through me. My legs were jelly under me, barely supporting my weight.

He dropped to his knees, taking my soaked panties down with him. Grabbing the hem of my shirt, he shoved it up my chest, exposing my stomach and bra, which disappeared like a figment of my imagination. He ran his bristly cheeks across my stomach. My nipples pebbled and ached at his slow torture. Taking one into his mouth, he rolled it between his teeth, running his tongue over the tip. My other nipple got the same treatment. Rippling waves of pleasure made me light-headed, and every nip of his teeth and swipe of his tongue sent me higher.

He placed his hand into the center of my chest to steady me and looped my legs over his shoulders. My skirt bunched around my waist, and I was exposed to him completely. My thighs rubbed against the soft cotton of his T-shirt. His hot breath skirted across my wet thighs. Each exhalation sent another shudder through me.

Like he had all the time in the world, he kissed his way along my parted legs. His hands cupped and squeezed my ass like the world's most inappropriate chair. Each touch of his lips brought him closer to my heated core. He was the master of anticipation.

I licked my lips and sank my fingers into his hair.

He growled and bit down on the inside of my thigh.

I yelped and hissed, and my pussy spasmed at the empty feeling inside. My fists clenched in his hair, yanking at the roots.

"You're going to come on my mouth." His words rasped against my skin, coarse like the brick wall behind me.

It was a fact, a foregone conclusion. It probably wasn't going to take more than a swipe of his tongue. I squeezed my eyes shut, trying not to be embarrassed by my body's reaction to him.

"Look at me, Liv. You need to tell me if it's too much." The deep growl in his voice sent the sparking electricity coursing through my body even faster.

I stared down through the valley of my breasts, past his

hand pressing me into the wall, and into his eyes. The hunger swimming in them made my head spin. A shuddering breath escaped through my lips as I locked eyes with the man I'd wanted since I'd known that was even a thing, and I nodded.

His mouth clamped onto my pussy. Sucking on my clit, he hummed a sound of appreciation before painting my skin with his tongue. He was a man starving, and I was his banquet.

It was the sweetest invasion, and my walls clamped around his tongue with unadulterated pressure. It was maybe five seconds, possibly less. If I had been a dude, I'd probably have been embarrassed by how quickly I came. The shuddering tension racked my body, and my legs shook.

Placing a tender kiss on my sensitive clit, he massaged my ass, holding me in place. "If you keep coming like this, I'm not going to be able to stop." Another swipe of his tongue across my heated button, and my toes curled.

"I don't want you to stop. I'm not going to be able to stop coming." My words were a keening cry on the tail of a seemingly never-ending orgasm brought on by one more gentle flick of his tongue.

Then I was floating, not only metaphorically but actually as he carried me in his arms, moving us across the room up into his bedroom.

He gently tossed me onto the soft comforter on his bed. I bounced and tried to catch my breath. Staring up at the exposed rafters, I sucked in a shuddering breath. Every jingle of his belt buckle made my mouth water. He'd already given me more orgasms in an hour than I'd had in a long time; returning the favor was the least I could do. I climbed up onto my knees and reached for him.

He stepped back, evading my touch. "No, not yet. Don't move." He pinned me with his stare.

I sat on my heels hungrily, impatiently waiting for him to come to me, needing to finally feel him inside of me, inside my mouth, inside my pussy. The ache between my thighs could only be sated by him.

He shucked off his jeans and boxers. His thick erection slapped against his stomach when it was finally freed.

I inched closer to the edge of the bed. He made a disapproving sound. "Liv." The warning in his voice sent a zing straight to my clit. Goose bumps erupted all over me. "Don't." The command in his voice could not be disregarded.

A shiver of delight raced down my spine. I nodded. Words escaped me.

Hefting his cock in his hand, he slid his hand down my legs, untangling them and grabbed my ankle. The bed dipped as his knee hit the bed.

"You've pushed me to my breaking point with your teasing." He pulled off my skirt and reached up to take a lock of my hair between his fingers. The back of his hand skimmed along my collarbone as he traced it to the end of my hair.

"Desperate times call for desperate measures." I bit my bottom lip.

"Do you have any idea—" He shook his head. "This can —" A flicker of doubt reflected in his eyes.

I pressed my fingers against his lips. "This—I need this. I need you. Please." There I was begging him to fuck me and I wasn't even ashamed. I might climb out of my own skin soon if I didn't get to feel him.

"Ford." Tilting my head up, I bridged the gap between us. The fiery-hot sparks of electricity overwhelmed me. His hold on me loosened as he devoured my mouth. His lips were demanding, drawing every breath from me like there was nothing else to keep him going. My body was on the verge of another explosion.

His hands ran along the side of my face and up into my hair. I gasped and opened my mouth wider at the sharp tug of his fingers looping through my hair. Shifting, I leaned into him, ready to devour him right back. He tasted like every sweet cocktail that went straight to your head.

He tugged off his tight T-shirt stretched over his muscled chest. "You wanted to see me, Liv. Here I am." He held his arms out at his sides, showcasing himself. His body in all its muscled glory on display for me to soak all of him in. The show was over too quickly, but forgotten once he dropped down over me. The weight of him settled between my legs, his hips spreading my thighs, opening me to him.

I stared down between us. He slid his cock along my soaking-wet opening, teasing and tormenting me with his control. I shuddered and fisted the sheets beneath me.

Digging into his discarded pants, he slipped on a condom. If I could've, I'd have flipped him over and impaled myself on his ever-growing member.

He lifted his head and caught my eye. "Hold on to me."

I wrapped my arms around his neck, and he held me close. His arms wrapped around my back. I breathed him in with my nose pressed against his neck. My heart thudded against my chest as he guided himself into me without his hands, our hips and legs meshing together perfectly.

I tightened my hold as he spread me open. The air in my lungs whooshed out as the head of his dick stretched me to my limit. He sank into me like an unrelenting force pushing me closer to the edge with each inch, joining us together.

"You're too sweet, Liv."

I wanted to reply, but I didn't have the words. Only

moans licked across his shoulder as I held on, fearing I'd break apart into a million pieces if I let go.

He bottomed out in me, lighting up parts of me only I'd been able to find.

Lifting his head, he stared into my eyes. "Are you okay?" Concern creased his brow.

I nodded as my head fell back, relishing the gentle thrusts of his hips.

"Let me hear the words, Liv."

His tone pulled me out of my daze, and I licked my dry lips. "Yeah, I'm good."

Then the softness was gone, flew straight out the window. His hips pistoned in grinding thrusts. It was unlike anything I'd ever felt. Every part of me was being lit up by him all at once. Every drag sent pleasure through my swollen flesh, drawing out the sensations until they rolled together in one cascading wave that stole my breath away.

The release was like nothing I'd ever experienced. A brutal climax ripped through me, so sharp and over-whelming tears filled my eyes. My scream was suspended in my throat. I ran my nails down his back, raking across his skin. It was every blissful feeling rolled up together and presented to me on a platter, a platter so heavy I could barely breathe.

I sucked in a sharp breath and released my arms from around him. I was dead weight, but the driving force of him continued. Flipping me onto my stomach, he lifted my hips. I moaned and tried to help as much as someone with bones made of jelly could.

His fingers dug into my skin, tightening as his hips slammed into me. His cock expanded, stretching me to the max. The pulse of his driving erection had me teetering on the edge of a blackout. Ford roared as he came, holding me in a viselike grip against him as he came into the latex between us. His weight settled onto my back before he rolled us to our sides.

I was still coming back from my mission to space when he pulled out, the breezy air of the room cooling the super-heated flesh between my legs. I could have passed out and not woken up for a month. The bed dipped, and then he was around me, pressed against my back, his arms holding me. He murmured into my hair.

His gentle touch brushed back the hair sticking to my face. He rolled me over.

"Liv..." His words died in his throat. His Adam's apple bobbed up and down.

"Don't. Just let us have this tonight. If nothing else, at least give me that."

He nodded and grabbed the blankets, dragging them up over us. I sighed as he wrapped his arms tighter around me. I snuggled in deeper to his chest and shut out the nagging doubts trying to push their way into my head.

I'd deal with them the next day. I'd show Ford this could work. After what we'd just had together, how could he deny it? Deny me?

25

FORD

Hair brushed against me, tickling my skin, a slight weight resting on my arm. It all came back to me in a rush. I cracked my eyes open and smiled. The tightness in my chest I woke up with so often wasn't there. Liv's brightness surrounded me, and her soft, even breaths made me want to never get out of the bed. I buried my face in her hair and breathed her in.

I slid out of bed and picked up my pants. Liv rolled over, clutching the pillow to her chest. The sheets slipped down, exposing her back and the smooth arc of her hip. The warm bed and her delicious curves called to me. I shook my head.

My fridge was an embarrassment after being on the road for so long. I needed to grab something for us to eat before she woke up. Jogging down the steps to the living room as quietly as I could, I spotted my phone. I grabbed it off the counter and checked the time. Being programmed since the eighth grade for practices at dawn still hadn't reset itself after all this time.

I grabbed a piece of paper and scrawled out a note before making my way quietly back into the bedroom.

Running the backs of my fingers across her cheek, I stuck my note on the pillow beside her. I buttoned my jeans and grabbed my keys off the counter.

Being recognized was never on my list of things I liked. But now? I definitely didn't want to field fans with Liv warm and waiting in my bed. Looking out of my massive windows, I stretched as the early morning sun peeked from between the city skyline. After tugging on my shoes, I stepped into the hallway and made my way out of the building.

There were a couple places around the block open that early. With a bag of freshly baked bagels, three types of cream cheese, coffee, and orange juice, I headed back to the apartment. My phone rang in my pocket. Balancing the cups and bag in one hand, I took it out with the other.

"Hey, man." The voice I'd been dreading blasted out the other end way too loudly, his words slurred.

"Hey, Colm." I stopped on the street corner. A few delivery trucks dotted the street.

"Are you in the middle of something?" The clink of ice against glass filtered through from his end.

"No. What do you need?"

"I can't call my friend?" The word dripped with disdain.

"Why are you awake this early?" Gritting my teeth, I held the phone against my shoulder.

"Where are you?"

"Out getting breakfast."

"You just snuck out of some chick's place, didn't you? Fueling up after a long night."

"I was home, and I'm heading back there." Checking for traffic, I started the walk back to my place.

"You brought someone back to your apartment? Thought that wasn't your style. Aren't you more of a hit-and-run type of guy?" There was an unmistakable edge to his voice.

Stalking to the end of the block, I stopped. *What the hell is going on?* "Why are you up so early?"

"I'm not up early—I never went to sleep." He slurped from his glass with more ice clinking. "Can't sleep."

"Is your knee keeping you up?" Rehab had been going well from what I'd heard.

"Eloise bailed, packed up her shit and left a few hours ago...or maybe it was yesterday. I don't remember."

I cursed under my breath. "How much have you had to drink?"

"Not enough. Not nearly enough. She decided LA is where she belongs and she wants to pursue acting, hooked up with some producer guy, and that was that. I'd outlasted my usefulness." A humorless laugh tore out of his mouth.

I winced. His relationship track record was not stellar. With everything going for him—family money, pro career, and his looks—he always ended up with users. I knew that better than anyone. Bile rose in my throat.

"I'm sorry, man."

"Par for the course, right? At least this turned out better than the last time. At least she didn't leave me for you."

I grimaced. "That's not how it was. I'd never have tried something with Felicity, never in a million years if I'd known. It wasn't a competition."

"You're right. You didn't even know someone else was in the running, but you still won."

The Felicity situation was like a ticking time bomb in our friendship, always there, each second counting down until the next explosion. "Get some rest, man. You're drunk."

The sharp clink of ice against glass nearly drowned out his laughter. "And why the hell shouldn't I be drunk? My knee still fucking hurts. My girlfriend left me again. My sister's hiding from me, and my best friend can't even take time out of his busy puck-bunny-fucking schedule to speak to me."

"You need sleep." My jaw tightened. Even though he didn't know who was in my bed, him mentioning the word in the vicinity of Liv made me want to hit him.

"Where's Olivia and why won't she answer my calls?"

"I don't know." She hadn't said anything about ducking him, but with her near panic attacks over medical school, I could see why she would.

"Weren't you supposed to be talking to her? Finding out what's wrong with her? And now she's stopped talking to me."

"Maybe she doesn't want to deal with your shitty attitude."

"Maybe I shouldn't have trusted you to help me out."

I squeezed the phone so tightly my fingers ached. "If this is how you're talking to her, I don't blame her for avoiding you."

"Did she say something to you?" His voice sharpened.

"She's fine, better than fine, and she's got her head on a hell of a lot straighter than you right now."

"She's still a kid. She's my responsibility."

"She's an adult, a woman—maybe it's time you started treating her like one." My voice echoed off the pavement, and the woman behind the newspaper stand jumped.

"Sorry."

"Don't think I haven't seen the way you look at her." His whispered words dripped with a silent threat.

My stomach knotted. Drunken Colm was likely to do some serious damage if he knew Liv was in my bed. This was a conversation we needed to have in person, sober. I swallowed past the lump in my throat.

Dead silence from his end, and then he let out a deep sigh. "Listen, I'm sorry. There are some lines even you wouldn't cross." The anger evaporated from his voice in an instant. "This shit with my knee has messed me up. Every time I put on my skates, I'm freaked out I'll tweak my knee again. Eloise blindsides me, and now Olivia's dropped off the face of the planet. I can't handle all this at once."

I stayed silent. What the hell was I supposed to say?

"All this crap out here's got me thinking about what happened with Felicity. It wasn't your fault, just sucks I lost to someone who didn't even know he was in the race. Fuck, I'm so drunk."

Some of the tightness in my chest ebbed away. That was the first time he'd said those words, *it wasn't your fault*. And that would all be erased once he found out. The vise grip in my chest was back with a vengeance.

"Just get some sleep. It will all look better in the morning."

"You're right. Sorry for waking you up. Head back to your latest conquest and have some fun. I'll talk to you later."

"Later."

I ended the call and stood in the middle of the sidewalk a couple blocks from my building, frozen like roots had grown out of the bottoms of my shoes. Liv was upstairs nice and warm in my bed. I wanted to rush back up there like I hadn't just had that call. In the light of day with the sun rising over the horizon and peeking out from between the buildings, my fuckup slammed into me so hard it nearly knocked me off my feet.

I'd hurt him once without even meaning to, but Liv had

been anything but a mistake. It wasn't like we'd fallen into this. I'd gone for her, couldn't get enough of her. Maybe if we'd waited, if I'd been able to hold off until repairing my relationship with Colm, then he'd be able to accept Liv and me. He may be realizing I wasn't a prick for sleeping with Felicity, but there was no way in hell he'd forgive me for sleeping with Liv. Not in his current emotional state. This wasn't something I'd be able to come back from.

The slicing, bitter cold from the winter had eased up, but the wind tunnel between the buildings still churned. I walked the last steps to my place. My hands were still full with Liv's breakfast, so I shouldered open the front door of the building. My phone vibrated again, and I took a deep breath. *Please not another drunk Colm call.*

My eyebrows furrowed when I spotted the name on my screen.

"Grant?" I stood in the lobby of my building balancing my breakfast haul.

"Morning, big brother."

"Why are you calling me so early?"

"You always bitch about me not telling you when I'm coming over, so here's your warning. I got stranded on this side of town last night."

"You're coming to my place? Where are you right now?"

"At your front door. I'm coming in."

My stomach dropped.

I burst through the lobby and took the steps two at a time to get to my floor. Hot coffee and orange juice sloshed onto my hand. This was not how I wanted him to find out. *Damn it!* The door to my apartment was cracked. Shoving it open, I skidded to a stop inside. I threw the bag and cups onto the table beside the door.

Grant stood in the middle of the living room, Liv a few

steps from him, wearing one of my T-shirts that hung to her knees.

He slowly turned to me, his nostrils flaring and a watery sheen over his eyes. Betrayal burned so bright it singed my skin.

"You're fucking Liv?"

26

LIV

The front door opened. "What took you so long? I'm freaking starving." I bounded down the stairs and turned the corner to the kitchen. "A certain somebody wore me out last night." Skidding to a stop, my body tensed, my smile falling off my face as I locked eyes with Grant.

He stood beside the kitchen, about to toss his keys onto the counter. They dropped to the floor with a muted *thud*. His eyes widened as he took me in. His gaze dropped to my feet and traveled up my body. I crossed my arms around my waist, folding in on myself. Like that would help. There was no mistaking why I was there and what I'd done.

The door flew open again, and Ford burst into the apartment. His eyes were wild and bounced from me to Grant.

"You're fucking Liv?" The pain in Grant's voice stung like a thousand paper cuts.

I dropped my head and squeezed my eyes shut. This wasn't how he should've found out.

He turned back to me. The tears in his eyes sliced

straight through me. "You're sleeping with him?" His voice cracked.

I opened my mouth, but the words died in my throat.

"After everything I told you? After how he hurt you? And now you're sleeping with him?"

"It just happened. We didn't mean for it to." I winced. The lie was clear even to my own ears. I closed the gap between us, but Grant backed up.

"Do you think I'm stupid?"

"Grant, calm down. We can work this out." Ford took a step farther into the room.

"Work what out?" Grant whipped around, jabbing his finger toward Ford. "You knew how I felt about her. I told you and you still did this."

"We didn't do this to hurt you." Ford stepped close with his palms up.

"We? You're a *we* now? How long has this been going on? How long have you two been laughing behind my back when I've come to you asking for advice?" Grant's words bounced off the rafters. His chest rose and fell, and his hands opened and closed into fists at his sides.

"I'd never do that." Ford's eyes pleaded with him.

"There are a lot of things I thought you'd never do." Grant turned his head and stared straight through me.

My stomach knotted, and I stood there wishing I could disappear into a puff of smoke.

"I never meant to hurt you. I... What you shared with me —I never laughed at you. It was never like that. I know how hard it is growing up with someone like them." I nodded toward Ford.

"Then what was it like? It didn't stop you from falling into bed with him." He blinked back tears.

My shoulders sagged.

"Let's talk about this." Ford put his hand on Grant's shoulder.

He shrugged it off. "What's there to talk about? Once again, you've proven to me that I'm second best and always will be." He dropped his head and peered over at me. The hurt in his eyes slammed into my stomach. Things were never supposed to go this way.

"I'm sorry." The words caught in my throat.

The muscles in his neck strained and he looked between me and Ford. Shaking his head, he bolted from the apartment.

I jumped at the earsplitting *bang* as the door slammed so hard it bounced back open. The lights suspended from the ceiling rocked and swayed with the force of his exit.

Wrapping my arms around myself, I picked up my clothes, which were dotted around the apartment, and held them to my chest. Ford stood staring at the door in stunned silence.

Tears filled my eyes, and I wiped my nose with the back of my hand. We were never supposed to hurt anyone. I walked into the bedroom and threw my shirt on over my head. My fingers trembled as I buttoned my skirt. Sitting down on the bed where I'd woken up happier than I'd ever been, I dropped my head into my hands.

The mattress dipped beside me. I lifted my head and stared at Ford's long legs beside me. He ran his hands up and down his thighs. What Grant had confided in me should've been enough for me to stop what had happened with Ford. I'd still done this. How shitty of a person did that make me? All I'd been focused on was me and Ford, how much I wanted him, how good it would feel.

"He's hurting." I sniffled.

Ford nodded.

"I'm sorry." My words came out thin and reedy.

His head snapped up. "Stop saying that. It's my fault."

I blew out a long breath to try to hold myself together. "It's both our fault, then." Putting on my shoes, I stared up at the ceiling. On shaky legs, I stood from the bed. I walked past Ford, and his hand shot out, wrapping around my arm.

"Liv, don't go." His hand slid down, and he ran his thumb over the inside of my wrist.

"How can I stay? You saw the look in his eyes." Tears welled in mine. "That's not something he's going to forgive."

"I can talk to him."

"You're the last person he wants to talk to. This is just another example to him of how you always come out on top. You might not know it, but people are drawn to you." I stepped between his knees and ran my fingers across his cheek. "You fight it tooth and nail with the beard and the quiet words, but people still flock to you, and he's always felt second best."

"I've never tried to make him feel that way." He stared up into my eyes.

"Of course not, but that doesn't mean he doesn't feel it, and I just added to it—another example of how you always get exactly what you want because I didn't stop to think, really think, about how us being together might hurt him."

He covered my hand with his, the heat of his touch filling every cell in my body.

"I'm not ready for this to end."

"Neither am I, but I can't do this if it's going to rip you two apart. He's your brother. You love him."

His Adam's apple bobbed up and down, and his grip on my hand tightened. "We've got some amazing timing, don't we?"

I let out a watery laugh.

He squeezed his eyes shut and tugged me closer. Burying his face in my stomach, he held on to me. I wrapped my arms around his head and choked back the tears clogging my throat.

"It doesn't have to end like this." His fingers tightened around my waist, too tight, but I didn't say anything. Savoring this moment was all I could do. His smell invaded my nose, and we clung to each other.

"What other way can it end? Are we supposed to show up to Sylvia's together? What would she think of me?" I cringed. I'd driven a wedge straight through the relationship of her sons, the ones she loved so much. How could she not hate me?

"My mom could never hate you, Liv." It was like he'd read my mind.

"Maybe not, but she'd blame me, just like I blame me."

"This wasn't just you. It's not like you flung yourself at me. I'm right here with you." He stared into my eyes.

I brushed back the hair from his forehead. "I'll never forget last night." I buried my face in his hair, holding him close.

Kissing the top of his head, I let him go, and he dropped his arms from around my waist. Tilting his head up, I pressed my lips to his. The urgency and desperation of the kiss brought more tears to my eyes.

Breaking away from him, I snatched up my bag from the edge of the bed and ran out of the apartment. I took the stairs and shot out onto the street. Even in the open air, I could barely breathe. I ordered a car and prayed Ford didn't come outside. Leaving him once had been hard enough.

Climbing into the back of the car, I didn't try to stop the tears falling from my eyes. I leaned my head back against the warm leather seat. The comfortable interior didn't do anything to stop the sadness and guilt raging a war inside my chest. It wasn't only for the way his heart had made mine sing, but also to mourn the loss of the friend I'd just gotten back. There was no going back there. In the blink of an eye I'd lost the man I loved and the friend I'd been able to count on for most my life.

I blew my nose and wiped my eyes. The driver glanced back at me a few times in his mirror. Somehow I'd get Grant to forgive me, and maybe someday Ford could be a part of my life again.

27

FORD

"Next game you play like that, Atherton, I'm pulling you," Coach shouted at me when I climbed into the box at the end of the period. We'd won—barely. They might as well have had a cardboard cutout zip-tied inside the goal for all the good I was doing.

The team trudged to the locker room, and I chucked my pads. I couldn't breathe in those things. Shoving everything onto the bench, I grabbed my clothes and stormed into the showers.

My phone sat at the bottom of my duffel. Calls and texts to Grant had gone unanswered. I hadn't used the phone much in days, which was a complete 180 from how much I'd talked on it over the past few weeks. The lack of routine calls at night between Liv and me left another hole in my life that I couldn't fill with practice, booze, or other women.

I hung up my clothes and towel and peeled off my drenched uniform. Dumping it in a pile in the back of the shower, I turned on the water. The hard spray seemed more like a power washer than a shower. I cranked up the heat, my version of self-flagellation.

The pain in Grant's eyes and the way Liv had buried her face in my hair before walking out on me replayed in surround sound in my head. Maybe it was for the best; Colm wouldn't have to know. I wouldn't have to stand in front of him and tell him I'd broken his trust again and crossed a line we both knew was there. Maybe if I kept telling myself that, I'd believe it was true.

It had been almost a week since we'd ridden to my apartment together. She'd looked so peaceful in my bed. With my head propped up on my arm, I'd watched her sleep, her golden hair fanned out across my navy sheets. Squeezing my eyes shut, I pushed the thoughts aside. It only made the hurt so much worse. Turning off the water, I rested my forehead against the cold tile. I got dressed just going through the motions.

I picked up my duffel, and my phone rang. My stomach knotted with each step closer to the phone. It was Colm's ringtone.

"Hello." Was this drunk Colm? Pissed-off Colm? Depressed Colm? Maybe I'd hit the jackpot and get all three.

"Hey, do you have a minute?" Stone-cold sober Colm.

I waved to the guys, ducked out of the locker room, and headed to my car. "Just finished up a game."

"Right. The time difference still has me all screwed up. I keep thinking 'what's the point of getting used to the time when I'm coming back,' and then my rehab gets extended."

"Must be messing with your head." I unlocked my door and got into my car.

"You have no idea. I rented this big house for Eloise, and now I'm rattling around the thing constantly reminded of my stupidity."

"You're not stupid. You've got a big heart."

"A big, stupid heart that can't pick a faithful woman to save my life."

My throat tightened. I didn't turn the car on, just sat there waiting for the other shoe to drop, for the digs to start.

"Sorry I'm dumping all this on you."

"It's what friends do—they listen when you need them to."

"You've been listening to my shit since ninth grade."

"I never complained before." Finally turning the car on, I pulled out of the lot.

"No, you haven't. I've been a shitty friend. I've put some shit on you that wasn't your fault. Being out here on my own...damn. Playing in Boston without you for a year was bad enough, but there's not even a team out here. Day in and day out I'm on my own. It's made me realize a few things. I'm lucky to have you guys."

"We know." The corner of my mouth lifted.

"Douche."

"I'm not the one repeatedly calling people at the ass crack of dawn."

"Shit, I know. Sorry."

"Stop apologizing. Just make sure you take care of yourself. Lay off the booze, fix that knee, and get your ass back here."

"I'm on it, and sorry for pushing the whole Olive thing on you."

My hands froze on the steering wheel. "Don't worry about it. Don't worry about anything until you get back here. There are some things I want to talk to you about." *Like squashing this Felicity thing between us once and for all and telling you how much I care about Liv, even though my own brother ended up as collateral damage.*

Damn, things had been a hell of a lot simpler back in high school. Back then, my biggest worry had been standing up in front of a class to give a presentation or screwing up so royally in hockey I'd lose my Rittenhouse Prep scholarship.

"You're right. I've got to head to my early PT session in a few. We can have your deep mysterious talk when I'm back in town." He chuckled.

I ended the call with Colm and pulled into the parking garage of my apartment. The solitude I'd found comfort in only served as a reminder of what I'd lost and what I'd continue to lose. As I opened the door, my phone lit up again.

Mom: *Do you have time to stop by this afternoon?*

I'd been avoiding the house since the Grant situation. Had Grant told Mom what had happened? Was she going to rip me a new one the second I stepped in the front door? Even if she did, I'd still go. Being alone didn't have the same comfort it usually did. Instead I was left alone with my thoughts...thoughts of Liv.

The fridge and walls were covered with new artwork from the kids. Frames I'd mounted with little slots at the top made it easy to swap out their pictures. The freshly-baked-cookie smell filled the entire room and took me back to when I was a little kid, or even better, when she'd sent me to practice with a tub of them for road games back in high school. I'd been a king among Kings when the Tupperware lid came off.

"Here, try this." She slid a piping-hot cookie off the spatula and into my hands. I tossed it back and forth, taking a bite with every other toss. The melted chocolate coated my tongue, its deep, dark flavor mingling perfectly with the brown sugar and vanilla.

"As good as always, Mom." Eating had been the last thing on my mind for the past few days, but damned if these cookies didn't help at least a little bit.

"I talked to your brother. He came over to do some of his laundry, and he was pretty upset." She looked at me over her shoulder from the stove.

Shoving more cookie into my mouth, I stalled. I'd been lured by sweets right into a trap.

"It's always been hard for him living in your shadow." She put in another tray of cookies and closed the oven. "And I didn't help things." Her shoulders sagged.

"It's not your fault, Mom."

Her lips curled into a small smile. "That's exactly whose fault it is. When your dad left..." She put her hands on the counter and dropped her head. "When he left, keeping busy was the only way I kept myself from falling apart, and what will make you busier than ever? Being a hockey mom. All the games and the practices and everything else that went along with it. I threw myself into it because it was what I needed to keep my mind off your father.

"But it came at a cost. Your brother was always the taga-long. He didn't get to do a lot of things because I couldn't be in two places at once, so he got shunted off to the sidelines to make room for your schedule and my fear of slowing down." She let out a deep sigh.

"Did he tell you why he was upset?" I swallowed past the lump in my throat.

She shook her head. "Not exactly, but I have an idea. He told me it had to do with you, about always coming in second to you."

"How'd I not realize he felt that way until now?"

"Because you're living your life. You're out there doing your own thing, making your own mistakes, blazing your own path. I want you to know this will pass. He'll be okay."

"I need to talk to him."

"Yes, you do. I love you, and I want you to be happy—both of you." She walked around the island and hugged me, kissing me on the cheek. "And I want Olivia to be happy too."

I choked on the cookie in my mouth.

"I'm not blind, you know." She waved her spatula in my direction.

"Mom—"

"I've seen both of you with her, and it doesn't compare. There's a spark there you can't hide—maybe from other people, but not from me, honey." She ran her hand along my cheek. "I know how rare that kind of connection is."

"It doesn't mean I can hurt Grant that way. He's always had a crush on her."

"A playground crush isn't the same as true chemistry and you know it. Don't worry about him. He'll figure things out, and you'll be happy to know, I took back your key." She winked at me. "I need to get things ready for dinner. Do you want some risotto?"

The knot I'd had in my stomach eased up the slightest bit. Maybe the cookie had unlocked it with some magic powers. "Sure."

The timer dinged on the oven, and she took out the next tray of baked goodness.

"Hey, Sylvia—" Liv came to an abrupt stop in the doorway to the kitchen. The smile dropped off her face the second her gaze landed on mine.

"Olivia, come in! I'm so glad you're here." Mom spun

from the counter, sliding the cookies onto the cooling rack, then giving Liv a bear hug.

"I can see you're busy. I'll come back later." Liv backed away.

"Busy? No, I invited you over." Mom's hand waved away Liv's concerns and tugged her into the room. "I'm just talking with Ford."

Liv's gaze darted to mine. My heart thundered in my chest. Had it only been a week since I'd seen her? Heard her voice? It felt like a hell of a lot longer than that. The days had stretched out in front of me in a long winding path without her, and I didn't have a map.

She broke our connection and stood beside my mom at the stove.

"I need to run upstairs and help out one of the teachers who's shorthanded during lunch. Can you stir this risotto, Liv? I figured you'd be sick and tired of sandwiches every time you came by. Keep stirring until the stock is incorporated and then put in another half cup and do it again. You can't stop stirring or it'll ruin it." Mom turned to me and handed over the spatula. "And Ford, can you finish the cookies?"

Liv's mouth hung open, then snapped shut. "Sure, Sylvia." The muscles in her neck jumped. Her hand clasped the wooden spoon in the pot, and she tightened her grip around it like she might snap it at any second. Turning her back to me, she stirred the pot like a portal into hell might open if she stopped.

Mom dropped a hand on my shoulder, nodded toward Liv, and then she was gone. She wasn't pissed, hadn't been the least bit angry. Maybe her heart-to-heart with Grant had helped calm him down.

I'd call him as soon as I left. Picking up the mini ice cream scoop, I stood beside her and dropped dough balls onto the cookie sheet.

Her stirring slowed when I reached into the bowl for another scoop.

The timer dinged, and I picked up the cookie sheet. "I told Colm we need to talk when he gets back."

Liv stepped back and leaned forward to keep up her stirring as I opened the oven. The heat blast from inside washed over both of us. I slipped in the new tray on a lower shelf and took out the finished one, sliding it onto the stove beside the pot Liv stirred. My shoulder brushed against hers.

She swallowed, her throat tightening. "To talk about whatever's come between you two?"

"That's part of it, and also to talk about you."

The spoon jerked in her hand, and a few grains of rice shot out of the pot. She grabbed a towel and wiped up the mess.

"Why me?" Her gaze stayed riveted to the whirling rice and broth.

I swallowed past the lump in my throat. "Whether there's an us or not, I need to tell him how I feel about you."

"That's a terrible idea. Why make this worse?" The spoon in her hand *thunked* against the side of the pot, beating out a steady rhythm. "It's bad enough that Grant got hurt and I've come between you two. I don't want you sacrificing your relationship with Colm too for something we both agreed was a mistake."

"I never said it was a mistake." Stepping in behind her, I grabbed the ladle from the pot on the back burner and poured another cup of stock onto the rice. "Do I wish things had happened differently? Yes, but don't ever think I look back on that night and think it was a mistake."

Taking her free hand in my own, I laced our fingers together. She didn't pull back or jerk away. Maybe we could still fix this.

28

LIV

I stood in front of the wall of mirrors like I had hundreds of times. Sweat dripped down my face as I pushed myself harder and harder. The chill in the air was washed away when my body had hit its limit. The dance studio was the only thing that could bring me out of a funk, but this wasn't a mood brought on by a bad exam grade or the pressure I put on myself about following the path I'd been set on. This was a crushing pain that seeped down deep into my bones.

Ford's words rang in my head. I'd bolted the second Sylvia got back to the kitchen, making my escape. Disentangling his fingers from mine had been like unstitching a part of my soul, but I couldn't breathe when he was so close. I'd closed the door in her shocked face and ran two blocks before ordering a car to come get me. I couldn't go back there. What if Sylvia found out what had happened between me and Ford and Grant and she kicked me out of her life?

I mourned the loss of the refuge in her house. That was what I got, right? That was my penance for crossing a line

I'd known would cause problems. I'd been so blinded by Ford's touch and the need to feel him.

Frustration mounting, I packed up my stuff. With my bag over my shoulder, I walked back to my apartment, trying to lose myself in equations and chemical reactions. Those were easy to understand after a good ninety hours of studying. Another cold snap had hit, and I tightened the collar of my coat as I rounded the corner to my apartment.

I dug my hand into my pocket and looped my finger through my key ring. Pulling it out, I ran through the problem sets I needed to complete tonight. My keys glinted in the fading light, and I looked up. A shock shot straight through me and I couldn't feel my fingers anymore. My keys dropped to the ground. I stood back up, I froze as a figure sitting on the front steps of my building stood. The small panic faded away, replaced by a knot in my stomach. His long, lanky limbs were unmistakable even in the shadow of the setting sun. My heart pounded in my chest, and I swallowed back the guilt welling in my throat.

"Hey, Liv." Grant stood up and shoved his hands into his pockets. His cheeks and nose were red from the lip-blistering winter air.

"How long have you been sitting out here?"

His gaze dropped. "Long enough."

"Why didn't you call me to tell me you were coming?"

"I figured you'd probably look for any chance to get out of seeing me, kind of like the dance you've been doing for the past two years." A pained look shot across his face.

The muscles in my neck tightened. I blinked back the tears building in my eyes. The hurt in his eyes that morning slashed at me. "I'm really sorry. I want you to know that. There's a lot I wish I could change, and hurting you is at the top of that list." I squeezed my lips together.

His face softened. "Can we walk?" He took his hands out of his pockets and held one arm out to the sidewalk.

"Why don't we go inside? It's freezing." I shoved my hands deeper into my pockets.

His gaze swung up to my building. "I'm good with walking, if you are?" He turned back to me with the streetlights catching the uncertainty in his eyes.

I nodded and fell in stride beside him. We walked in silence for a couple blocks. Every few steps, I'd glance over at him, trying to figure out why he'd shown up. The texts I'd sent him had gone unanswered, but he didn't seem angry now. He turned the corner, and I fidgeted with the buttons of my coat.

Looking up, I froze, coming face-to-face with the chain-link fence.

The corner of his mouth lifted. "Saw it on the map. I had a little time to kill while I waited." He walked inside the playground, going right over to the swings and sitting on the hard plastic seat swaying in the wind.

I followed him and sat on the one beside him. The chains rattled as I plopped down on the freezing-cold seat.

He wrapped his fingers around the chains and angled himself sideways. "These things are a lot smaller than I remember." He shifted, trying to fit his lanky body into the seat.

The gentle sound of the links of the chains rubbing against each other as our swings swayed back and forth added a soundtrack to the evening air.

"You've grown a lot since the last time we sat on these."

He pinched his lips together and nodded before taking a big breath. "I wanted to apologize."

"You have nothing to apologize for," I rushed out.

"No, I do—"

"Please—"

"Stop interrupting, Liver." He looked up at me and smiled a little more.

"Sorry." I pushed my feet off the ground, swinging back and forth.

"When I saw you at Ford's—" He broke off and swallowed, staring down at his hand. "I lost it."

I resisted the urge to apologize again, and let him say what he needed to say.

"But you don't owe me anything just because I like you. Just because I've always liked you doesn't mean you have to. I'm not one of those 'nice guy' assholes who turns on a dime the second his feelings aren't returned."

"I know."

"No, you don't, but that's how I felt. I was so angry at both of you, so hurt."

The pain in his voice frayed the edges of my resolve, and I opened my mouth, then snapped it shut when he looked up at me.

"But that was as much to do with me as it was with you two. I knew you didn't feel the same way about me that I felt about you. I've known that since the first day on the playground when I gave up my swing to you and you hugged me. I'll admit, I totally went for it after Declan's wedding when I saw my opening. Ford hurt you, and I thought maybe then I'd have my shot to show you how good we could be together, but I knew from the first kiss, it wasn't lighting you up like it did for me."

My throat tightened, and I blinked back the moisture in my eyes. "I'm sorry."

He shrugged. "It's not like I can force you to care about me."

My hand shot out, and I grabbed his arm. "I do care about you. Of course I do."

"Just not that way."

I stared into his eyes. No more hiding. No more half-truths. I shook my head and dropped my gaze to the frozen wood chips on the ground. "It would have been so much easier if I did."

He let out a chuckle. "Tell me about it, for you and me both. Then I wouldn't have to do this grand gesture of giving you two my blessing."

My head snapped up, and I stared at him wide-eyed.

"Not that you need it. I mean, you don't need my permission for whatever you do, but I wanted you to know I'm okay —" He took a deep breath. "I'll be okay. Just please don't start making out in front of me." He laughed, but the undercurrent of pain was there. "I'm nowhere near ready for that yet."

"Thank you, Grant." I got up and hugged him. "I appreciate it, I really do, but I don't think it makes a difference." My words were muffled by his shoulder.

He jerked back. "Why not?"

"Because I made my decision. I'm going to go to med school, and I need a clean break. I need to start over without all these threads to my childhood I've been trying to hold on to. Maybe I'll go to California or Chicago. I kind of shoehorned myself into Colm's life, taking over his friends and coming back to Philly, and then I'm pissed when he keeps trying to dictate what I do. I need to stop deferring to him and show him that I'm an adult. I need to stop trying to say the words and actually do it."

"I hear you when it comes to constantly living in the wake of someone else's life."

We swung for a few more minutes as the sun set,

sending streaks of light through the gaps between the buildings.

"While this has been fun, I need to get inside before my balls actually fall off my body. It's freezing." Grant hopped off the swing.

"How long were you waiting outside?"

He squeezed the back of his neck. "Too long. If I'd known how long it would be, I'd have taken one of your neighbors up on letting me sit inside the stairwell, but I figured finding me on your doorstep would be more dramatic." He bumped into my shoulder.

I laughed and we walked back to my apartment. On the front steps of my building, I fixed the collar of his coat.

"Thanks for coming to talk to me." I wrapped my arms around his neck.

"Thanks for being a friend." He squeezed me tight, dropping his head into the crook of my neck before straightening up. "I know you said things were done with you and Ford, but he really cares a lot about you. He's beat himself up about that one for a while. I figured he'd never make a move from how much he'd always fought against it."

"Sometimes you fight against things because you know how big of a problem they can be if you give in."

"I'm not standing in the way anymore."

"It's not just you."

Grant's lips thinned into line. "Right, Colm."

"And if I'm trying to prove to him I'm not a kid anymore, falling back into middle-school-crush mode isn't going to help my case. I'll talk to him when he gets back."

"Good luck." Grant waved and walked off down the street.

Climbing the steps to my apartment, I dropped everything the second I stepped inside. The place was quiet. I peered through Marisa's cracked bedroom door. She'd passed out in her bed surrounded by flash cards. Her desk light flickered, so I unplugged it. Small char marks were burned on the outlet. That was the third time this month. I wasn't moving and giving Colm the satisfaction of being right about this place. Making a mental note to send a message to the landlord about all the stuff that was always on the fritz, I tiptoed to my room.

I changed into my pajamas, and while my bed called my name, I opened up my laptop. Firing up the spreadsheet of med schools Colm had sent me almost a year earlier, I stared at the screen. My fingers hovered over the keys. Before I could second guess myself, I deleted every choice listed. A blank slate. My stomach knotted as I pulled up the med school rankings and I filled out the sheet again.

Another seven (or more) years of school. I could do it. How many people would kill to be in the position I was in? I had the chance to become a doctor. I'd worked hard for the grades. I'd worked my ass off and sacrificed every spare minute I could, consistently sitting down and burying myself in the books.

It doesn't make you happy. Well, happiness is overrated.

Happiness had gotten me into this mess. After what had happened to my parents, you'd think I'd have learned happiness was an illusion. I'd been so happy for a spare ten minutes to actually speak with my parents. I'd been happy for one kiss from Ford. I'd been happy with one night in his bed. Maybe that was all I got, little glimpses to keep me going.

Saving lives could make me happy. It was important work. What was more important than holding someone's life in your hands? How long could I really make it as a dance instructor, anyway? Which made more sense in the long run? What was more stable and sensible? Of course it was medicine. It felt like a mistake right now, but in time I'd see it was the right choice. The long hours in the hospital would be more than enough to keep me company. Go in for a thirty-six-hour shift, help people, pass out as soon as I got home, rinse and repeat.

It was time to stop running from the future that had been laid out in front of me. I needed to prove to myself, my parents, and Colm that I could do this. Happiness could come later, and I just had to hope when Ford found someone who didn't come with the baggage I did, I could swallow that suffocating pain of seeing his hands on someone else, plaster on a smile, and be happy for him.

29

FORD

Standing on the porch of the college-row home, I knocked and stepped back from the door. The days were dragging now, each one adding another tally mark to my days without Liv. I shoved my hands into my pockets and rocked back and forth on my heels. Little bits of green stuck up from the branches of the trees lining the street, and I hoped the cold snap wouldn't kill them off. My plane had landed a few hours earlier. Our almost run at the playoffs had died between my shitty goaltending and a general breakdown in team performance. At least that meant no more travel until the next season. Eighty-two games a season didn't get easier.

The door swung open, and one of Grant's roommates took a look at me, then yelled over his shoulder.

"Grant, it's for you." He held the door open, and I stepped inside.

Heavy footsteps on the stairs shook the floor. His steps slowed at the bottom of the stairs when he spotted me.

"What are you doing here?"

"I came to talk."

"There's not much more to say." He crossed his arms over his chest.

"There is."

"Fine, but I need beer for this." He walked past me into the kitchen. Following him, I cleared my throat. He opened the fridge and grabbed two beers. The bottles still inside rattled as he kicked it closed. He flicked the caps off using the edge of the counter and handed me one.

"Thanks." I picked at the label. "Mom said you two talked."

He gulped down some of his beer. "We did."

He leaned against the counter, and I sat on the edge of their table, jammed against the wall.

"Talk," he said sharply. "Or did you come all this way just to bum a beer off me?"

He wasn't going to make this easy, and why should he?

I took a deep breath. "And to apologize."

He stared at me, stone-faced.

"Not for being with Liv. I can't apologize for that." I drummed my fingers along the side of my bottle. "But I should've told you how I felt about her. She's not a dirty little secret, and I shouldn't have treated her like one."

"No, you shouldn't have." Grant gave me a hard look. I met his gaze. He shook his head and stared up at the ceiling.

"I didn't realize how much you felt like you were living in my shadow growing up. It never crossed my mind that Mom being there for me meant she wasn't there for you. I'm sorry. I'm your big brother, and it was selfish of me to not even think about how all that would affect you."

"You're right." He stared at me, and I grimaced. "I spilled it all to Mom, too." He ripped the label off the bottle in his hands. "I have a feeling I'll be getting extra helpings of cookies from now until the end of time. I also told her I was having girl troubles again. I didn't say it was about Liv specifically, but she eventually figured it out."

"She's not exactly subtle. She sprung surprise invites to come over to the house on Liv and me."

"I know." His lips thinned into a hard line. "Damn, I hate being the gracious and understanding brother."

My eyebrows pinched together.

"I already talked to Liv and Mom. You're off the hook, golden boy." He slapped my shoulder.

Shaking my head, I was tempted to slip my finger into my ear and wiggle it to make sure I'd heard him correctly. "Just like that?"

He chuckled and took another sip of his beer. "Not just like that at all. Trust me, there were a good few days where I wanted to beat the crap out of you." As he stared into my eyes, I saw a flash of the anger still in his. "But I had a long talk with Mom, finally got some stuff off my chest that's been bothering me for a long time."

"Stuff like me being the asshole brother who gets all the attention, takes over the family with his cost-and time-intensive sport, and then falls for a girl you've had a crush on since you were ten?"

He nodded. "Something like that, though it's been since I was nine. You have to admit, I did like her first."

"She was nine when you met. I was fifteen. Everyone would have been a hell of a lot more concerned if I'd fallen in love with her back then."

"You're not wrong, and I can't say the fact that she was the one girl I knew you liked who'd agreed to date me didn't play the tiniest part in why she stuck in my head for so many years."

"I can't blame you for that. She's unlike any woman I've ever known before."

He peered over at me. "You love her?"

"I wouldn't have done what I did if I only kind of liked her. I've been in love with her since Declan's wedding, maybe a little before that, but then you two went out on a couple dates and I didn't want to—I didn't want to make it worse. I tried not to."

"And here I thought I was getting the short end of the stick on this one." He drained the rest of his beer. "You're in love with her, and she's dead set on staying away from you. Pretty ironic given how hard you've been pushing her away since forever." Setting his empty down, he looked me dead in the eyes. "She said she doesn't want to come between us, but running off to the West Coast for med school isn't the solution. You haven't been able to talk any sense into her?" He peered over at me.

My stomach dropped. The West Coast? She was leaving? I'd always assumed I'd have more time. She was leaving. Could lungs collapse without anything touching you? Because it was nearly impossible for me to breathe at that moment.

Maybe one day we could get the timing right, smooth things over with Grant and Colm and work it out, but if she left, there was no chance, no "accidental" run-ins. Med school wasn't right for her. She'd be in a new city, doing something she hated, trying to find where she fit.

No one had panic attacks because they loved something so much they couldn't live without it. Grant and I shared a beer, and I left, giving him a big hug before hopping into my car. The night air wasn't freezer-blast cold anymore, but damned if this winter wasn't clinging on for dear life.

I stopped in at Fish's to grab a burger, and a few people spotted me on the way to my spot at the far end of the bar. That hadn't happened before. A couple pictures and an autograph later, I was left alone. While that was normally exactly how I wanted things, now it made me restless. The quiet and solitude meant I didn't have to try to carry on a conversation or pretend to be interested in stuff I didn't like, but I missed conversations with Liv. I got my food wrapped up and headed home.

During our late-night calls, she'd gone on about whatever new dance she was working on or the students in her class. I'd tell her about my search for the next best bottle of bourbon. Even if I had no idea what she was talking about, I was always interested because it was important to her. Her plans might have included med school and a move out of state, but I wasn't going to let her go without a fight.

I lay in bed, staring up at the ceiling and trying to figure out how the hell to get her to see that there was no escaping us. She'd known it earlier than I had, but with how smart she was, I should've known she'd figure it out before me. We belonged together. Colm would have to see reason when it came to us and medical school.

My phone lit up on the table beside me. I glanced down, and my heart skipped a beat. Tapping the button, my heart raced at the name blazed across the screen.

I picked it up. A wail of sirens blared out of the speaker, and my blood thundered through my veins.

"Liv!" I jumped out of bed. The muffled voices made it hard to hear anything other than the sirens and commotion. I shoved my finger into my ear, my heart hammering against my ribs. "Liv!"

"Ford!"

30

LIV

T he commotion going on outside the ambulance felt so far away, like something happening on a movie set. I tried to clear my throat, but that only sent the smoke in my nose shooting deeper down into my lungs, like I'd stuck my head inside a chimney or inhaled the burnt toast Marisa always made. The wail of the sirens had died down. They didn't need them anymore, all the fire trucks having already arrived.

I'd made it out, and that was the most important thing, right? So why did I feel like a part of me had died? Like I'd lost something I'd never be able to get back? I shuddered and wrapped my hands tighter around the scratchy blanket draped over my shoulders. *What time is it?* The paramedic put the stethoscope in his ears.

"Liv!" I heard the voice I'd recognize anywhere, even through the walls of an ambulance. I jumped off the gurney, knocking into the paramedic. "Liv!" The urgency in his voice made my skin break out in goose bumps that had nothing to do with the cold.

Pushing open the doors of the vehicle, I scanned the area for him.

"Ma'am!" The urgent request of the paramedic behind me didn't stop me.

I hopped out of the ambulance. My feet hit the freezing wet pavement, sending a shiver through me. "Ford." My voice croaked. Smoke and droplets of water filled my nose.

"Liv!" His shouts were cut off. I spotted him. What looked like five firefighters and police officers had grabbed hold of him. He was still trying to move forward, toward the burning building. Someone had their arm around his neck to try to keep him back.

"Ford!" Icy water from a puddle slipped into my shoes. Cupping my hands over my mouth, I screamed his name again.

His head whipped around, and the entire weight of the pack shifted and collapsed into the ground. He scrambled out from under the pile of pissed-off first responders, rushing toward me.

Droplets of water created a fine, freezing mist as the battle against the fire raged around me. Everything moved in slow motion. The fog in my head wouldn't lift as I stared at the building I'd called home, engulfed in flames. They'd taken Marisa to another ambulance. I needed to find her. *Where is she?* Hysteria bubbled toward the surface of my mind.

Ford's eyes were wild when he got to me, pushing past anyone in his way. The fear ebbed away a bit now that he was there. His arms wrapped around me, crushing me against his chest. The thundering of his heart pounded against mine. His hold tightened, and I could barely breathe. I banged on his back, and he loosened his grip.

"Are you okay? What happened?" His voice was frantic.

"We got out before it got really bad." It could have been so much worse. We could have died. The tears I'd managed to keep at bay rushed to the surface. A panic I'd pushed aside while I was sitting outside in the blistering cold slammed into me, and I swayed on my feet. *I could have died.*

His hands tightened around my arms. Letting me go for a second, he slipped out of his coat and wrapped it around my shoulders, tugging it around me.

I needed to feel him. Pressing my face against his chest, I sucked in a shuddering breath. "I got into bed after getting back from the studio. I tried to get some sleep. Marisa's light was on the fritz, but stuff like that's been happening for weeks so we didn't think anything of it.

"I finally fell asleep, and then I woke up coughing. When I opened my eyes, I could barely see anything. The smoke was so thick, and I rolled off my bed onto the floor. I slipped on some shoes, picked up my phone, and shouted for Marisa. She sleeps like the dead, and I had to drag her out of her bed. Once she hit the floor, she woke up and we both crawled out of there. There was fire in the stairwell. I thought we were trapped." My fingers trembled as I wrapped my hands around his back. His muscles tightened, and he rested his chin on the top of my head.

He squeezed me even tighter, and this time I needed it. We sat there, wrapped up in each other until the paramedic came over, insisting he finish looking me over.

The paramedic tried to get Ford to go, but he refused to leave my side.

"It's okay. He can stay." My fingers wrapped tighter around his arm.

"I'm not going anywhere." He stared into my eyes with an intensity that snapped me out of my building panic. They closed the back of the ambulance, and the paramedic pulled the stethoscope from around his neck. I focused on my breathing and Ford being so close to keep myself from losing it while they finished the exam. Ford held my hand as the paramedic checked me over. His thumb traced a path along the back of my hand.

His black thermal was stretched tightly over his chest, every muscle on full display. It was a lot easier to distract myself from the thoughts of what could've been by looking at him.

What would Colm have done if something had happened to me? He'd have been all alone. A shiver shot through my body. What the hell would we do without each other? And Ford—what about the things left unresolved between us? There were so many things left unsaid.

"No major smoke inhalation. Your lungs and heart sound fine. You're free to go, if you have somewhere to go, but you need to get to an emergency room immediately if you have any difficulty breathing—and I mean *any*." His eyes bored into me. The seriousness not lost on me, I nodded.

"She's coming home with me." The words shot out of Ford's mouth not even a second after the paramedic finished his sentence.

"I need to find Marisa. I don't know where she is." My phone buzzed on the gurney beside me.

Marisa: I couldn't find you. Are you still here? Are you okay?

I tapped on her name. She picked up in the middle of the first ring.

"I'm fine. They just finished checking me out. Where are you?"

I strained to make out her words. "Outside now. LJ is here, and he's about to get his ass kicked. He's hovering like I'm going to drop dead at any second."

The paramedic opened the door, and Ford held out his hand, guiding my way out of the back of the ambulance. I gasped at the freezing wind whipping around my legs. Pajama pants weren't exactly meant to be worn in temperatures approaching freezing. As I climbed down, her voice was in surround sound. Ford adjusted the blanket around me over his coat, and I swung around the side.

A pair of arms wrapped around me, and Marisa squeezed me against her. Spitting her dark hair out of my mouth, I hugged her back.

"I was so worried when you disappeared on me." She rocked us back and forth.

"I could say the same about you." I leaned back, smiling at her. Tears clouded my eyes.

"Stop crying—you'll make me cry, and then he'll lose it again." LJ stood close by her shoulder like he was ready to swoop in if her legs gave out. "He's trying to get me to go back to the Brothel, but I'm not leaving you here."

"Liv can come too." His baritone filtered through the noise around us.

"It's okay. I know the football house is cramped as it is. I'm going to go with Ford." I peered over my shoulder at him.

He stared into my eyes. "She's coming with me. You can too, if you need to," he offered to Marisa.

"I'm good. I'll go with LJ." Marisa eyed me. "Are you sure?" We'd spent more than a few hours over the past couple weeks rehashing my last night with Ford.

"I'm sure."

"Then I'll see you on campus? We need to figure out a more permanent living situation and what the hell we're going to do about our stuff..." She stared up at the still smoldering building.

A pit plunged deep in my stomach. Our stuff...my pictures... I wrapped my arms tighter around myself.

"Let's just get through the night and figure everything else out tomorrow. I need to take a shower. I reek of smoke." Marisa pulled her shirt away from her body

I sniffed my hair. "And I need to go to sleep." My energy ebbed away, drained like a vampire had attached itself to my neck. Adrenaline no longer coursed through my veins, leaving me dead on my feet. The wind at my front competed with the heat radiating off the building behind me in between blasts of wind.

Ford wrapped his arm around my shoulder and tucked me in close to his side. He was so warm. I slid my arms around his waist, and he wrapped the edge of his coat tighter around me as we navigated through the crowd and news crews to get to his car.

He opened the door, and I slipped inside. Resting my head against the headrest, my eyelids fluttered. He got in, and the engine started with a purr. It still had that new car smell.

My eyelids got heavier by the second as the streetlights filled the car with a rhythmic yellow strobe.

"Get some sleep, Liv. I'll wake you when we're home." His hand ran along my leg from my knee to my thigh like he was trying to warm me quicker than the heater. *Home.* Home with Ford.

I yawned and turned in my seat to face him. The soft fabric cushioned my cheek. His beard had grown longer. I hadn't watched the games since *the* night, but I knew their season was over. I couldn't help but feel partially responsible.

He glanced over from staring straight out the windshield and ran his hand along the side of my face. "Close your eyes.

You're safe now." His strong fingers tucked my hair behind my ear. Dropping his hand back to my leg, he held on to me like he was afraid I might disappear into a cloud of smoke, and I supposed I almost had.

Now I was going home with Ford, and we'd figure everything else out in the morning.

Careful not to wake her, I lifted her from the car. My heart drummed against my chest as I carried her into the elevator and into my apartment. It took everything in me not to crush her to my chest. I could've lost her tonight. She didn't stir the entire time. The adrenaline crash was a bitch. Kicking the front door closed behind me, I took her into my bedroom. Laying her down, I got up to get her something to sleep in, and her hand shot out and wrapped around my wrist.

"Don't go," she murmured.

"I'm not going anywhere. I'm just getting you something to wear. Your clothes are all smoky."

She looked down at herself and her soot-covered clothes, then tore at them like they were on fire.

"Shhh, let me do it." Catching her legs, I slid her shoes off. They hit the floor with a *thunk*. I hooked my hands under the waistband of her pajama pants and dragged them down her body. She stopped flailing and watched me, lifting her hips to help me get her undressed. Tears glittered in her eyes.

Her sweatshirt and T-shirt were tangled with my coat still half on her. I peeled all the layers off until she was completely bared to me, slowly and methodically checking her over even though I knew the paramedic had already done it.

"Do you want to get cleaned up so you can sleep better?"

"Can you come with me?"

"Of course." I picked her up from the bed and walked her into the bathroom. She rested her head against my shoulders, her hand braced on my arm. I never wanted her to leave the safety of my embrace again.

"Let's get you in the shower to get all the smoke off you."

She nodded. "Then can I have a bath?"

"Anything you need." I cupped my hand to her cheek.

"Will you get in with me?"

Even inside my apartment, there was fear in her eyes, the kind of haunted look I couldn't have turned away from even if I'd wanted to. I set her down and turned on the water.

Without another word, I kicked off my shoes, shoved down my jeans and shorts, and then whipped my shirt up over my head. I turned on the water for the bathtub to let it fill. Taking her hand, I walked her into the shower, running it over her body and hair. The water beaded on her skin and soaked into her hair. When all the sooty streaks on her skin were gone, I let her out of the shower.

She slipped into the warm water of the tub without waiting for it to fill completely. I grabbed us a couple towels and a washcloth, setting them beside the tub. The tension in my shoulders eased as she closed her eyes and laid her arms along the ledge.

I ran back to my room and grabbed a T-shirt from my drawer for her, then darted back into the bathroom.

She had her knees pulled up to her chest, and her head rested on top of them. Sitting on the edge, I slid in behind her. The water rose along the sides, and she turned it off when it threatened to crest over the edge.

When she sat back down, it was directly on top of my lap. The erection I'd been trying to keep at bay was now nestled between the soft globes of her ass.

"Sorry, just pay him no attention and he'll go away." I took the washcloth and rubbed soap on it before running it over her back.

"Maybe I don't want him to go away." She braced her hands on the side of the tub and lifted herself to angle my dick straight for her opening. Even in the swirling water of the tub, I could feel her wetness coating my head.

I wrapped my arm around her waist. "Liv, you're tired, and you've been through a lot tonight."

"I know. I could've died." Her voice cracked.

Tugging her close to me, I wrapped both arms around her, but she had other ideas. When I moved, she shifted her hips and sank down onto me. She clenched around me, and I groaned. The electric ecstasy of being inside her again nearly snapped my control.

Bear-hugging her against my chest, I nipped at her shoulder and squeezed tighter when her ass was fully seated on my lap, her tight, velvety hold sending blissful shudders throughout my body.

"We skipped a few steps." I ran my teeth along the curve of her neck.

"There'll be plenty of time to make up for that. But right now, I need you." She stared at me over her shoulders.

As if I could deny her anything. Lifting her, I drove my cock harder into her. My arms were braced across her chest, and she held on. I dropped one of my hands into the water and ran my fingers along her clit.

"I knew you had it in you to improvise." Her laughter bounced off the walls of the tiled bathroom. Water sloshed over the edge of the tub as our fevered motions increased.

"I'm not going to miss a single opportunity to make you come." I pinched her clit, and she hissed. Her legs shot forward, and her pussy clamped around my driving cock. I bit back a curse and kept up my rhythm. Her fingers dug into my forearm, but I kept going, determined to shove the bad memories from her mind.

"Ford!" she screamed and shook against me. The brutal grip on my dick nearly pushed me over the edge. I drew out her pleasure but left her sensitive clit alone. Teasing and pinching, I rolled her nipples between my fingers as she shuddered in my arms.

My fingers ran over her stomach, stroking her as I slipped into a more leisurely pace, changing the angles of my thrusts. Her head dropped onto my shoulder, and she shook as a slow, steady orgasm coursed through her.

As she reached another peak, I let myself go and squeezed her tighter against me, pumping into her. Her soft pants bounced off the tile walls.

"I'll always be here for you. Don't ever think I'd be better off without you." I hugged her against me, wishing I was looking into her eyes.

She nodded. Her damp hair rubbed against my chest.

I grabbed the cloth and soap again. Her eyelids fluttered as I washed her up. I helped her out of the tub, careful of the water spilled all over the floor, and toweled her off. Sliding the T-shirt over her head, I let my fingers skim over her skin. I took her hand and got her into my bed, exactly where she belonged.

∽

I'd never been happier the season was over. We stayed in bed for a solid two days. Jack begrudgingly supplied us with burgers from Fish's, and I dug out my laptop and set it up in the bedroom so we could watch movies. Take-out boxes littered the floor around my bed. The first night, she'd woken with nightmares, and I'd taken the long, leisurely route to banishing those thoughts from her mind with panting, soul-shattering orgasms.

She nibbled on her bottom lip, sitting cross-legged on the center of my bed. I lay back with my head propped up on my arms behind my head. My gaze tracked every parting of her lips as she tried to get her thoughts together. The gears were turning in her head.

"I'm not going to med school," she blurted out.

Keeping my expression neutral, I sat up. "Why not? Grant said you'd made up your mind."

"I had. I'd started looking up application deadlines, even finished a few online the night of...you know." She picked at the blankets beneath her.

"What changed between then and now?"

She looked at me. "The fire. I was so sure going down that path was the safest. It was what was expected of me. It was the path I needed to take to prove to myself that I could do it, and when I was choking on the smoke and crawling out of my apartment with the whole world on fire around me, do you know what went through my head?"

"Run?"

She smiled and lobbed a pillow at my head. "Well, after that. It was you. It was you and Colm, Heath, Declan, Mak, Kara, Emmett, Avery, Sylvia—" Her throat tightened. "Grant. It was that I wouldn't be able to dance again if something happened to me. I wouldn't get to touch you again, and I wouldn't get to make margaritas for everyone or kick your ass at Scrabble. That's what's most important to me. That's what I need to cherish, not run away from by burying myself in my books for the next seven years and never having enough time for anyone. I always wanted to be like my parents, but I don't want that anymore. They weren't ever there for me and Colm, not like they should've been. Trying to live up to some ideal they had in their minds is insane. I don't want that."

"Good." I covered the back of her hand with mine. "You'd be an amazing doctor, but that's not who you were meant to be."

"Now I just have to figure out how to tell Colm." She flopped back on the bed, sending her hair flying across my bed in a golden cascade.

"We can do it together." I threaded my fingers through hers and tugged her across my lap. "Then you can teach me a few moves, and maybe I'll join in on your next class. I can be your assistant."

She threw her head back. "I thought you hated people staring at you."

"For you, I'd make that sacrifice." I sat up and peppered her face with kisses. Her laughter was the most beautiful thing in the world, and I'd spend the rest of my life making sure she did it every day.

I jumped out of bed and fished out some sweatpants for her. After cinching them at the waist and rolling up the legs about ten times, they were serviceable. I needed to get her some clothes, not that I didn't love watching her walk around my apartment in my clothes—or better yet, in nothing.

Standing side by side in the kitchen, we made breakfast.

Music blared from my phone, and we danced as we cooked sausages and eggs. Toast popped up out of the toaster, and she took over buttering duty.

We sat at the table, both eating with one hand, staring out the window and watching the clouds part, revealing a beautiful blue sky. Sitting in separate chairs after being in bed almost constantly felt too far apart. She rubbed her thumb over the back of my hand. I wanted this for the next seventy years. She drained the last of her juice; then I lifted her plate and stuck it in the dishwasher. Liv's phone went off on the counter. She picked it up and crunched on the last piece of bacon.

My phone pinged with each incoming message to the group chat someone must have set up. I scrolled to the top of the chain.

Mak: Liv! We saw the news, are you okay?

Avery: Liv, where are you?

Kara: This happened 2 days ago and we're just now finding out?!

Declan: Do you need anything?

Heath: Is this you trying to get out of your exams?

Liv: I'm fine, thanks for checking in on me.

Emmett: Where are you?

Kara: Are you safe?

Liv: I'm safe.

She paused and glanced over at me.

Liv: I'm staying with a friend.

Mak: Do you need clothes? Do you need to replace your text-books? Email your professors?

Liv: All of that, but I can handle it.

Avery: At least let us take you to get some new clothes. *Hugs*

Emmett: Avery volunteering to shop. Hell yes, take my credit card!

Me: She can use mine

Heath: Welcome to the convo, sleeping beauty!

My lips pinched together.

Liv: Thank you for all the offers, but I know everyone is busy.

Mak: Don't even try it. Hockey season is over. Tell us where you are and we'll come get you.

Her head shot up, and her eyes got wide.

Liv: I can meet you in Rittenhouse Square.

Kara: In an hour?

Liv: Perfect!

I wrapped my arms around her from behind.

Liv: And can everyone please not tell Colm? He'll only freak out and fly back here when there's no reason for him to.

Everyone replied that they'd keep it to themselves.

"I was going to take you shopping."

She laughed and pushed against me, no doubt feeling the insistent nudge of my cock against her back.

"I'd prefer to not get arrested for indecent exposure."

Nibbling on her earlobe, I palmed her ass. "I'm incredibly discreet."

Turning in my arms, she ran her hands along the sides of my face. "I have no doubt of that, but it will be good for me to see them. Maybe I'll even pick up a couple surprises for you." She winked.

I searched online for somewhere we could go once Liv's semester ended, somewhere to take a break and reset, leave our phones at home and just be together.

My phone rang beside me. Sliding my finger across the screen, I lifted it to my ear.

"Have you seen Liv?"

"Hi, Colm. I have. She's shopping with the girls right now."

"Shopping? She doesn't have enough clothes?"

I gritted my teeth. He didn't know about the situation, and I'd promised Liv I wouldn't tell him.

"She's tagging along. A break will be good for her. She's worked hard this semester."

"But she can do better."

"Why are you always on her case? It's a nonstop barrage of expectations and never good enough with you. Give her some space."

"What the hell makes you an authority on this? She's my sister. I want what's best for her."

"You want what's best for you. You want her to cut a piece of her heart out to fulfill this ideal vision you have in your head that doesn't exist." I shouldn't have said it, but she'd been through a disaster and had almost died. She needed a break from his pressure before she broke.

"Is that what she's telling you?"

"She doesn't need to. Anyone who's seen her dance knows how important it is to her."

He scoffed. "That's not a real career."

"Maybe it can be. She's a hell of a teacher, and she can do whatever she needs to for that to work."

"She doesn't teach. This is not up to you."

"It's not up to you either. It's up to her, and she'd go through with med school just to please you." Jumping up out of my chair, I threw my hand up in the air. "She'd put herself under soul-crushing pressure for something she doesn't want. You should be happy she's not going to med school because if she were, it would be halfway across the country to get away from you and your expectations. You're trying to shove her into that little kid box and run her life, and what you're doing is pushing her away." My heavy breath filled the silence of the room.

He was quiet for a moment. "She's not going to med school?"

I winced and squeezed my eyes shut. *Fuck!*

Dragging my hand through my hair, I collapsed into my chair. "Out of everything I just said, that's what you focus on? You're pushing her away and pushing her too hard."

"I'll see her when I land at the end of the week." He ended the call, and I dropped my head. Add another point to the column of Ford fuckups.

I had the next couple of hours to go over it in my head. The front door swung open, and I berated myself as I took a deep breath. Liv came back from shopping with a few bags filled to the top, and I dropped the oven mitts at the distress on her face.

She set the bags down and backed away from them like they were filled with live snakes. "They said it was payback for all the makeovers I've done for them over the years." She picked at her thumb. "I kept saying I didn't need this much. I told them I'll get new credit cards from the bank. I can replace all my stuff myself..."

A rainbow of colors and fabrics spilled out of the bags.

"They're worried and wanted to do something nice for you. You've been through a lot. They want to spoil you." I wrapped my arm around her and skimmed my fingers along her collarbone. "I want to spoil you."

The final triumphant music drifted from the laptop, and the scene cut to black. Names scrolled up the blank screen. The Wet Bandits had always freaked me out when I was little, but watching it now, Kevin McCallister pretty much committed attempted murder at least fifteen times in that movie. Ford made fun of me for still watching through the credits. These people had contributed to the movie, so the least I could do was watch their names run across the screen.

"I can't believe you don't have a TV in your bedroom," I shouted, scrolling my finger across the trackpad on his computer.

"My living room is literally three steps from my bedroom," he called out over the bedroom wall that stopped ten feet up.

"But you don't have a bed in your living room."

"I'm not putting a TV in the bedroom." The microwave beeped. Buttery, salty goodness floated through the air into the lofted bedroom. The sounds of Ford banging around in the kitchen filtered in as well.

Laid out in the middle of the bed, I scrolled through the list of movies to find another one. Movies and binging tv shows had helped keep me distracted, not to mention Ford's own distraction techniques.

I'd been on a strict communications embargo since the fire. Everything seemed so much louder and more chaotic since that night. I needed to be tucked away in a cocoon. The calls from Colm were getting to be too much. I sent him a text.

Me: I love you, I'm dealing with some stuff right now, and I need you to trust me that it will all be okay.

Lying to him had never come naturally; therefore there was only one solution. I turned off my phone. *Ha!* And he thought I wasn't a good problem solver. He'd be in town at the end of the week, and I could sit him down then to talk it all over in person. Actually, maybe that wasn't such a good idea.

Maybe I could send a carrier pigeon and have it deliver a note from me while he was at the airport in LA. Being locked inside a metal tube for eight hours was bound to help him cool down. Nowhere to run. Or I'd suck it up and have the conversation, get him to understand how much forging my new path meant.

The neck of Ford's oversize T-shirt—well, oversize on me —hung down over my shoulder. Ford bathed my neck in kisses, raining them down over me and setting my skin aflame. He slid the bowl of popcorn onto the table beside the bed and closed the laptop. "What are you thinking about?"

I turned my head and he captured my lips never missing a beat. How had I gone weeks without this? "You," I whispered against his mouth.

"You're going to have a hard time getting rid of me now."

My stomach flipped. I didn't ever want to be rid of him. It wasn't just the way he spoke to my body; it was the life he breathed into my soul. There was a part of me that came alive whenever he looked deep into my eyes.

Unhooking my bra, which I'd only had on for about twenty minutes, he made a disapproving sound and pulled it from around my body. His fingers dipped under the soft jersey cotton, and he shoved the shirt up to my neck. My skin broke out in goose bumps as the cool air rushed over my breasts. He lowered his lips to my nipple, sucking it into his mouth and teasing it with his teeth.

I gasped and ran my hands along his back. My pussy throbbed, clenching and calling out for attention. I ran my hands through his hair, tightening my grip with each nip. He switched sides, rolling my nipple between his teeth and swirling his tongue around my taut peak.

Lifting more of his weight, he sank lower, dropping down my body until his fingers toyed with the waistband of the sweatpants I still wore even though I had my own now. Like the pants and underwear weren't even there, he had them both down and off me in no time, tossing them over his shoulder.

He ran his hands down my thighs. "There are three more days until I need to leave this apartment. I'm keeping you in bed until then."

"What about my classes?" I pushed up on my elbows.

"Fine, you can go to class, but I'm picking you up from there and bringing you right back here." Sparks of excitement rushed through my body. When we were apart, touching myself had only made me think of him and of our near-nightly calls that had always ended with me screaming my release into my pillow. I didn't need to muffle my sounds now. He rested his hand on my stomach and nudged my knees apart with his shoulders.

"What about studying?" My words came out in shuddering pants.

"The only one studying will be me—studying every inch of you and trying to see how many ways I can make you come." He trailed his fingers from my stomach and teased my clit.

I stared at him between my legs with my head swimming. Hooking his hands behind my knees, he lifted my legs, opened them wide, and pushed them up toward my chest. I was completely exposed and at the mercy of the delicious promise in his eyes. If I made it through the night without losing all of myself to him, it would be a miracle.

My muscles clenched in anticipation of his touch. His breath skimmed across the wetness coating my thighs and pussy.

"I've missed you."

I laughed, and his gaze snapped to mine. "Are you talking to me or my pussy?"

"Both," he growled before dropping his head, painting my opening with his tongue. My body trembled as he sucked on my clit in a long pulsing rhythm that made my toes curl. I clawed at the bed beneath me and screamed, digging my heels into his shoulders. He dropped one hand from behind my knee. Using his thumb, he rubbed my clit and sank two fingers into me, plunging them deep and stretching me, but nothing filled me up like his cock.

"You know what I want."

My thighs tightened around his head, the soft brush of his beard scraping against my oversensitive skin. My back arched off the bed, and I screamed his name. It echoed off the industrial-height ceiling, and I bucked against him. Planting one more kiss on my clit, he let go of my legs. I shuddered and dropped them to the cool blankets beneath me.

He kissed his way up my body and to my mouth. The heft of his erection nudged my already slick folds open.

Lifting his body, he caged me beneath him. The grind of his hips meant I never fully recovered from my last orgasm.

"You didn't say you missed me too." His latex-covered head stretched me. Guiding it in like a heat-seeking missile, he didn't even need his hands.

"It's been days. I thought you knew." My eyes rolled back, and my eyelids fluttered. I gasped at his sharp thrust and moaned. Hitching my legs around his waist, I opened myself even more, digging my heels into his muscled ass.

"You need to say it." He nipped at my chin.

His pubic bone ground against my clit, sending toe-curling shots of pleasure racing through my body. I clawed at the bedding beneath me and at his back, at the fabric bunching under my grip.

"I missed you too." I slipped my arms under his and grabbed the backs of his shoulders. I bit down on his shoulder, screaming into him as I shook and shuddered. His thrusts sped up, grinding into me and drawing out my orgasm until my vision winked in and out.

He tightened his grip around my back, groaning into my neck. The pulsing of his cock sent another orgasm ripping through me. I was coming apart at the seams. Unraveling at the unending climax that stole my breath away.

Rolling to his side, his throat worked up and down. He pulled me in close against his chest. Our hearts pounded in unison as we came down from the explosive high.

I rested my head against his chest and ran my fingers

along his skin. Contentment settled in deep to the cracks in my soul I hadn't known were there. There was no restlessness or worry that I needed to do something. There was only the rise and fall of his chest and his complete possession of my heart.

Leaning over the center console, I kissed Ford again. He held on to the back of my neck and pulled me over onto his lap. I jumped at the sharp horn honk when my hip banged into the steering wheel.

"I'm taking you out for your birthday tonight."

I grinned. "You remembered."

"I could never forget."

"With everything that's happened, *I* almost forgot about it. The girls reminded me when we were shopping, and they already beat you to the punch—Mak and the guys invited me to go out with them. When I turned my phone back on, Marisa was so pissed." I'd make it up to her.

He tightened his arms around me and rubbed his nose against mine. "Then I get to take you for your first drink."

I pecked him on the lips and reached for the door handle. "Deal!" Flinging it open, I hopped out of the car. If I didn't make a break for it, we'd end up making out in the car. "I'll call you when I'm finished." I pushed the door closed, and he rolled down the window. Leaning in, I ran my fingers through his hair. "Only a couple hours."

"You sure you don't want me to wait with you?"

I laughed and rested my forehead against his. "I can handle it. Meeting with my dean isn't the hard conversation. This feels right, like a phoenix reborn from the ashes." If I hadn't been up late and smelled the smoke or had smelled it but had brushed it off like the other times that burning smell invaded our apartment, where might I have been right then? Dread bubbled up, and I shoved it down. The what-ifs would only drive me crazy. They'd driven me crazy after my parents died, and I wasn't going to do that to myself. These were the first steps in my new life.

"Go do your thing and I'll be here when you're finished."

I let go and stepped back onto the curb in front of my academic dean's building, I waved to Ford. He stared back at me as I climbed the steps. This should've been scary. It should've been insanity. Changing majors at the end of junior year? Who does that? Me, that's who.

My leg bounced up and down in the waiting area. This was what I wanted. What was there to be nervous about?

My mouth was so dry I grabbed a paper cup and filled it to the top. The receptionist called my name. I choked on my water, spewing it all over my shirt. My palms were clammy and felt like I'd been running them under a faucet.

The dean opened his door and invited me in to take a seat. My hands shook, and I perched on the edge of the chair. Taking a deep breath, I word vomited the whole thing out before he could say a word.

Completely out of breath, I sat back in my seat and braced myself for the judgment.

"I'm glad you're safe. If you need anything from this office or your professors, please let us know. We're here to make sure you're not handling this difficult time alone."

"I have friends and family helping me out."

"Good, but don't hesitate to send a message. I'm not just saying it to be nice."

I nodded.

"What major were you thinking?" He turned halfway in his chair and clicked away at his computer.

"That's it? You're not going to try to talk me out of it?"

"Do you know how many premed students come in here needing a new major? You're not the first, and you certainly won't be the last. I can't say most of them have anywhere near the grades you do, but only a small percentage of people who think they want to be doctors go on to be doctors. Don't worry about it." He waved his hand like it was no big deal.

A giddy laugh burst free from my lips.

"Not the first one of those I've heard either. With your grades and some of the electives you've squeezed in, you can switch majors to just about anything. You'll need to take some summer classes depending on which you choose. There are a lot offered online now, but you'll still be able to walk at graduation with the rest of your class. What did you have in mind?" He spun in his chair to fully face me.

My mouth hung open, and I racked my brain. With medicine off the table, I drew a blank. *Nice going, Liv.* I could've at least actually come up with a plan for what the hell would come next.

I blurted out the first thing that came to mind.

Thirty minutes later I was officially a business major. I ran down the steps, practically skipping. Business was the perfect combination I needed. I wouldn't want to teach forever, but running my own dance school had some real possibilities. Maybe that would convince Colm I was serious about this. I wouldn't just be a dance teacher, but a business owner.

The money in the trust was sitting there, and now I had a plan for what I could do with it. Any fear about what I'd do when I wasn't on the path set out for me melted away.

With a couple of online summer classes, my graduation would be delayed until the next summer, but that wasn't a big deal.

Any course load after the one I'd just taken would be a cake walk. I'd finish out the last of this semester strong to keep my GPA up, and a new chapter of my life would start in the summer.

I grabbed my phone and tapped on my contacts.

She picked up on the first ring, sounding groggy even though it was after two p.m.

"Are you still asleep?"

I jerked the phone away from my ear at her massive yawn.

"You try getting any sleep when these guys have parties so often it's like they think it's an Olympic sport."

I laughed. "The Brothel not the bastion of quiet nights you expected?"

Marisa sighed. "I didn't believe them when they said the parties appear out of thin air, but I've seen it happen. Now I believe. People bring their own kegs and just set them up in the living room. It's insane."

"Other than getting no sleep, how are you?"

"Hiding indoors. I got extensions on any work I had due this week, so I'm hibernating and making LJ feed me to keep his overprotective tendencies in check."

"I'm glad he's there for you."

"Me too." I could barely make out the words. "How are you handling the study disruption? Have you made Ford create a study den for you at his place?"

"Nope, I just left the dean's office. Guess who's a business major now."

"About freaking time! If I had to hear about your obligation to become a doctor one more time, I was going to strangle you."

"Hey!" I stepped off the curb and walked across the street toward the coffee shop right off campus.

"The landlord called and said we should be able to get into our place to see what might be recoverable tomorrow."

The heat of the flames licking at my arms as we rushed down the stairs came back to me. What would be left? "That's number one on the list of things I don't ever want to do."

"Not all of us can replace all our worldly possessions at a moment's notice."

I cringed at how shitty my words had sounded. "Sorry."

"Don't worry about it. You're allowed one privileged rich girl comment every so often. I'm fine sporting LJ's boxers and T-shirts until my next paycheck comes in."

Now I really felt like a shitty friend. "We can go shopping once my new cards arrive. Think of it as a birthday present for me."

"I thought *I* was supposed to give you something for your birthday."

"Nah, I get to choose what I want, and I want to get you some stuff."

"I'd normally say no, but seeing as most of my stuff is probably a charred pile of rubble, I'll let it slide this time. So, where am I taking you for your birthday?"

"The Kings are taking me out. I can send you a message on where to meet once they tell me."

"Sounds good. Someone just left the bathroom. These guys are worse than chicks and I need to take a shower, so I gotta go. Talk later." She ended the call, and I ordered my coffee.

Maybe Ford would be up for a vacation somewhere. We

could spend the summer in a place with a good Internet connection so I could take my class, and we could laze by the pool, eat amazing food, and spend as much time as we wanted in bed. Whatever it was, things were finally falling into place. I couldn't wipe the grin off my face. Everything was perfect.

33

FORD

I'd tried to call Colm, but he let every call ring out. Liv wasn't freaking out, so I hoped that meant he'd decided to stick to what I'd asked him to do and wasn't going to say anything to Liv until he landed, until I'd gotten a chance to talk to him.

She stepped out of the bathroom and did a twirl in the hallway. Her makeup made her look like Liv, but not Liv.

"I told you I had a surprise." She rested her hands on my chest, and in her heels, she didn't have to stand on tiptoes to kiss me. I wrapped my arms around her. My hands traced up and down her back. The smooth fabric glided under my touch, and I wanted to peel it off her with my teeth.

"What if we just stayed here for your birthday? I'm sure I can make it a celebration you won't forget."

"Don't even think about it. I'm going out for my first legal drink and you're buying it for me, remember?" she said against my lips. She tasted like strawberries.

"If that's what you wanted, maybe you shouldn't have worn that dress." I palmed her ass and lifted her up on her toes.

Laughing, she pushed against my chest until I let her down, and then she picked up her bag. "Let's go." She led the way across the street, and I rested my hand on the small of her back, guiding her into Fish's.

Her tight green dress turned more than a few heads. I was equal parts proud and ready to growl at anyone who looked too long, but she was on my arm for the night, and she'd be in my bed in a few hours.

Jack dropped off a couple of glasses at my usual spot on the far end of the bar. I picked them both up and held one out to her.

She stepped in closer, the light catching the color of her eyes and reflecting off her dress, illuminating her like a jewel.

"Thank you for my first legal drink." Her lips curled in a mischievous smirk, the same kind she knew drove me crazy. Letting her fingers linger on mine, she took the glass from my hand.

The background noise of the bar faded away. Our quiet little corner became my whole world. There were no booths back there. It was my favorite spot where, even if it got busy, I never had anyone around me.

"Happy birthday." I kissed out each syllable against the side of her face. Fish's was the perfect place to take her for her first drink. It was quiet, although a recent review from the *Philly Mag* about its quaint off-beatness had brought in new arrivals.

Flashes went off at the front of the bar as people took selfies and pictures of their plates. Apparently bar food that actually looked like bar food was the new trendy thing. A couple heads had turned when we'd walked in, but other than that, no one seemed to notice me, which was just how I liked it. I didn't want to deal with fans on this night, not when I had so many plans for Liv.

"I say we skip the group celebration and just go back to the apartment." She traced her hands along the bottom of my shirt. Her fingers skimmed my skin, and blood rushed to my cock.

I wrapped my fingers around her wrist. "Is this a test? You're the one who wanted to come out. You're not going to tempt me."

The noise of the crowd got louder, and more flashes went off at the front of the bar. The place was turning into a photo shoot.

"What's the fun if I don't?" She lowered her hand, bringing mine with it. Angling her back to block the view of anyone nearby, she slipped my hand between her thighs.

I traced my fingertips along the soft skin between her legs. I cupped one hand over her ass to keep her dress down and ran my fingers higher. She sucked in a shuddering breath and wrapped her hands around my forearm.

Bracing my back against the wall, I stared into her eyes. They burned with a desire I'd come to know so well, one I had tasted on my lips and couldn't wait to taste again. I pushed my fingers higher and brushed against her bare skin. She wasn't wearing any panties. The evidence of how much she liked my teasing coated her inner thighs. My thumb brushed along the seam of her pussy.

She let out a long breath and her hold tightened on my arm.

"Once I get you home, I'm not stopping until I've wrung every last orgasm from you." I ran my other hand along the back of her neck and pressed my mouth against her ear. Wetness coated my fingers, and I pushed two inside her. Her pussy clenched around my invading digits.

She licked her lips. "Is that a challenge?"

Her body trembled and her knees dipped. I wrapped my arm around her and held her up. "I'm going to spend the whole night with the smell of you on my fingers. Every time I take a drink or a bite to eat, I'll be thinking about you and making my plans for what happens when my front door closes behind me."

Her lips parted, and she stared back at me with a dazed look in her eyes. She rocked harder against me.

I flicked my thumb across her clit, and she stifled her moan. My cock strained against my jeans, but the discomfort was totally worth it. I ran my thumb along her jaw; her pulse thundered against my palm. My dick throbbed at her soft mewling and the way she barely maintained her composure. Her ankles wobbled in her high heels. I cupped her pussy and dragged my thumb across her clit again.

She shook and her hand shot out, grabbing my shirt. Clutching the fabric in her fist, her back bowed and her eyes fluttered shut.

"I think you liked that," I whispered against her ear.

Her low moan and almost collapse into my arms confirmed it. I tugged down the skirt of her dress, making sure no one got a flash.

"I think I've created a monster." She laughed and rested her cheek against my shoulder.

The taxi pulled up to the curb of the club. Liv looped her arm through mine, and the bouncer lifted the velvet rope. We walked inside past the long line of people stretched down the block. The music thumped and pounded, slamming into my chest.

"Do they have to make it so loud?" I stuck my finger into my ear.

"Says the old man." She bumped her hip into my leg. "That's the whole point—to make it so loud no one can think about their bad decisions."

Tugging me across the dance floor, she walked up the steps to a small raised area that was roped off. The people around us moved like an undulating sea of drunken mayhem. She let go of my hand, and I fought back the urge to grab hold of it again.

Telling everyone else about us before we told Colm wasn't right. The rest of the night was strictly hands off. I ran my hand over my chin and smelled her on me. It was as intoxicating as any drink. I'd be Liv drunk by the end of the night.

She waved to the Kings plus their queens beyond the rope, and the second level bouncer let us through. Everyone wore grim looks on their faces. Glancing over her shoulder at me, her eyebrows dipped.

I shrugged.

"Why do you guys look like you just found out the truth about Santa?" She grinned at them.

Their eyes darted between the two of us, and my stomach sank. They knew.

Emmett pulled out his phone and handed it to Avery like he didn't want to be the one to deliver the news directly. Avery slid it into Liv's hand as Mak and Kara closed ranks, wrapping their arms around Liv's shoulders.

I moved in closer, and Declan shoved his hands against my chest, keeping me back. "What the fuck is going on?" I asked.

"It's not good." Heath shook his head and looked like someone had told him he couldn't stargaze anymore. He almost always found a way to look on the bright side of things, so him not doing so now had a ball of dread forming in my stomach.

Liv's hands shot to cover her face, and Emmett's phone dropped to the plush navy carpet. Knocking everyone out of the way, I gently wrapped my hands around her arms. "What is it?" I looked from her to the video replaying on the screen on the floor.

Bile rose in my throat as I watched the intimate moment between us at the bar replaying on social media.

"Shit!" Liv stared up at me, and I folded my arms around her. I'd failed her, had been so stupid. There were cameras everywhere, all the time, and I knew that. I'd lived that.

I'd been too lax at Fish's when I should have kept my guard up. I knew I should always keep it up when it came to protecting Liv.

The ladies spirited her off to the bathroom. I sank into the leather couch that ran the length of the cordoned-off area and dropped my head into my hands.

"I take it this means you two are a thing?" Heath rocked back and forth on his heels and rubbed the back of his neck.

I nodded.

Emmett cleared his throat. "You might want to break that to Colm sooner rather than later, especially if this is floating around out there."

Floating around—that sounded so casual, like it was no big deal that anyone with a phone could pull up a video of her holding on to me as I teased her, like I didn't already have enough to tell Colm, secrets that gnawed until the only thing left was bruised and beaten limbs.

Everything around me moved like we'd been plunged into the ocean. Maybe that was why I felt like the air in my lungs had been replaced by water from the inky deep. I shot up from the couch and followed after where the girls had disappeared to.

Knocking on the bathroom door, I squinted as the bright light from inside poured into the small hallway. Avery opened the door, her lips tight in a grim line.

"How is she?"

She opened the door wider and lifted her chin with her eyes darting back into the room behind her. My stomach knotted. I wanted to run to Liv and break something at the same time, wanted to go back to Fish's and tear the place apart, then dismantle the phone of whoever had done this.

Kara and Mak stood protectively outside the only closed stall. Their arms were crossed over their chests like sentries at their posts. My stomach knotted and my footsteps echoed along to the distant muffled beat of the club. People were outside laughing, dancing, and drinking like our world hadn't been flipped on its head, like someone hadn't stolen a moment from us and left it forever tainted.

"We all reported the video." Mak held out her phone. "I don't know what good it will do, but it's a start."

"She'll be okay." Kara rested her hand on my shoulder. Comfort wasn't what I deserved right then. If anything, it was a kick to the chest that knocked the wind out of me, but that had already happened. I was still underwater, and I didn't even want to push to the surface.

I knocked on the heavy wood of the closed stall door with my knuckles.

"We'll leave you two to talk." Mak, Avery, and Kara left. The restroom door banged shut, leaving only the muted music from outside and the silence in there with me and Liv.

The toilet paper dispenser rattled, and her trumpeting nose blowing hit sharp notes in the small bathroom. When she opened the door, the redness ringing her eyes made me want to throw myself into the charred remains of her apartment.

I tugged her into my arms and squeezed her tight against me. Her hands came up to my chest—I thought she meant to push me away, but instead she tucked her arms in, letting my body blanket her.

"Seems we weren't as stealthy as we thought." She let out a tight laugh, the kind that only comes after tears so blinding you can barely breathe.

"I think you're right." I brushed my hand down over her hair. "I can't tell you how sorry I am."

She stared up into my eyes. "Let's just go home."

It was her suggestion from earlier that I'd teased her about, one I should've eagerly accepted because then we would have avoided all this. Instead I'd let her talk me into taking her out for once. I'd opened her up to the laser-focused gaze of thousands of people without being on my guard, and this was what had happened. They'd seen the way her body shuddered and how she held on to me, the way I looked at her like I was ready to devour her.

I took her hand in mine. Everyone crowded around the bathroom and helped us get out the back door exit to the club and into a taxi. Their words of comfort didn't do much, but Liv's head resting against my chest may as well have been a whip across my back. She burrowed into my side like I had any protection to give her, like I hadn't already exposed her to the world, like I hadn't already exposed even more of her secrets.

34

LIV

I lifted my head and cracked my eyes open. My head pounded. The tears had stopped falling sooner than I'd expected. Being around the Kings, attention was never in short supply, but it had never been focused on me. Even the previous night it hadn't been; it had been focused on Ford. He'd been the target, and his hesitancy about exposing himself, his need to burrow deep inside made even more sense.

For the rest of the guys, they thrived on the attention that came from playing hockey. It kept them going and amped them up. I'd seen firsthand how it drained Ford, though. It sucked something out of him that was only recharged when we were alone and cuddled up together. Our flirting at the bar had felt so private, which was stupid, but Fish's was like an extension of his house. He felt safe there. It was one of the few places he felt that way, and it had been taken from him—not just taken, but ripped from him.

My eyes adjusted to the low light. The warmth of the bed wasn't complete without him. Ford's back to me, he sat on the edge of the mattress. Pushing the sheets down, I leaned over and ran my hand over his back.

He jumped and turned. The grave expression on his face was like someone had died.

Getting up onto my knees, I draped my arms around his neck and ran my lips along the side of his face. He covered my hand with his and rubbed his thumb in small circles.

"Can't sleep?"

"What gave it away?" He smiled the kind of forced smile you give at work when you're barely hanging on. But I wasn't a work colleague. I didn't want him to ever think he had to hide anything from me.

Sitting beside him, I pulled his arm into my lap and ran my hands along the underside of his forearm. The sinewy muscles tightened and relaxed under my fingers.

"I screwed up." His gaze was locked onto the floor like a hundred-pound weight was looped around his neck, dragging him down, drowning him.

"I was right there with you. Hell, I practically shoved your hands up my dress. Come to think of it, I actually did." I rubbed my face against his neck. He smelled fresh and clean, like newly folded laundry.

He made a sharp noise and shook his head.

"You're not the protector of the world. You're not the creep who decided to film it. It was a stupid mistake. No one saw my face. Maybe in the morning I'll feel differently, but I'm sure in another day, this will be old news and someone else will have done something way more scandalous."

"How can you be so calm about this?" He tilted his head, the sheen on his eyes catching the dim light from the living room. "People saw me touching you. I let them see you vulnerable like that, so trusting and open."

I lifted his hand and raised it to my mouth. "No one

watching that was focused on my openness or trust." A small laugh crept out of my mouth. "They saw me, saw how much I enjoyed it and the look on your face when I came on your fingers. As far as sex tapes go, they didn't even get a flash of the goods." Somehow him being so freaked out let me put the whole thing in perspective. It could have been worse, a lot worse, but learning this lesson hadn't been nearly as painful as it could have been.

He jerked back. I tightened my hold. "You can't hide from everyone forever." I kissed the words into the back of his hand, trying to apply a salve to the pain radiating off him and leaching into the air. "And I don't want you to hide. Just think of how not scary any other public appearance you make will feel after this." I snorted.

"I need to go for a walk." He stood up, but I held on to his hand.

"Come back to bed. It will all be better in the morning."

He stared down at me, his eyes boring into mine, peeling back the layers of himself for me, and that raw ache brought tears to my eyes.

"It'll be okay."

He nodded. "I know. Go back to sleep. This will help clear my head." He freed his hand from mine and ran it along the side of my face, cupping my cheek. "I won't be long." Trailing his thumb along my bottom lip, he stared into my eyes. My heart squeezed at the uncertainty and worry in his eyes.

He dropped his hand and walked from the room with his hands shoved in his pockets. The front door closed a few seconds later, and I burrowed deep into the blankets. This was a speed bump, and we could handle it. Once he got back, we'd figure out how to face this together.

Morning came far too early. The video was down. It hadn't been up for more than a few hours overnight. Most people hadn't seen it, and most people couldn't even tell it was me. The guys hadn't even known it was me. That had made me laugh in the VIP room bathroom when Mak and Avery had told me they'd had to point it out to them before we even got there.

It gave me some solace that the thousands of people who'd seen Ford doling out digital pleasure in the bar might not put two and two together. I tugged down a strand of my hair. Maybe a dye job was in order. It wasn't the end of the world. I could still walk and talk. No one had come to the door with pitchforks ready to put me in the stocks, but damn was it embarrassing. This took having a nightmare of standing in front of your entire school naked to a whole new level.

Ford's face when I'd opened the stall door had looked like someone hadn't just kicked his dog but a whole litter of puppies. He'd crawled back into bed not that long after he left, slipping his arms around me and tugging me close. I hadn't been able to sleep without him there anyway, but I didn't want to pile on more guilt. Sleep had overtaken me when his breathing evened out.

Sometime close to dawn, I propped myself up on my elbow and brushed my hand across the hair on his fore-head. So strong and so fragile, he had the biggest heart and so much fear about letting people see all of him. There were rare moments when he let himself go, a rare moment like the night before when some of who he was alone with me saw the light of day. Now I'd be lucky if he didn't throw that piece into a trunk, lock it up with chains, and chuck it into a river.

Resting my head on his chest, I let my eyes close. We'd had a long day, and if we didn't deserve a snooze, I didn't know who did.

~

A thundering pounding shook the whole apartment. It was like someone was trying to knock down the entire building through the door. I rushed to it, hoping to stop whoever it was before they woke Ford. *Why the hell are they banging like that?* A small pang of fear hit me that the building might in fact be on fire.

I wrenched it open, and all the blood drained out of my face. Standing in the hallway like a bull ready to charge, Colm stared back at me like he'd seen a ghost. One second I was in the doorway and the next I was lifted off my feet.

"Thank God you're okay." His words came out in a rush. "I went to your apartment to see the place half gutted by fire. You weren't answering your phone. I freaked the hell out. I've never been more scared in my life." His grip tightened on my shoulders, and I could barely breathe. He buried his face in my neck, tremors racking his body.

"You aren't supposed to be here until the end of the week. I'm okay," I croaked out after drawing the slightest bit of air into my lungs. Not giving him a heads-up was my screw up. I should have let him know, but I'd known exactly what he'd have done: gone into overdrive protection mode and tried to bulldoze his way into making it right. I held him tighter and ran my hands over his back.

"Happy birthday, Olive." He squeezed me tighter against him, spinning me around.

"Thanks, big brother." Under my hand, his heart pounded like he'd run a marathon. "Colm, I'm okay."

He loosened his grip and set me back down. "What are you doing here? I'd have thought you'd be with Marisa. Is she okay?" His gaze traveled over me, and the pieces clicked into place like a combination lock.

Bare feet—*click*. No pants—*click*. Wearing Ford's T-shirt —*click*. Rumpled hair—the lock swung open.

Colm's eyes widened, and his gaze bounced from my feet to the top of my head.

My gaze darted over Colm's shoulder. Ford stood behind him with his arms crossed over his chest. The tension radiated off him like someone waiting for a cobra to strike.

I winced. Ford crossed the room and stood beside me. His arm brushed against the oversize sleeve of the shirt I had on, the gentle contact grounding me while Colm stood in front of us looking like he was seconds from losing his shit.

"Let's get some breakfast. We have a lot to talk about." Ford dropped his hand onto Colm's shoulder.

Colm shot back like he'd been burned, and his gaze jumped from Ford to me.

"You're fucking Olive?" Anger shot through his words like venom.

"You've had a long trip. You're tired." Ford tried to corral him toward the kitchen, but Colm shoved him back.

"Don't patronize me. You think this is because I'm tired? This is because you fucking lied to me—again." Colm's shoulders shook as his rage built.

"Calm down." Ford put his hands in front of him, moving them up and down like they could fan away the tension in the air. Instead they fanned the flames.

"I get on the first plane I can after they finally free me

from my rehab prison, and what do I show up to? Liv's apartment is a smoldering pile of rubble, and you don't even call me?" His gaze shot back to me. "And you won't answer my calls. Do you know what happened when I showed up at your apartment? I thought you died." They could probably hear his voice three blocks away. "How the hell did I know that didn't happen last night? I called every freaking hospital on the way here. I was searching newspapers online looking for your name in some kind of death notification." Rage and anguish battled for dominance with every breath.

I winced.

He shoved against Ford's chest. "Not only are you screwing my baby sister, you don't even warn me about the fire or tell me she's safe."

"We didn't know you were coming back early."

"I don't care!" Colm roared. "I don't care if you thought I was coming back in a day or a week or a month. I deserved to know."

"There was nothing you could do. Mak, Kara, and Avery took me shopping for clothes. They gave them to me as a birthday present. My textbooks were replaced, and I'm fine here with Ford."

"Wow, sounds like everyone else knew about this but me. Everyone else is taking care of me—except me. You'll take their help, but you won't let your own brother sort things out for you." Hurt tinged his words.

"They were here and offered their help. Telling you would have just worried you and made you freak out."

"Look what not telling me did." He pointed at the center of his chest. "Look what finding out my former best friend has been fucking my little sister behind my back has done."

Ford stood still as a statue as Colm went after him, but the bunch of his forearms and the strain in his neck told me he was barely hanging on. I stepped in between them, putting my hands on Colm's chest.

"This is why we didn't tell you. I knew you'd freak out."

"And why shouldn't I? After what he did, he's lucky I still speak to him."

Ford's body went rigid like someone tightening a screw to the point that the threads started fraying. His breathing picked up, and he opened and closed his fists at his side. I pressed one hand into the center of his chest to try to calm him and kept one on Colm's to keep them apart.

"What *did* he do? What the hell could he have done to drive this wedge between you two?"

Colm's fiery gaze dropped from Ford's to mine. "He slept with my fiancée."

Things slowed down. If there had been a hummingbird in the room, I had no doubt I'd have seen every flap of its wings.

My head whipped around, and I stared into the horror-filled gray-brown eyes I thought I knew so well. "You slept with Felicity?" If Colm had told me this was Ford's evil doppelgänger who'd gotten rid of the real Ford years ago, I couldn't have been more shocked.

I jerked my hand back from his chest. His fingers wrapped around my wrist to keep me put. "It wasn't like that. I didn't know who she was."

My voice shot up an octave. "How could you not know?"

"I didn't know he was dating her."

"But once you found out, did you tell me? Did you confess the whole thing and come to me asking for forgiveness?"

Ford dropped his head as his grip on my wrist tightened. My chest burned like I'd been drowning and kicking for the surface, dying for a gasp of air.

"No, I didn't tell you."

"You'd have kept that a secret and let me marry her. I trusted you." Colm's gaze bounced back to me. "But I can see once again that trust was misplaced."

"Felicity wasn't my fault. How many times do I have to apologize? She promised me it was a lapse in judgment, a one-time thing, said it would never happen again. You were so happy."

"Happy in a lie! It should've been my choice. Instead I had to find out from someone else, sitting there with humiliation burning in my gut as some other guy talked about you two sleeping together."

"I thought I was doing the right thing."

"And then I ask you to figure out what's going on with Olive and not only are you sleeping with her, but she's not going to medical school? You can't help but fuck up my life."

Their words volleyed back and forth. My chest was so tight it was like someone had slipped me into the jaws of a vise, but then the words finally registered.

I snatched my hand from Ford's grip.

"Seems he's good at keeping some secrets after all— secrets where he's covering his own ass." Colm seethed behind me. If he could have breathed fire, I'd have ducked for cover.

I stared up at Ford in disbelief. "You told him about med school?"

35

FORD

They were the words I'd known were coming. Secrets balanced on top of lies, sprinkled with omissions—it had only been a matter of time before the crash. They clattered to the ground around me, leaving splintered shards scattered all over my life.

Liv looked back at me like she was seeing me with new eyes, and why wouldn't she? I'd slept with her brother's fiancée. I'd gotten her plastered all over social media and told her brother the one secret she'd needed to tell him herself.

"I didn't mean to. I was trying to show him how the pressure he was putting on you was driving you away."

"You think you know what she needs more than me." Colm slammed into her back, coming for me, nearly toppling her over into me.

I grabbed her shoulders, steadying her. "Yes! You keep trying to shove her into this twelve-year-old-sized hole in the old life you had, and it won't work anymore. She's an adult. She deserves to live a life that makes her happy."

"You two stop talking about me like I'm not here." She

shoved both of us away and stepped back. "It wasn't your place to tell him."

I squeezed my eyes shut and clenched my fists in front of my face, slamming them into my forehead. "I know. I was trying to tell him that he was pushing you away, that you love him but this pressure he's putting on you is making you so unhappy. It slipped out."

"That slips out but you can't tell me I'm about to marry someone who'd cheat?"

"And how would that have gone down, Colm? You finally tell me about the girl you've been secretly dating. You're happier than I've ever seen you and I show up at that table and...what? I tell you what? That she's a cheater? You'd have wanted to know how I knew, and I'd have had to confess that to you, would have had to break the heart of my best friend. You'd have never forgiven me." My voice was raw as the words tumbled out, choking me.

Colm glared and paced. At that moment a pin drop would have sounded like a jet engine.

Liv stared at me like I was a different guy than the one she'd wrapped around last night, like I wasn't the person she thought I was, and maybe I wasn't.

"Last night, you could have told me. When I was going on and on about having that talk with him, you could have told me you'd already said something." Liv's hurt echoed in her voice.

"Last night—" Colm froze with his hand halfway in his hair. Every muscle in his body went rigid, and then something snapped. He rushed forward. "It was you. The video... the video all over social media last night—it was you." He held out his shaking hand to Liv.

She shied away, dropping her chin to her shoulder like she'd been smacked.

"Are you trying to completely fuck up her life?" Colm roared at me before rounding on Liv. "Are you trying to screw up your life? Is this your way of making sure you don't get into med school? A sex tape?"

"It wasn't a sex tape. You can barely see anything. You didn't even know it was me until now."

"What would Mom and Dad think if they were here? How would you explain it to them?"

She jerked back and stared at him wide-eyed. Shaking her head, she threw her hands up. "I'd probably schedule an appointment and wait a week just to have them cancel it on me and never even notice."

"Is this your way of getting back at them? Of getting back at me?"

"Back at you for what? You're my brother and I love you, but I just want to live a life I love. I want to do something that makes me happy. Why is that so hard to understand?"

Colm spun around and shoved his hands into his hair. "If you do this, if you don't go to med school, and whatever this thing is with Ford—if you do this..." He stared at her over his shoulder. "I'm cutting you off." Turning, he crossed his arms over his chest like his word was the end of the discussion. I'd never wanted to see this ugly, controlling side of him, but I supposed it had always been there. He's only ever been supportive of his dreams for Liv. She'd hidden such a huge part of her life from him. He talked about her dancing like a throwaway thing that didn't matter, but it mattered to her.

She made a sound like someone had hit her right in the chest. I'd heard that sound before when I took a puck straight to the solar plexus. "This is *my* life."

I stepped in between them. "Don't do this, man."

"I'm not going to let her ruin her life and throw away

everything she's worked for—*we've* worked for over the years."

"I know you feel guilty, but her going to med school isn't going to bring your parents back." In the dark days after the funeral, he'd nearly buckled under the intense guilt that clawed at him. It wasn't only the pain of losing a parent. I'd seen that pain cutting deep into Liv, but Colm's was different. His was guilt, and I knew it because I'd felt the same kind of crushing guilt before.

"This doesn't concern you. This is between me and my family, me and Liv." His jaw popped.

"You're not going to have a family left if you keep pushing her like this. Let her make her own choices." I went toe to toe with him. Colm trying to resurrect their parents through Liv would crush her. She already had so much to deal with without him trying to fix something that could never be fixed. We stared each other down, breath coming out like two charging animals ready to tear each other apart.

"A choice I'm perfectly capable of making myself."

We both glanced to the side at the sound of her voice.

Liv stood at the foot of the steps to my bedroom fully dressed, and the backpack on her shoulder made my heart plunge straight to the pits of despair. Her gaze burned into mine. "I told you everything, all the ugly little things I'd hidden away or kept locked up, and you kept this from me." She lifted her chin. "I asked you directly what happened between you two, and you shrugged it off. Then you go and tell Colm about med school before I can tell him. After last night, I thought we could handle anything as a team, but I can't trust you." Her fingers tightened around the strap of her bag. "And Colm, I can't be who you want me to be. Killing myself to follow in the footsteps of two people who never thought we were worthy of their attention...I can't live with that in the back of my head anymore. If you want to cut me off, fine. I'll do it myself."

"You can do it; you can be a doctor. Just stick to what we told them we'd do. We made promises to them, Liv."

"I was in the hospital, too, right there beside you, but you can't expect me to follow a plan created back when I was a kid."

"I can. Don't make me do this."

"You're doing this. You both are. Looks like you two are a hell of a lot closer than you thought. You both think you're the only one who knows what's best for the people you claim to love." She stared into my eyes with a pain and hurt that lashed at my skin, and then there was nothing but blank space where she'd stood.

Colm rounded on me the second the door slammed shut. "You did this."

"You did this to yourself." My blood pounded in my veins like a cascading rapid. "And now she's gone." I gritted my teeth and met his eyes fire for fire.

"I asked you to do one thing, and you couldn't even do that."

"I'm sick of apologizing for things I'm not to blame for. Should I have told you about Felicity? Yes, but sleeping with her wasn't wrong. I didn't know she was with you. You kept your relationship from me. If I had known, I wouldn't have gone anywhere near her. Since then, it's been a string of failed relationships for you. You say it's because you have trust issues, but maybe it's because you're finding the exact type of women you deserve. You're an asshole who just cut off the only family he has because of some obsession with fulfilling the dreams of your parents who are long gone.

"They are gone. There's nothing you and Liv can do to bring them back. She needs you. You're the only family she's got. Don't do this." I dropped my hand onto his stooped shoulders.

He shook off my hold. "You don't think I know that? I have a responsibility, though. I promised them she'd be safe, promised them I'd protect her, and look what I come back to. She wants to teach dance." He spat the words like nails splitting wood. "She wants to be with you, a friend I can't even trust to not bang her in public?"

I clenched my fists at my side. "It was a mistake, something I'll regret for the rest of my life, but it was a mistake I'll never make again. I love her, man."

There was a split second where his eyes lit up, and I thought maybe that had been all he needed to hear: that this wasn't some fling between me and her, that I loved her with all my heart and I'd do anything for her.

That was before his fist connected with my jaw.

Pain exploded on the side of my face, and I stumbled back. The metallic explosion of blood filled my mouth. I wiped the back of my hand against my lips and stared at the blood smeared on my skin.

Colm stood in front of me with his chest heaving and his hands dancing at his sides. "You don't get to take someone else from me. Stay the hell away from her." His words were low and dangerous. It would have been better if he'd yelled and shouted at me, but he hadn't. He stared at me like he wanted to melt the flesh off my bones. "I forgave you once, but this..." He glanced around the apartment. "You don't get a pass on this. Stay away from her, and stay the hell away from me." The walls rattled as the door slammed behind him. It was becoming an everyday thing; maybe I needed them to reinforce the walls or something.

Tugging the freezer open, I grabbed a handful of ice and dropped it into a kitchen towel. I rang Liv. Her phone went straight to voice mail. The silence of the place roared in my ears. Sitting on my couch with the ice on my face, I stared at the pictures on the wall.

So many things I should have done differently.

So many mistakes made.

So much I needed to fix.

36

LIV

I stood on the sidewalk outside Ford's place shaking like the ground beneath me was shifting. Colm had just cut me off, Ford had slept with Colm's fiancée, and I'd ended things with Ford. I had no place to go.

Walking the streets with my bag banging against the back of my leg, I tried to clear the cloud in my mind. The cold snap from the night of the fire had melted away like the frost on the ground. Spring had finally arrived. The birds chirped their early morning song, and people went about their day like the world hadn't just imploded.

I'd been prepared for the lost feeling after the fire. Everyone had seemed so surprised I'd bounced back like I did. Even the video had rolled off my back, but this was so much more. The person who had been a foundation of my life had just sliced the line that bound us like it was nothing.

I turned on my phone and touched the first name on my list.

"Morning." Her groggy voice was the anchor I needed.

"Hey."

"What's wrong?"

"Nothing's wrong."

"Don't bullshit me. What's wrong? What happened? I can hear it in your voice."

"I kind of need a place to stay."

"What about F—oh. Okay, let me know where you are."

I glanced around at the street signs and told her the cross streets.

"Getting dressed now, ordered a car, I can be there in twenty minutes."

Nodding, I looked for a spot to wait. "There's a coffee shop on the corner. I'll stay in there until you get here."

Concerned faces from behind the coffee shop counter made me want to turn around and bolt. Instead I ordered my coffee and sat by the window, waiting for Marisa. I sipped on the black coffee and tried not to burn myself. Staring out the window, I caught a look at my reflection. Now it made sense why everyone was staring at me like I was a sideshow freak. My eyes were red, and my hair was a mess. My brush was back at Ford's.

Marisa burst through the door like a superhero making her grand entrance. Her eyes scanned the people sipping their coffee and typing away on their computers. She had on gray sweatpants rolled up a bunch of times at the ankles and an oversize white T-shirt she'd knotted at the waist.

The second she spotted my face, she rushed over to me. "Let's get you out of here." She wrapped her arms around my shoulders and guided me out like the paramedics had right after the fire, like I looked like I was on the verge of losing it. It was appropriate because I was.

We got into the car, and she gave the driver our old address. I glanced over at her.

"Our landlord called. We can go back into our place and salvage what we can."

"Let's go."

Standing in front of the building we'd called home, I couldn't let go of the gratitude that we'd made it out. Most of the windows along the front were shattered, and char marks had licked their way up the brick exterior of half the building.

My stomach sank when I thought about Colm pulling up to the front of this building and not being able to get ahold of me. Hiding from your problems wasn't how you fixed them; it only made them that much worse when they were brought out into the light of day.

Marisa threw her arms around my neck, apparently trying to cut off the blood flow to my brain.

"What the hell is that for?" I said against her arm, which was squished against my cheek.

"For getting me out of there. I'll never complain about you staying up so late to study again."

I laughed and disengaged her arm lock. We walked around the back of the building to the back stairs. Caution tape cordoned off the areas that were off-limits. So many apartments had the tape across their doors. In the grand scheme of things, we were lucky we could even go back and see what was salvageable.

Empty doorways showcased the charred remains of furniture and belongings blackened and blanketing the floor. Many objects were no longer recognizable, and the smell of burnt plastic and wood overwhelmed every other sense.

Pushing open the broken door, we stood staring at the waterlogged remains of the life we'd built together there. Her fingers wrapped around mine, and we walked inside.

"Wow." Marisa glanced around our living room—well, what was left of it. The couch LJ always bitched about was a shell of itself. The paint was peeling off the walls, and scorch marks lined the ceiling.

She went inside her bedroom, and I froze outside mine, following the blazing trail of destruction with my gaze. The door, broken from the hinges, leaned on the other side of the doorway, propped up against the wall. My bed, my desk, and everything else looked almost normal. The wood groaned under my feet, and the wooden planks creaked where they'd buckled.

The books on my desk were stacked how I'd left them, but the edges were warped. I picked one up, and the entire cover fell off. The words on the page were blurred and faded.

Opening my closet door, a small flood of water came rushing out, having been trapped behind all the clothes stuffed inside. The strong smell of mold hit me. Unsalvageable.

"Looks like your room missed most of the fire." Marisa stood in front of the door with a few things cradled in her arms and her weighted down backpack slung over her shoulder.

"But not the fire hose." I closed the door and spotted the boxes under my bed. Like my feet were encased in cement blocks, I walked over to my bed. Everything slowed down, but my breathing pitched higher and faster with each shuffle of my feet.

Marisa's gaze followed mine, and she winced, taking a step farther into the room.

Crouching down, my fingers trembled as I dragged the crumpled boxes out. The printed cardboard collapsed more with each inch I moved them. Peeling a lid off, I stared into the box of childhood memories. The watery smiling face of my mom and dad stared back at me. Lifting the picture, a few more came with it, stuck to the back. The ink shifted, sliding the entire photograph off onto my fingers. I choked back a breath, the image swimming even more as my eyes filled. Memories I'd held on to washed away in an instant...it was like having the images physically erased slowly, chipping away at the clear picture of them in my head.

Marisa gasped and covered her mouth with the tips of her fingers. "Oh God, Liv." She wore the same face people had at my parents' funeral, like she was watching me lose them all over again—and she was. I was losing the mental picture I'd built up of them assembled from boxes of photographs and slivers of their time. Colm hadn't even wanted to keep these pictures. Maybe he'd been right. These weren't the truth; these were part of the fabricated past I'd tried to create for myself to get me through my broken future.

Everything in there was a part of the old Liv. Some of the recent pictures would still be saved on my phone, and I could make new memories not weighted down by the past I'd always been trying to measure up to. I dropped the boxes from my numb fingers. Swallowing back against the thickness in my throat, I wiped my eyes. This was it. The last of them I'd carried with me since the day they died. The house was gone, and now the pictures I'd clung to in order to preserve those memories were gone. It was hard to catch my breath. Where did this leave me? What happened now? "Let's go."

"There's nothing you can salvage?"

"There's nothing here for me. Let's go."

The car ride to LJ's was pin-drop silent. Marisa and I stared straight ahead like we'd both just run away from our own weddings, shell-shocked and trying to figure out what came next. While I'd never really thought money mattered to me before, part of the reason was that I knew it was always there. Colm was there to bail me out if I ever screwed up royally. If I needed anything, it was a matter of *when* the money reached my account, not *if*.

I had ten shirts, five pants, a couple of pairs of shoes, some socks, panties, a couple bras and textbooks. My entire life fit into the duffel bag on my lap. After years of wanting a place to call home and trying to build a stable life for myself, I was sitting in the back of a taxi with no money, no home, and almost no belongings.

"I put in the renter's insurance stuff, but I have no idea how long it will take them to get us a check."

"Once school's over, I can work more at the dance studio, pick up as many classes as I need to."

She turned to me with her eyebrows sky-high. "Why the hell would you need to do that? I'd have thought Colm would get you everything you need."

"It's a long story." The cab pulled up to the front of the Brothel, and we climbed out.

"Spill."

Standing outside LJ's house, she paced back and forth like a fighter preparing for the heavyweight title. Throughout the recounting of what had gone down that morning, Marisa let out a string of familiar curses and a few newly invented ones.

"I'll kill them both. Seriously, I'll wrap my fingers around both their necks at the same time and choke the life out of them."

A few people walked by and stared at her, likely trying to figure out if they needed to call campus security. The few items retrieved from our apartment sat on the steps to the Brothel, and she threw her hands up in the air.

"No, that's too good for them. I might just tie them both

together, cover them with honey, and leave them right beside an ant hill." The intensity of her expression and the fact that her brain came up with that scenario sent a laugh leaping from my mouth.

"Is she promising to bury someone up to their neck and smear peanut butter on their head to attract woodland creatures and bugs?" LJ walked down the last couple of steps and sat on the bottom one behind her.

"Close."

"These types of punishments are only for people who really deserve it, and right now Ford and her brother deserve it."

"Remind me never to get on your bad side." I leaned against the railing leading up to the front steps.

"She's all bark, no bite," LJ stage-whispered.

"Her brother cut her off. One year before graduation and he pulls the rug out from under her unless she goes to med school. That's total bull in my book."

Pushing off the bottom step, I raised my finger in the air. "I agree."

"That blows, Liv. Sorry about that."

I shrugged. "Marisa mentioned you might have a spot for me here? If not, that's totally fine, but if you do, I'd really appreciate it."

"Of course." He shielded his eyes from the afternoon sun. "The couch is free." He held up his hand as Marisa tried to interrupt. "And we can get you new blankets for it."

"Why don't you want to stay with the other hockey guys? The Kings?" Marisa peered over at me.

"It would be the first place Ford or Colm would come looking for me. I need some space."

"Let's head inside. Nix and Reece are grilling out back."

"Grilling?" It was barely spring.

"They grill even if there's two feet of snow on the ground." He held the door open for us.

We gathered up our stuff and went inside. The house looked a lot different when there weren't two hundred drunk bodies packed wall to wall. There was a leather lounger that looked like it had seen better days, two couches covered in more stains than I cared to think about, a TV mounted on the wall, and a few video game consoles. LJ went out back to check on the food.

"You can keep your stuff upstairs." Marisa stood at the base of the steps. "I'll show you."

"I'll get you two some burgers and drinks." LJ came back into the living room.

"I'm going to let Liv stash her stuff in our—your room. We'll be right back."

We climbed the steps. A guy with shaggy brown hair walked out of the bathroom with steam billowing out behind him. His towel was wrapped low around his waist, showing off that killer V and abs for days. I averted my eyes and glanced over at Marisa.

"Hey, Berk." She rolled her eyes and pushed open a bedroom door, dragging me inside. There were a couple posters up on the wall and a desk in the corner. Marisa plugged her phone in on the table beside the bed. The sheets were rumpled and balled up in the corner of the bed.

"You can put your stuff in here." She opened the top dresser drawer. "LJ cleared it out for me but I don't have any stuff yet, so you can use it."

"You can wear any of the stuff I have. What's mine is yours. So, where do you sleep?" There wasn't a couch or futon or anything up here.

"The bed." She made herself busy taking my clothes out

of my bag, folding them—even though they were already folded—and putting them in the drawer.

"And where does LJ sleep?"

"It's a big bed." She shook out a shirt and continued folding.

"You two are sleeping together?" I couldn't hold back my smile.

"Not *sleeping* together, but sleeping together. We did it all the time back in middle school."

"Back in middle school he wasn't a hottie with a rock-hard football body."

"He's okay." She shrugged and her eyes darted to the rumpled sheets.

"I feel like after nearly dying together, I deserve the truth. Plus I could really use some fun gossip right now. Please? I need this." I squeezed her hand.

She sighed and peered over at me. "Okay, it's a little different than middle school."

We were huddled together, and she gave me the rundown of the few late-night surprises that had poked her in the back during their sleepovers. And there was the time she'd walked in on him in the shower. Let's just say that was a big surprise—huge. She told me how his roommate, Berk, had a secret sex pen pal, and how Nix kept disappearing now that football season was over. We'd long since finished putting away my limited articles of clothing when LJ knocked on the door.

We jumped at the sudden intrusion.

He leaned in, swinging from the doorjamb, his brown hair ruffled just right and his light eyes twinkling with amusement. "Burgers are ready, ladies."

"We'll be right there," Marisa chirped way too loudly.

He knocked his knuckles against the door and smiled before running back downstairs.

"Seems I'm not the only one making waves lately."

"Don't get me started. It's nothing. Nothing at all. Come on, I'm hungry."

She grabbed my hand and dragged me down the stairs. Those few minutes had helped me forget what awaited me afterward.

37

FORD

Not even the smell of the cookies in the oven could drag me from the thoughts I hadn't been able to outrun, didn't want to outrun.

Liv had disappeared. Every call and text went unanswered—not that I'd thought she'd pick up, but I'd have welcomed an earful right then. None of the guys knew where she was. It wasn't like I could ask Colm, though I doubted he'd heard from her either. I'd staked out the dance studio for a few days, and she hadn't even shown up there.

She was hiding, going to great lengths to make sure I couldn't get down on my knees and beg her forgiveness, which I would've done without a moment's hesitation.

A plate of piping-hot cookies slid across the table and stopped right under my nose. I looked up at my mom. She pulled out a chair and sat down opposite me at the table.

"It looked like you could use those."

"Am I that out of it? When did you even make the dough?"

She smiled and jerked her thumb over her shoulder

toward the fridge. "I make big batches and then freeze them, ready to go for moments just like these. One of the kids gets a bump or something and these do wonders for their mood."

"Is that what you're doing for me?" I picked one up. Warm chocolate coated my fingers.

She shrugged. "Desperate times call for desperate measures. What's going on?" She covered my hand with hers, that little gesture of love and comfort. My first memories were of her crouched down in front of me when I picked myself up off the ground after my first attempts at the big kid slide. Her eyes softened around the edges, crinkling in the corners, and my chest tightened.

"I screwed up." I swallowed and looked down at the plate.

"Tell me something I don't know. You didn't even come in here looking like this when you got knocked out of the playoffs."

I dropped the cookie to the plate and leaned back in my chair. "Couldn't even get that right."

"Stop it. That wasn't a dig, but what I'm saying is you weren't even this upset when your season ended. What is going on?" The laughter of kids filtered in through the walls. "It's Liv, isn't it? Something happened? I talked to Grant, and I thought he was okay."

Nodding my head, I stared at the chocolate and cookie crumbs on my fingers. "He is. This time it's all my fuckup."

"I'll go get the pliers if I need to, or are you going to tell me willingly?"

"Do you think you'd have been happier not knowing Dad was having an affair?" I peered up at her.

Her face transformed. The small smile disappeared, swallowed up by those hard memories from our past, and

326

MAYA HUGHESMAYA HUGHES

then just as quickly as the stricken sadness had appeared, it vanished.

"Do you wish I'd never told you?" I whispered the question I'd never been brave enough to ask, the words catching on the way out. I truly wondered if she wished I hadn't imploded our family by telling her what had happened. My dad had promised it would never happen again, but the anger that had burned inside of me when I'd seen him kiss that other woman had been all-consuming. I couldn't have stopped myself if I'd wanted to—and I hadn't.

The noise Mom had made when I'd told her still haunted me. I'd never known what it was like to break a person, but standing beside her while she was on her knees planting the new flower bed of begonias, I'd found out.

I squeezed my eyes shut, refusing to let the tears fall.

She shot around the table and crouched beside me, holding on to my hand just like I was five years old again.

"Honey, none of what happened with your dad and me has ever been your fault. Of course I'm glad you told me. I know things were hard for a while, but I never would've wanted to stay with your father after that. I couldn't handle it again." Her voice was hoarse with emotion, just like it had been when she'd sat me and Grant down and told us Dad would no longer be living with us.

Then her words clicked in my head, like a key turning the lock of a door that was nearly rusted shut. My head jerked back. "Again?"

She patted the back of my hand, grabbed her chair, and slid it back toward me. "Again." She shook her head and ran her hands over the backs of mine. They were soft and a little dry, showing her age, even if her face didn't.

Nodding slowly, she looked up at me. "You probably don't remember, but it wasn't the first time. While I was pregnant with Grant, we went to live with Grandma for a while."

Vague memories of playing in their backyard one summer trickled in. "It was over the summer?"

"Your dad cheated. I caught him and I left." She let out a deep breath, the kind you exhale like you're breathing out a part of your soul. "And then I went back." Her lips pinched. "He came back after a couple of months, begged for my forgiveness. He made promises and professed his love, said it would never happen again.

"You were six. I was pregnant with Grant and I wanted us to be a family, so I went back. Things were good, great even, for a while. That's why when you told me—when you told me, it broke my heart." Her eyes snapped to mine, and her grip tightened. "*You* did *not* break my heart. Do you understand me? It had nothing to do with you, nothing at all. You did nothing wrong, but your father broke my heart.

"When you told me—when someone rebuilds your trust, that break hurts even more because not only are you hurt and betrayed, they also make you feel like a fool. I needed to know, though, and thank you for being brave enough to tell me." She wrapped her arms around my neck and squeezed me tight. It was the kind of mom hug that threatened to break your back. Even when you'd long since dwarfed her, she still showed you who was boss.

She patted my back and rubbed it like the late nights when I was a kid and had been up all night with a fever. "That was one of the proudest moments in my life. You knew what was wrong, and you came to me and trusted me with what you'd found out. That's all a mother can ask for."

Guilt pounded harder against my ribs. I hadn't done that this time, not for Colm.

She sat in her seat and picked up the plate until I took a cookie. "Now will you tell me what's going on?"

I started spilling out the entire story, and Mom stopped me halfway.

"Okay, this calls for milk." Two short glasses of chilled milk later, she sat back in her seat. "Wow, well that's quite a pickle you've gotten yourself into."

Dragging my fingers through my hair, I sat back in my chair. "After what happened with Dad, I defaulted to keeping secrets locked up. I locked them down tight and tried to protect the people I care about."

"The pain doesn't just come from the thing, sweetheart. Some of it comes from the lies, from the secrets and second-guessing you dismiss because you don't want to be that paranoid person who can't open their heart up to the people around them." I hung my head, and she ran her hand over my shoulder. "Now you've got some fences to mend and promises to make. It's not often people get a second chance, but if there's anyone who can, it's you." She cradled my cheek with her hand, rubbing her thumb along my scruff.

"I don't know if she'll even want to talk to me. It's not just that I told him about med school. I hurt him. Even if she's pissed at him, he's still her brother, and worse, I lied to her about it. She asked me flat out what had happened between us, and I said nothing."

"You're going to have to get her to believe it will never happen again."

My head snapped up. "It won't. This secrets thing..." I squeezed the back of my neck. "That's finished. I'd rather face the fallout than have that panic, guilt, and worry in the back of my head."

"You'll be okay, then. It might take time, but eventually she'll see straight into your heart and know you mean it.

You're both still so young, practically babies. You're almost to your twenty-sixth birthday, and Liv's only twenty-one. There's so much more to learn."

I left Mom's house and drove the streets. Without meaning to, I ended up back at Liv's dance studio. I gravitated there more than I should have, like a stalker hoping for a glance of her. Pulling up to the curb, I kept my eyes trained on the people coming and going. I shut off the car and stared out my windshield. People floated in and out of the building in body-hugging clothes. The warmer temperatures meant winter coats were no longer needed. I rested my head against the headrest. *What am I doing here?*

I turned the key in the ignition, and the engine purred. I threw it into drive, swinging my car out of the parking spot. A horn blared from a car beside me, and I slammed on the brakes. The golden wisps of her hair stuck out from under the hat that was way too warm for the temperature disappeared into the dance studio. She looked like someone in the witness protection program, someone hiding—from me. I threw my car back into the space, bolted from the car, and crossed the street. I raced after her into the building.

Bypassing the front desk, I shot up the stairs. Taking them three at a time, I made it to the second floor. A door swung closed, and I rushed to the small window. Peering inside, I watched her take off her hat and stick it in her bag, shaking her hair out. Swallowing against the rising fear clawing at my gut, I opened the door. How did I keep going if she was out there and never forgave me? My sweaty palms nearly slipping off the doorknob, I walked inside.

"Class isn't for another twenty minutes," she said without looking up from the speakers she fiddled with. When she finally glanced over her shoulder, her polite smile fell, the kind of expression reserved for coming back to your car to find it had been rear-ended and there was no note in sight. "What are you doing here?" She tugged her long-sleeved shirt off, balled it up, and threw it onto her bag.

"I needed to talk."

"I don't have anything to say."

"There's something I need to say to you."

She stood with her back to me. Her muscles were tight, like a rubber band pulled taut enough to snap. "Talk."

"Are you safe? Do you have a place to stay?"

She tilted her head to the side. "I'm staying with friends. I'm not a kid. There's no need for you to worry."

"It's not possible for me not to worry, not when you won't talk to me."

"You survived just fine without me speaking to you before Colm asked you to spy on me for him. Just pretend we're back there. Pretend you're still ignoring my existence and any feelings you might have for me. You're good at that."

"I'm shit at that, Liv. Denying my feelings for you was slowly chewing me up inside."

"It didn't sound like it from the stories of Ford's great conquests. Hell, even Colm's fiancée fell victim to it. I'm sure you can find someone to fill the space in your bed." Her words came out rapid-fire, like bullets slicing through their target, and they had—me.

"If there was a way for me to erase it all, just wipe away those years, I would, but there isn't. Felicity...she was a mistake that will haunt me forever, but not because I slept with her."

Liv winced.

"That's bad enough, but I can't take all that back. I wish I could, but I can't. But I didn't even know she and Colm were dating when she and I slept together. It was a one-night stand, and then I found out she was his girlfriend when he introduced us to each other after we'd already... It will haunt me because I didn't tell Colm once I knew who she was. I believed her when she promised she'd never hurt him like that again. I wanted to protect him. I've seen what happens when someone cheats, how it can chew someone up from the inside out, but now I know that's better than letting them think they can't trust the people close to them. Keeping secrets is something I learned to do early."

38

LIV

I'd avoided him for this long. I knew what would happen the second I was within five feet of him. Once the anger burned away and the adrenaline wore off, I'd want to forgive him. I'd want his arms around me and to sink into that peaceful cocoon we fell into where things were always going to be all right.

"You were supposed to be the one I could share anything with. You were supposed to be the person I never had to pretend with, the one who promised not to keep things from me."

"It's a reflex, like catching a falling knife even though you know it's going to slice you to the bone. I've been keeping secrets since I was little, and the one time I said enough, that's when he left. I refused to lie for my dad anymore. Looking my mom in the eye knowing what he'd done killed me. That wasn't the type of shit you heap on a kid, but my dad wasn't winning any parent of the year awards."

I tilted my head. "What are you talking about?"

He ran through the whole sordid story about his dad,

how he'd told his mom about his dad's affair, the way she fell apart, and the guilt he carried with him over that. That anyone could cheat on Sylvia was mind-boggling to me, and it made me want to track his dad down and unleash Marisa on him. He'd kept that bottled up inside and had never spoken about his dad much before, even Grant had been tight lipped, just saying he'd left.

"But his cheating was keeping secrets, Ford. Just because someone isn't sleeping around doesn't mean hiding things can't hurt someone—someone they love." I stared into his eyes.

"There are so many other ways I wish I could've told you."

"How about any other way?" I crossed my arms over my chest, grasping on tightly to my shirt. His crisp ironed shirt was stretched tightly across his biceps and chest. The same ones I'd fallen asleep encircled in. The same ones I'd longed to feel again. "And what happens the next time you try to play protector and keep me in the dark?"

"I won't. From now on, it's one hundred percent open and honest. I have no more secrets. There's nothing else about me you don't know, and if you want to know something, ask and I'll tell you. Anything. Everything."

"There's too much I need to figure out right now." *Like how I'll survive next year without any financial support.* The financial aid office had already informed me that because the trust was technically mine, the money in it counted against me getting aid. The fact that my brother wouldn't let me touch it didn't matter.

Maybe once Colm had cooled off, things would change, but the email I'd gotten from the lawyer's office letting me know I wouldn't be getting my next semester paid for had seemed pretty final. My brother's words about it being me and him against the world were bullshit. It was me and him against the world as long as I followed along with his plan for my life to a T.

I didn't have a credit history, and private student loan interest rates were insane. There was a tiny voice in the back of my head that wanted to say screw it and go the easy way —ha! Had anyone in the history of mankind thought of medical school as easy? If I went along with his plan, he could then also pick out my husband, where we'd live, and when I'd have kids, dictating the rest of my life until I died.

I needed this. I'd needed this for a long time, but fear had held me back. This was me standing on my own two feet and figuring my life out.

"I can help. Let me know what you need."

I shook my head. "No, I've been relying on everyone else to make decisions for me for too long. It's my fault. I let it happen. I let everyone else's expectations decide what I did, and I can't do it anymore. I won't."

"So where does that leave us?" His gaze darted from the floor up to mine.

My throat tightened at the longing and sadness in his eyes.

I cleared my throat. "I don't know, but I need you to let *me* figure it out."

"I can do that. I'll do whatever you need me to do."

Staring back at him, I let him know this wasn't his problem to fix. He didn't flinch or shy away. He met my eyes, almost pleading with me to believe and trust him again. The words were there, the ones I'd thought a million times and had finally learned were real. This was beyond a crush, had blown straight past infatuation and become something I couldn't live without. He was someone I couldn't live without.

His Adam's apple bobbed up and down under his buttoned collar.

I crouched down and took my things out of my bag for class. It was the only way to keep from reaching out to him. Now that I had the whole story about Felicity, I couldn't blame him for sleeping with her, no more than he could blame me for anyone who came before him, and the lies—those were harder to swallow, but I understood why they were his misguided version of protection.

"There are a lot of things I wish I could change, Liv, but being with you will never be one of them. Whatever you put your mind to, there will never be anything that can stand in your way. You think you've let other people drive your life, but you're the most determined person I've ever met.

"Colm will come to his senses, and you're not alone, Liv. You're never alone. Even if you don't want to come to me for help, please don't think Emmett, Heath, and Declan won't be there for you in an instant. Mak, Kara, and Avery will rally together and get you anything you need."

"I know." My voice sounded small and far away. I'd missed them. Turning on the speaker, my fingers shook as I played with the buttons. I'd wanted to call them, but dodging Ford hadn't been my only reason for avoiding them. I'd busted up the Kings, driven a wedge between Colm and Ford. How would they react? I was just the taga-long little sister. I was great to have around like a team mascot, but what happened when the mascot screwed things up?

"I'll do whatever I need to do to prove you can trust me again." He backed away toward the doorway. "I'm sorry I lost your trust in the first place. If I need to stay away for you to do that, I'll do it." He sucked in a breath, and our gazes collided.

And then he was gone. With him, all the air left the room. The door banged shut, and the pin-drop silence of the space surrounded me.

I pressed my fists against my lips, staring after the spot where he'd stood. People milled around outside in the hallway. We'd already walked away from each other so many times. I'd already lost too many people. Could I do it again after I'd given him my whole heart?

Someone opened the door, and my chest filled with hope that it was Ford coming back. One of the dancers came in and paused in the doorway, glancing backward.

I wiped at my eyes, at tears I hadn't even felt soaking my cheeks, and went back to the front of the class. Right, I was supposed to be teaching, trying to support myself and living the life I'd always said I wanted.

$$\sim$$

FORD

I made it to the bottom of the stairs and yanked at my collar, but it wasn't the claustrophobic fabric choking me; it was knowing I'd lost her. Dropping down, I sat on the steps. People came in through the front doors and up the steps, flowing around me. They stared, probably trying to figure out who the hell the guy sitting there about to lose his shit was, but I didn't care.

Being put on display came in a distant second to having my heart ripped out of my chest. I'd do whatever she needed. I'd make sure everyone else knew what was going on with her so she wouldn't be alone. I never wanted her to think she'd lost out on being a part of our group, a part of our Kings family because of what had happened.

I pushed off the steps, the cold stone driving the emptiness in my heart even deeper. *Keep going, Ford. Show her how much she means by keeping your word.* My hand wrapped around the door handle, and I stood, frozen. Someone came up to the door and tried to pull it open, but my grip kept it closed.

They raised an eyebrow at me like I was a crazy person, and I was. My heart hammered against my ribs, and the thought of leaving this place without her made the floor shift beneath my feet.

Spinning around, I raced for the steps. It couldn't end like this. Our timing had always been shit, but guess what? I didn't care. Bumping into someone, I skidded to a halt at the bottom of the steps when, halfway up, Liv came up onto her tiptoes, stopping as our gazes collided. Other people stood on the stairs, along the railing up above her and behind me.

"You were coming back," she said, the smile in her voice so bright it banished the dreariness in my heart.

"I was. I am."

"I thought you said you were going to leave."

"I was, but I couldn't. I couldn't open the door."

A woman's voice came from behind me. "He really couldn't. Like, he was holding it closed. I thought he was a psycho or something trying to rob the place."

I let out a laugh that sounded more like a bark.

"Why couldn't you leave?" She came down a step, and I went up one.

"There are a lot of promises I've made to myself over the past week, and one of them is that I'm not lying anymore, not just to other people, but to myself, and saying I could stay away from you was a lie—the biggest one I've ever told. There's nothing in this world that I want more than to be there for you, to love you and show you how much you mean to me."

"What if I don't want that?" She came down a step, and I went up another. The people around us stared. No one said a word. Every eye in the entire place was on us, and more people came in behind me. The voices died as other people whispered retellings of what they'd seen so far. Any other day, it would've sent me running for the door, but for her, I'd endure anything.

"I'd do whatever I could to convince you that you don't need to do this alone. You're strong enough to, one hundred percent, but *I* can't do this without you."

My slow ascent and her slow descent met halfway. She was one step up, her head level with mine.

She swallowed. "What if I'm afraid of losing you again?"

"I'm just as afraid that one day you'll realize this is only a childhood crush and you'll want nothing to do with me."

"We're well beyond crush territory." She moved to the edge of her step, her body even closer to mine.

"What territory are we in?" I leaned in.

Her hands settled on my chest. "Love." With her eyes open, she pressed her lips against mine, the red tinge around her eyes melting away as she sank into the kiss.

I tugged her against me, holding her tightly around her waist. The heat of her body pressed against mine, and I held on to her and what we'd almost lost. She closed her eyes and leaned into me even more.

The tightness in my chest gave way to a blissed-out feeling that didn't compare to even the biggest comeback win on the ice. She was in my arms. Her warmth pressed against my skin, and I wanted nothing more than to brand this kiss into her mind so that she'd never be able to go a day without my lips on hers again.

Everyone around us erupted in loud cheers and clapping. Running my hand up her back, I cupped her neck and dipped her. If they wanted a show, we'd give them a show. She laughed, holding on to my shoulders.

"I think we have an audience," she whispered against my lips.

"I don't give a shit." Kissing her again like she deserved to be kissed, my world centered on her. Every touch. Every taste. Every breath.

The people around us didn't matter to me one bit. I wanted them to see us. I wanted my love for her on display for the world, and I wanted her to know it would always be there.

39

FORD

Liv stood in front of her class wrapping up another sweat-filled, nonstop session. I sat in my chair off to the side out of the way. Her students didn't stare as much anymore. I'd become a classroom staple.

If I wasn't at the rink or conditioning training, I was there. She moved with even more confidence, passion, and grace than the last time I'd seen her. It wasn't even that she danced for me; she danced for herself, and I couldn't help but want to watch her every minute I could. I'd even swung a few private dances at home on some extra-special occasions.

After people filed out, she ran over, a little out of breath. Sweat was shining on her skin, and strands of hair fell out of her ponytail and stuck to the sides of her face. Her eyes were soft and cast a spell over me, one I never wanted to be free from and that would forever be a part of my soul.

With my arm wrapped around her shoulders, I led her out of the studio after she changed. Anyone who saw her dance could see that it breathed life into her. We went back to my apartment, and I showed her exactly how much I'd appreciated her performance. A couple of burgers ordered in from Fish's was the cherry on top.

Lying in bed, tangled in the sheets with her against my chest, I ran my finger up and down her arm.

"I'm talking to Colm tomorrow."

She lifted her head and stared at me.

"I need to smooth things over with him. He's my best friend whether he wants to be or not. Maybe I can get him to stop being such an asshole when it comes to you."

"I doubt it. He's probably more stubborn than you on most things and especially when it comes to anything to do with Mom and Dad. He's always been so concerned about their legacy, about making them proud, but when I think back to whether or not they saw us as individuals or just as extensions of themselves, I honestly don't know.

"Dad played hockey when he was younger, before he settled on medicine. Colm was my dad's clone, and then with me, medicine became my crutch. It was the only way to spend time with them, and even then it was scraps.

"Colm goes back and forth between hating how they were and putting them up on a pedestal. He sold the house without even asking me." She dropped her head back down and ran her fingers along my chest. "Just showed up one day and said it had sold. It's like he wants to leave their shadow behind, knows both of us need to be freed from the promises we made to them, but he can't."

I kissed the tip of her nose. "We'll figure it out, one way or another."

∿

I walked from the locker room on my skates. Walking like that was always so damned awkward. My ankles always felt like they might break at any moment while balancing on the plastic guards that protected the blade of my skates, but it felt good to have them back on again.

With the season over, I hadn't taken to practicing solo like I usually did in the off-season, not when Liv was waiting for me at home. I'd volunteered for a few charity events for the team over the past few weeks, visiting hospitals and attending dinners to raise money for local animal shelters. Having a more public profile wasn't as horrible as I'd imagined it would be, especially not with Liv on my arm.

She shined at those types of events, rubbing shoulders with people from her social circle, and it gave me a chance to spoil her and buy her some new dresses. She'd been adamant about me not paying her troubles away, and standing on her own two feet was what she needed to do. It had taken me almost a month to convince her to move in with me.

At least she hadn't been at the Brothel, as she and Marisa called it, for more than a couple of weeks. The second she let that name slip, I was ready to kick down the door to get her out of there. Every one of those fuckers was too good-looking for his own good, and they reminded me too much of the Kings and our college antics. I didn't think I had a decent night's sleep until she was out of there. I trusted her, but I wasn't so sure about those guys, or the randoms crashing their parties.

Now coming home to silence filled me with unease. I loved walking in to her talking on the phone, watching TV, or jamming to some study tunes while she went through her coursework for her summer classes.

She still worked hard, but she didn't have to chain herself to her desk. We explored the city. I'd grown up here, but I'd never seen half the tourist attractions. The zoo, cannoli at the Reading Terminal Market and extensive research into the best cheesesteak in town were at the top of the list. So far it was a tie between Jim's and Woodrow's Sandwich Shop.

With her hand in mine, I didn't care if we were in the middle of a bustling restaurant or sitting at home on the couch. Anywhere with her was where I wanted to be.

The rest of the guys had been busy. Emmett and Avery were preparing for the wedding of the century later in the summer, and Declan and Mak squeezed in a quick trip before she went back to med school. Kara got invited to a summer writer's residency up in New York, so Heath tagged along. It had been ages since we'd had a Kings friendly match.

"What took you so long?" Declan called from the ice.

Heath whipped around the rink at Mach 5, always a bundle of energy.

A loud curse echoed off the rafters of the practice rink. Skates sliced across the ice, and the seriously pissed-off face of Colm appeared between the open doors to the rink.

"Is this your bullshit attempt to get us to kiss and make up?" Colm threw his stick down into the box, and it cracked off the side of the bench.

"I don't want to fight with you." I held up my hands.

"Maybe I want to fight with you." His words were clipped and spit like nails.

The rest of the guys stood behind him on the ice like they were on the way to a funeral. Maybe they were. Maybe it was the death of the Kings as we knew them.

"Where's Olivia?" He jerked off his glove and threw it down.

"She's not here." I backed up, waving my hands in front of me.

"Where is she?" he growled.

"She misses you, man."

He dropped his other glove and looked over his shoulder. I thought maybe he'd come to his senses. Instead he whipped back around and charged at me. His glance back had been to make sure the guys were far enough back so he could get to me, but this time I was ready for him. He threw the first punch, and I leaned back, dodging it.

"Colm, stop, damn it. She's home." At least until we decided to move somewhere else.

His face contorted, and this wasn't the Colm I'd grown up with, the one who'd taken me under his wing as a freshman in high school. This was a wounded animal. He rushed toward me, slamming his shoulder into my stomach. I tucked my hand under his arm and shoved him away to avoid engaging in a fistfight.

There was a sickening crunch and a howl. One of his legs stuck up out of the top of the box. My brain raced to piece it all together. When I'd shoved him, he must have fallen back over the wall to the box. Peering over the waist-high wall Colm had flipped over, I stared down at him, wide-eyed.

He clutched his knee, shouting. Bile rose in my throat. I'd probably just ended his career. My hands shook. I rushed toward him.

I slid my hands under his arms to try to lift him.

"Get your fucking hands off me," he yelled, writhing in pain. The rest of the guys crowded in.

"It's okay, man. We've got this." Heath put his hand on my shoulder, looking more serious than I'd seen him look in a long time. I backed up and let them get Colm to his feet. Declan ran off and came back a few minutes later with Bailey, our team physical therapist, while I stood there helpless with my hands braced behind my head.

They got him strapped into a stretcher and out to an ambulance. His eyes caught mine, and he looked ready to jump up and break my nose. I was pretty sure he would've if he hadn't been strapped down. Emmett went along with him. Heath, Declan, and I stood there shell-shocked as the ambulance drove away.

"We all saw what happened. No one blames you." Declan turned to me with somber eyes.

"I shouldn't have pushed him."

"He shouldn't have charged you, especially not when he's only been back on the ice for a few weeks."

"Shit, man, what the hell do I tell Liv?"

Heath looked over at me. "The truth."

I nodded and we all got changed in silence. This wasn't how the day was supposed to go.

"We're heading to the hospital. We'll let you know the news."

The drive back to my apartment was the longest in history, other than when I'd rushed to Liv's apartment the night of the fire. Each notch on my key sounded like an anvil dropping. I turned the knob and walked inside.

Music played on the Bluetooth speakers, and Liv's voice filled the room. I turned the corner to the kitchen where she danced around, singing into her spatula. My lips tilted up.

She spun around and her eyes lit up. Looping her arms around my neck, she stood on her tiptoes.

"What's wrong?" Her gaze ran over my face.

"Colm was there."

Her arms dropped from around my neck. "How is he?" She rubbed her fingers along the back of her hand.

"Hurt. He got injured."

Her eyes widened. "What? What happened?"

I relayed the whole story to her after she grabbed me a beer and sat down on the arm of the couch beside me.

"It doesn't sound like it was your fault. Colm's going through some stuff." She stared up at the ceiling. "Maybe I should go to the hospital to see him." She squeezed her hands in her lap.

"Emmett, Declan, and Heath are all there now, and they said they'd send over an update once they knew something."

My stomach churned. What did she think of me? I'd not only alienated her from her brother, but now I'd put him in the hospital.

"Hey." She grabbed my chin and turned my face toward her. "I don't blame you. I know you'd never intentionally try to hurt him. It's his fault for flying off the handle." She ran her fingers along the scruff on my cheeks. "I love you, and nothing is going to change that." Leaning into me, she pressed her mouth against mine. Parting her lips, she let me inside, opening herself to me, and I drank down her beauty one gulp at a time. "He'll be okay. It's just going to take some time."

I ran my hand along her hair. "I hope you're right."

EPILOGUE

LIV

"Roll up your sleeves, you cheater." I lunged across the table and grabbed at Grant's arm. My fingers caught on the end of his sleeve.

"I'll do no such thing. How long have we known each other, Liver? How could you ever think I'd do something like that?"

"Sylvia—"

"You're going to call my mom on me?"

I tugged harder on his sleeve. The jingle of Scrabble tiles was a dead giveaway.

"How did those get in there?" His eyes widened in mock shock.

I pursed my lips and held out my hand as he shook his contraband out onto the table. "It seems the Scrabble tile fairy decided to pay you a visit, huh?"

"Must have." He whistled and stared up at the ceiling.

"Did someone call my name?" Sylvia breezed into the kitchen and checked in the oven. The double chocolate

348

MAYA HUGHES

chunk brownies baking inside made my mouth water. She used a knife to test their doneness.

"Nope. It was Liv sneezing." Grant gave me the death stare that only came from daring your friend to get you in trouble with your mom.

"And it had nothing to do with you cheating at Scrabble?" She pulled the knife out of the center of the brownie pan and set them on the counter.

His mouth dropped open.

The click of the front door saved him from a sputtering excuse. Ford walked into the kitchen. His T-shirt stretched tightly across his broad chest, and I wanted to climb him like a tree.

"Look who I found outside." He held out his arm.

The tall, lanky brunette popped her head out into the doorway with a huge smile on her face. Grant rushed over to her, nearly knocking me into the table. What am I, chopped liver?

He wrapped his arms around her and swung her around.

Ford shook his head and laughed before making his way over to me. He planted a toe-curling kiss on me.

I pressed my hands against his chest and broke the connection. Panting, I stared into his eyes. Practices had started up again, which meant our lazy days at home were over.

"Could everyone stop making out with their significant others so we could eat?"

Sylvia spoke to us with her back turned.

"Let me help you with that," Grant and Ford said at the same time.

"By all means, boys." She stepped back from the counter and let the two of them get everything ready for dinner.

Sitting at the table, she poured me and Laura some white wine.

"You two need to come to dinner every night, if it gets them doing all the work." Sylvia winked and took a sip of her wine.

Laura leaned in, glancing between us like we were planning a heist. "I say next time, we get them to cook."

Sylvia threw her head back. "I knew I liked you."

The guys brought over the dishes, and we all sat down, devouring the meal Sylvia had made for us. My stomach had been rumbling after my four back-to-back classes at the studio.

Across the table, Grant and Laura were exchanging little glances and touches. My heart filled with the feeling that only came from truly being so happy for someone else's happiness.

"They're good together." Ford's words caressed the shell of my ear.

"I know." I held out my fork and gave him the last bite of my lasagna.

"You're just trying to fill me up so I won't be able to eat brownies."

I touched my hand to my chest and gasped. "I would never do such a thing."

He laughed.

Sylvia pushed her chair back from the table. "Everyone ready for more?" She picked up the plate piled high with brownies.

"More than ready." Ford threaded his fingers through mine under the table and squeezed my hand.

~

Ford's arms wrapped around me, wrinkling the navy fabric of my dress. His smell washed over me as he peppered my neck with kisses. I held on to his arms, rocking back and forth to the music from the speakers.

"We should've stayed home." He tucked some of my hair behind my ear and stared into my eyes like he was ready to take a bite out of me.

My stomach flipped, and I squeezed my thighs together. The beard burn between my legs sent a sweet, throbbing ache pulsing through me. Flickers of pleasure tingled along my skin. My fingers tightened along Ford's back.

"You have to stop doing that to me." He dipped his head, bringing his nose an inch from mine. His thumbs rubbed against the sides of my face with a fire burning in his eyes, and I nearly fanned myself.

"What did I do?" I stared up at him with all the innocence I could manage.

His fingers slipped under the fabric of my backless dress. The lace around my hips tightened as his hand ran down over the curve of my ass, palming it and squeezing me tighter against him.

"You know exactly what you do to me." The insistent nudge at the front of his pants increased, pressing into my stomach. My mouth watered, wanting to taste him.

"Hey, enough of that. We don't need another one of those videos going around," Heath called out from the top of the steps.

Ford's arm tensed around me, and he slid his hand out from under my dress.

I ran my hands along his shoulders. "It was a joke."

Kara followed Heath down the stairs, her pale blue dress flowing with each step. Emmett and Avery burst out of the kitchen, his mouth covered in lipstick smudges. The left side of his hair stuck straight up, and Avery reached up to pat it down, her cheeks glowing a non-blush-colored pink. I couldn't tell if it was from her near mauling or embarrassment—probably a combination of both.

The front door opened, and Declan held it open. "Hurry up, the car's waiting." All the ladies grabbed their bags, and the guys picked up their suit jackets.

"We're one staircase picture away from looking like we're headed to prom." Mak laughed from inside the limo, her hand on the open door as it idled curbside.

The guys exchanged looks, and we all went right back inside the house. The limo driver was nice enough to serve as the cameraman for the couples shots, along with the all-guys and all-girls pictures with us standing along the staircase. I knew they would look good on my wall of pictures, the new memories I was making with my new family.

With tears of laughter in my eyes, I slid into the limo sandwiched between Emmett and Ford. "I can't believe you made us do that."

Mak tapped away on her phone. "I ordered five framed prints, and they'll be delivered by the end of this week." She leaned back and ran her hand along Declan's leg.

The slow realization of why she'd ordered five sent silence creeping through the car. She looked up, her eyes darting to me and Ford.

"Sorry." She shoved her phone into her bag. "Have you spoken to him?"

I shook my head. It had been almost three months. Classes started again for me in a few days. "Every time I try, he shuts me out." Ford tightened his hold on my shoulder, his touch keeping the sadness at bay.

"Did Bailey ever get him to take his new rehab seriously?" Mak scooted to the edge of her seat.

"They'll cut him if he can't get back on the ice by mid-season." Heath's usually sunny voice cast a darker cloud over our group.

"His voice mail box is totally full. He won't respond to any messages." I stared into the eyes of everyone there, and they had the same lost look I had in mine.

"He needs someone from outside to get his ass in gear." Declan threaded his fingers through Mak's, and she held them on her lap.

"What about Imogen?" Avery's head popped up from Emmett's shoulder.

"Imogen?" Kara's eyebrows shot up.

"She just finished her training as a physical therapist and rehab specialist. She went back to school after...after Preston." Declan's last words came out as a hoarse whisper.

"After all she's been through, you want to subject her to a surly and pissed-off Colm?" Heath settled his hand on Kara's lap.

"What's the other option? Do we let him sulk and be an asshole to the point that he throws his career away? Or do we go for a Hail Mary pass that maybe she can knock some sense into him?" Declan looked to me, then Ford. "She's the one person he might not automatically snap at."

I stared up at Ford and the grim set of his mouth. The night had started off so well, but it was always something in the back of our minds. I'd hoped Colm would come around like Grant, but he seemed bound and determined not to even speak to us—hell, to any of the Kings, let alone try to reconcile with me or Ford.

Ford looked to me and nodded. "Call her, if you think she can help."

I stared into Ford's eyes before turning to Declan.

"We can call her tomorrow." Mak offered a weak smile.

The limo pulled up to the entrance of the art museum. A red carpet covered the stone steps and photographers lined the path up to the massive bronze double doors at the top of the staircase.

"Here goes nothing." Emmett shouldered the door open and held out his hand for Avery. She took it and stepped up.

The tension in Ford's body radiated off him. I ran my hand over the back of his hand and laced my fingers through his. His hate for these events had lessened recently, especially when it was for charity. But it still wasn't easy for him.

"It'll be okay." I smiled at him and scooted closer to the door.

He tugged me back against his chest. Everyone else climbed out, and flashes from the cameras filled the limo with light every few seconds.

I looked over my shoulder at him. His eyes were fixed outside the limo through the partially closed door. The rest of the Kings and their queens stood outside the door, waiting for us.

Turning, I ran my fingers along his chin and pulled him closer. "Don't worry about the cameras or the people screaming your name. You can do this."

His Adam's apple bobbed, and he locked eyes with me. The tension creasing his forehead eased some, and his pulse, which was pounding against my hold on his hands, slowed. "I love you, Liv."

"I know." I grinned and shifted on the seat.

He pulled me back. "That's all you've got to say to me?" Growling against my ear, his fingers tightened around my waist.

"We don't want to keep your adoring fans waiting." Slipping out of his grasp, I hopped out of the limo. Ford followed behind me, his presence unmistakable, along with the laser lock of his gaze.

Our group climbed the stairs of the museum. The guys were directed down the line of reporters and cameramen by the event organizers. Ford had microphones shoved in front of his face and answered each question, but his eyes never left me.

Kara, Mak, Avery, and I walked alongside them, soaking up the energy of the crowd.

"They look good, don't they?" Kara sighed with a dreamy look in her eyes. Heath winked at her over his shoulder.

"They clean up nice. Maybe next time I won't have to bribe Declan into a suit." Mak clasped her hands around her clutch in front of her.

"More like bribe him out of one. I swear Emmett was born in a tux." Avery tugged at the fitted waist of her dress. She'd have shown up in jeans and a T-shirt if she could have.

Ford glanced over his shoulder, his eyes promising retribution for my love snub. I welcomed it. My smile widened as he walked over to me, holding out his arm for me to take while we entered the gala.

Bypassing our table, he led me out onto the dance floor. One hand traced the small of my exposed back, the other holding my hand. I held on to his shoulder, my heels bringing me up to chin height.

"I know what you're doing," he whispered into my ear. We glided across the dance floor with other couples as the band played a classical cover of Coldplay's "Viva La Vida."

"What am I doing?"

"You're holding out on saying you love me too to keep me distracted and to make me crazy so I won't pay attention to the cameras, the photographers, and being in a room of a couple hundred people." His words caressed the shell of my ear, and now *I* was wondering why we were there instead of at home.

"If you know what I'm up to, why let it make you crazy?" My breath caught at the hungry look in his eyes.

"You do that anyway. No matter what, you always make me think I'll go out of my mind if I can't talk to you, touch you, taste you."

I bit my bottom lip.

He pulled back and stared into my eyes, still dancing across the floor. "But two can play at these games, so let's see how you fare." His words brushed across my glossy lips, and I wanted to devour his minty ones.

The song ended, and he led me back to the table with his hand never leaving its spot on my back. His thumb dragged across my skin in insistent circles, the same kind he used on my clit that left me sweaty, shaking, and unable to remember my name.

My clit throbbed, and I bit my lower lip. He pulled out the chair for me, and I remained standing, unable to move.

"You okay?" he whispered against my ear. A shiver shot through my body.

I nodded, sweeping the back of my dress aside and finally sitting on the navy-covered chair.

"Your napkin fell." He crouched down and picked up the folded navy fabric on the floor. Dropping his hand, he stared into my eyes, and a shiver raced down my spine. He picked up the napkin and used that as an excuse to brush the backs of his fingers along my ankle, which was wrapped in the thin straps of my heels.

His eyes lit with a fire that could have burned down half the city. I sucked in a sharp breath. It was the same look he gave me when he looped my legs over his shoulders and feasted on me like I was his last meal.

My thong was seconds away from disintegrating off my body. I swallowed against the boulder that had taken up residence in my throat.

His smile transformed. Resting one hand on the table and one on the back of my chair, he caged me in. "See? I can play too." He sat in the seat beside me and lifted a bottle of wine, pouring a glass for me. My brain fogged over, and there was only one thought running through my head. It all centered on him. I wanted to jump up on the table and scream out my love for him in the middle of the crowded room, but where was the fun in that?

The corner of my mouth lifted. We'd be lucky if we made it back into the limo before he ripped this dress off my body. I squeezed my thighs together. I must have made a noise, because Mak leaned over and rested her hand on my arm.

"You okay?"

Ford peered over his shoulder with a wide grin. *Oh, it's on.*

"I'm fine, Mak. Just got a slight chill." Scooting my chair in closer to the table, I ran my hand over Ford's knee under the tablecloth. His muscles bunched under my hold, and he peered over at me, his breath catching as my fingers trailed higher.

Taking a sip of wine from my glass, I laughed at the joke Heath told across the table. Ford's gaze bored into my cheek, my hand shifted along his thigh, and he choked on his drink. The electric smile set my stomach off in flutters that threatened to carry me away.

His smile was enough to wash away those tinges of sadness that crept in when my mind drifted to Colm.

We'd fix it together.

We'd been through so much over the past—how long had it been? That didn't matter now. He was the only one for me. The universe had finally given us our break and I wasn't letting that go. With Ford, it was always and forever. And ever.

Thank you so much for reading Ford and Liv's story! These two had so much chemistry, I thought my keyboard was going to combust. I had such an awesome time being back with the Kings. For an extra special day with Ford and Liv, you can check out their bonus epilogue HERE!

The final King has arrived!

Heartless King - A Friends to Enemies to Lovers

Two blue lines. That means not pregnant, right? Right? Oh, sh*t.

Five years ago, Colm Frost asked me to marry him and I ran. I ran from my painful past too raw and fresh to escape. He was the only one who looked at me like I wasn't broken and made me believe it. He made me feel it.

Heartless King is LIVE! Grab your copy of the last book in the Kings of Rittenhouse series!

AUTHOR'S NOTE

It feels good to be back with the Kings! Thank you so much for reading Ford and Liv's story. Theirs was one that popped into my head back when I started writing the free prequel novella, The Kings of Rittenhouse. I loved the idea of having that person you've been crushing on finally realizing what they're missing and what it would be like with all the complications only growing older and dealing with family can bring along with it!

Ford and Liv were so much fun to write and I swear, I wanted to throw my laptop just as many times as you wanted to throw your screen with roadblock after roadblock stopping these two from finally getting their hands on each other! It probably has something to do with me and Mr. Hughes attempting to find some quiet time alone, but that's in short order with 3 kiddos. Oh trust me, we've been blocked WAY more times than Ford and Liv! :-D

I've got an exciting slate for the rest of 2019. I'll have the next FULTON U book out in the late summer/early fall. It'll be an enemies to lovers book featuring our favorite quarter-back, Nix, in The Second We Met. Then not too long after that release, I'll have the next and final [I'm totally not teary, I swear :-(] Kings of Rittenhouse book.

This is Colm's book. We've been building to this since he spotted those little glances at Ford from Liv back when the Kings were in high school. And now Colm's hurt. He's alone. And he's angry. He's going to need someone who knows what it feels like to lose everything and have their life turned upside down to snap him out of this. But he's going to be a serious grump about it!

He's going to need some serious TLC and I know precisely who he'll get it from!

There's an excerpt from The Perfect First after my note, so you can see what all the fuss is about :P

Until next time!

Maya xx

P.S. Grab the Fearless King extended epilogue!

P.P.S. Add Colm's story, Heartless King, to your Goodreads!

EXCERPT FROM THE PERFECT FIRST

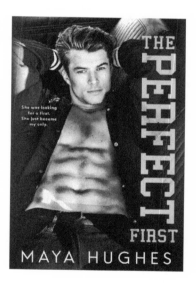

"How long do you last in bed?" Those were her first words to me, swiftly followed up with, "And how big would you say you are?"

"Let's get started." *Just rip the Band-Aid off.* Clearing my throat, I tapped the cards on the table. A few heads turned in our direction at the sharp, rapping sound. "When were you last tested for sexually transmitted diseases?"

Setting the bottle down on the table, he stared at me like I was an equation he was suddenly interested in figuring out. And then it was gone. "At the beginning of the season. Clean bill of health." He looked over his shoulder, the boredom back, leaking from every pore. *Wow.* I'd thought guys were all over this whole sex thing, but he looked like he was sitting in the waiting room of a dentist's office.

"When did you last have sexual intercourse?"

His head snapped back to me, eyes bugged out. "What?" I had his full attention now.

"Sex? When did you last have sex?" I tapped my pen against the notecard.

He sputtered and stared back at me. His eyes narrowed and he rested his elbows on the table.

I scooted my neatly lain out cards back toward me, away from him.

"No comment."

"Given the circumstances, it's an appropriate question."

The muscles in his neck tightened and his lips crumpled together. "Fine, at the beginning of the season."

"What season?" I looked up from my pen. That was an odd way to put it. "Like, the beginning of fall?"

"Like football season."

The pieces fit together—the body, the looks from other people around the coffee house. "You play football." That made sense, and he seemed like the perfect all-American person for the job.

"Yes, I play football."

"When did the season start?"

He shook his head like he was trying to clear away a fog and stared back at me like I'd started speaking a different language. "September."

"And..." I ran my hand along the back of my neck. "How long would you say it lasted?"

His eyebrows dipped. "It didn't last. It was a one-night thing. I don't do relationships."

Of course not. He was playing the field. Sowing his oats. Banging his way through as many co-eds as possible. Experienced. Excellent.

I cleared my throat. "No, I didn't mean how long did you date the woman. I meant, how long was the sex?"

The steady drumming on the table stopped. "Are you serious?"

I licked my Sahara-dry lips. "It's a reasonable question. How long did it last?"

"I didn't exactly set a timer, but let's just say we both got our reward."

"Interesting." I made another note on the card.

"These are the types of questions I'm going to be asked for the draft?" He took the lid off the bottled water.

The draft? Pushing ahead, I went to the next line one my card and cringed a bit. "Okay, this might seem a little invasive." I cleared my throat again. "But how big is your penis? Length is fine. I don't need to know the circumference, you know—the girth."

A fine spray of water from his mouth washed over me. "What the hell kind of question is that?

Reece and Seph have only just begun! Grab your copy of The Perfect First or read it for FREE in KU!

ACKNOWLEDGMENTS

It's always so hard to me to write the acknowledgements because I try to tell the people who've helped me along the way thank you every chance I get.

My words don't come out gleaming and shiny in my first drafts. It's always a very messy affairs. There are tears, threats of throwing my computer out the nearest window and staring at my screen through my fingers when I get my manuscripts back from my editors. I thank them so so much for all their help throughout the process. Tamara Mayara, Lea Schaffer and C.Marie.

Every message, email comment and recommendation to a friend helps spread the word in so many ways, so I wanted to say thank you to everyone who's taken their time to live with these character and introduce them others.

I'm still blown away with how much the Kings have touched so many people and I love hearing about it. You keep reading and I'll keep writing!

M

CONNECT WITH MAYA

Sign up for my newsletter to get exclusive bonus content, ARC opportunities, sneak peeks, new release alerts and to find out just what I'm books are coming up next.

Join my reader group for teasers, giveaways and more!

Follow my Amazon author page for new release alerts!

Follow me on Instagram, where I try and fail to take pretty pictures!

Follow me on Twitter, just because :)

I'd love to hear from you! Drop me a line anytime :)
https://www.mayahughes.com/
maya@mayahughes.com

Made in the USA
Monee, IL
22 May 2020

31700929R00215